QUEERVILLE

SEX, CARS & DOO-WOP

"Queers vs. Squares"

PROLOGUE

Anthony Calhoun stepped confidently into the dimly lit, quite obviously illegal shop. His entrance caused a ripple through the crowded room as he glared around.

"Who's the owner of this establishment?" Anthony was usually more barbaric, but tonight he felt a sense of calm. "This is my place and who the hell are you, beatnik?" a small man from across the room retorted.

Anthony circled around to see who spoke. *A frail little man, such harsh words from a twerp,* he thought.

"I'm Anthony Calhoun..." Anthony stated bluntly.

Silence filled the air. People gulped. Anthony was young, and his youthfulness didn't necessarily intimidate people, and being a melanated man in 1955, neither did his skin color. However, the name Calhoun alone sparked fear into the hearts of people.

No one moved.

No one dared.

His brutality had only been matched by his unwavering determination.

"...and I'm here to inform you that this establishment is now closed indefinitely," Anthony snarled.

"Well listen here, Anthony... The Calhoun's are no longer running..." Before he could finish his sentence,

Anthony had brandished a revolver, in one swift motion he had drawn his weapon and put two holes in the twerp's head. Anthony towered over his corpse and placed his hand to his ear, mocking the man beneath him, "Calhoun's are what?" He confiscated the brown paper bag protruding from the man's suit jacket.

"There will be no drugs sold in Queerville. Tell your dealers to stay out or get carried out!" Anthony hollered.

As the terrified people stampeded through the shop and out the door, Anthony grabbed a bottle of alcohol and splashed it around every inch of the illegal shop, leaving a trail leading to the front door. He stood gallantly at the entrance and reached into his denim jeans to retrieve his lighter. He sparked it and tossed it inside. The place was immediately ablaze with color. White hot flames shimmered through fierce yellow and into burnt orange. A blanket of smoke enveloped everything.

Anthony retired into the night with the flames dancing in the background. He stood by his chariot with a content smile, thinking about the wad of cash he had in the brown paper bag. He peeled off a few twenties from the top, but there were more.

He raised his head as he heard footsteps approach him from behind. He twisted to the side...

"Now what are you..." Anthony was surprised by the sudden noise, "...doing over on this side?"

The last thing Anthony saw was his killer. The last thing he felt was three bullets piercing his chest.

CHAPTER 1

Anthony laid guilelessly in his casket. His mother sat before him, her eyes red-rimmed and glassy. You could see the anguish in her eyes as tears streamed down her cheeks. Everyone sat in silence, all in disbelief, nothing but grief and loss written across their faces. The town of Queerville mourned the loss of their beloved and respected Anthony, and his death darkened the town and intensified the rivalry between Queerville, O Town and Bronxville. If one wanted to witness pain, they needed only to look at all their faces; if they sought sorrow, they could find it in his mother. As for rage and merciless vengeance, all eyes turned to Zack, Anthony's trans masculine, non-binary sibling.

Zack walked in, their skin kissed by the sun, sporting a rockabilly hairdo. They removed their dark sunglasses, revealing dazzling eyes, the prettiest shade of emerald. Zack was striking, as if angels had chiseled their features. It was evident that they were the offspring of two very attractive parents. Every head turned to see them. Some were shocked to see Zack, while others were thrilled, for they knew what Zack's presence meant. Revenge.

Slowly, Zack made their way down the aisle, their heart pounding in their chest. As they drew closer toward Anthony's casket, it still wasn't quite real to them. Zack looked at Anthony incredulously. Seeing him in that casket will haunt them forever. Tears fell down their face as they kneeled at his casket. Zack wept for Anthony. They had always been reserved; this was the most public display of emotion they had ever shown.

A sudden fury filled their heart. Zack leaned over, "I'm going to find whoever did this to you and put them in the dirt right next to you," Zack quavered. They kissed Anthony on the forehead and stood up, embraced and kissed their mother, then headed to the door with fire in their eyes.

Every Queerville gang that was present stood up and followed Zack out. A war was coming, and they all wanted to take part in it.

All the gangs in Queerville then gathered at Charlotte's club. Each gang sat at their own round table. The Red Dragons were the largest gang composed of the toughest men and women in Queerville. The Scorpions were the gay boys. The Lipsticks were all beautiful pin-up femmes. Two Souls were the bisexuals and House of Prosperity were the elders. Charlotte, with her six-foot commanding presence and fiery personality, was no wonder she was the most respected Drag Queen in the Midwest. She considered everyone in town her babies and treated them so. Charlotte had known Zack and

Anthony since they were children, she was like a second mother to Zack. She took the mic.

"Thank you all for coming to support Zack and the Red Dragons in their time of grief. The house would like to acknowledge Two Souls, Scorpions, Lipsticks, The House of Prosperity, and my fellow Drag Queens…"

The gangs nodded in support for Zack.

"…I think it's safe to say we are all mourning the loss of our good friend, Anthony. Anthony was so full of life and always kept a smile on his face no matter what. He could turn your worst day into your best day. He had that effect on you. That's why it's never easy when these horrible things happen to such beautiful people. Anthony will truly be missed. God bless him… and may God have mercy on his killer. Because he will not find any in Queerville," Charlotte stated firmly.

The hypnotic power of Charlotte's voice grabbed them. A surge growing in the faces of the crowd, you could see their rage building up as she continued.

"With the tragic loss of Anthony, we are without a leader. The only living member of the Calhoun bloodline is now Zack. This means Zack will have full command and leadership of Queerville and the gangs. Anyone who opposes this say nay."

The room fell silent.

"Zack is officially in command." Charlotte solidified the occasion by placing the Red Dragons jacket on Zack.

The gangs cheered and stomped their feet in favor. Charlotte slammed her gavel to silence the room.

"Now, what do we know about Anthony's murder, Scorpions?" Charlotte turned her attention to Freddie, with his flawless cinnamon brown skin and duck butt hair.

"Nothing, Bronxville cats ain't talking," Freddie replied.

Charlotte then looked at Halle, the leader of Two Souls. "What can you tell us, Halle?"

"Same as Freddie, no one is talking," Halle reluctantly admitted. No one wanted to disappoint Zack, but right now, no one had any answers about who killed Zack's brother.

"I say now that Zack is back, we remind everyone what Queerville is all about," Freddie blurted out.

The room erupted; the crowd hungry for revenge.

"Cut the gas and settle down!" Charlotte shouted, trying to quiet them.

Maria, a fierce and passionate Latin beauty, also Zack's ex, exchanged a warm look with Zack.

"I say we ask Zack what they would like us to do." Maria suggested. All heads turned to Zack.

Zack stood up.

"My only brother is dead. And unless these cats suddenly lost their tongues, I don't want to hear that they're not talking. So, I say we give them some initiative," Zack said with a menacing grin.

The crowd roared in agreement. Everyone jumped out of their seats and stormed out. The gangs raced into the street, hungry for blood, fueled by a thirst for revenge, hopping into their vintage 50s chariots and peeling off.

Bronxville, USA

Lisa, a young brown beauty, was kissing another girl in the front seat of a yellow 1955 Cadillac convertible. Their hands were exploring each other. A Bronxville greaser happened to be walking by. He stopped in his tracks, shocked by what he saw. He looked around, sure it was a joke, but no one else was present. He popped the collar to his black leather jacket and, with a smug smile on his face, confidently approached them. Robin, an ebony knockout, hazel eyes, slim frame; the other girl in the make-out session, spotted him approaching from the corner of her eye.

"Woah, you Betties look like you're in need of some assistance," he said, grabbing his crotch. The girls continued making out, ignoring his presence. Lisa caressed Robin's backside as their tongues connected; stalling for him to get closer. Once he was near, he said, "Let's play some backseat bingo."

Suddenly, Zack emerged from the back seat brandishing a handgun. "Sorry cat, this backseat is taken." Lisa and Robin were also wielding handguns aimed at the Bronxville greaser.

"Woah, what's your tale, nightingale?" the greaser said, raising his hands in fear.

"Where are they?" Zack asked solemnly. Staring down the barrel of three guns, he thought it best not to negotiate. But once he recognized Zack, he knew better not to tell them what they wanted to know. Zack grew impatient and pressed the gun against his temple.

"Okay. Cool it, Zack. I'll tell you where they're at," the greaser muttered, fearing for his life.

A group of Bronxville Devils were gathered at a secret location. A location that was just given to Zack and their crew. Seven chariots pulled up in the distance surrounding them. They hadn't noticed. Queerville gangs exited their rides and made their way toward the large group, wielding bats, chains, switchblades, all types of makeshift weapons. They approached from all directions. The Bronxville gang took notice and started to break and run every-which-way. The crowd dissolved into panic. They made a run for it but were met with force. The Scorpions led the charge, swinging on any

Bronxville Devil they encountered. Freddie threw blows like a pro boxer, delivering powerful punches. Maria and her Lipsticks gang were pulling hair and cat fighting with the women of Bronxville.

Two Souls were engaged in a fierce switchblade fight. Val, the youngest stud, was sucker punched from behind by a Bronxville cat. Zack charged him, their eyes flaming with the weight of their fury, and pistol-whipped him, causing him to collapse to the ground. Stunned, seeing stars, blood trickled from behind his ear. Zack and Val stomped on him until Lisa intervened and pulled them off. Suddenly, police sirens blared in the distance.

"Zack, c'mon, let's burn rubber," Lisa urged, attempting to drag Zack away, but Zack had a message for the Bronxville cat. Zack grabbed him by his shirt with both hands with a ferocity that burned through him.

"Tell your boss I want to speak with him, or we'll be back here with more bats and even more blades. Every day until someone tells me what happened to my brother!" Zack shouted, delivering a powerful blow to his face, cracking his jaw. Lisa finally managed to pull Zack away, and they quickly hopped into their ride and sped off.

O Town, USA

The birds were chirping. The sun was shining. All the hedges were neatly pruned, and the lawns were perfectly manicured. All the men were in earth-toned suits, while the women were dressed in pastel colors, holding dainty purses in gloved hands. Impeccably groomed youngsters made their way to school.

At the high school, teens walked and skipped their way through the doors, all wearing their usual attire of poodle skirts, sweaters, and short-sleeve button down shirts, like some psychotic scene from a black and white horror film.

Suddenly, they heard *Tap, Tap, Tap*, screeching feedback over the speakers. The teens covered their ears till it stopped.

Principal Skinner, a short, stocky, older white woman with a deep southern accent, and a strong conservative demeanor, addressed the students over the PA system.

"*Good morning, O Town's finest and brightest. God loves you and he's always watching. Ladies let's pull up those poodle skirts and brush off our sweaters. Gentlemen, you stay sharp as we are here to serve you.*"

The halls were crowded with boys in letterman sweaters, all cheery and pleasant looking. Amongst the sea of poodle skirts and sweaters, Kelly stood out.

Kelly was the prettiest girl in school, but she was not your typical blonde. She was also the smartest teen at O Town High. She embodied a square, but she was far from it. Her retro polka-dot dress only accentuated her 50s bombshell figure. All the boys stared at Kelly, following her with their eyes glued, hoping she would look their way. Kelly was strutting the hall with her three best friends; Rose, the flirtatious redhead; Dawn the rebel; and Mary Sue, the Bible lover.

"Did Principal Skinner just say that we are here to serve them?" Dawn asked, appalled.

"I feel like this town gets weirder and weirder each day. I mean just look around..." Rose added.

They glanced at all the teens in their pastel colors and smiley faces.

"... I can feel the cool being drained out of me," Rose sneered.

Mary Sue turned and faced Kelly.

"As student body president, I can tell you that you had ninety percent of the votes for this year's prom queen."

"Prom is eight months away," Dawn sighed.

Kelly was amused but it was not something that was on her bucket list. Sometimes she felt like her beauty was a curse. No one had ever seen Kelly for who she truly was.

Rose tapped Mary Sue on her shoulder and said, "Well, that's no surprise Mary Sue."

She motioned for Mary Sue to scan the hall. All the boys were gawking at Kelly.

Mary Sue was grossed out by all the boys lusting after Kelly.

"God can hear your thoughts, you know. He will punish thy eyes," Mary Sue shouted furiously. Rose rubbed Mary Sue's back to help her relax.

"Mary Sue, breathe. God has already punished them. Not one of those boys has anything to offer, trust me," Rose retorted. Kelly and Dawn chuckled.

Kelly removed her pom poms from her locker.

"Will someone please remind me why we signed up for cheerleading?" Kelly asked.

"But you're the captain of the cheerleading squad," Mary Sue replied.

"Well, I signed up to look at boys in their shorts," Rose admitted.

"I needed a skill for my college application. I'm sure I probably won't use it but hey, my parents are happy," Dawn chuckled.

The one thing they all had in common was overbearing parents who had already decided their futures for them.

"Hey, let's go to Paradise Road tonight," Rose suggested.

"Is it race night?" Dawn asked excitedly.
Mary Sue clutched her chest and exclaimed, "Paradise Road is dangerous with all those gangs and greasers."
"Well, that's why I'm going honey. I love a bad boy," Rose confessed. Mary Sue rolled her eyes at her.

Kelly, looking for some excitement in her life, decided to go too. "Can you pick me up?" Kelly asked.

Rose became excited. "Oh gee, Kelly I'm glad you've finally decided to come with us."

"Yeah, we've been trying to get you to come with us since last year," Dawn added.

Dawn and Rose hugged Kelly.

"This is going to be so much fun," Rose confessed.

Principal Skinner was making her morning rounds through the halls with her megaphone, causing teens to scatter in fear. During her walk, she came across a teen boy wearing a white t-shirt with his hair slick back. In her usual melodramatic fashion, Principal Skinner switched on her megaphone and shouted, "Hey you, commie!" The teen froze and rolled his eyes in annoyance. "What's in your hair? Is that the devil's grease?" she asked as a teen girl in a short skirt walked past simultaneously. Principal Skinner immediately yelled out, "Stop right there, hussy!"

She pulled out her ruler and measured the length of the girl's skirt. "This skirt is three inches too short, Missy. Both of you, to my office right now. We're going to ring your folks and see if they're aware that their children are Judases."

The frustrated teens rolled their eyes as Principal Skinner firmly grabbed their arms, leading them to her office.

Queerville, USA

Queerville was a strange Utopia, a vibrant version of "Pleasantville," after David and Jennifer shook up the town. The only place in all the Midwest with palm trees. A symphony of 50s life; bright outfits and rebellious teens smoking, relaxed hair and Cadillacs. Lesbians and gay boy's displaying affection, while the cacophony of car radios compete with one another. Their hormones running crazy.

Charlotte's Diner was just as colorful as the rest of Queerville. At any given time, you could find teens from all over enjoying a milkshake, they were the best in town. The diner was dead—just the regular customers who liked to sit and make googly eyes at Sandy.

Sandy was the epitome of a 50s pin-up girl, like something out of a fairy tale book. She was unrivaled in beauty, captivating anyone who laid eyes on her. A young, beautiful, sultry, curvaceous, yellow bone. She was every single man's dream girl and every married man's fantasy. Her beauty was so intimidating that men dared not approach her, which is why she remained single. Sandy was stocking up the pastries on the counter and could feel Rickey, the James Dean doppelganger, seated in the corner, staring at her.

Charlotte emerged from the back.

"Sandy, is that poor soul still sitting there?"

"Yeah, he's still here nursing that milkshake. I think he's tried everything on the menu. It's kind of cute," Sandy replied, smiling.

"Cute, doesn't pay the bills. Go see if he wants anything else, off the menu."

Sandy, playfully annoyed with Charlotte as always, rolled her eyes and grabbed her pen and pad.

Rickey watched Sandy approach as if she were moving in slow motion. He scanned every curve of her body, his heart racing as she got closer. To him, it felt like she was miles away, but it was really only a few steps. He nervously adjusted his clothes and cleared his throat.

"How was your shake?" she asked.

"It was swell, really swell. The milk was fresh, best shake I've ever had," Rickey rambled on, nervously.

Sandy was amused by Rickey's nervous behavior.

"Is there anything else I can get for you?" she asked with a radiant smile.

Rickey gazed up at Sandy, her gorgeous amber eyes pierced his soul. She had the voice of an angel, and her smile could warm even the coldest heart. She was so beautiful, and he wished so bad she was his. He had waited long enough, and now was the time to ask her out.

"You probably don't think I should be asking you this. I mean, we don't know each other well and all..."

At that moment, a group of teens burst in, distracting Sandy. "I have to go and take their order. I'll be right back," Sandy said, and Rickey nodded. He was relieved and didn't want to go through that awkward moment again. He sneaked out so Sandy wouldn't see.

Zack sat in the kitchen icing their hand. Mama Zack walked in, still wearing her clothes from the funeral. She noticed the bruises on Zack's knuckles, something she was all too familiar with. There was an awkward silence in the air. The last time Zack was home was not a good memory for either of them. Right now, the only thing that connected them was the loss of Anthony. Somehow, Zack also felt responsible for that.

"Let me guess, you fell?" Mama Zack said, her comment dripping with sarcasm.

Zack didn't respond to the snarky comment, instead asked a question of their own. "How was the burial?"

Mama Zack paused before answering, "I buried my first born today. How do you think it was?"

"I couldn't go there. I couldn't watch them lay my brother in the dirt," Zack said, desperately fighting back tears, trying to stay strong.

"I know. That's why I didn't ask you to come. What I am going to ask you to do is, please go back to school. I don't want you to throw your life away like your brother did."

"He didn't throw his life away. Anthony was a good man," Zack insisted.

"He was a twenty-one-year-old dropout who stayed in the streets looking for trouble. I guess he found what he was looking for," she scowled.

Zack stormed out and entered the garage to cool off. They took a moment to admire Anthony's chariot. Zack placed their hand on the chariot and closed their eyes. They could hear their brother's voice trash talking at one of his races.

Zack snapped out of it and walked over to their own ride, which was covered by a dusty tarp. Zack removed the tarp to reveal a red 1954 Hudson Hornet Hollywood Hardtop with a custom paint job and modifications, making it one hell of a race machine. Zack marveled at it then hopped in and peeled off.

O Town, USA

Kelly was frantically searching for threads through her closet, while Dawn and Rose were primping.

"Hey, do you think those Bronxville cats will be there tonight?" Rose asked.

Dawn shook her head and asked, "What is it with you and greasers?" "I just love bad boys," Rose smiled.

Kelly seemed to be curious about this topic; she'd never dated a greaser or anyone other than a square. She went over to them and took a squat before asking Rose, "What's it like being with someone who's not a square?"

Rose was more than happy to share her experience with Kelly. "Well, it's not for the faint of heart. But if you can handle the danger and the violence. It's exhilarating, and the sex is incredible, afterwards it puts you right to sleep."

Kelly was even more intrigued now, as she had never had sex before. She was a virgin square, ready for sacrifice. It's not that she hadn't had offers or had opportunities. Kelly had never been attracted to anyone sexually, something she had struggled with throughout her adolescence.

"I've only dated squares. My parents would lose it if I brought home a grease head," Kelly admitted.

Dawn had always suspected that Kelly was different, but she never confronted her. She allowed her best friend to figure it out on her own.

"Well, there are far more exciting people out there other than grease heads," Dawn gave Kelly a cheeky look, almost to say she knew her secret.

Kelly jumped up and changed the subject. "I just can't find anything to wear," she blurted out. Rose rushed into the closet to help Kelly pick out an outfit.

Kelly's twin brother, Max, with his blonde hair and blue eyes, poked his head in. "Hey girls' what trouble are you getting into tonight?" he inquired with a smirk.

Dawn's face glowed when she saw Max.

"Hi Max, there aren't any girls in here, only us ladies. I haven't seen you at school," Dawn stated.

"I've been around," Max replied.

Kelly was mortified when she saw Max. "Max, get out of my room. I am undressing," she shouted.

"Cool it, Kelly. I know where you guys are headed to-night," Max shouted back. "Hush your mouth, don't let mama hear you," Kelly said softly.

"Gee whiz, Kelly," Max said, getting a little annoyed.

"Hey, Max, are you going to make the scene to-night?" Dawn asked.

"No. I had a long day. I'm headed to bed early," Max yawned.

"Sweet dreams Max," Dawn said flirtatiously.

Max winked at Dawn and shut the door.

"Kelly, your brother is so dreamy," Dawn sighed and tossed herself back onto the bed.

Kelly emerged from the closet in a mohair sweater and a poodle skirt. Under the sweater she was wearing a bullet bra.

Dawn laughed uncontrollably.

Kelly looked at herself in the mirror and said, "I don't know about this, Rose."

* * *

Queerville, USA

Sandy exited the diner after a long shift and found Rickey waiting for her. She was delighted and a bit curious. "Ms. Sandy, I figured you'd like some company on your walk home," Rickey said as he approached her.

"Is that right?" she remarked.

"I mean it being late in all. No lady should walk alone in the dark," he added.

Sandy liked him, but she wanted to make sure he knew that she was a transwoman. "Lady, huh? Do you know what I am?"

"I would like to think you are the same as me, one of God's creations. I don't judge. You can't help who your heart desires," Rickey explained.

Sandy was enchanted by Rickey. "What's your name?" "Rickey, but you can call me Rick," he replied.

Sandy extended her hand, which was snugly wrapped in a white glove, and added, "Pleasure to meet you, Rick." They exchanged handshakes, and Rickey joined Sandy on her stroll. "So, you haven't been coming to the diner because you like our shakes?" Sandy teased Rickey. "Your shakes are swell in all, but it's the view that I can't get enough of," Rickey said shyly.

"You really know how to make a lady feel special, Rick." Sandy went on to say.

"Do you think I can take you to see a flick or to a hop some time?" Rickey inquired.

Sandy was flattered by the offer, but she was otherwise distracted. "I don't know, Rick. I really have a lot going on."

Rickey wrote his phone number down on a napkin. "No rush, it's no rush at all. Give me a ring," Rickey handed Sandy the napkin and extended his arm. Sandy obliged, and they continued walking.

Paradise Road River Basin

A fleet of cars lined the river basin as different gangs from all over the state flooded in for the love of racing. One outlandish set of outfits after another made it easy to tell who was from where. Everyone was there for fun, hundreds of rough, menacing young men and women. 50s tunes blasted from the radio as the racers were already competing, but everyone was eagerly waiting for Zack to show up.

Kelly, Dawn and Rose arrived at the scene. Kelly glanced around, taking in all the different people and styles. Besides a few visits to the Queerville diner, she had never really been outside of O Town. It was like a social shock, but she was excited to learn about all the different cultures and people.

Rose and Dawn swayed to the music that was blasting. Kelly, on the other hand, kept adjusting her clothes, visibly nervous, and not dressed appropriately for this crowd.

Dawn noticed Kelly's nervousness and spoke up, "Kelly, cool it, would you? Here, have a drink and relax." She offered Kelly some of her beer.

"Dawn, you know I don't drink that stuff," Kelly replied.

"Fine, suit yourself," Dawn said dismissively.

Kelly attempted to remove her bullet bra, but she was struggling. Dawn noticed and decided to assist her. Rose felt embarrassed by their behavior.

"You two are attracting the wrong attention," she scolded.

"You mean the attention isn't on you," Dawn retorted.

21

"Oh, please, the spotlight is always on me. I simply allow you to share the stage," Rose replied, checking herself out in her pocket mirror.

Dawn rolled her eyes at Rose's comment. Meanwhile, a hunky grease head smiled at Rose, who noticed and returned the gesture.

"Excuse me ladies, I see someone who seems to be looking for heaven." Rose strutted over toward him.

She circled the hunky guy, teasing him, and making him work for it. "Didn't your mama ever teach you that it's rude to stare?" Rose asked.

"No ma'am, I didn't have a mama growing up. I had no one to teach me right from wrong," the hunk replied.

Rose's face lit up.

"That just sounds awful." Rose stopped in her tracks, grabbed the hunk by his leather jacket and said, "Tell me more," as she dragged him away.

Engines revved in the night as Zack pulled up in their custom Hudson Hornet. The crowd went crazy, thrilled to have their race champion back. Zack, still the undisputed race champ in all the Midwest, stepped out of the car, exuding the same intimidating energy. The crowd blaring with adlibs from guys and girls shouting their name. It was clear that Zack was very popular. Zack joined their Red Dragon gang and grabbed a beer. It felt good to see so many people excited about them, but there was still a void in their chest.

Lisa approached them.

"What's buzzin, cuzzin? Everyone came out to see your race tonight. You better not lose," Lisa urged.

Zack gave Lisa a blank look and said, "I'm a Calhoun. We never lose." They joined Roy and the other racers, Danny and Roger.

"Listen up, this will be a go for pinks, winner gets both losers' ride. I'm going to hold the pink slips and hand them over to the winner at the end of the race," Roy explained.

A long line of sleek spectators' rides followed. Zack sped up to the starting line and suddenly stopped, screeching to a halt. Danny stopped, aligning his bumpers with Zack. Roger stopped too late.

Roger backed up to the others. A dozen cars fanned out with practiced choreography towards the finish line. Roy stood between the waiting racers.

Kelly was looking at all the commotion. This was her first race, and she was fascinated by all the different chariots and designs. She had only seen things like this on television.

"What exactly is going on?" she asked, trying to peer through the crowd to the strip.

Dawn looked at her innocent best friend who seemed lost, and said, "You are about to witness the greatest race ever. Zack is racing! We came on the perfect night."

Kelly looked at the cars lined up at the starting line.

"Who is Zack?" she asked, she couldn't see anything.

"Come on, you don't want to miss this," Dawn grabbed Kelly's hand and they made their way down to the strip.

Danny had beads of sweat on his forehead as his engine snapped and popped hungrily. He looked over at Roger and grinned. Roger checked the time. Nervous. Mouth dry. He glanced over at Zack who stared back with piteous disregard, treating Roger as a mere nuisance to be ignored.

Roy slowly raised both arms, while Zack's left hand grabbed the steering wheel, their left foot on the clutch, right hand on the gearshifts, and their right foot lightly on the gas. As Roy's arm dropped the engines screamed and the three cars burned rubber. With the clutches up, the tires spun and caught, propelling the three cars forward.

Roger was slammed into his seat as the rpms climbed. He watched the shift lights, and at the perfect moment, he took his foot off the throttle, pressed the clutch in, shifted to 3rd gear, and released the clutch. The car accelerated faster and faster, reaching 80MPH. The car was shaking, jalopy chaos, smoke filled the car as the engine strained. Meanwhile, Zack was in the lead with Danny close behind and Roger gaining ground, his exhaust shooting flame. The crowd at the finish line was elated. Zack led with precision, mechanical skill, reaching — 100mph.

At the perfect moment, Zack floored it. Stunning acceleration. Smooth sailing, a beautiful waltz to Roger's frantic jalopy. The road ahead seemed inviting and open, and Zack's engine howled its controlled war cry. Danny's Cadillac peeled off with Roger on his bumper. Zack was driving with Zen precision. The harmony of man and machine. Zack cast an almost lazy glance at Danny's bright green Cadillac alongside. Zack threw the car into 4th gear.

As the finish line approached, Zack nosed ahead, with Roger a couple lengths behind. Danny slammed it into 4th gear, causing it to shudder. Danny crushed the wheel in his hands as the speedometer climbed. He was nose to nose with Zack, and his car seemed like it wanted to tear itself to pieces. The finish line was just ahead, and Danny and Zack were dead even. However, Zack managed to pull ahead and crossed the finish line first, winning the race. Danny screamed "NO!" in frustration, while Roy, at the finish line waved his arms. Danny lagged behind by a few thousandths of a second.

Several car lengths behind, Roger crossed the line. The racers slowed down, made U-turns and returned to the finish line. The car tires were hot, and Danny's Cadillac was smoking. Spectators rushed forward.

Roy pulled up and handed the titles to Zack, who casually folded them and tucked them into their pocket, never expecting any other outcome. Lisa was the first to greet and congratulate Zack, while all the girls swooned over Zack. Danny and Roger stood defeated by their cars.

Zack strutted up, feeling cocky and said, "What can I say, boys? Welcome to Queerville, sex, cars, and doo-wop. I don't want your wheels, but I will take your money. We'll be racing for green from now on. I have enough cars."

Danny and Roger exchanged glances, both relieved. They would rather pay than give up their cars.

"Gimme some skin," Danny exclaimed with glee.

Zack slapped five with Danny and headed toward the crowd, onto the strip, just as Dawn and Kelly were driving up. Kelly, on the passenger side, was looking around at the crowd when she turned and locked eyes with Zack.

Kelly was speechless, she literally stopped breathing. The crowd had disappeared, the noise had quieted, and time stood still as she gazed at Zack. Zack was mesmerized by Kelly's beauty. They stopped in their tracks and watched Kelly cruise by. Zack had never seen anyone more beautiful, neither one of them blinked. Kelly leaned her head out the window to maintain eye contact. It wasn't until Zack was out of sight that Kelly snapped out of it. "Wait. Who was that? Go back please, Dawn," she said in a panic as she opened the door before Dawn could even stop and hopped out and started searching desperately through the crowd for Zack.

LOVER'S LANE HAD A BEAUTIFUL TREE-LINED POND WITH a picturesque willow tree in the foreground. The moonlight danced on the water's surface, creating a mesmerizing sparkle. Soft moans of pleasure drifted through the air, mingling with the glistening allure of the pond.

Rose sat with the hunky guy on the edge of the grass, their gaze fixed on the serene water. Even in the moonlight, the colors were vivid. Rose's laughter filled the air as she shifted on the grass, playfully hiking her skirt above her knee, revealing a long, tanned leg. The hunky guy watched as she kicked off her shoes, relishing the sensation of the cool grass beneath her feet.

In her most seductive voice, Rose asked, "What's it like where you're from?"

"Bronxville? I don't know... It's different," he replied.

"How so?" Rose inquired, genuinely curious.

"Where I'm from there's nothing much, it's really just sadness and misery in Bronxville," he confessed.

Rose understood all too well, "Sounds like O Town," she said.

Suddenly, and without warning, Rose unbuttoned her cardigan sweater, allowing it to slip off her shoulders. She arched her back, exposing her breast, which captivated the hunky guy's gaze. Clad in a light cotton blouse, even in the moonlight, it formed a tantalizing silhouette. She got up and streaked towards the pond, diving in. The hunky guy immediately took his clothes off and joined her in the pond. They laughed and splashed water on each other, then Rose leapt into his beefy arms, locking into a deep kiss.

KELLY WAS STILL LOOKING FOR ZACK THROUGH THE CROWD. The gangs were dancing, enjoying the warm fall night. Zack was sitting having a beer with Lisa on their lap, laughing and engaged in a coy conversation. "So, you and Robin really went for it," Zack teased. Lisa was feeling sheepish, "Anything for the crew, right?" she shrugged. "Oh, is that what it was?" Zack remarked.

Robin approached and handed Lisa a beer.

"Here you go Lisa. I got you a fresh one."

Robin smiled and handed Lisa the cold beer. They locked eyes... Lisa grinned and took the beer.

"Thank you," Lisa murmured.

Zack gave her a cheeky look.

"Don't say a word," Lisa whispered to Zack who was smirking as she hid her face in her hands. It was clear she had feelings for Robin.

The Scorpions were doing their doo-wop acapella of; "*My Babe*" by Little Walter and the Lipsticks were swaying to the harmony.

Kelly walked through the crowd and finally spotted Zack. She froze in place, watching. She studied their every move, their eyes, their smile, their style. She was mesmerized by Zack.

Suddenly, Dawn came up behind her, out of breath, "What is with you, Kelly?" she asked, panting as she followed Kelly's gaze and saw Zack. "Oh, I see. Do you have something you would like to tell me?" Dawn inquired slyly.

Kelly never took her eyes off Zack.

"Do you know if they're going steady?" she asked Dawn, referring to Lisa sitting on Zack's lap.

Dawn chuckled and replied, "Steady? Does Zack look like the steadying type?"

Kelly looked back at Dawn. "Zack? So, that's Zack?"

Kelly was elated to finally learn the name of the beautiful soul that had just stolen her heart.

"Do you think I should go over there?" Kelly asked. Dawn examined Kelly's threads before saying, "Not dressed like that."

"What's wrong with my clothes? You are really stressing me out," Kelly said, feeling anxious.

"Here, go have a smoke. You'll look like a badass. Zack might like it. Go ask one of those cool cats for a light," Dawn suggested.

Kelly reluctantly took the cigarette and went searching for someone with a lighter. She found a greaser and motioned for a light. She took a drag and turned around so Zack could see her, but Zack was gone. Disappointed, she turned back around and came face to face with Zack.

The moment their eyes met; speech deserted her. Zack gazed into her eyes, the bluest of blue, as if they recognized their soul. Kelly was lost in Zack's eyes, the prettiest shade of green. She had never met anyone more breathtaking, male or female. She could hardly breathe around Zack.

"Hi," Zack said, flashing a million-dollar smile that gave Kelly goosebumps.

Suddenly, Kelly coughed from the smoke wafting up from her cig.

"That's why I don't smoke those things," Zack remarked, plucking the cigarette from Kelly's hand and flicking it onto the ground, stepping on it. Zack handed Kelly their beer. "Here, drink this."

Kelly, still in a daze, snapped out of her trance and took a sip of the beer, gagging slightly. She took a breath and just stared at Zack, speechless.

"Feel better?" Zack inquired, teasingly. Kelly nodded her head yes.

"Do you speak?" Zack jested.

As soon as Kelly opened her mouth to speak, Lisa approached abruptly. "Zack let's hit the road. The heat is coming," Lisa said, looking at Kelly then back to Zack, "What are you doing with the librarian?" Lisa gave Kelly a nasty look. "Nice sweater," Lisa snidely remarked as she pulled Zack away.

"You owe me a beer!" Zack yelled out to Kelly.

Kelly smiled then examined her clothes.

Zack was getting into their ride when they were approached by Dennis, a street kid from Bronxville but not affiliated with any gangs, he was the guy that always *knows a guy.*

"Zack, welcome home. I need to speak with you in private," Dennis said. Zack walked off to the side.

"What's the big secret?"

"It's about your brother," Dennis replied. Zack's interest was piqued. "I spoke with some Bronxville cats. They know something, but they're not talking. All I can tell you is what I have heard," Dennis stated. "Which is what?" Zack asked. Dennis seemed scared to share the info, knowing Zack's disdain for O Town.

"They say your brother was killed by someone from O Town. If you want to know more, you gotta get those Bronxville cats to talk."

Zack's eyes filled with flames as anger consumed them, intensifying their already-existing hatred for O Town. Now, they wanted to paint the town and everyone in it in blood.

CHAPTER 2

O Town, USA

Early afternoon at the High School Gymnasium, the boys were in their O Town jerseys, white sneakers and red socks. Johnnie, the handsome jock, entered the gym feeling a bit groggy. He hadn't gotten much sleep because his dad had been pressuring him to study and practice for the upcoming game against Queerville. As he looked up, he noticed Max talking to Ronnie, who had a reputation of being hot headed. They were huddled up with the rest of the team at the far end of the gym, each holding a basketball under their arm. Max was in the center of the group, so Johnnie decided to join the boys.

"What's the trouble?" Johnnie asked Ronnie. "Those Queerville freaks gave those Bronxville cats a knuckle sandwich last night," Ronnie replied.

"What were they doing in Bronxville?" Johnnie asked, confused.

"Looking for whoever killed Anthony Calhoun. This could be bad for us," Max warned Johnnie.

"Why do you say that?"

"We're playing against them in two days. If they're out for blood, we don't stand a chance against them," Max said.

As the captain, Johnnie felt it was his responsibility to reassure everyone. "No, our quarrel with Queerville is about basketball, that's it," Johnnie shouted to the team as he snatched the basketball and started dribbling while the team broke out into formation.

MR. BOOKER, THE MAYOR OF O TOWN, STOOD AT THE PODIUM beneath a permanent banner that read *"O Town Chamber of Commerce."* As the only legally constituted body in O Town, it was a natural place for a town meeting. The atmosphere was far from bright and cheery, with floor lamps in each corner casting huge, looming shadows along the walls. Mr. Booker stood at a lectern with a rotary insignia on the front. He spoke confidently but compellingly to a hundred attentive men and women.

"The events that took place yesterday in Bronxville were unfortunate and second rate," he snarled.

There was some jeering from the crowd.

Mr. Baker was also sitting up on the stage, in an honored position right behind Mr. Booker. Mr. Baker was a full-fledged member of the Chamber of Commerce. He sat stoic and upright, lending a sense of safety and reassurance.

Mr. Booker spoke sternly into the mic and said, "Obviously, certain 'changes' have been happening. Up until now, things in O Town have always been Christian. And recently, certain things have become...un-Christian like. Now, it seems to me, the first thing we must do is to separate ourselves from the things that are un-Christian. That's why I'm motioning to cancel our upcoming game against Queerville this Friday."

Citizens rose to their feet, there were shouts from the audience. Mr. Booker lifted his hands in the air and the crowd quieted down a bit. He turned to Mr. Baker,

"Jim, maybe you want to take this," he suggested.

Mr. Baker stepped onto the podium.

"While I do agree with Mr. Booker about these un-christian-like activities that have been going on, I do not, however, agree with canceling our upcoming game. Our kids have practiced day and night for this game. It's a game we haven't played against Queerville in over five years. We need this game for the town and for the future of our academics," Mr. Baker explained.

There was a loud murmur and nods of agreement. Some citizens didn't like the idea and shook their heads in disappointment.

"I say we take a vote," Mr. Booker urged.

JOHNNIE STROLLED OUT OF SCHOOL AND SPOTTED ROSE sitting with Kelly, Dawn and Mary Sue, animatedly describing something that was holding their rapt attention.

Rose was giving a very vivid description of her night with the hunky guy. "His touch, his lips, the way his hands caressed my body," Rose said.

Mary Sue was listening intensely. Rose's words were making her temperature rise. She'd never experienced such things before, and her curiosity was getting the best of her.

"The way his lips pressed against mine made my butterflies shiver," Rose continued.

The girls were captivated by Rose's words, but none more so than Kelly, who had always wanted to experience such a thing.

"I've never had butterflies before. What does it feel like?" Kelly asked with eyes wide.

"It feels like sin bubbling in your tummy," Mary Sue blurted out before Rose could respond to Kelly.

"That wasn't butterflies," Dawn chuckled.

Rose looked at Mary Sue and teased, "Mary Sue, you should let Johnnie explore your body. You might relax some."

Johnnie approached and gave Mary Sue an unexpected hug. "Oh, Johnnie, you startled me," Mary Sue exclaimed. "What are you all jazzed about?" Johnnie asked. "Nothing, just girl business," she replied.

Kelly looked around for her brother, Max.

"Hey, Johnnie, have you seen my brother?"

"Yeah, he should be coming out soon," Johnnie replied.

Mary Sue experienced some hunger pains and her stomach growled. The girls laughed.

"I'm sorry I haven't eaten all day," Mary Sue apologized. "I could take a coke and fries," Johnnie offered.

"Girls, you want to come with?" Mary Sue asked.

Kelly was happy to see Zack again. "Yes, but I need to go home and change first. I don't want to go to Queerville in this."

"Ok, see you later girls," Mary Sue and Johnnie said as they left. Kelly turned to Rose. "Will you guys help me pick out something," she touched her sweater and said, "a little less square? Something that will get the hippest cat to notice me?"

Rose was excited. "Oh my god! A makeover?"

"Just a hip outfit, nothing greasy," Kelly replied.

"Don't worry, Kelly. We'll have the hippest cat, meowing at your feet," Dawn said with a cheeky grin.

Queerville, USA

Mary Sue and Johnnie entered the diner and Johnnie hurriedly up to a table and pulled out a chair for her. As she sat down, she accidentally brushed against him. Johnnie stared at Mary Sue from across the table and reached out to hold her hand.

"Hello, can I take your order?" a voice said.

Johnnie looked up at Sandy, who was initially startled but then smiled at Johnnie.

"I hear your milk shakes are the best in town," Mary Sue inquired.

"Yeah, they are, we make them fresh to order," Sandy replied.

"I'll have a strawberry shake and a burger," Mary Sue said.

Sandy looked at Johnnie. "Okay, and for you?"

"Um, (clears throat) I'll just have a coke," Johnnie seemed to be very uncomfortable.

Sandy took the orders and went back to the kitchen.

O Town, USA

Kelly was frantically going through her entire wardrobe in her closet, trying to find the perfect outfit to enchant Zack. Rose was helping her try on different looks, while Dawn rated each one. Kelly tried on every dress, as well as every poodle and pencil skirt in her closet. After a few moments, Kelly emerged from the closet in a new outfit. Dawn and Rose were left speechless.

* * *

Mr. Booker continued speaking to the citizens about the votes. "Most of you have voted to have the game, but make no mistake, the people can and will protect themselves and their businesses against these Queerville hooligans in any way they see fit."

The place exploded with shouting and anger. Someone yelled, "No Queerville freaks!"

Queerville, USA

Zack came home to find their mother sewing, something she hadn't done in years. "Mom, what are you doing?" Zack asked.

"I just thought I'd get back into sewing," Mama Zack replied. "What are you making?" Zack asked curiously.

"A sweater for you."

Zack was amused that their mother was actually sewing them a sweater. "Mom," Zack sighed, annoyed.

"It's red, don't worry," Mama Zack said, sensing Zack's disapproval, causing Zack to chuckle.

"No, Mom, I don't wear sweaters. Only squares wear sweaters," Zack muttered.

"Don't worry it's not your typical sweater. I'll make it keen enough for someone as hip as you," she assured Zack.

Zack took a seat next to Mama Zack.

"Any more thoughts on going back to school?" she asked.

"School sucks the life out of people, mama. It just fills you with fear and doubt and trains you to be a worker for the rest of your life. I don't have a high school diploma, but people still come to me for their cars. They pay me to customize their rides. I don't need a diploma. I have skills," Zack explained.

"When I had you, you were born into so much pain, so much hatred. Yet you were a happy baby. That's when I knew you were special, and I knew life would be hard for you. Happiness is your birth right. You can't give up every time things get hard."

"So, I have to endure it?"

"Not endure. Push through it. Life doesn't get easier, baby; it gets harder. You have to get stronger. Do you know what today is?" Mama Zack said, leading Zack toward the backyard. A brand-new Triumph GT Thunderbird sat waiting with the sun beaming over it. Zack walked out behind Mama Zack, shocked, their jaw dropped. "Mom. What?" Zack exclaimed.

"Happy Anniversary," Mama Zack said. Zack was confused. "Anniversary?" Zack inquired puzzled. Mama Zack cupped Zack's face and said, "Two years ago, today, you showed me your true self. You allowed me to get to know… Zack. I just want to say thank you and I love you."

Zack was taken aback by those words. Zack grabbed their mother, hugged her and whispered, "I love you, mama."

JOHNNIE AND MARY SUE WERE JUST FINISHING THEIR FOOD as Sandy stared at Johnnie intensely. Mary Sue was looking at Johnnie like she wanted to tear his clothes off. Her conversation with Rose earlier had ignited her hormones, sending them into a frenzy. Johnnie was oblivious to it all.

"Hey, have you talked with your parents about what college you'll be attending next year? My dad is pestering me about making a choice," Johnnie revealed.

"My parents don't think college is for me. I'd be better as a homemaker," Mary Sue confessed.

"Shouldn't you decide what's best for you?" Johnnie asked as he looked up and noticed Sandy's intense gaze fixed on him, making him extremely uncomfortable.

"Hey, do you want to get out of here? This place is freaking me out," Johnnie suggested, feeling uneasy.

"Yes, and I know exactly where I want to go," Mary Sue responded eagerly, taking Johnnie's hand as they rushed out.

THE RED DRAGONS & SCORPIONS WERE ADMIRING ZACK'S new motorcycle. Freddie was more excited than Zack. "Zack, you have to let me take this for a spin," Freddie urged. Zack chuckled in response. Lisa was also infatuated with the motorcycle. "Boy this thing is a beauty, better than a rag top," she remarked. Val turned to Zack and asked, "Can you race with this?" "Probably, yeah," Zack replied, and they all chuckled.

"Let's go grab a burger, I'm starving," Zack shouted.

Freddie let out his war cry, and the Scorpions all hopped in their rides. "Can I ride with you?" Lisa asked. "Hop on," Zack replied as they revved their motorcycle and peeled out.

THE DINER WAS PACKED WITH A MIXTURE OF QUEER TEENS, grease heads and squares. Doo-wop music was blasting from the jukebox, and teens in their hip outfits were dancing.

A slim figure in skintight blue denim and a small polka dots halter top entered the diner, wearing red platform shoes with chunky heels. It was Kelly, and her rockabilly Rosie hairdo made her even harder to recognize. As she walked in, everyone in the diner took notice and stared at her. Rose and Dawn followed behind her and took a booth by the window.

"You sure know how to make an entrance," Dawn said to Kelly. "I'm still me, these are just clothes. It's like playing dress up," Kelly replied. Rose looked around at the crowd. "It's pretty rocking for a Wednesday night," she said.

"The town is really excited about the game this Friday," Dawn told her meanwhile, Kelly was anxiously looking around for Zack.

"Oh, I can't wait. I love those Queerville fellas," Rose added.

"You aren't the only one," Dawn murmured causing Kelly to kick her under the table. "Ouch!" Dawn wailed as Charlotte approached the table.

"Well, aren't you ladies just the prettiest bunch," Charlotte said. "Gee, thank you, Charlotte. I still wish I had your fashion sense," Rose replied.

"Well, Rose, you are my inspiration," Charlotte said as she swirled around, flaunting her bright dress.

The praise delighted Rose.

"Rose is the best," Kelly added.

Charlotte did a double take since she didn't recognize Kelly at first. "Kelly? Is that you?" Charlotte asked, taking Kelly's hand in hers and pulling her up, swirling her around admiring her new look. "I haven't seen you in forever. You look amazing," Charlotte continued. "Thank you, Charlotte," Kelly replied with a warm smile.

"You ladies should come to our talent show this Saturday. It's going to be really jazzed only the cool cats allowed."

Rose was instantly excited; not too many people were invited to hang out with the Queerville gangs.

"Oh, we will be there," Rose said enthusiastically.

Kelly had never been to one of Queerville's parties. She was never allowed to leave O Town. Her parents' myopic views kept her very guarded, but she always knew there was more to life, and she planned on seeing more, especially now that she would soon be off to college.

"I would love to come, thank you," Kelly said with her heart full. "I have the perfect dress for that night," Dawn wiggled her fingers together excitedly.

"We should all wear the same color," Rose suggested. Kelly and Dawn both looked at Rose and shouted, "No!"

The sounds of engines and motorcycles approached the diner. The girls looked out their window to see the Scorpions and Red Dragons pulling up. Zack was riding up on their motorcycle with Lisa on the back. Kelly, looking out the window, saw Zack and smiled. She could feel her heart racing and her knees getting weak. She noticed Lisa getting off the motorcycle with Zack and felt a little disheartened.

After they settled back in their seats Kelly turned to Rose and asked her a question, "Hey Rose, you know the

Queerville gangs pretty well, don't you?" "Yes, I do,"
Rose replied.

"Is Zack and that girl an item?" Kelly so desperately
wanted to know.

"Who, Lisa? No. Zack just arrived back in town.
They're not seeing anyone. You know Zack's brother
was just killed, right?"

Kelly was saddened to hear such a thing, her heart
ached for Zack. "What? Oh my god. That's just awful,"
she sighed.

"Yeah, a bunch of them went up to Bronxville and
gave those fellas a pounding," Dawn added.

Kelly had never witnessed violence before, and here
she was keen on the most violent person in Queerville.
She had some compassion for Zack due to her own
closeness with her twin brother Max.

"That's so heartbreaking. I couldn't imagine losing
Max," she sighed.

Zack walked in with Lisa, followed by their gang.
Every teen took notice when Zack entered; heads
turned, and a path cleared for them. Kelly watched Zack
intently, tracking them with her eyes. She was so intrigued by Zack, she wanted to go to them, but she
didn't know what to say. After learning what Zack was
going through, she could only imagine the rage that
had built up inside of them. However, when she looked
at Zack, she saw something that no one else did she saw
love.

Charlotte came to greet them, "Look at my babies.
Are y'all hungry?" she asked. "That's why we're here,
Charlotte," Freddie said sarcastically. Charlotte
clutched her chest and gaped as she said, "I thought you
came to see muva." Robin smiled at her.

"We came to see you too, Charlotte." "Thank you, baby." Charlotte blew her a kiss. "Cheeseburger and Fries for me," Zack ordered.

"Vanilla milk shake for me," Lisa shouted.

"I'll take a coke and a slice of pie," Val blurted.

Zack scanned the diner, reminiscing about old times. They looked up and spotted Sandy approaching from the back. Zack hadn't seen their best friend in over a year, they were elated and dashed over just as Sandy turned around. Her face lit up with a huge smile when she recognized Zack. "Oh my god, Zack!" she screamed. Zack hugged Sandy, lifting her off her feet.

Kelly, who was watching, was immediately envious. "Great. How many beautiful women does Zack know?" Kelly whispered to herself. Waiting for the right moment to approach Zack, Kelly was still hoping Zack would see her and come over, but she was now realizing just how popular Zack was.

Sandy and Zack were all smiles. "Sandy, how are you? You look fantastic." "Well, thank you," Sandy replied, doing a 360-degree turn to show off her body as Zack twirled her around. Sandy's curvaceous bombshell figure only made Kelly more envious. She continued to watch them no matter how much torture it brought her.

"Zack, when did you get back in town?"

"A few days ago."

Sandy was shocked. "A few days! And you didn't come see your best friend?"

Zack's expression became solemn. "I just went straight to the funeral," Zack sighed.

Sandy cupped Zack's face with her hands.

"Sorry to hear about Anthony. I was out of town. How are you holding up?"

"I'm dealing with it. My mother on the other hand is keeping up a good face."

"You know if you ever need anything. I'm here for you."

"I know, I know. What about you? What's new?" Sandy gave Zack a cheeky grin. "Do you have time?"

"For you? Always."

Sandy took Zack by the hand, and they stepped off toward the counter.

LOVER'S LANE WAS CRAMPED WITH PARKED CARS WITH their occupants' holding hands. Johnnie's car was parked at the end. He sat stiffly at the wheel staring straight ahead. Mary Sue was draped languidly across the seat beside him, she stared at Johnnie with a less-than-innocent look. Rose's talk from earlier was still playing heavily in Mary Sue's head. *This is not like me*, she thought. *I'm a good Christian woman.* She tried to resist her urges, but her body was in heat and Johnnie looked so damn cool. He glanced over at her and noticed the lust in her eyes, causing him to gulp nervously. In an instant, she pounced on him.

* * *

Rose and Dawn were finishing their food. Kelly sipped on a glass of water gawking at Zack. Rose looked concerned. "Kelly, are you sure you don't want anything to eat?" "She doesn't want to bloat before she shows off her new look," Dawn informed Rose. Confused, Rose asked, "To whom?" Rose was lost, Dawn however, fully understood the situation and was thoroughly enjoying it.

Suddenly, the song *Maybellene* came on the jukebox, and all the teens hit the floor. Freddie grabbed Lisa and shouted, "Let's get this place rocking." and started dancing. "This is my song." Val took Robin and started dancing.

Sandy and Zack were oblivious to the chaos around them. "Wow!" Zack said, after hearing Sandy's big secret. "Yeah. I don't know what to do," Sandy sighed. "You should give this cat a shot," Zack urged her.

"You think so?"

"Yeah. You like him, right?"

"I do. I really do but..." Zack cut Sandy off, "Stop. That doubt is always going to hold you back. You deserve happiness, you deserve love. Bet on the one that shows you, not the one that tells you." Sandy mulled it over. "I'm going to take your advice and give him a ring. Thank you, Zack," she said, excitedly as she rushed off to the back.

Rose and Dawn were distracted by some hot guys while Kelly watched as Sandy walked off, so she decided to cease the moment and make her move. She stood up, adjusted her clothes and headed over. Her heart was pounding, and she felt incredibly nervous, but there was something drawing her to Zack. She couldn't resist it, she had to see Zack.

"Hi," Kelly spoke softly, almost a whisper. Zack almost didn't hear her, but her presence was undeniable. Zack turned around, and their eyes met. Kelly was stunning, and it left Zack the speechless one now.

Her beauty was evident from her blonde hair to her captivating blue eyes and luscious lips.

"Do you remember me from the other night? I was choking on a cig, and you gave me your beer," Kelly said, her lips drawing Zack's attention.

Zack just wanted to grab her and kiss her, but they managed to regain their composure.

"Oh yeah, the mime," Zack replied.

"I'm not a mime," Kelly corrected them.

"No, no you're not," Zack said, looking Kelly up and down, admiring her outfit.

"Well, they don't sell beer here, and even if they did, I couldn't buy it anyway. So, I bought you this milkshake instead," Kelly smiled as she handed Zack the milkshake.

"You have a beautiful smile." Zack told her.

"Thank you," Kelly said, blushing.

"Thank you for my milkshake."

"Thank you for your assistance."

They both stood there, smiling at each other. Zack motioned for Kelly to join them, and she happily obliged. It didn't feel real to her; she couldn't believe she was actually sitting there with Zack.

"I'm Zack, by the way," Zack introduced themself.

Kelly chuckled to herself, thinking, *Oh, I know who you are.*

Zack extended their hand to Kelly, and the moment their hands touched, sparks flew. They both felt it, like two electrical sockets connecting and causing a spark. Both of their bodies were a volcano of emotions. Kelly's touch was like kryptonite to Zack. They were at her mercy. Zack was taken aback by the spark but didn't show it. Kelly was on the verge of losing control; she desperately tried to remain composed. Still holding hands, they stared into each other's eyes, trying to process what was happening. Wondering if the other felt the same, Kelly slowly came back to reality.

"Nice to meet you, Zack. I'm Kelly," she said.

"I've lived in Queerville for most of my life. I've never seen you before. And I know everyone from O Town to Bronxville. Are you from here?"

Kelly desperately tried to think of an answer. The one thing she knew about Queerville was that they detested O Town folks. She didn't want to lie, but she knew if she told the truth she would never see Zack again. And that's all she wanted, to see Zack again, and discover what these emotions were.

So, she lied, "No, I'm from across the tracks."

"We get a lot of people that come here and fall in love with our palm trees and colorful scenery. Until they figure out what this town is all about and who we are. Do you know who we are?" Zack continued grilling her.

Kelly was captivated by Zack; she found them very charming. Kelly hung on their every word. She knew what Zack meant. Her whole life she'd heard what freaks Queerville people were, because of who they love and how they look. She never gave in to those hateful assumptions mainly because she felt like one of them. Kelly had never been attracted to anyone. She always felt different, like maybe she was asexual. Kelly knew what being Queer was, and no matter what her parents said, they were not bad people; they were not freaks. They were humans with emotions and feelings who only brought joy to everyone they met.

"Yes, I do, actually," Kelly said, smiling at Zack.

"And you're okay with that?"

"Yes, I am."

Zack studied Kelly's eyes, attempting to read her before grabbing a straw and inserting it into the milkshake. They took a sip, then slid the glass to Kelly. Kelly watched Zack's gaze, then picked up the glass and took a sip from the same straw. Kelly, to her surprise, was becoming more comfortable with Zack.

"Did I pass your test?" Kelly asked with an impish smile.

Zack smiled at Kelly. They weren't used to having someone challenge them. Kelly was amazed by Zack's smile. "Wow, you have a beautiful smile."

"Beautiful?" Zack questioned.

Kelly was embarrassed, she thought she had offended Zack. "I'm sorry, was that not the right word to use?" Zack chuckled. "No, it's fine. Just no one's ever called me beautiful before."

Kelly felt relieved. "Good, that means I'm the first." They shared a warm glance.

Zack stepped down from the stool and offered their hand to Kelly, assisting her down. Zack didn't let go, and Kelly didn't appear to mind. They stood there, holding hands, gazing deeply into each other's eyes, almost as if they were in a trance and unable to move.

"It was nice meeting you, Kelly," Zack said softly.

"You too, Zack," Kelly replied faintly. They continued to lock eyes, lost in the moment.

* * *

BACK AT LOVER'S LANE, THE LOW GUTTURAL MOANS OF two teens coupling drifted out over the evening air. All the other cars had their occupants primly holding hands in a tender silhouette. However, in Johnnie's car Mary Sue's leg was sticking out of the window. A letterman sweater was hanging over the door and the windshield was completely fogged. The car was rocking, and from the sounds coming out, it was clear that Mary Sue was no longer a virgin.

O Town, USA

It was another gorgeous sunny day at O Town High. The Cheer Squad was practicing their routine in the gymnasium. The girls were stiff and sloppy. Dawn and Rose tried their hardest but fell short of the routine.

Kelly watched courtside; she was faced with an arduous task today. She blew her whistle, and the girls came to a standstill in the center.

"Ladies, there's no other way to put it, that was a disaster," Kelly laughed. "We apologize, Kelly. We're having a hard time getting into a rhythm," Dawn exhaled a sigh.

"Yeah, can you show us one more time?" Rose requested. The Squad's eyes were all puppy dogs.

"Sure," Kelly replied.

She took center, chanted the school cheer, and performed the eight-count routine beautifully. She swung her hips rhythmically. Kelly's movements astounded the girls. She ended up cartwheeling into a split. The girls were left gawking at how effortlessly Kelly executed the routine.

After rehearsal, the girls were changing in the locker room. Kelly's moves continued to astound Rose.

"Kelly, you must reveal your secret to me. I wish I could move my hips like that," Rose admitted.

"We can practice at my house if that's what you want. Come by anytime," Kelly offered.

Principal Skinner's voice came over the P.A. You could hear the southern conservatism in her voice as she spoke, "*Good morning, O Town's finest and brightest. Thank the lord for another day in this beautiful all-American town. Don't forget America's Bandstand is in O Town tonight. We will be making some announcements and look forward to seeing all of you cutting the rug.*"

"God, are we going tonight?" Dawn asked, annoyed.

"It's America's Bandstand! We could be on television," Rose exclaimed, reminding Dawn.

"That show makes hell look like fun," Dawn remarked.

"Dawn, how can you say such a thing?" Kelly was appalled by Dawn's comment.

"People watch that show to be bored to death," Dawn added.

Kelly, listening to her friend complain, decided to be the positive voice. "Let's just go and see how it is. Maybe it'll be fun." "Doubt it," Dawn replied.

———————————

FREDDIE WAS CRUISING IN HIS JALOPY SINGING ALONG to some doo-wop tunes, when his radio suddenly conked out and smoke filled his car.

"Damn it," Freddie coughed from the smoke. A police car came up behind him signaling for him to pull over. "Shit, here comes the fuzz." Freddie pulled over to the shoulder.

Officer Whitey, the youngest officer in the department, handsome, and married, slowly approached Freddie's jalopy.

"What can I do for you, Officer Whitey?" Freddie asked. "You can step out of the vehicle," he replied.

Officer Whitey opened Freddie's car door, and Freddie got out. They walked toward the patrol car.

"Put your hands on top of the car please," Officer Whitey demanded.

Freddie smirked and placed both hands on the roof. Officer Whitey kicked Freddie's feet apart, frisking him very carefully and getting a little handsy.

He finished frisking him and patted him on the back. Freddie turned around.

"Are you done?" Freddie asked irritated.

"No, I think you might be concealing something. I need you to step inside the vehicle," Officer Whitey urged.

Freddie rolled his eyes and got on the passenger side. Officer Whitey got in and did a quick look around.

"I'm not concealing anything," Freddie said.

Officer Whitey suddenly grabbed Freddie and kissed him. Freddie pulled away and gave a *this is not our first-time* glare at Officer Whitey. He then smiled and kissed him back.

Afterwards, Officer Whitey was panting, trying to calm down. Freddie desperately searched for something to clean his hand with.

"Glove compartment. There are some tissues in there." Freddie reached into the glove compartment and retrieved a tissue. He wiped his hand. Officer Whitey fastened his pants with a look of satisfaction and morbid embarrassment.

"Officer Whitey, we must stop meeting like this. You know I do have a home with a bed," Freddie remarked.

"I'm a married man," Officer Whitey scowled.

"Funny, how you men always remember your wives, after." "I'm not doing this with you today. Look, get out of my car."

"Next time you want a release, go home to your wife then." "Maybe I will. Get that damn jalopy fixed."

Freddie hurried out of the patrol car and slammed the door.

NIGHT FELL ON THE HOP AT O TOWN HIGH SCHOOL. The basketball nets were swung back, and an *O Town High School welcomes America's Bandstand* banner hung high. The waxed floor was being polished and pounded by stockinged feet as a seething mob of adolescents joined in that ancient rite, the Hop.

A camera crew angled around the gymnasium and students gathered around excitedly. As the camera passed students, they checked their hair and made fleeting adjustments to their already elaborate outfits.

A hundred teens were dancing and swaying in unison like some over rehearsed church performance while the band performed on a raised platform. Kids on wooden bleachers watched the whirling and spinning mass of ponytails and concrete hair, button-down shirts, poodle skirts, and saddle shoes.

Archie and the Heartbeats, wearing their matching red blazers, rocked into their masterpiece *O Town blues*… "Oh…Oh…Oh… O Town blues… I got those Oh…Oh…Oh… O Town blues."

The girls were in the lavatory. Kelly stood in front of a mirror in a line of other girls. She was brushing her hair, staring rather despondently at herself in the mirror. Dawn and Rose were fixing their appearance.

"This hop is like a waiting list for hell," Dawn shouted.

"I just want to get this pretty face on the tube," Rose said.

"Seriously, why do we keep coming to these? Nothing but eggheads and bible whores," Dawn continued.

Kelly had to agree, the hop was dead.

"Because we're insane. We keep waiting for something to change and it never does," Kelly murmured.

"Dullsville," Dawn added.

The girls tumbled out the lavatory and abruptly cooled it as they saw Principal Skinner. They then ran into Ronnie as he was coming out of the boys' lavatory with Johnnie. They all went together to watch the dancers as Archie and his band moaned through a slow number, *"Smoke Gets in Your Eyes."*

Ronnie attempted to take Rose's hand, "Come on, Rose." "Come on what?" Rose snatched her hand away.

"I want to dance," Ronnie said.

"Who's stopping you?" Rose asked.

"I want to dance with you." Ronnie tried relentlessly to put his arm around Rose, but she rejected all his advances.

"Ronnie, why don't you go take a long walk off a short pier," Rose suggested as she shoved Ronnie away from her.

The show then took a commercial break and Principal Skinner got on the stage and took the mic.

"Now the next dance is going to be a snowball and leading it off is Captain of the basketball team, Johnnie Baker, and this year's head cheerleader, Kelly Hamilton."

There was applause, whistles and cheers from the crowd. A blue spotlight floated over the dance floor and then landed on Johnnie and Kelly. Johnnie looked reluctant to go, Kelly saw everyone's eyes on them.

"Oh, Johnnie please, everybody's watching. Smile or something." Kelly pulled him to the floor.

Johnnie gave a sick smile as she dragged him out onto the floor.

* * *

Outside the Hop, the Queerville gangs were attempting to enter but were met with resistance by the security guards.

Zack and Freddie stood chest to chest with the guards. "We just want to show the world what we can do," Zack pleaded. "I told you, you guys are not allowed in," the guard replied. "Why is that? Because we're negroes?" Freddie scoffed. "No, because you're queer!" the guard shouted, causing Freddie to punch him in the face.

A tussle broke out.

Zack spotted a back door and motioned for everyone to follow them.

Back inside the Hop, Elvis Presley's 1954 version of *Blue Moon* blared out as Johnnie and Kelly danced in the center of the floor.

Johnnie and Kelly argued, whispering in each other's ears. "You think I care that you're with Mary Sue now? You think I'm going to crack up or something? Are you conceited?" Kelly asked, fed up with Johnnie's accusations. "Well since we're no longer going out. I'm just trying to make sure there are no hard feelings," Johnnie replied.

"Going out? Johnnie, you're scared of your own shadow. We agreed to go to the spring formal together, that's it. We were never a couple."

He held her tighter, and they circled the floor, the gym echoing with *Blue Moon.*

Rose and a random boy were holding each other, hardly moving, sharing a passionate kiss, they continued to circle slowly until Rose felt a poke in her side; it was Principal Skinner.

"Alright, Rose, break it up. You know the rules. If you and your panting boyfriend want to do the devil's tango, you'll have to do it somewhere else."

The red light came on the camera. The show was live again.

The band members were briskly yanked off the stage, one by one, and replaced by a Queerville teen.

The Queerville band took the stage.

A record needle scratched...

Suddenly, boom – the doors flew open, Zack and the Red Dragons stormed in. The O Town students looked stunned and lost. Rose and Dawn were excited to see the Queerville teens crash the hop. Kelly spotted Zack and was swooning but desperately tried to hide her face. Kelly ran and hid behind the bleachers, looking on. She still was hiding her identity from Zack. *How stupid could I be to show my face on a national televised program,* she thought.

"Hey, O Town let us show you how it's done. Step back, clear a hole and make room for some sooo-ouuuuul." Zack and the band performed an original funky doo-wop song. The Queerville teens lined the center floor and did a sick rendition of the Lindy hop, with some modern-day step moves infused.

They were spinning, swaying, dipping and stepping in formation to the beat. Their step moves were captivating. Freddie looked on through the camera; it was some sick choreography. The Queerville teens looked great on T.V. The O Town teens had never seen such a performance. Some students were overwhelmed; others were enjoying the show, feeling exhilarated.

Rose and Dawn were in the back trying to mimic the step moves, failing terribly. Kelly couldn't take her eyes off Zack. Ronnie was not amused and took it as a sign of disrespect.

"Hey, these Queerville freaks can't just run amok at our hop," Ronnie scoffed.

Johnnie looked at Ronnie and said, "Do you want to go tell them that? Just enjoy the show, look how they move." "What do you expect? They're negroes," Ronnie remarked.

The Queerville teens finished their routine.

"Thank you, O Town. Remember, do not attempt these moves without taking your melanin," Zack sneered.

The Queerville crowd stormed out, with security running after them. Principal Skinner was trying desperately to get the producers of the show to cut to a commercial. Dawn and Rose saw Kelly and they screamed in excitement.

"That was so cool!" Rose shouted.

Kelly had never seen anything more riveting.

"That was so amazing."

"Let's blow this joint and go to Queerville. I'm feeling groovy," Dawn said, exhilarated. The girls rushed out with big smiles, ready to have fun.

———————

Everyone at the diner was pumped up after crashing America's Bandstand at O Town High School. The teens were doing the jitterbug, the place was live. Zack was talking with Sandy. Charlotte was taking orders. Freddie, Lisa and the gangs were all cutting up and enjoying themselves.

Kelly, Dawn and Rose arrived at the diner, excited to see the place so lively. Kelly anxiously looked around for Zack. Some hotties snatched Dawn and Rose to dance, and another one attempted to grab Kelly, but she waved him off. She was annoyed and just wanted to see Zack.

Kelly couldn't stop thinking about them. She could barely sleep and was obsessed with when she would see them again. Kelly sat alone at the booth while Rose and Dawn were cutting it up on the dance floor.

Zack spotted Kelly sitting in the booth. What was it about her that had them at her mercy? Maybe it was her sweet, mellifluous voice or her irresistible smile, or perhaps it was Zack's soul recognizing its counterpart. Zack wanted to see beyond her obvious pulchritude and get to know her. So, Zack walked over, and just like two magnetic fields, Kelly felt Zack approaching.

Kelly looked up and a wide smile spread across her face. Before she even realized she had moved, she was face to face with Zack.

"Hey, I didn't think I would see you again, so soon," Zack said. Kelly smiled and replied, "Sorry to disappoint you."

They shared a moment, gazing into each other's eyes before Zack asked, "Would you like to dance?"

"I thought you'd never ask," Kelly replied, her smile growing even bigger.

Zack led Kelly toward the jukebox; Lisa seemed visibly upset. The song changed to *"I only have eyes for you." by The Flamingos.*

Zack took Kelly's hand and drew her in closer, wrapping their arms around her. The moment Zack touched her, her body trembled. The tighter Zack held her, the faster her heart raced. Kelly reciprocated by wrapping her arms around Zack, and they wayed to the music. Lost in each other's gaze, like they were the only ones in the room. Everything around them faded away, and they were consumed by the moment. The song complimented the scene, but they were too absorbed in each other to hear the melody. All they could hear were their own heartbeats and the deep breaths they both took.

Dawn observed them with a smile, glad that the secret was finally out. Rose looked shocked, in disbelief, her mouth hanging open. The hot guy whispered something in her ear, and she turned to kiss him, forgetting everything she had just seen.

Zack continued to stare into Kelly's eyes.

"You know, I normally don't dance, drink milkshakes or give my beer away," Zack confessed.

"Say it isn't so. Why the sudden change?" Kelly teased.

"I'm not sure, Kelly. I can't seem to get my mind off you since we met. There's something about you. I'm not quite sure what it is," Zack explained.

Kelly grinned; her heart fluttered at Zack's words.

"I can say the same about you," Kelly admitted.

"Have you ever danced with someone like me?"

"I've never met anyone like you before."

"Oh, so you think you know me?" Zack replied defensively. Being cautious was second nature to Zack as they had learned at a young age not to trust easily.

"No, I don't know anything about you, and I won't pretend to. But I would like to know everything there is to know about you Zack," Kelly said with determination.

She wanted to know all the good, all the bad and all the ugly. She wanted to know their strengths, weaknesses, and everything in between. She wanted to study Zack, and she knew she would excel at that task.

"Is that right? Why?" Zack asked.

Kelly looked deep into Zack's soul, "Because you're special," she whispered, gazing at Zack with total adoration.

Zack was caught off guard. Besides Mama Zack, no one had ever told them they were special. Kelly had only known them for a day, yet she saw something in them that no one else did.

Zack wanted to learn more about her, so they asked, "Where are you from again?"

Kelly's eyes grew big; there it was, that dreadful question she had kept trying to avoid. She didn't want to ruin the moment, and she hated lying to Zack. Especially now with Zack's arms wrapped around her so perfectly. One last time, she thought, after they spent more time together, she would tell Zack the truth.

"Um, just across the tracks," the words reluctantly left Kelly's lips.

"North side?" Zack inquired.

"Um, yeah," Kelly lied.

Zack was impressed. The north side was a nice suburbia. They weren't square, but they weren't greasers either. The cost of living was higher, but it was a nice place, and no one messed with them.

"I've been there once or twice. Nice cars."

"Is that what you do, cars?" Kelly changed the subject. "Yeah, I customize and tune up cars. It takes me all around the country. I've seen so many beautiful towns and fat cities."

Kelly was impressed by how much Zack had seen.

"Wow, I've never been further than Queerville."

"Well, we need to change that. There's a big, beautiful world out there you should see it all," Zack suggested.

"That's my dream, to travel the world with someone special." "Have you found that someone special?"

Just then, Lisa abruptly approached them.

"Zack, those Bronxville devils are cruising. C'mon, let's get them," Lisa urged, pulling on Zack's arm as they held onto Kelly's hand.

"Can I see you tomorrow? Are you free?" Zack desperately asked Kelly. "Yes, yes, I'm free. I would love to see you again," Kelly replied hastily, her face glowing, with a wide smile.

"Wait for me tomorrow," Zack requested.

"Okay, I'll be here," Kelly agreed.

Zack and the gangs stormed out of the diner, chasing after the Bronxville gang. Kelly was left on cloud nine.

Sandy approached her and looked straight into her eyes. "Hi! If you hurt Zack, I hurt you. Love this outfit, you look great," Sandy said, winking before sashaying off. Kelly didn't take offense to Sandy's threat. She knew what Zack meant to the people in this town.

* * *

THE RED DRAGONS CAUGHT UP TO THE BRONXVILLE guys, and there was an all-out brawl in the middle of the road. Zack caught up to one of them, kicking him in the groin, followed by a kick to his knee, and then tossing him to the ground. Zack twisted his arm, contorting it like bubblegum, until he submitted.

"Tell me who killed my brother!" Zack demanded to know. "I don't know," the guy denied.

His denial infuriated Zack. Zack squeezed harder, causing the guy to scream in pain.

"All I know is that your brother was killed by someone you know," he grunted.

Zack was frozen, they stared at him with a sense of incredulity. "What did you say?"

"Someone witnessed what happened to your brother. But he skipped town; he was too scared. He mentioned that the person who killed your brother was someone that you know," he grunted.

Zack continued to hit him, fueled by agony and rage. "Who was it?" Zack hollered.

"I don't know. All he would say was that the person who killed your brother was wearing an O Town sweater, that's all," the guy replied.

Zack's rage grew considerably.

CHAPTER 3

O Town, USA

Burt Campbell opened his hardware store like he did every morning, only today, there was a slight difference. He swung open the door, put out the lawn mowers and fans, then prominently displayed a newly handwritten sign in the front window, that read, **NO QUEERS!** As other businesses on Main Street opened, an increasing number of signs with the same message appeared in their windows, alongside the donuts, fishing poles, and beside the newspapers that featured the Queerville teens on the front page with the headline, *America's Bandstand Disaster.* Everything else looked frighteningly the same.

————————

Kelly confidently walked down the school halls, radiating beauty in her form fitting white Capri pants and a pink blouse. Her petite victory roll hairdo added to her overall charm. She was all smiles and glowing. She couldn't contain her excitement to see Zack after school. She knocked on Principal Skinner's door and asked, "Principal Skinner, you wanted to speak with me?"

Principal Skinner glanced up at Kelly's attire, paused, raised an eyebrow, and then looked back at Kelly with practiced disappointment.

"Yes, Kelly, come in dear and have a seat," she said, exasperated.

This was Kelly's first time being summoned to the principal's office, and she nervously took a seat. Principal Skinner's southern accent seemed a bit thicker today. "Kelly, for the past few days, I've noticed that you haven't been wearing your usual attire to school."

Kelly looked at her clothes, annoyed by everyone's opinions on her style. "Well, there is no standard dress code policy." "Well, child, we've never needed one. The kids just oblige."

Kelly rolled her eyes, "Well, Principal Skinner..."

"Hush child. Someone with authority is speaking..." Irritated, Kelly crossed her arms and legs and shook her foot, drawing attention to her Capri pants. Principal Skinner's eyes went big, and in classic form got melodramatic.

"And what are those, petal pushers? Oh, the monstrosity, and your hair; what have you done to your hair? It's just not Christian, like," Principal Skinner shook her head.

"Now you have a problem with my hair?" Kelly murmured.

"Less petal pushers, more poodle skirts, and where are the sweaters?" Principal Skinner continued to nag. Kelly rubbed her head in complete agony as Principal Skinner nagging persisted.

"In O Town, our kids wear sweaters and poodle skirts." "Can I go to cheerleading practice now?" Kelly asked, growing impatient.

Principal Skinner couldn't believe her ears.

"Practice?! You need to get your GPA up before you worry about practice."

"I have the highest GPA in the school," Kelly reminded Principal Skinner.

"Yes, I know. So, you're not the dumbest."

Kelly dropped her head back in anguish.

———————————

Johnnie was packing up his jersey to head to practice when his dad, Mr. Baker, poked his head in. "Are you ready for your big game tomorrow?" Mr. Baker asked.

"Yes, Dad, I'm headed to practice right now." Johnnie had grown accustomed to his dad's harshness, so it didn't bother him anymore. He knew his dad expected nothing less than perfection, and he wouldn't settle for anything less.

"I went against the council so you could play this game. You need to win in order to secure the scholarship for college next year," Mr. Baker reminded Johnnie.

"I know what this game means to this town. We trained hard every day just for this game. We will go out there and give it everything we got," Johnnie noticed his dad wasn't wearing his wedding band.

"Dad, where's your wedding ring?" he asked.

Mr. Baker hadn't even realized he wasn't wearing it.

"Oh, I... must... I guess I left it by my bedside," he replied.

An awkward silence filled the room as they exchanged curious glances. Mr. Baker then stood up and walked out, leaving Johnnie wondering.

MAX CREPT INTO AN ILLEGAL SPORTS BAR. AS HIS EYES adjusted to the dim light, he saw a group of hardened men on stools at the small bar. Max pretended to be at ease and sat down. The bartender was busy polishing glasses. "A fellow at the barber shop in town, Beck Charleston, told me this was a place someone might make a wager," Max stated.

The bartender assessed Max, "How old are you, boy?" Max felt annoyed, "Old enough to be in a bar on a school day." "What are you looking to bet on?"

"How about the fight of the week? Jeffrey versus Sanchez. Jeffrey to win." "Give you three to one odds."

Max was disappointed, "That's it? What about Sanchez for the win in the fifth round?"

"I'd say six to one," the bartender replied.
Max liked those odds, "Well, hell I'm going to go for it."

The Bartender glanced briefly at the end of the bar. A small, pinched face man met his glance and gave the bartender an almost imperceptible nod.

"Are you sure about that, kid?" the bartender asked.

"That's a bet. Fifty dollars," Max replied.

The pinched-face man, spoke quietly, "I'll cover that bet. What's your name, boy?" "Max Hamilton," Max answered. "My friends call me Machete Mike. Let me buy you a drink."

Machete Mike gave Max a sinister look. Max felt a chill run down his spine. He instantly realized his mistake in making a bet with a man named Machete Mike. Nervously, he pulled up a chair and took a seat.

Queerville, USA

Charlotte was overseeing preparations for the upcoming Talent Show with Patty, a fellow Drag Queen. She was meticulous about the planning. Crews were rehearsing; there was a lot of hammering, power tools and terrible singing.

"Patty, I need these lights brighter and these banners need more color," Charlotte pointed out.

"Noted," Patty jotted down notes.

"Where are the balloons?" Charlotte asked.

"They'll be here by Friday," Patty replied.

"Friday is cutting it too close, that's a day before the show."

"It was a huge order, Charlotte."

"Fine. They better not be late. Those mics sound horrible, can we fix that?"

"I'll get the guys to check the mics," Patty took more notes down.

"Is everyone signed up? Because this will not be an open mic night."

"Yes, all the acts have signed up, three minutes each, song selection and wardrobe have all been logged. We should be good."

Charlotte observed a group rehearsing an awful performance. The group was just bad, they couldn't sing or dance and were just tripping over each other. Charlotte looked at Patty and said,

"Make sure to keep the tomatoes in the back."

O Town, USA

Johnnie was practicing with his team, but they were making small mistakes with passing and shooting, which frustrated him. "Come on guys, get it together. We can't make these mistakes come Friday," Johnnie warned the team.

Ronnie, however, didn't appreciate being scolded.

"Relax, we got this in the bag. Those Queerville freaks don't stand a chance," Ronnie replied arrogantly. "Those Queerville guys are way more talented than we are. We're going to have to practice our butts off. If we plan on beating them. College scouts will be there," Johnnie scowled.

"What's the matter, Johnnie? Scared your daddy won't love you anymore if you lose?" Ronnie's snide comment angered Johnnie. "What did you say?" he growled.

Just then, Max stumbled in, clearly drunk.

"Woah! Let's go!" Max shrieked.

Johnnie turned around to see Max belligerent, yelling and waving his arms around.

"Are you drunk?"

"No... No... Gimme some skin," Max denied it and held up his hand to give Johnnie a high five but Johnnie didn't oblige, causing Max to fall on his face.

Queerville, USA

Kelly arrived at the diner, filled with excitement about soon seeing Zack. She looked stunning, catching the attention of every fella in the diner, which was no easy feat when Sandy was around. She took a seat at the counter just as Sandy appeared from the back to take her order. Kelly felt slightly nervous about seeing Sandy.

"What can I get for you?" Sandy asked.

"Oh. I'm not getting anything. I'm just waiting for Zack. Is it okay if I wait here?" Kelly replied, with a broad smile. Sandy smiled back, noticing Kelly's admiration for Zack, it was seeping through her pores.

"If you're with Zack, then you're good here."

"Thank you. I'm Kelly, by the way," Kelly introduced herself. "Sandy," Sandy responded.

Kelly was delighted to finally meet Sandy officially. She had witnessed countless men groveling at Sandy's feet, and she greatly admired her style and confidence.

"Yes, I know who you are. The guys all come here just to stare at you. You're incredibly beautiful," Kelly remarked. "Thank you, but I could say the same about you." Sandy gestured to Kelly to scan the room. All the boys were ogling her. Kelly wasn't particularly impressed by their superficial interest. She yearned for a deeper connection.

"None of that matters if it's not from the one you truly desire," Kelly sighed. "That would be Zack, right?"

Kelly's face instantly lit up at the mention of Zack's name. "I meant what I said," Sandy reminded Kelly.

"Oh, you don't have to worry about me hurting Zack. I'm peachy keen when it comes to Zack," Kelly reassured her.

"That's good to hear. I was genuinely surprised when I saw you two dancing. Zack is usually very reserved. I suppose you both are peachy keen on each other," Sandy said. Kelly beamed, hoping Sandy's words held true.

FREDDIE WAS FRENZIED REHEARSING WITH HIS CREW. Carl, Jerome, and Theodore. They were not in sync, the vocals were squeaky, and the guys were missing steps, Freddie was getting frustrated. "Who keeps stepping on my shoes?"

"Carl," Jerome shouted.

"You know he got two left feet," Theodore whispered. "Well, then go right," Carl shrugged.

"Look, we need to get these steps correct. Then we can work on these basic ass vocals," Freddie scolded.

"I can't carry y'all on every note," Jerome stated.

"Jerome, you're bass. What note are you carrying?" "You ain't carrying shit," Theodore yelled.

Freddie interjected, "Come on, let's get this. Ready, 1...2...3..."

Freddie led the dance routine, starting off good, then Carl tripped up Freddie. "Take ten," Freddie shouted.

ZACK ARRIVED AT THE DINER TO FIND SANDY AND KELLY at the counter laughing. It brought them joy to see their best friend and Kelly getting along. "Well look at you two," Zack said. Kelly turned around; her eyes grew big. "There you are," she said, beaming with joy.

"Have you been waiting long?"

"Not too long. Sandy kept me company."

"Thank you, Sandy," Zack nodded at Sandy, extending their hand to Kelly. "Are you ready to have the best night of your life?" Zack asked.

Kelly looked at Zack, their gaze burned her with its intensity. She happily took Zack's hand.

Zack's motorcycle was soon speeding down the road into the beautiful sunny afternoon with Kelly on the back. Kelly was super excited, smiling ear to ear, holding tightly onto Zack. Her face pressed into Zack's neck, cherishing every second.

Main Street turned into a winding country road as they left the town behind and headed off into the dirt road. They passed a sign with a happy Queer family on it that read, *Now Leaving Queerville.* And just like that, Zack had already taken Kelly further than she'd ever been.

Zack rode up to a beautiful, secluded pond area with the greenest grass, clearest water and incredible view. No sound rang out from the shimmering emptiness; it was quiet. The area was lined with pine trees and the whiff of mint wafted through the wind. The idyllic scene took Kelly's breath away. She was amazed by the scenery. She climbed off the motorcycle and took in the breath-taking view.

"Wow, it's beautiful here, Zack," Kelly exclaimed.

Zack grinned at the excitement in Kelly's eyes. They unlocked an old shed where they had some supplies stored. Zack took out two fishing rods and gave one to Kelly to fish with.

She was nervous but excited to learn. She kept casting the rod incorrectly. Zack helped her, but she was too distracted by Zack's arms around her. She kept staring at them. Zack forced her to focus on the rod. She was amused by Zack's determination to teach her how to fish. She smiled hard; she had never had so much fun. She finally got one on the hook, and Zack helped her reel it in. Kelly was so happy and proud of herself. She jumped into Zack's arms.

Zack dug a hole, placed twigs in it, and attempted to start a fire. Kelly watched in amazement, impressed by

Zack's skills. She'd only seen such things on the Davy Crockett show. The fire finally sparked, and Zack cooked the fish in a pan.

"Wow, I've never seen anyone make a fire before. How did you learn to do that?" Kelly asked, filled with wonder.

Zack saw the wonder on Kelly's face but knew it was not the story she wanted to hear.

"Well, when you're a street kid, you learn a variety of skills. I used to come here to get away from my dad. I spent so many nights eating and sleeping here," Zack explained, their voice tinged with sadness.

Kelly could hear the pain in Zack's voice. She wondered how much pain they were holding in. She wished she could drain it all out.

Zack placed the food on a red blanket, surrounded by soda pops, chips, and pie. Kelly looked at the spread in awe. She found it so romantic. No boy had ever done anything like this for her.

This was not what she was expecting from Zack, but she was impressed and started to feel like there was more to Zack. Kelly took a bite of the fish, it was delicious, she licked her fingers and smiled at Zack.

"I know it's pretty corny having fish on your first date," Zack admitted, feeling foolish.

But Kelly was beaming from hearing that this was a date. But what else could this be? Of course, this was a date. Why did hearing Zack say it make it more real to her? She was an emotional wreck.

"You brought me to this beautiful place, taught me something new, and cooked me some delicious fish. This date is ideal, in my opinion," she said, winking at

Zack, before continuing to ask, "So, is this our first date?" Kelly flashed Zack an impish grin.

RICKEY'S CADILLAC CONVERTIBLE ROLLED UP TO THE CURB with Elvis playing on the radio. He ran a comb through his hair before grabbing the bouquet of flowers next to him and headed up the walkway. Rickey rang the doorbell and, a moment later, Sandy's silhouette appeared in the doorway. Sandy looked stunning in an all-white form fitting dress that showcased every curve of her body. Her make-up was flawless, with full lips painted in the perfect shade of red lipstick. Rickey was in awe.

"Oh, wow! Sandy." Rickey marveled at the sight of her, his eyes scanning her from head to toe. He handed her the flowers.

Sandy smiled, familiar with this reaction from men. She still got a kick out of it. She knew how attractive she was, but she never used her body as a weapon.

"Thank you, Rickey," Sandy said, taking the flowers and kissing him on the cheek.

Being the gentleman that he was, Rickey escorted Sandy to the car, opened the door for her and she got in. They took off into the sunset.

O Town, USA

MAX WAS HOME, LISTENING INTENSELY TO THE BOXING match on the radio, *"Buster Henderson is yelling instructions from Jeffrey's camp, but Jeffrey can't seem to get off. Thirty seconds to go in this round. Grazing shot. Jeffrey still walking, stalking forward."*

"Ugh he's taking a beating," Max murmured to himself. *"Jeffrey still game, still carries the big bomb, still can* unleash that heavy leather, but Sanchez is taunting him with very fast moves," the commentator continued.

"Come on please, please," Max pleaded with the radio. "And ladies and gentlemen, we are seeing Jeffrey turn it around!"

"Fuck!" Max shouted.

"A flurry of uppercuts - beautiful shots all the way, each one finding its mark! Sanchez is stunned!"

"No! No! Come on," Max pleaded.

"He's down, Flat on his back. Wait - he's up on his haunches but no, Sanchez is down in five, six, seven, eight, nine-- (bell) The fight is over! The fight is over! Jeffrey has knocked out Sanchez in the sixth round! Nobody saw this coming!"

On the radio, the crowd goes crazy. Max screamed, grabbed the radio and shattered it against the wall.

THE POND GLISTENED IN THE MOONLIGHT, AND THE POLE lights along the way created the perfect romance. They glided in a rowboat in the middle of the water, with Zack rowing. As the boat plowed through the water toward the center of the pond, Kelly couldn't stop smiling. Zack put the oars up and Kelly couldn't stop herself from saying, "I have to say, this is not what I was expecting from you." Kelly was being sincere, but Zack took offense.

"Let me guess, I'm supposed to take you to some greasy bar and get matching tattoos," Zack answered sarcastically.

Kelly replied with a straight face, "Yes."

She was joking, but Zack was not amused. Mostly because Kelly was correct. Even when they were with

Maria, the most Zack ever did for her was take her to the diner for dinner. It was strictly sex with Maria, as it was with every other girl who threw themselves at Zack, and there were far too many. Maria was happy with the physical aspect; she wasn't the romantic type. Zack once bought her flowers, but she lit them on fire, claiming she was allergic. None of them ever sparked this side of Zack, maybe because they simply weren't Kelly. That was a fact even Kelly knew. There was something magnetic between them.

"Are you always this defensive?" Kelly asked.

"Are you always this nice?" Zack replied.

"I don't know how to be any other way," Kelly replied.

Zack took a long look at Kelly trying to figure her out… "I can't read you," Zack confessed.

"Stop trying to," Kelly remarked.

Zack wanted to be angry and offended, yet they weren't. Instead, they glared at Kelly and felt their heart melt. Zack respected how Kelly refused to back down, and for some reason, they couldn't be mad at her. Somehow it felt … wrong. So, they decided to let down their guard.

"I usually come here by myself. I find the water so calming, and it's a great place to write."

"Oh, do you write?" Kelly asked, surprised.

"It's the only way I know how to express what I'm feeling. Poetry heals the scars created by life."

"Do you have anything with you now? I would love to hear something," Kelly said anxiously.

"Stop joshing me, Kelly," Zack chuckled.

"I'm not joshing you. I'm serious, Zack."

Kelly glanced at Zack with genuine yearning; she longed to hear Zack's writings.

"I've never let anyone read my writing," Zack confessed. Zack was attempting to escape the hole they had dug, but Kelly persisted. "I won't tell a soul, if you don't," Kelly smiled softly at Zack. How could they resist Kelly's sweet innocent face? Zack took out their little notebook, and nervously gave Kelly a glance.

Kelly listened attentively as Zack cleared their throat, with their eyes glued to their book as they read,

"In the beginning, God made two flames. One to experience joy, the other pain. One to know love, the other only loss. One to be happy, the other sad. One to be good, the other bad. Once these two flames met, they soon turned lovers. When they asked God why, he told them, I couldn't create one, without the other. Twin Flames."

Kelly was dumbstruck, she looked at Zack in amazement. "That was beautiful Zack. That was the most beautiful piece of poetry I've ever heard. Did you really write that?" she asked curiously with a newfound respect for Zack.

"Yeah."

"I really enjoyed it. Thank you for sharing it with me Zack. I must ask, what is a twin flame?"

Kelly had never heard of such a thing but if Zack knew what it was, she wanted to know as well.

"A twin flame is two halves of the same soul."

"Like soul mates?" she wondered.

"No, a soul mate is just someone you're compatible with. A twin flame is more intense, more of a magnetic connection. You feel drawn to this person, like you've experienced past lives together. Reincarnated to find each other over and over again."

Kelly was awestruck by Zack.

"I'm not sure who I thought you were, but I'm so glad I get to see the real you," Kelly said softly with profound admiration for Zack. "It's almost time," Zack told Kelly as they switched sides and sat next to her.

"Time for what?" Kelly asked, baffled.

Zack was being evasive, they just looked up at the sky with a sneaky grin on their face, then... Boom!

Fireworks filled the sky. Kelly was startled at first but then laughed, hiding her face in her hands. She smiled at Zack as the fireworks exploded in the moonlight sky. Kelly stared at Zack, admiring their profile. She'd never fallen so hard or so quickly for anyone before. *Is this love? No, maybe not love, it was too soon for that.* But there was something magnetic about Zack. It was familiar and comforting. She was enjoying the moment.

They rowed back to land where the radio was playing, *The Madison.* Kelly sought to teach Zack how to do the 'Madison' dance. Zack was flabbergasted by Kelly's movement; she had great rhythm for a white girl and was a natural moving her hips. Zack quickly picked it up quite easily and the two enjoyed a dance break before being interrupted by the D.J.

"This one goes out to all you lovebirds out there," the D.J said as he played; *"I only have eyes for you." by The Flamingos.*

"I think this is officially our song," Kelly chuckled.

Zack slowly walked up to Kelly and offered their hand. "May I have this dance?"

Kelly was more than happy to take Zack's hand.

Zack gently placed their arms around her waist. No one had ever held her like this before; it felt good to feel like she was part of Zack. She gave Zack an ever so welcoming smile, a look of pure love like she would do anything for Zack. She wondered once more if it was possible to fall in love overnight. Zack's gaze made her tremble; those beautiful, alluring emerald eyes pierced her soul.

Zack cursed at how vulnerable they felt with Kelly. The warmth of her body against theirs...the sensation of her arms around them...Zack was frozen. The moonlight glistened over them as Zack spoke softly, "Thank you for coming." "Thank you for asking. And you were right, this was the best night of my life," Kelly murmured. "Have you been on many dates, Kelly?" It was an innocuous question.

"A few," she replied with a shrug.

"Yeah, where'd you go?"

"Boys only ever take me to the drive-in. They spend half the night doing everything to get into my pants but nothing to get into my heart."

"Well, that's why we call it the passion pit."

"Oh, here I thought it was a place to watch a flick." Kelly loved being sarcastic. It made Zack laugh, something they hadn't done in a while.

"You are funny. I will give you that. Your turn, you can ask me anything you want."

Kelly took a minute to think. She had so many burning questions ready but now her mind was blank. She wanted to know everything but didn't know where to start. "How many girls have you brought here?"

"None," Zack replied.

"So, I'm the first?"

"Yes."

"And what made you bring me here?"

"Because," Zack mumbled as they averted their gaze. "Because what?" Kelly returned Zack's face back to her gaze. Zack was drawn into Kelly's eyes, the sincerity in those angelic blue eyes scorched Zack.

Zack was extremely reticent about their feelings. Kelly wasn't leaving the question without an answer, Zack had figured that out at this point. She was very persistent. She stared at Zack waiting for a response.

"Because you're special," Zack whispered.

Kelly lit up like a Christmas tree. Now she knew the feelings were mutual. She held Zack a little tighter, gazed a little deeper, she was hypnotized by Zack's amber aroma. Zack smelled like a mixture of lemon, lavender, mint, and bergamot. Every time she inhaled; it was like taking a hit. She couldn't get enough.

"I just have one more question," Kelly said.

"I'm listening," Zack replied.

"Are you ever going to kiss me?" Kelly asked ever so softly.

Zack smiled then lifted their hand to her chin, leaned in slowly, as Kelly met them halfway. Their lips touched, and Zack kissed Kelly with passion but gentleness, capturing her lips like they enjoyed the taste. Kelly's entire body exploded with heat and need. A need she had never known before. The intensity of the kiss... the sensation of Zack's hand caressing her back... it was intoxicating. Kelly melted into Zack, pulling them in closer, kissing passionately as if she'd been waiting her entire life to kiss Zack.

With the moon in the rear, the fire burning near the motorcycle, they were the cover of their own romance novel.

Their lips finally parted… "Wow, so that's what it feels like," Kelly whispered. "What?" Zack wondered. "Butterflies," Kelly said faintly as she gazed into Zack's eyes.

Queerville, USA

The Night of the Hunter was playing on the cinema screen. Rickey sat nervously, staring straight ahead, occasionally stealing glances at Sandy from the corner of his eye. Sandy was fully aware. She admired how much of a gentleman Rickey was being but decided to make the first move. Leaning closer toward him, Sandy tried to catch his attention. Rickey, still watching her from the corner of his eye as she cleared her throat. After gaining some courage, he raised his arms in a poor attempt at a yawn, casually draping his arm across the top of the seat. Although his arm didn't completely encircle Sandy, she found his effort amusing.

Sandy smiled and reached for the popcorn, placing it between them. Suddenly, a jarring jump-scare from the movie startled Sandy, causing her to clutch onto Rickey. In that moment, he was able to effectively wrap his arm around her. Sandy smiled and held onto him tightly.

ZACK RODE UP TO THE DINER TO DROP OFF KELLY… She still hadn't told Zack the truth about being from O Town. Lying to Zack was difficult, especially after such a romantic night, but she didn't want to come clean now. Zack found it a bit odd dropping her off at the diner at this hour. "I can take you home; I really don't mind." Kelly tried to think of a quick response. "No, it's okay. It's just that my friend is meeting me."

"Are you sure? It's kind of late," Zack said, looking worried.

Kelly was trying her best to lie. "Yeah, she's having boy trouble. I promised her a girl's night," Kelly explained. "Oh, okay. I'll wait with you," Zack offered.

"No! You don't have to. She'll be here soon. I'm sure of it. It's okay, really," Kelly insisted.

Zack could tell she was hiding something but didn't want to push it. "Ok then, if you say so."

"Thank you for tonight. It was truly amazing. I will never forget it as long as I live," she said with her heart ready to burst.

Zack took Kelly's hand and interlocked their fingers.

"Can I see you tomorrow?" Zack asked.

She had a wide-eyed smile, full of joy that Zack wanted to see her again. But the O Town basketball game is tomorrow, and she needed to cheer alongside her team, so she lied...again.

"I would love to, but I have to study."

"You North side girls are always studying."

"North side girls are the best, woo hoo!" Kelly attempted to lighten the mood but failed. She was terrible at lying, especially to Zack. She knew she had to come clean soon.

As Zack leaned in for a kiss, Kelly gladly obliged. They shared a sensual kiss that sent shivers down Kelly's spine. Zack kissed her in a way that no boy had ever kissed her before, gentle and sweet, as if they shared one breath and their tongues danced together as if they shared one mouth. The heat rose in her cheeks as Zack kissed her with more intensity, more determination, like they were searching for the electricity between them in Kelly's mouth. Her knees became weak, and she was left breathless, as if Zack had snatched her very soul.

Opening her eyes, she momentarily forgot where she was until she heard Zack's voice whispering...

"Goodnight, beautiful."

Those were words Kelly had heard far too many times in her life, but in that moment, they held immense meaning. Zack made her feel truly beautiful. Kelly gave Zack a warm smile before watching them speed off.

RICKEY ARRIVED BACK TO SANDY'S HOUSE. HE DREADED walking her to the door, he didn't want the night to end so soon. He helped Sandy out of the car and accompanied her to the door. She returned his jacket that she had been wearing.

"I'm sorry I had to cut our night short, Rickey. I have to be at work early tomorrow, and I'm doing a double shift due to the big match with O Town," Sandy explained.

"It's okay, Miss Sandy. I'm just lucky you went out with me at all," Rickey replied, blushing, and turning cherry red.

"I had a really good time tonight, Rickey."

"Really? I'm happy to hear that. I enjoyed myself as well."

"You're a real gentleman and that is hard to find these days."

"Well, you make it easy, Sandy. A woman of such beauty should always be treated with the utmost respect," Rickey's compliment made Sandy smile brightly. "Can I see you again, Sandy?"

Sandy pulled Rickey in and kissed him before saying, "Ring me. Goodnight, Rickey." Rickey left with the biggest smile on his face. "Goodnight, Sandy," he replied, falling over his own feet in amazement from his kiss with Sandy. Rickey was seeing stars like some cartoon character who had been knocked in the head.

* * *

Rose was excited to hear about Kelly's date with Zack. They were both fangirling in the car on their way back to O Town. "Oh my god! I'm so jealous, that sounds amazing. Fireworks, a rowboat, a picnic, that's a dream date. All a guy has ever done for me is, let me order first," Rose began rambling. Kelly was still on her high from her date with Zack.

"Oh, Rose, it was. It was just the best date ever."

"...the farthest a guy has ever taken me was to the diner. And don't even get me started on fishing. I don't think a guy has ever taken me to eat fish," Rose continued to ramble.

Suddenly, worry washed over Kelly. She was concerned about how people close to her would react to her and Zack. She turned and sat up. "Honestly, Rose, how do you really feel about Zack and me? Is it weird for you?" "As long as you're happy and Zack keeps treating you like the princess you are. I'm just jazzed for you both." Kelly felt relieved to hear that from her oldest and closest friend. "That really means a lot to me. I don't know how my parents are going to take it."

"Is that why I'm picking you up from the diner?"

"There's that and... Zack doesn't know I'm from O Town," she mumbled underneath her breath.

Rose slammed on the brakes, bringing the car to a sudden stop. She glared at Kelly.

"What? Kelly, don't you think Zack will find out? Zack hates O Town, everyone knows that. You have to tell them."

"I know. I just... I wanted a chance, a real chance with someone outside of O Town. I don't want O Town to be all anybody sees when they look at me. I'm nothing like my parents or those squares in O Town."

Rose wasn't like the squares in O Town either; that's how they became best friends. Rose was also the most understanding and compassionate person Kelly knew.

"Well, you've got that right. I understand; just don't wait too long," Rose warned her, and Kelly nodded her head.

* * *

Max returned to the illegal sports bar, desperate to plead for his life. The weight of his debt was crushing him, but he couldn't bring himself to confess to his parents. The last thing he wanted was for his father to discover the extent of his colossal mistakes. As Max walked in with a long face, Machete Mike noticed him. "Well, well, well, if it isn't, Mr. Max. I was starting to think I'd have to send my guys after you," Machete Mike snickered.

"I don't have it," Max whispered.

"What do you mean you don't have it? Rich kid like you from O Town," Machete Mike asked with his blade clutched tight in his hand. Max found himself

surrounded by goons, feeling terrified, he stayed vigilant. "I'm not rich, my parents are rich," Max explained.

"Oh. I see. Let me guess, your parents cut you off? So
now you go around making bets you can't pay. Hoping
to buy yourself some fancy car, am I right?" Machete
Mike taunted.

"Something like that. Look, I'll do whatever it takes
to repay you," Max promised.

"Oh, the price just went up and I expect payment
every week. Each week you don't pay the interest goes
up."

"I'll get you, your money, okay," Max said, turning to
leave.

"Oh, and Max!" Machete Mike shouted causing Max
to turn around. "The first payment is due now."

Without warning, one of Machete Mike's goons
punched Max in the eye, and he fell to the floor. The
other goons joined in delivering relentless blows to
Max. He curled up, enduring the brutal beating.

CHAPTER 4

THE SUN ROSE OVER BRONXVILLE AS ZACK WALKED TO the site where their brother's body was discovered. Anthony's blood still stained the ground. Zack kneeled and touched it. Anthony's smiling face popped into their head. The agony of knowing they would never see Anthony again overwhelmed Zack with despair. While Lisa and Val were chatting, Zack examined the ground, contemplating what may have taken place.

"Have you seen the newspaper?" Lisa asked.

"Yeah, they called our performance a disaster," Val replied. "Those folks don't even season their chicken. So, how are they gonna taste our flavor?" Lisa chuckled and Val agreed with a high five.

"We've been way too easy on those O Town punks. They've been coming over here eating at our diner, going to our shops."

Val was always the hot head Zack pondered.

"I say the next O Town punk we see we put the screws to him," Lisa urged.

Zack gave them both a stern look before saying, "Charlotte extended an open invite to O Town and everywhere else, to come to her diner. Charlotte's is mutual grounds. We must respect that."

"So, they just keep coming to our town and we don't do anything about it? They come and go as they please?" Lisa grunted irritably.

"Zack, we need to do something about this. Pretty soon those squares are going to take over our turf and Queerville will be just like O Town. How many more of us are going to disappear or get killed in the streets?" Val pleaded. "Disappear? What are you talking about?" Zack asked, curiously. "Some Queerville kids went missing," Lisa elaborated. "And the police aren't doing much to find them," Val added. "Neither are their parents for that matter." "Remember the little tomboy that used to follow you around?" Val asked Zack. "Yeah, um Carmen," Zack replied. "Yeah. She just went missing with a bunch of other kids."

Zack couldn't believe the news. "What?" They were baffled. "What is going on?" Zack shook their head.

"I don't know, but whatever it is, I'm sure O Town has something to do with it," Lisa snarled.

"You're right. The Bronxville cat that saw Anthony the night he was killed said he was with someone wearing an O Town sweater. Maybe we've been going after the wrong people." Zack gave Val a vicious look.

O Town, USA

MARY SUE INDULGED IN HER DESIRES OF THE FLESH AND HAD sex with Johnnie once more. She couldn't seem to stop herself even though knowing it contradicted everything she'd been taught. It wasn't like her to defy God but trying to maintain her perfect Christian image was daunting. Is it premarital sex if she intended to marry Johnnie? She was mentally negotiating her sins.

"How about we go to the cinema later?" Mary Sue was eager to spend more quality time with Johnnie. He'd been so preoccupied with practice and studies. She hardly saw him anymore. It's as if he vanishes off the face of the earth.

"I can't. I have to train before the game tonight."

"Practice isn't all day."

Johnnie became irritated, "Look, you know I have a big game tonight I need to be focused."

"Oh, is that what we were just doing, staying focused?"

"Damn it, Mary Sue!" Johnnie shouted frustrated.

"All you care about is basketball." Johnnie's tone and attitude didn't sit well with Mary Sue.

"If that's how you feel then why are you with me?" Johnnie stormed out, leaving Mary Sue sobbing.

KELLY WAS IN HER BEDROOM WRITING IN HER JOURNAL about her memorable date with Zack. She wore the biggest smile just thinking about it when Max came storming in. "You need to stay out of Queerville," Max exclaimed. Kelly slammed her journal shut. "Max, could you knock for once," she scowled.

"Look, I know you and your friends like going to that diner there. But things are getting heated between O Town and Queerville, especially with this game tonight. I just think it's best for you guys to stay clear," Max said with concern, but there was no way Kelly was staying out of Queerville, not now that she had found Zack. "Max, it's just a basketball game."

"Not to the people in this town, Kelly."

Kelly rolled her eyes. She disliked the people in O Town and their views almost as much as Zack did.

"These people treat O Town like the Salem Witch trials," she retorted. "Kelly, this is no joking matter." Max glared at his sister, and she took a closer look at her brother and noticed he had a black eye. "Where did you get that shiner from?"

"Nowhere I was just goofing around." Max tried to hide his eye from his twin sister.

"Did someone from Queerville do that to you?"

"What? No, those cats don't bother anyone unless you bother them," Max stated.

Kelly felt relieved to hear that. She had heard about Zack's reputation and couldn't bear it if they ever harmed her brother.

"So, who did this to you?"

"I got it practicing, it's nothing," Max replied, although his mind wasn't clear due to all his drinking. Kelly could smell the alcohol coming out of his pores.

"Have you been drinking? Are you just getting in?"

"I have to go," Max said as he stormed out.

"Max, wait!" Kelly ran after her brother, shouting.

Queerville, USA

THE QUEERVILLE AUTO SHOW HAD ALL THE TEENS showing off their tricked-out rides. A row of jalopies, Cadillac's, Fords, and convertibles, each uniquely designed, caught everyone's attention. People were admiring the rides, while doo-wop music played from the cars. However, the biggest crowd had gathered around Zack's custom red Hudson Hornet with a Hollywood hardtop. The town hadn't seen it this close in years, so everyone was marveling at it. Zack's ride was the most popular ride in town.

Zack stood proudly by it having made all the customization themselves. Zack's skills were in high demand, and Val, Lisa and Robin came to get a closer look. "Zack, please customize my ride. I need an upgrade," Robin pleaded.

"Yeah, because I know the ladies ain't giving you any play in that trash can," Lisa teased.

Robin looked at her car then back at Lisa. "Hey, she can hear you."

"When I get my ride, Zack, can I hire you?" Val asked.

"You can't afford it, fuzzy duck," Lisa chuckled.

Robin came and stood next to Lisa, she had a little crush on her but clearly, she hadn't noticed.

Maria strutted in wearing her sexiest pin-up girl threads like the Latin hottie she was, turning every horny teen's head in the process. She squeezed through the crowd surrounding Zack's ride, passing Val, who was crushing hard.

"Hey, Maria," Val's voice cracked.

"Hey, Val," Maria replied with a wink.

Val blushed as Robin and Lisa laughed at her expense. "Not a chance," Lisa mouthed to Val, causing Val to flip her the middle finger. Maria stepped to Zack and gave them an affectionate embrace. "Hey, Zack, I never properly welcomed you back home," she said, planting an unexpected smooch on Zack.

"Damn Maria, I see you haven't changed," Zack wiped their mouth. Maria licked her lips and gave a seductive stare to Zack.

"So have you broken that bad boy in yet?" Maria asked. Zack looked at their ride…

"I raced the other night. I guess you must've missed it." "I'm not talking about the ride," Maria looked down at Zack's crotch and caught a tantalizing glimpse of Zack's package. "Last time I checked you like pussy," Zack remarked. "I like whatever is between your legs." Maria replied, feeling enticed.

Zack's bottom surgery had been two years prior. At the same time that Maria and Zack had their last fling. Maria had a soft spot for Zack that she was too afraid to admit, but everyone knew. She never got over Zack, but they were completely over her.

"C'mon, Zack, I know you're dying to find out what pussy feels like," Maria whispered into Zack's ear, while groping their crotch. She was trying her hardest to seduce them. Zack considered it for a second then immediately thought of Kelly. "Put an egg in your shoe and beat it," Zack said removing Maria's hand and motioning for her to walk away. She sucked her teeth and sighed, "You'll come to your senses eventually," before she sashayed away.

A car in desperate need of a tune up sounded abruptly. The crew turned to see a jalopy pulling in. The car didn't actually stop, it just kind of wound down. Freddie, beaming with pride, opened the door and got out. The door hinge gave way and hung at an angle. Freddie gave it a yank and lifted it into place.

"What cha think?" Freddie happily asked.

"What a hunk of junk," Lisa said.

"How much did they pay you to take this off their hands?" Robin asked.

The others looked at the car dubiously. Freddie looked defensive. He took out his bandana and attempted to polish the rusted paint.

"It beats walking or riding in the back of the bus. Besides, I have a best friend who knows how to turn jalopies into hot rods." Freddie smiled convincingly at Zack.

Robin examined the inside. "Zack can't fix this."

Val looked under the hood. "Probably could use it for parts." They all burst out in laughter.

Freddie looked desperately at Zack. "Well?"

Zack circled the jalopy and assessed the damage and possible repairs. The crew watched, patiently waiting for Zack to say something. "I can fix this. Some new upholstery. Slap on a paint job, install a new carburetor, and soup up the engine. She'll run like a champ." Freddie was ecstatic. "My race is this week. I need this baby to fly," Freddie said.

"Fly? It barely starts. What a jalopy," Lisa said as she laughed.

Freddie cast her a vicious look. "Don't make me key your car."

"Relax, don't be so sensitive. Zack it's going to take a miracle to fix this," Lisa teased.

"Two miracles," Val added.

"So, y'all don't have faith in me? Like I'm not the go to, the pros go to. How quickly you forget I built my own ride from the ground up," Zack strolled between Val, Lisa and Robin like a parent scolding their kids. "Give me my respect or you can give me your money."

"Uh Oh!" Freddie smirked.

"What are you saying?" Val asked.

"Just a friendly wager. If I can transform this jalopy into a respectable race car, you guys have to pay up."

"I'll take that bet. I bet this car burst into flames before you can get it off the curb," Lisa giggled.

"Laugh now, but you're going to pay later." Freddie gave Zack a high five. "Can this thing make it to my mom's pad?" Zack whispered to Freddie. "We're about to find out," he replied.

FREDDIE'S JALOPY BARELY MADE IT INTO MAMA ZACK'S garage. Zack immediately started working on it. Zack and Freddie removed all the waste, including the worn-out seats, and burnt-out radio. They jacked up the car and removed the old tires. Zack looked under the hood and salvaged what they could use. Mama Zack brought out some beverages.

"Here you guys go, stay hydrated," Mama Zack insisted. Zack and Freddie were more than happy to gulp down the lemonade. "Thank you, Mama Zack."

"Thanks Mom." Zack kissed their mother on the cheek. Mama Zack looked over Freddie's jalopy. "And what do we have here?" "My Scorpion mobile," Freddie said causing Zack to spit out their lemonade and giggle.

"Is that what you're calling it?" Zack was amused. "Yeah, why not?" Freddie was being his usual pesky self. "Well, I'm happy you finally have your own wheels." "Thank you, Mama Zack."

"Freddie, don't you graduate this year?" Mama Zack asked. "I hope so, or else I'll be the only eighteen-year-old in the senior class next year," Freddie remarked.

"Maybe you can talk some sense into Zack."

Freddie looked nervously at Zack, "Yes, I'll have a talk with Zack," Freddie said with a nervous grin.

"Zack can hear you," Zack scowled at Freddie.

"I'll leave you to it," Mama Zack returned inside the house. "Can you make my car blue?"

"I can turn your car into an airplane if you want," Zack said with conviction. They were excited to customize Freddie's car for him. Freddie had always been a good friend to Zack. Besides Sandy, Freddie was the closest person to Zack. "Oh, and scorpions going across the side?" "Are you sure you want scorpions painted on your car?" Zack was perplexed but given that they were the Red Dragons' leader and drove a red car, it made sense that Freddie, the scorpions' leader, would want scorpions. "Yes, I want everyone to know whose hot rod this is." "It's your car," Zack shrugged.

Freddie had never raced before and had always wanted to win just once. So, this car meant everything to him. He could envision himself flying past the finish line, but he would need Zack's help.

"Can you make my car go faster than yours?" he asked. "That's not possible," Zack replied, and they both laughed. "I saw you talking with Dennis. What did he have to say?"

Zack stopped working and glanced around for Mama Zack before answering. "He told me that my brother was killed by someone from O Town," Zack revealed, shocking Freddie.

"Really? Who?" Freddie asked, bewildered.

"I don't know. All he said was that it was someone wearing an O Town sweater."

Freddie gave Zack a puzzled look.

"There's no way. No one we know would be foolish enough to lay a finger on Anthony."

Zack looked at Freddie and said, "Yeah well, someone did. I need to clean up if we're going to make it to this game."

* * *

Johnnie was packing his uniform for the game when he overheard his father whispering on the phone.

Intrigued, he moved closer to eavesdrop...

"Yeah, I can make it tonight after the game. Same place? Okay, I'll be there. See you soon," Mr. Baker whispered into the phone.

Johnnie struggled to understand what he had just heard. *It couldn't be an affair, there was no way.* Thoughts raced through his mind, but he knew he couldn't dwell on this before his big game. Frustrated, he stormed out.

THE QUEERVILLE TEENS ARRIVED IN O TOWN FOR THE big game. A procession of Chevrolets and custom jalopies paraded down Main Street into O Town, their eyes big with excitement.

However, their smiles quickly faded from all the overwhelming; "*No Queers*" signs posted throughout the town. O Town folks gave them dirty looks while locking up their shops. Some folks were making threatening gestures, holding rifles, and wielding bats. Despite feeling dispirited, the Queerville teens brushed it off and continued to the high school to support their team.

The gym was plastered with banners and support signs for the O Town Team. The entire town had turned out for the game. The Queerville team, in their midnight blue and taffy pink uniforms, faced boos from the crowd. The Queerville football team, in their midnight blue and taffy pink letterman jackets, came to show support and tried their hardest to make their voices heard. They stood and cheered for their team.

The O Town team, in their classic red and white colors, made their entrance and the gym erupted with excitement.

Mr. Baker was front and center and expected nothing less than a victory.

Kelly, Rose, Dawn and the rest of the cheer squad kept the crowd entertained with their routines. Kelly, relishing her role as head cheerleader, at least for tonight, shouted their cheer and energized the crowd...

"*O.T.O... O.T.O... O.T.O... It's the O Town Show... O.T.O... O.T.O...*" The crowd roared in support of their team's cheer. The teams took the floor. Johnnie was centered and focused, with Max right beside him.

Ronnie had a devilish look on his face.

Jump ball. Johnnie received the ball, and scored first, causing the crowd to explode. O Town started off strong, running up the score, dropping buckets, and pumping up the crowd.

However, the situation shifted when Max made a turnover, allowing Queerville to score. Additionally, Johnnie failed to make any of his three-point shots.

The Queerville team suddenly became alive, making impressive three-point shots, dunking the ball, and flipping the bird to the hecklers in the bleachers.

Later in the 4th quarter;
Scoreboard: O Town 90- Queerville 88 Time: 00:59

Both teams were in an intense huddle. The crowd was divided, with O Town folks cheering and Queerville folks looking hopeful. The cheerleaders took to the floor. Kelly led them out with a huge smile on her face when suddenly she saw Zack in the bleachers.

She got a pain in her stomach and her smile instantly disappeared. Zack couldn't believe their eyes; they stood up for a closer look at Kelly in her O Town uniform. Zack was furious, they stormed off. Kelly froze on the floor clutching her stomach as she watched Zack storm out. She didn't hear the faint sound of Rose calling her name.

"Kelly!"

Kelly snapped out of it, dropped her pom poms and took off after Zack. She ran like a gold medalist out of the gym, through the halls and to the front of the school. She had never run so hard for anything in her life, but she was too late. Zack was already on their motorcycle.

"Zack! Wait! Please wait!" Kelly screamed.

Zack sped off.

Kelly was devastated. She had just lost the most precious thing in her life. *How could it be over this soon when it had only just begun?* she wept.

The game continued with Queerville in possession of the ball. Johnnie tried to play defense, but the Queerville point guard was too quick. He ran the ball up the court, and at the three-point line, dribbled the ball between his legs. With the *shot clock at 5 seconds,* he shot and scored.

Queerville won with a buzzer beater.

The team celebrated, and the few supporters in the crowd cheered, but it was lost amongst the boos. The drag queens in the crowd began to vogue. The crowd grew unruly, ripping the banners down and tossing trash cans onto the court. The Queerville team was rushed out. Mr. Baker was disappointed with Johnnie;

he shook his head and stormed out. Johnnie was left feeling like a failure. His college scholarship, gone. The boys, back in the locker room, were devastated by the defeat. A lot of long faces and somber glares.

Johnnie quickly changed and rushed out with Max yelling after him. "Johnnie!" Johnnie ignored him and continued out.

Members of the team wanted blood and Ronnie was leading the charge.

"We need to make those Queerville freaks pay. They come into our house and embarrass us in front of the entire town."

Ronnie was getting the boys riled up.

"Come on guys, this isn't a good idea." Max tried to defuse the situation.

Ronnie ignored him and kept lighting the fuse.

"My dad told me what those freaks are all about. They don't even go to church. Let's go bring down the wrath of God upon them."

Max grabbed Ronnie and made a desperate plea to get through to him, "I'm telling you this isn't a good idea."

Ronnie gave Max a menacing look and said, "You're either with us or with them." The rest of the team stood behind Ronnie.

———————————

Charlotte popped a bottle of champagne. The Diner was packed in celebration of the team's win. "We won bitches!" Charlotte shouted with glee as she went around pouring champagne for everyone. The team was dancing and celebrating. Freddie was dancing with a guy; Lisa and Val were dancing when Robin came over to interrupt. "May I cut in?" she asked with a seductive smile. "Sure," Lisa smiled.

Robin took Lisa's hand, leaving Val, feeling left out, she felt a tap on her back and turned around to see Maria. Val's face lit up. "Vamos a bailar!" Maria grabbed Val and they jitterbugged.

While everyone else seemed to be having the time of their lives, Zack sat in a booth, sipping a beer. Sandy saw Zack from across the room and could tell something was wrong. So, she went over to check on them.

"You know, you're not allowed to bring in outside drinks," she teased, "Are you okay, Zack?"

Zack was ruminating over Kelly's truth.

"I'm just tired of people lying to me. Like, why is it so hard to be honest with people?" Sandy rubbed Zack's back as she sat on their lap. "Okay, what happened?"

"I just found out Kelly is from O Town."

Sandy chuckled.

Zack wasn't in a joking mood.

"She wears poodle skirts and sweaters, Zack. Where did you think she was from?" Sandy retorted.

Zack shot Sandy a look. "She said she was from the North side. How was I supposed to know? They all look the same. Ugh, I hate O Town."

Sandy lifted Zack's chin up to meet her gaze.

"She's not O Town, Zack. She's Kelly."

"I can't trust her, she lied to me."

"True. But you know what Mama Zack would say? We only forgive the ones we love." Zack shrugged, not sure what to say. "Come on, let's dance." Sandy stood up and took Zack's hand. "Sandy, you don't dance with anyone." "Well, I want to dance with you, so come on."

Sandy pulled Zack and led the way to the floor.

O Town, USA

Johnnie followed his dad to a motel on the other side of O Town. The night sky painted a dark and mysterious ambience. He observed as his dad exited the car and made his way to a motel room. Mr. Baker knocked on the door and anxiously glanced around. A mysterious blonde woman greeted him with a smile as she opened the door. Mr. Baker quickly surveyed the area before stepping inside. Filled with anger, Johnnie clenched his fist and pounded it against the steering wheel, letting out a scream. He started his ride and sped away, the tires screeching.

Queerville, USA

Kelly rushed into the diner, which was jam-packed; she had to work her way through the crowd.

She was stopped in her tracks when she saw Zack dancing with Sandy. The dancing was innocent, but Kelly couldn't help but feel jealous. After all, Sandy was every man's fantasy, and now she had her hands wrapped around Zack. Kelly didn't like feeling jealous or seeing Zack with someone else. Before she could react... the O Town boys stormed into the diner and started throwing punches. They attacked the Queerville team and multiple fights broke out. Kelly was forced outside, where more fights were occurring.

Zack backed Sandy into a corner, shielding her from the brawls. Charlotte couldn't believe the violence that was happening in her place of business. Everyone knew Charlotte's diner was neutral ground, so this was a huge sign of disrespect.

"Oh, no. Not in my house." Charlotte headed toward the back.

Zack ran outside and immediately grabbed an O Town teen and gave him a beating. Ronnie snuck up and punched Zack in the face. Kelly was mortified seeing Zack get struck.

"No!" Kelly jumped onto Ronnie's back; he tossed her on the ground. Zack saw Kelly on the ground and lost it. Wham! Zack nailed him with an uppercut, clacking Ronnie's teeth together. Ronnie threw a series of punches, but Zack blocked them all, waiting for an opening. In one reflexive blitz, Zack punched Ronnie in the face, kicked him in the groin, and tossed him to the ground.

Max rushed to help his sister up. Charlotte came out brandishing a shotgun and let off two shots in the air. "If you're not from Queerville get the hell out now!" Charlotte shouted.

The O Town teens scattered like roaches as the police sirens filled the air. Lisa pulled Zack to leave, while Max pulled Kelly to leave. Zack and Kelly were fixated on each other. Kelly pleaded with her eyes, "Zack!" she quavered desperately.

Zack shook their head and ran off with Lisa. Kelly wept as Max dragged her away.

ON A SECLUDED ROAD SOMEONE STRUCK A MATCH AND ignited a fire in a steel barrel. The fire grew, and they tossed an O Town sweater into the flames. The sleeve draped over the barrel, there was blood on it. A mystery guy stood there watching it burn. When they turned around, the bright light revealed... Freddie.

CHAPTER 5

Queerville, USA

The birds chirped, the sun shone brightly, and a gentle breeze rustled the curtains as Zack enjoyed a bowl of cereal in the kitchen. Mama Zack entered the room with a wide smile.

"Good morning, dear, You're up early. I would've made you some breakfast. Why didn't you wake me?"

"I can make my own breakfast, Mom. Besides, I need to work on Freddie's ride. That's why I got up a little earlier."

"How is that going?"

"It's going swell. It'll be ready soon."

"Well, that's just wonderful, dear," Mama Zack said, pleased that Zack was being productive. She wouldn't admit it, but she was thrilled to have Zack back home.

"I was thinking if I decide to stick around, I could make good money fixing up people's rides," Zack suggested, hoping a job would suffice their mother's desire for them to return to school.

"Like some oily mechanic?" Mama Zack questioned. "No, Mom. I don't just tune up cars. I customize them. No one in the state can do what I do," Zack explained.

Mama Zack still wasn't completely convinced. "And you'll treat my driveway like your personal garage. No! You will finish school and then go to college."

Zack stared at their mother, contemplating their words. "I'm not him, Mom. I never wanted to go to college. That's why I stopped attending school the first time." "Well, you're back in school, so..." Zack interjected, "Mom, that's what I'm trying to tell you. I'm not going..."

"Enough of this; I have errands to run. We will finish this discussion later," Mama Zack stormed out.

Zack was left feeling like they would never make her proud. A constant reminder that they were a screw-up.

Zack went to the garage to work on Freddie's car. The Radio News was playing,

"Bank robbers got away with ten thousand dollars today. Eyewitnesses say they escaped in a 1940s black Chrysler Crown Imperial headed West..." Zack turned the radio up and listened intently.

O Town, USA

Kelly laid in bed, weeping and heartbroken over lying to Zack and getting caught. The thought of Zack not speaking to her made her feel sick to her stomach. Max knocked on the door.

"Go away!" Kelly hollered.

Max entered anyway. "Are you not going into town today?"

"I don't want to see those monsters," Kelly sat up, ready to give her brother a piece of her mind.

"And you, what were you doing there last night? You guys went there looking for trouble."

Max became defensive.

"I went there to stop them. Then I saw you... and the way you looked at Zack."

"You have something to say about that? Let me guess, you don't like Zack?"

Max didn't respond to her angry tone.

"I don't think you understand what those people are capable of," Max said, with a concern stare.

"What? Where is this coming from? I thought *Queerville doesn't bother you if you don't bother them?*" Kelly mimicked Max's voice.

"Kelly, you don't know what's happening out there. There's a war starting, and you don't want to be caught in the middle of it," Max warned her.

"What is that supposed to mean?"

Max looked at his sister, genuinely concerned for her. "I don't want to see you get hurt."

"Zack would never hurt me," Kelly assured Max. Max shook his head and cupped Kelly's face.

"Zack is a Calhoun. Zack is dangerous. You don't know what you're getting yourself into," Max stated as Kelly pulled her face away.

"You and Zack come from two different worlds. You can't be together. It'll never work," he murmured.

Kelly gazed at Max, tears streaming down her cheeks, her eyes crimson from the agony of deceiving Zack. "A world where Zack and I can't be together, is a world I don't want to live in," she said as she drew the covers over her. Max stood up and noticed Kelly's gold necklace on her dresser and snatched it.

Queerville, USA

Charlotte was going over last-minute preparations with Patty before she opened the doors for the talent show. "Where is Sandy?" she asked, irritably. "I haven't seen her," Patty reluctantly replied. "I swear, that girl is always sneaking off somewhere." Patty looked away as if she knew something Charlotte did not. "I can tend the bar if need be. You'll just have to open."

"Fine. Have we finalized the lineup?"

"Yes," Patty replied, looking over the list.

"Are all the acts here?" Charlotte looked over the list double checking everything was in order, she was a bit of a perfectionist. "All but one," Patty sighed.

"If they're not here on time, I'm giving their set away."

"Don't worry, we got this. It's going to be a great night," Patty reassured her.

MAX RETURNED TO SEE MACHETE MIKE TO DISCUSS HIS payment options. The bar was just as dark and dull as the first time he had come. Machete Mike and his goons were shocked to see Max back. "School boy comes back for more," Machete Mike chuckled.

"I'm here to pay off my debt." Max dropped the gold necklace onto the table. Machete Mike didn't even glance at the necklace.

"Do I look like some high school skirt? Are we going steady? This is junk," he said while his goons laughed. "Hey, my parents paid a pretty penny for that necklace. It was a gift for my sister," Max said, defensively.

"You stole your sister's necklace? You got some spunk in you after all." "So, what do you say? Are we even now?"

Machete Mike chuckled. "Even? You know, I lost a lot of money because of you boys in that Queerville game. So, no, I wouldn't say we're even. And this necklace just bought you another week."

Max's expression turned furious. "Come on, that necklace is worth…" "The necklace is worth what I say it's worth," Machete Mike interjected. Max noticed the goons closing in on him.

"And I say it's worth a lesson."

"A lesson?" Max's voice cracked dreading another beating.

"A lesson to remind you that I am not a fucking pawn shop!"

The goons rushed him and took him down; Max curled up on the floor, grunting, as they trampled him.

"Come back here again with this foolishness, and I'm going to show you why they call me Machete Mike."

Queerville, USA

Kelly was determined to win Zack back, so she asked around to find out where they lived…

She arrived at Mama Zack's home and softly tapped on the front door. When Mama Zack opened the door with a pleasant smile, she couldn't help but notice how much Zack favored their mother. Mama Zack was a natural beauty; good looks must run in the family, Kelly reasoned.

"Hello, dear, how may I help you?"

"Hello, I'm Kelly, I was hoping to speak with Zack."

"Well, hello, Miss Kelly. Zack isn't home at the moment."

Kelly seemed distraught. Mama Zack noticed the sadness in her eyes. She instinctively wrapped her arm over Kelly's shoulders and brought her inside.

"Come in sugar. Let's get you something to drink."

Mama Zack prepared a cup of tea as Kelly poured her heart out, "I just wanted to tell Zack why I lied and that I never meant to hurt them," Kelly wept.

"Zack's disdain for O Town comes from personal experience. One day in O Town, Zack and their brother Anthony were both assaulted. Zack was badly beaten."

Kelly gasped and covered her mouth in disbelief of what she was hearing about her hometown.

"Anthony spent two weeks in a coma. Zack stayed by his side every day. The trauma those two went through took a toll on them. Eventually Anthony woke, and they made a pact to never trust anyone from O Town again. Zack's physical wounds healed, but their mental scars did not."

Kelly was heartbroken to learn this. She resented her parents for keeping her so sheltered. How could this have happened in her town, and who was responsible for this horrific crime?

"I never knew anything about this. No one has ever said anything. No one, not even in the newspaper," Kelly wept and took a tissue to wipe her tears.

"If you're planning on being in Zack's life. You need to know something. Zack gives love, but Zack does not know how to receive it."

Kelly was starting to understand Zack a little better now.

"Zack has never forgiven the people that put them and their brother in the hospital. Zack accused the town of covering it up." Kelly shook her head and said, "Zack is never going to forgive me." "Oh, I wouldn't say that," Mama Zack said as she took a tissue and dried Kelly's tears. "Why not?" Kelly asked.

"Because you always forgive the ones you love." Kelly had a sudden realization. "What is today?" she asked excitedly. "Saturday, dear," Mama Zack replied. Kelly leapt up. "Thank you for everything but I have to go," Kelly said, hugging Mama Zack before hurrying out.

ROSE AND DAWN ARRIVED AT THE QUEERVILLE TALENT show. They were feeling a bit nervous, but the Queerville folks greeted them with warm smiles, making them feel welcome. Although it was evident that Rose and Dawn were squares, they were not the only White people in the space.

There were people from all backgrounds, all colorful, Northsiders and even some greasers. They snatched up two front-row seats just as Charlotte took the stage.

"Well, hello beautiful people!"

The crowd gave Charlotte a nice welcome and applause. She spotted Rose and Dawn in the crowd and waved, "Hey babies, I'm glad you made it." They waved back with huge smiles.

"I want to thank all you cats for coming out. We have some incredible acts for you to enjoy. So, drink up, eat up and SHUT UP!" the crowd recited with her.

"Our first act coming to the stage are the only people on earth that possess two souls. So, make sure you double your applause. Welcome to the stage, Two Souls." The applause carried.

Two Souls came to the stage and did their rendition of, *"Stupid Cupid."* The crowd was enjoying the performance as more people arrived. Rose and Dawn were having a ball, they hopped on stage and sung along.

Charlotte was backstage, inspecting wardrobes. All the acts were lined up, eagerly waiting to perform. The groups were dressed in custom designs tailored personally for them.

* * *

Zack rushed into their room and immediately began changing into their casual outfit. They kicked off their shoes and unbuttoned their shirt. Mama Zack poked her head in, soaking in the moment of having Zack back in their old bedroom.

"You had a visitor today," she told Zack. "Who?"

"A Miss Kelly."

Zack looked shocked and a little amused that Kelly had found them and had the guts to show up at their house. "What did she want?" "You know what she wanted dear." There was an awkward silence, almost as if Zack was embarrassed to tell their mom the truth.

"She's from O Town, Mom," Zack said through clenched teeth.

"Yeah. And what do you think the people in O Town are telling her about you? What about her parents? What do you think they'll tell her about you?"

Zack gave Mama Zack a disconcerting look. "Still, she came here to fight for you. You could at least hear her out," Mama Zack left Zack to ponder.

The Scorpions performed, *"I'm Your Hoochie Coochie Man." by Muddy Waters* while wearing matching tuxedos. Freddie played the guitar, and they killed it with their exceptional stage presence and vocals. The performance ended with a round of applause and Charlotte took the stage once more.

"I love a tall, dark and hung-some man." The crowd chuckled. "I mean handsome, sorry y'all. But if y'all think that was sexy, wait till you see this next act. Welcome to the stage the two toughest bitches in Queerville, the first ladies of the Red Dragons, Lisa and Robin."

The applause was noisy, and whistles came from the crowd as Lisa and Robin performed a sexy and seductive rendition of *"Shave 'Em Dry." by Lucille Bogan*- but their version was called "*Eat me dry.*"

Lisa and Robin grinded against each other. The crowd gaped at them as they delivered their raunchy lyrics. Rose and Dawn fan themselves, as the performance was scorching hot.

Finally, they concluded their act and gracefully exited the stage, leaving the crowd chanting for an encore. They made their way backstage, while Charlotte took the stage.

"Lovers' lane will be rocking tonight. Are y'all ready for the divas to take the stage?"

The vibrant crowd roared. Three other drag queens graced the stage. They began their over-the-top dramatic performance of "*That makes it*" by Jayne Mansfield.

Zack arrived at the club, slapping high fives on their way in. Patty came over and escorted Zack to a table right in the center. Zack grinned at Charlotte, who was on stage. Charlotte's performances were always extra. She soon finished her act.

"Whew! I need a drink. Can we turn down the lights for our next performer? She's kind of shy."

The spotlight dimmed. The room fell silent.

Charlotte continued, "This next performer was invited by me personally. So, you all better give her a warm round of applause. Welcome to the stage, Miss Kelly."

The crowd gave a warm welcome. Rose and Dawn looked at each other, then back on the stage. They couldn't believe their eyes, it was Kelly.

Kelly anxiously took the microphone. Her vision dimmed as she looked out into the crowd. Her heart began to race, and her hands began to shake. She spotted Zack in the center, she focused on them and calmed down. Zack appeared befuddled. But Kelly had their undivided attention.

The track *"Only you (And you alone)" by The Platters* came on. Kelly belted out the first few lyrics and the crowd was left stunned. She sounded fantastic. Rose and Dawn were impressed by Kelly's singing, but not more than Charlotte, whose mouth was on the floor.

Kelly locked her gaze on Zack. She was singing to Zack and Zack alone. The crowd was impressed with Kelly's vocal ability, they rocked their heads and mouthed the words.

Zack was captivated by Kelly but was still holding on to anger. Kelly sang the entire song and received a standing ovation. Rose and Dawn jumped on stage and congratulated her.

"Well, that's one way to tell us you have a hidden talent," Rose teased. "Kelly, that was beautiful, you sounded amazing." They gave her a bear hug. She received another well-deserved standing ovation. "Thank you," Kelly said to the crowd as she looked for Zack, but they were gone. She continued backstage and was greeted by Charlotte. "You did so good baby girl. We're going to talk later," Charlotte gave Kelly a big hug and a kiss on the cheek.

"Thank you, Charlotte." Kelly looked over and saw Zack waiting. She smiled and walked over.

"Hey," she said almost shyly.

"I didn't know you could sing like that."

"I had a lot of motivation," Kelly replied with pleading eyes, screaming forgive me. The silence was killing her, so she took a deep breath and began her apology speech.

"I'm sorry, Zack. I should have told you the truth. I never should have lied. I understand if you never want to see me..."

Zack pulled her in and kissed her. Kelly shivered as she wrapped her arms around Zack, welcoming the kiss. Kelly clutched onto Zack as if she held an emptiness that only Zack could fill. She explored every inch of Zack's mouth with her tongue.

Their lips parted...

Zack pressed their forehead to hers and gazed into her eyes. "I missed you," Kelly said softly.

"Never lie to me again," Zack growled, fury burning in their eyes. Kelly could see the torment Zack was going through, wrestling with their soul in order to forgive her. In that moment, she knew she'd rather die than ever lie to Zack again.

"I won't. I promise. I'll never lie to you again," she hugged Zack tightly, not wanting to let go.

O Town, USA

Zack rode up to Kelly's home, which was big and lavish. Zack felt a little intimidated. Zack knew Kelly was a square but had no idea she was a rich kid. The house resembled more of a plantation. Zack could only imagine what conservative parents Kelly must have.

"Wow, you live here?" Zack exclaimed.

"Yeah, my parents like to think of themselves as royalty," Kelly sighed.

Zack noticed the family crest on the door, which read *Hamilton*. The Hamilton's were known as the richest family in the Midwest. There were folktales about how rich the Hamilton's were. Zack was speechless and started to feel overwhelmed.

"You're a Hamilton? Kelly Hamilton?" Zack asked, in disbelief.

"Yes, don't flip your lid please. It's just a name."

"Hamilton in this town means more than just a name," Zack said, astonished that Kelly seemed so ordinary, despite being the heir to the richest and most conservative family in the middle of the map. She was unscathed by it all.

"Well, it is to me," Kelly replied.

"Are you sure I should be dropping you off?" Zack questioned.

"Why not? I'm not ashamed of you, Zack," Kelly said, looking into Zack's eyes and meaning every word. She wrapped her arms around Zack to prove it.

"I just don't want you to get in any trouble."

"My folks are in bed asleep by nine every night and I really don't care what they would have to say," Kelly assured Zack. She didn't follow her mother's conventions when it came to her romantic life. Zack was witnessing that now. Kelly was quite unique. "I've never met anyone like you, at least not from O Town," Zack admitted, lost in her eyes.

"I'm glad you see that now. I don't care about where I come from or where you come from. I just want to be with you, Zack," Kelly said softly, her voice filled with passion.

Zack had given up hope of finding love, but here it was in the most unexpected of places - in the arms of a square. Zack could tell that Kelly meant every word. Zack could feel her heartbeat pounding between their fingers as they raised their hands to frame her jaw on both sides.

Kelly's lips pulsated with anticipation as she prepared to taste Zack's sweet kiss. They leaned closer, and Kelly parted her lips, ready to consume Zack's warm breath. Zack kissed her firmly causing her to let out an involuntary moan. They wrapped both arms around her, pulling her closer as she tangled her fingers in their hair, something she'd longed to do since the first time she saw them. They inhaled each other and Zack sank their hands into Kelly's hair, pulling it back as their tongues danced. Neither of them wanted to come up for air, they were completely consumed by the moment.

BACK ON LOVER'S LANE, LISA SAT IN HER CHARIOT WITH Robin, listening to tunes and gazing up at the blanket of stars that stretched to infinity. "We killed it tonight, Robin," Lisa said. "Did you see their faces?" Robin asked as she giggled. "I think we should take this act on the road," Lisa suggested. "We need a name." Lisa pondered then blurted out, "I got it, vagitarians... no wait, scissor sisters. Satan's mistresses," she chuckled. Robin blurted out, "Clam smackers!" They both burst out laughing.

Suddenly, the sound of two horny teens echoed out into the night. Lisa and Robin shared an awkward silence as they listened. "Sounds like someone is having fun," Robin said.

"It is Lover's Lane," Lisa replied, looking seductively at Robin, before asking, "Hey, Robin, you have a crush on me or what?"

Robin was completely caught off guard. Her eyes went big, she smiled sheepishly and looked away.

"What are you talking about?" Robin's heart was beating out of her chest. She refused to confirm or deny it. "Oh, I'm sorry I must've had you all wrong," Lisa remarked trying to reel her in. Robin turned around and said, "What do you mean, you had me all wrong?"

"Well, see I thought you were someone who goes after what she wants..." Lisa played with Robin's hair that was falling over her shoulder. "...I always thought you were beautiful. But now that I know you're not interested. I guess..."

Lisa ran her hand gently up Robin's thigh. Robin's temperature rose, she became breathy. Lisa's touch was turning her on. "...if I do this..." Lisa placed her hand underneath Robin's dress, between her legs, and rubbed her gently. "...it would do nothing for you?"

115

Robin tensed up... still unwilling to admit she liked Lisa... she looked Lisa in the eye and shook her head no.

"...yeah, I didn't think that would do it. Maybe if I try one more thing..."

Lisa pulled Robin's panties aside and slid her fingers inside of her. Robin's head dropped back, and she clutched onto the passenger door. "...you're so wet.

I guess I must really turn you off." Robin sighed; unable to hold back any longer.

She grabbed Lisa and kissed her passionately.

"I guess you don't have a crush on me after all," Lisa teased.

* * *

Zack arrived home to find Mama Zack up in the kitchen holding onto a letter. *This can't be good,* Zack thought. "Mom, what are you doing up so late?" Zack asked.

"I got this letter today. You already dropped out of school."

"Mom, I told you..." Mama Zack leaped up in rage and disappointment, something Zack was all too acquainted with. "You told me this morning that you were thinking about it. But you already went ahead and did it," she said disappointed. "Mom, school is not for me." "You cannot live in this house if you're not in school." "What are you saying?"

A tearful Mama Zack cupped Zack's face and said,

"I will not bury another child. Pack your things and get out." Mama Zack said sorrowfully.

* * *

Sandy opened her door in a stunning night gown. She was a knockout even with rollers in her head. She was not shocked to see Zack at her front door with bags of clothes. She simply stepped aside and welcomed Zack in.

CHAPTER 6

The Queerville gangs were gathered outside Charlotte's at Zack's request. They looked around wondering what this meeting was about. A horn rang out and Zack pulled up Freddie's new customized chariot. A blue monster with scorpions painted on the sides. They all came over and marveled at it. Val, Robin and Lisa were dumbfounded, they couldn't believe Zack had pulled it off. Zack hopped out. "Gimme some skin." Lisa slapped a high-five with Zack.

Val gave Zack two slaps and said, "That thing is bitchin'," Val was extremely impressed. "Zack you're the best."

Freddie came out and ran over to his ride, his eyes glassy. He was choked up. "Look at my baby! She's a hot rod now," Freddie said ecstatically, as he hugged Zack for doing such a great job.

Halle came over and was equally blown away as everyone else. "Zack, you have to do ours next," she insisted.

"No, you promised you would do the Lipsticks ride next," Maria interjected before Zack could respond.

"My mom kicked me out last night. I'm staying with Sandy for now, but as soon as I have a place to work on them. I will start taking orders. I had to get Freddie ready for his race tonight." Halle and Maria nodded in agreement.

"I want to break this baby in and see what she's made of. Scorpions! Let's burn rubber!" Freddie shouted.

"Red Dragons let's roll!" Zack shouted and the gangs all hopped in their rides and took off.

Paradise Road River Basin

The gangs were showing off their driving skills, burning rubber and performing tricks. Freddie was in his car, spinning donuts. He looked like a kid on Christmas morning, coming down the stairs and seeing the bike he had always wanted. His ride handled exceptionally well. Zack watched proudly, Maria approached and stood beside them.

"So, I heard you're dating a square now?" she remarked. "She's not a square," Zack said, defensive.

"C'mon, you can get cut on her corners, she's so square." "Maria! What did I say?" Zack scolded.

"Jeez, relax. If you want to date a square, that's your business. But you know the other gangs might have an issue with that."

"Yeah, well they can come see me about it."

"Zack, where's your jets, huh? That girl will never fit in here."

Zack turned to look Maria in her eyes.

"You don't know her. She's not what you think. She's not like them."

"Yeah, keep telling yourself that," Maria sneered as she patted Zack on the chest and walked off.

A two-toned white Ford pulled into the basin. It was an outside crew. They were white boys, wearing patterned button ups tucked into their cuffed dark denim pants, and black shoes.

"What's this? Are we early? I want to race the champ," one of them said excitedly as he headed straight for Zack.

The Red Dragons took defensive stances and stood behind Zack. "Who are you cats?" Zack asked.

"C'mon Zack, don't do me like this. It's me, Duffus, from the north side. You customized my ride," he said with a disappointed tone, realizing Zack didn't recognize him.

"Did you say your name is Doofus?" Lisa asked as the gangs all laughed. "No, sweet thang. It's Duf-fus," he corrected her.

Zack seemed to suddenly remember him and blurted out, "Duffy! I remember you." Zack grinned.

"See! We know each other. I've been doing what you told me. I haven't lost a race since you souped up my ride."

"Don't race against Zack and it will stay that way," Lisa warned him. Duffus turned his attention towards Lisa, admiring her beauty and not so subtly checking out her curves. "And what is your name, sweet thang?" Duffus said as he took Lisa's hand and cradled it. "Lisa," she said almost sarcastically.

"Well Lisa, how bout we blow this joint and go play some backseat bingo?" Duffus said with a cocky grin.

A black handgun was abruptly pointed at Duffus' temple. "Is that really what you want? Because she comes with three bullets," Robin said sternly.

Duffus let go of Lisa and raised his hands up in the air. "Woah, now I didn't know she was spoken for," Duffus said. "Well, clearly, I just spoke," Robin retorted.

Zack waved Robin's gun down. Lisa jumped into her arms, and they kissed.

Zack pulled Duffus to the side. "Zack, I didn't mean no disrespect," he confessed. "Ice it, Duffy. You always know how to clear a room." "What about that race Zack?" "I'm already racing tonight. You can't just come the day of, and challenge someone." Duffus was disappointed. "Man, I just heard you were back in town," he sighed. "Look, come back tonight, there will be others just as eager as you. Win a few of those racers and then we'll talk."

Duffus got excited and slapped Zack five, "See you tonight. Woah!" he shouted hopping back in his ride and speeding off. Zack stepped over to Lisa and Robin and said, "Well, it took you guys long enough." Zack opened their arms for Lisa and Robin, and they all shared a hug.

THE STATE FAIR WAS SANDY'S FAVORITE PLACE ON earth. So, it was only fitting that Rickey had brought her there for their second date. Sandy ran, holding Rickey's hand, and they quickly made their way to the Ferris wheel. As they reached the top, Sandy couldn't contain her excitement and showed her appreciation with a passionate kiss.

Rickey, wanting to impress Sandy, decided to showcase his skills at the free throw game. To his delight, he knocked in all his shots and earned enough points for Sandy to pick out a prize. They moved on to the next game, knife throwing, which turned out to not be Sandy's forte. In fact, she nearly took off the attendant's head.

To lighten the mood, Rickey took Sandy to the petting zoo where it was safe. Sandy's face lit up as she fed and interacted with the various animals. They also took some time to watch a show, and Rickey couldn't help but be captivated by Sandy's genuine happiness. It warmed his heart to know that he could bring her such joy.

As they continued exploring the fair, Rickey decided to indulge in some classic fair food. He bought them some funnel cake and a coke. Sandy took a moment to express her feelings, admitting, "I had gotten so used to seeing you, Rickey. I started to look forward to you coming to the diner. But I have to ask what it is that drew you to me?"

Rickey paused for a moment, contemplating his answer. "You remind me of someone," he finally replied.

"Who?" Sandy asked, curious to know more.

"My mother," he replied.

Sandy was stunned by Rickey's answer, and she wanted to know more about him.

"Aww, that's sweet. Is she still alive? Where is she?" "Oh no, mother is buried out in the Carolinas," Rickey replied sadly. "She passed? I'm sorry to hear that, was it polio?" Sandy asked sympathetically.

Rickey offered Sandy a seat so they could enjoy their snack. "Oh, no, polio didn't get mama. Mama died in her sleep from what I guess you can say was a heart attack.

She didn't suffer, it was quick, I doubt she even felt any pain," Rickey explained.

"Well at least she didn't suffer," Sandy replied, trying to find some comfort in the situation.

"Have you ever been outside of Queerville?" Rickey asked, changing the subject.

"Yeah, but not for too long. I'm not too welcome outside of Queerville," Sandy admitted.

Rickey was displeased to hear that. He truly fancied Sandy and couldn't imagine anyone not welcoming her anywhere. "You just want to stay in Queerville?"

"Pretty much," Sandy replied.

"There's a big world out there. You should see it. To hell with what people think," Rickey encouraged.

"There are a lot of evil people in the world. The only place I feel safe is Queerville," Sandy sadly confessed.

Rickey wondered about the evils Sandy must've endured to make her terrified to leave Queerville.

O Town, USA

Mr. and Mrs. Hamilton had just finished a discussion regarding Kelly and her recent change in behavior and appearance. Mr. Hamilton summoned her into the living room. "Kelly, get in here!" Impatiently, he waited with his hands on his hip. Kelly entered, chipper and dressed colorfully, something frowned upon in O Town. "Yes, pop," she replied.

"Darling, what is this gossip about you going to Queerville?" Mrs. Hamilton asked, hoping for a denial. "Who told you that, Max? Why don't you ask him where my gold necklace is." Kelly became defensive and prepared to fight for her relationship with Zack.

"It doesn't matter who told us. I don't want you going to that God forsaken town and mixing with those people," Mr. Hamilton said sternly, his choice of words only further enraging Kelly.

"Those people, Dad? Those people are human beings who just want to enjoy life and be left alone," she exclaimed.

Mrs. Hamilton intervened, placing herself between Kelly and her father. "Don't talk back to your father, Kelly. And what is with these clothes you've been wearing? Where are all your sweaters and pastel colors? This isn't how you were raised, young lady. Now, your father and I are trying to have a constructive talk with you."

Kelly grabbed a chair and plopped it in front of her parents. "You want to talk? Let's talk. Let's talk about the two Queerville kids who were brutally beaten and put into a coma by someone from O Town. Let's discuss that," Kelly said, her eyes burning with a fire her parents had never witnessed before.

Mrs. Hamilton clutched her pearls, dumbfounded that Kelly knew about the town's dark secret.

"That is not true, that never happened. Those people over there are reckless and godless. They're trying to corrupt you," Mr. Hamilton said.

"Corrupt me, how, dad?"

"With their sex, cars, and doo-wop music," he replied.

Kelly was shocked and appalled by her father's outrageous claims. "Oh my... Dad! By the way, I'm still a virgin." "What your father is trying to say is that you might get confused hanging around those people," Mrs. Hamilton clarified. Kelly looked her mother directly in

126

the eyes. "I'm not confused, Mom. I've been this way my entire life. You guys just never noticed," Kelly admitted.

"Never noticed what?" Mrs. Hamilton asked.

"Me," Kelly said in a dejected tone as she hurried back to her room.

* * *

Max walked through the dreary pawn shop, lined with televisions and radios on the wall for sale. As he met the owner's gaze, he felt a wave of guilt and shame wash over him even before revealing what he had brought. Reluctantly, Max approached the counter and took out all the jewelry he had taken from his mother's jewelry box. "How much for all of this?" he asked, his voice filled with apprehension.

The owner scrutinized Max, sizing him up.

"Where did you get all of this from, son?" he inquired, suspicion evident in his tone.

"Why does it matter?" Max responded defensively. The owner shot Max a sharp look.

"Because I don't deal in stolen goods," he retorted firmly. "Look, it's not stolen alright? It's borrowed," Max insisted, his voice tinged with desperation.

"Then I suggest you go borrow some cash," the owner suggested, his tone cold and dismissive.

Feeling a surge of frustration and anger, Max snatched his items off the counter and stormed out of the shop.

AT THE MOTEL, YOU COULD HEAR THE SOUND OF TWO bodies thrusting together. A man was moaning in pleasure.

It was Officer Whitey and Freddie...

Exhausted and breathless, they both collapsed onto the bed. "Hey, did I see you the other day in O Town?" Officer Whitey asked.

"O Town? No, it must have been another little brown boy," Freddie replied.

"Well, there aren't too many little brown boys in O Town. I just knew it was you." "Were you with your wife?" Freddie inquired. "Now, why did you have to bring her up?" Officer Whitey became upset; he jumped up and quickly got dressed.

"I was just wondering. Since you thought you saw me, why didn't you say hello?"

"You know damn well why I can't say hello."

"Why? Because I'm colored or because I'm Queer?"

"Take a got damn pick," Officer Whitey angrily stormed out.

* * *

FREDDIE RACED TO THE DINER TO SHARE HIS MOTEL rendezvous with Charlotte. He vented to her over a cold chocolate milk shake.

"Then the mofo got dressed and stormed the hell out," Freddie said, clearly irritated.

"Oh, he dick and dipped?" Charlotte teased. "What?" Freddie asked amused.

"He got some dick and dipped. He dick and dipped," Charlotte elaborated.

Freddie erupted with laughter. Charlotte had a knack for making anyone laugh, no matter what was going on in their lives. "I need to start dick and dipping," Freddie admitted.

"I thought you were. You need to leave ol' captain square America alone," Charlotte suggested.

"I know but I like a little cream in my coffee."

"Well, they say drinking it black is the healthiest."

They both giggled.

"I'm going to take a leak," Freddie said as he stood up and headed to the boy's room.

At the same time, Kelly rushed into the diner hoping to find Zack. The place was empty, and it didn't take her long to scan the room and realize that Zack wasn't there. However, she spotted Charlotte and thought that if anyone knew where Zack was, it would be her.

"Hello, Charlotte," Kelly said with a smile.

"Well, if it isn't the singing sensation, Miss Kelly. Hey, can I have your autograph?" Charlotte teased.

Kelly was delighted that Charlotte enjoyed her performance. It made her feel like one of her Queerville babies. "Thank you for allowing me to perform. I really appreciate it," Kelly replied. "Oh, you're welcome sugar. You did not disappoint," Charlotte reassured her. "I've never seen this place so empty," Kelly remarked.

"Yeah, everyone is at that damn carnival that's in town. I'm surprised you're not there. I know Zack doesn't like clowns."

"I'm actually looking for Zack. I've checked everywhere..." Kelly trailed off. "Sandy, sugar," Charlotte said. "Sandy?" Kelly mumbled, confused.

"Zack is staying with Sandy now," Charlotte revealed. Kelly's heart sank. *Why was Zack staying with*

Sandy? What were they doing all night? She was consumed with jealousy. "Oh, I had no idea," Kelly managed to say, attempting to crack a smile. "Here, sweetie, I'll write down the address for you." Charlotte wrote down the address and handed it to Kelly. "Thank you, Charlotte," Kelly said hurriedly as she rushed out.

RICKEY WAS CRUISING DOWN THE OPEN ROAD WITH Sandy. He gazed at her, marveling at her beauty, and felt like the luckiest man on the planet. She turned and smiled at him, giving him butterflies in his stomach.

"Thank you for taking me to the carnival. I try to go every year, usually alone. It's my happy place," Sandy said. "Why alone?" Rickey asked curiously.

"My friends think it's corny. They're all too badass to have fun," she retorted. "Sounds like you need some new friends." "Well, I have you now to go with me," she said with a smirk.

Rock Around the Clock, came on the radio and they both became excited. Sandy turned up the radio and they sang along, belting out the lyrics at the top of their lungs, until mid-song. Rickey wanted to have a serious discussion, so he turned off the radio and became solemn. "Sandy, have you ever been in love?" he asked. "Yes, I have," she replied. "What happened to that, if you don't mind me asking?"

Sandy stared out the window and took a moment to reflect before answering, "He wouldn't leave his wife."

"I don't fancy you as a homewrecker," Rickey remarked. Sandy glared at Rickey and said, "I didn't say I asked him to leave his wife. I said he wouldn't." Rickey confused asked, "Isn't that the same thing?"

"No. One's a choice; one's an option, and I don't play second fiddle," Sandy stated.

Rickey averted his gaze from her, wishing he could relate. He wished he had the guts and fortitude to put himself first, but he had always succumbed to the need to prioritize the wants and desires of others before his own. He respected Sandy for it; he was frail, while she was strong. He was even more smitten with her.

———————————

There was a knock on the door at Sandy's house. When Zack answered the door, they were overjoyed to see Kelly. She was beaming with delight and had an infectious smile on her face.

"Hey, beautiful, what a nice surprise."

Kelly embraced Zack right away. "Hi, I've been looking everywhere for you," she sighed.

Zack took Kelly's hand and led her into the living room where they took a seat on the couch.

"I would've given you a ring and told you where I was. But I didn't know how your folks would react."

"Good call that wouldn't have gone well."

Kelly looked around and asked, "Is Sandy home?"

"No, she's on a date," Zack replied.

Kelly was thrilled to hear that Sandy was on a date and not playing house with Zack. She couldn't shake her jealousy towards Sandy; the woman is a walking goddess. "Good for her," Kelly said, faking a smile.

"I'm glad you found me," Zack said warmly.

Kelly returned the contagious smile and murmured, "I'll always find a way to you Zack." Zack smirked before replying, "I believe you."

It was clear Kelly had something on her mind. Zack took her hand and asked, "You look upset. What's wrong?"

"I just had a huge argument with my parents. They just don't get it. I can't believe they're the same people who birthed me."

"What did they say?"

Kelly avoided eye contact with Zack, not wanting to tell them what her parents said, but she didn't want to lie again. "They forbade me from coming to Queerville," she groaned, anticipating Zack's annoyance.

Zack became agitated.

"I knew they would. No one wants us to be together. Not them, not my friends," Zack exclaimed.

Kelly knelt in front of Zack and cradled their face in her palms. "Hey, look at me. I don't care what anyone has to say. Not my parents, not your friends. There's no way I'm ever giving you up," she said softly, gazing into Zack's fiery eyes as she kissed them. The kiss became a touch too intense, leading Zack to pull away.

"It's really hot in here, maybe we should go outside," Zack suggested.

Kelly chuckled. The temperature in the house was fine; it was Zack who was in heat. They took a squat outside on the stoop.

"My mom wants me to stay in school and become this paper pushing bill collector. I don't want to do that. She's so stubborn that it's impossible to change her mind," Zack complained.

"What do you want to do?" Kelly asked.

"Wow, no one has ever asked me that before." Zack was taken aback by the question. It was the first time someone cared about what they wanted. Kelly smiled and held on to every word.

"Cars. I love cars and I'm good at it, Kelly."

"Freddie's car, the one parked in front of the diner with the scorpions, did you do that?"

"Yeah, I dropped it off to him this morning," Zack said proudly. "Oh my god! That car looks rad, you are good. You should do it, that's how you can make an earning." "You think so?" Zack asked doubtfully.

"Yes. You should open your own shop."

"My own shop? We'll see if I stick around long enough."

"You're not staying? I thought you moved back for good."

"I came back because my brother was murdered and to find his killer," Zack explained.

"I heard about that, I'm sorry," she said sympathetically.

Kelly was crushed to hear Zack might be leaving. She was so caught up in her emotions she never thought about the reason Zack was here.

"What happens after you find your brother's killer?" she asked, desperately wanting to know.

Zack took a long look at Kelly before whispering, "I'm still deciding." Kelly smiled at the hope she could persuade Zack to stay. She intended to do her best to keep them here.

"I have a brother—a twin, actually," Kelly lightened the mood. "You do?" Zack asked, surprised.

"Yes, his name is Max."

"There are two of you. So, he looks like you just with a buzz cut?" Zack inquired. "No, silly," Kelly replied giggling.

"Is he the cat that helped you when those O Town boys stormed the diner?" "Yes, that was Max. That was my brother."

"I can see it now. You guys do look alike. I'm glad you have someone looking out for you," Zack admitted.

Kelly wanted Zack to meet Max. She believed once Max had a conversation with Zack, he would grow to like them. There was so much more to Zack if only Max would give them a chance. But Max was keen on her staying away from Queerville.

"So, back to you starting your own business," Kelly said.

"I don't know how to run a business," Zack sighed.

"What do you think you've been doing? Every trip you've taken, from city to city, you've already been running your own business."

"That's different, managing and running, a whole shop. I don't know if I can do it," Zack expressed disinterest.

"I know you can. I believe in you," Kelly said encouragingly. Zack had never experienced such unwavering support. Kelly had only known them for a short time, yet she believed in their potential while their own mother feared the worst. Kelly made Zack do something they had never done before, believe in themselves. "I'll think about it," Zack said, shrugging.

"Who taught you how to fix cars?" Kelly asked.

"My dad," Zack replied after a brief pause.

"Was he a mechanic?" Kelly asked curiously. Zack found the question amusing and they chuckled slightly before murmuring, "No, he was a gangster." Kelly seemed surprised. Zack felt uncomfortable talking about their dad, so they changed the subject.

"Who taught you how to drive?" Zack asked.

"No one, I don't even own a car," Kelly replied.

Zack laughed and said, "Wait, you don't know how to drive?" "Don't laugh at me Zack," Kelly shouted as she threw a playful punch at Zack.

"How did you get here?" Zack asked.

"I took a taxi," Kelly said embarrassed.

"Come on," Zack said, taking Kelly's hand in theirs and escorting her to their car.

Kelly was behind the wheel while Zack sat in the passenger seat, giving her pointers. "Zack, I can't drive this thing. It's a race car." "Don't worry I don't have it in race mode. It's just a regular automobile. Keep eyes forward and hands on the wheel."

Kelly followed Zack's instructions.

"Okay, keep your foot on the brake," Zack instructed.

"Which one is the brake?" Kelly asked.

"The left pedal, Kelly," Zack replied.

Kelly applied the brakes. She was both anxious and delighted to finally learn to drive. Nobody had ever bothered to teach her before. "Alright, keep it on there until you're ready to move. Now, put it in drive."

Kelly put the car in drive.

"Now, slowly take your foot off..." Before Zack could finish, the car suddenly sped forward.

"Brake!" Zack shouted.

Kelly slammed down hard on the brakes, and the car came to a stop. "You told me to take my foot off," Kelly anxiously shouted. "When you're ready, take your foot off slowly. Then slightly press the gas," Zack clarified.

"You didn't say that," Kelly huffed.

"Let's do it again," Zack suggested.

Five minutes later... Zack and Kelly were arguing.
Ten minutes later... Zack and Kelly were kissing.
Fifteen minutes later... More arguing...

Zack spent the next two hours teaching Kelly how to drive, but Zack lacked one crucial quality as a teacher: patience. Kelly, being sensitive, found Zack's instructions to be more like those of a drill sergeant. As a result, they spent more time bickering than actually driving. However, they also found themselves making out more often than arguing.

An uncomfortable silence hung in the air. Kelly's arms were tightly folded across her chest and Zack avoided direct eye contact, staring out the window, occasionally stealing a sideways glance at Kelly.

"Do you want to go racing with me?" Zack eventually asked.

Kelly's eyes brightened with enthusiasm, and she said, "Yes!" with a broad grin, before grabbing Zack and kissing them.

SANDY STEPPED INTO THE DINER AND INSTANTLY started swaying to the doo-wop tunes. She oozed sultry sex appeal and exuded a vibrant energy. The men in the diner couldn't help but gawk at her, secretly wishing they could have her. Their dates, however, didn't seem to notice. Charlotte shook her head; she was far too familiar with Sandy's antics.

"Well, the beauty queen finally decides to show her face," Charlotte said, shaking her head in annoyance.

"Hello, darling," Sandy replied in her best boujee voice. "How was the carnival?"

"It was so much fun. But the day I find a man who can bring the carnival to me is the day I fall in love," Sandy romanticized as she clutched her chest.

Charlotte chuckled at Sandy and her dramatics. "Yeah, you're used to dating clowns," Charlotte mumbled, continuing the conversation she asked, "How is Rickey?"

"Rickey is such a swell guy."

"He's swell, is he?" Charlotte inquired, cynically. Sandy noted the tone in Charlotte's voice.

"Yes. What are you getting at?"

"You go M.I.A. for days and it's not with swell guy, Rickey."

"So what?" she remarked defensively.

"Be careful, Sandy. Karma is a bitch in heels with swollen ankles," she quipped. "What?" Sandy laughed heartily. Charlotte's funny quips always perplexed Sandy.

* * *

Paradise Road River Basin

Beatniks lined the strip, admiring all the custom colorful hot rods. Suddenly, an engine roared, causing nearby cars to tremble. It was Zack, cruising in their custom red monster. All eyes turned as Zack pulled in with Kelly in the passenger seat.

Kelly felt like a movie star, riding with the most popular person in town, who also happened to be the undefeated race champion in the state. She couldn't contain her joy, her smile stretching from ear to ear. Looking at Zack, she couldn't believe this was happening; it felt surreal. The crowd waved enthusiastically, thrilled to see Zack. Stepping out of the car, Zack was warmly welcomed by the Red Dragons. However, Lisa seemed visibly upset to see Kelly.

"Hey Zack, what's with the librarian?" Lisa snidely asked. Kelly heard Lisa's snarky comment and before Zack could defend her, she stepped to Lisa.

"My name is Kelly," Kelly said with a sneer.

Lisa would normally use her switchblade on someone for less, but she knew better. As long as Kelly was with Zack, she was off limits. The crowd was stunned with suppressed giggles from those who were impressed by Kelly but were scared to laugh at Lisa's expense.

She didn't know it at the time, but Kelly had just earned cool points with Lisa. She had to admit Kelly had guts.

The moment was interrupted by Freddie flying down the road in his new ride. "Oh, shit, look! It's Freddie," Val shouted. Everyone turned to see Freddie's blue car speeding toward the finish line.

Freddie was behind the wheel driving like a bat out of hell. He glanced at the fixes and customizations Zack had made to the car. Freddie's gauges were off the charts, he was clutching and shifting, burning rubber. His eyes were intense, filled with focus. He looked over at his opponent, showing no emotion, but he was about to shit himself.

"Come on Freddie, you got this. You got this Freddie. Come on baby," he mumbled to himself. He switched gears and slammed his foot on the gas pedal, forcing himself back into his seat. "Woah baby, she's flying. My baby is flying!" Freddie was grinning ear to ear as he sped past the finish line winning his first race.

The crowd went nuts for him. Freddie was screaming, he was so excited to win his first race. He started crying, but he wiped his eyes quickly before anyone could see him.

Zack looked on as Freddie won his race then turned to Val and Lisa. They were in shock.

"Nice work, Zack," Val slapped Zack five.

"Yeah, I don't know how you did it, but that baby was flying," Lisa said, impressed.

"Pay up. Both of you," Zack demanded.

Val and Lisa took out the money and attempted to hand it to Zack. "Give it to her," Zack nodded to Kelly.

Zack, with their arm around Kelly, smiled at her. They handed the money to Kelly. Lisa gave her a little smirk. Kelly took the money and stuffed it into Zack's pants pocket.

Zack turned to face her and said, "I want you to wear something for me." Zack took off their Red Dragons jacket and placed it around Kelly's shoulders.

She felt ecstatic, in her world, when a guy gave you his jacket, it meant you were together. She was overcome with joy.

"Does this mean we're going steady?" Kelly asked, overjoyed.

Zack just looked at her and laughed, they didn't really conform to the rules of the square world.

"Steady?" Zack teased.

"Yeah," Kelly said.

Zack found Kelly's remarks adorable, they grabbed her chin and planted a kiss on her.

Duffus and his crew arrived to witness the race.

"Just in time to see the race champ," Duffus exclaimed as he eagerly approached Zack, "Good luck out there, not that you'll need it."

"Duffy, I'm glad you came," Zack said, giving him a high five.

"I have to see this for myself and take notes," Duffus said, trailing off as he became fascinated by Kelly; his gaze moved over her body and back up to her face. She was a stunning blonde bombshell. He wasn't trying to be subtle in the least.

"Well, who is this betty here?" Duffus asked, attempting to take Kelly's hand, but she was not interested. She wrapped her arms around Zack's waist.

"Easy Duffy, this one comes with a toe tag," Zack cautioned with a harsh glare.

Duffus grew disappointed and exclaimed, "Are all the beautiful women in this town spoken for?"

"Are you here to race or chase skirts? Go watch from the sidelines!" Zack shouted.

"I got you next race Zack. Don't forget," Duffus said as he gracefully backed away.

Kelly fixed her focus on Zack. She admired how they stood up for her and defended her. She never needed anyone to, but it made her feel special, something she had never felt before.

At the starting line, the guys examined each other's cars; the doors, hood and trunks. Afterwards, Zack came face-to-face with Roger; he gave an ultra-macho shrug. Zack clearly did not take him seriously. Kelly liked this nonchalant side of Zack.

Zack and Roger talked trash to each other. "You like losing money," Zack snidely said to Roger. "I got you this time, Zack. I have a new carburetor and engine," Roger scoffed.

"But you still have those same old ass tires and you're still the same double foot egghead," Zack replied, causing the crowd to laugh at Roger, but he brushed it off.

Zack and Kelly hopped into Zack's car, ready to start the race. Kelly's excitement overshadowed any thoughts of danger. She had complete trust in Zack, devoid of any fear.

"How many girls have you let ride with you?" Kelly asked.

"None," Zack replied, revving the engine to show off. They leaned in for a kiss, and Kelly eagerly accepted. Zack kissed her passionately, with Kelly gently caressing Zack's face as she savored their connection. Kissing Zack made her body tremble and her heart flutter.

Zack made sure Kelly was safely buckled in, then put on a Chuck Berry track.

Roger and another car joined the line while Roy stood in front of the cars with his arms raised. They revved their engines ready to take off.

Roy dropped his arm...

Zack bolted, leaving tire tracks and flames in their wake. Roger became blinded by the smoke. He took off late and pulled out, but he eventually caught up to Zack. They were virtually neck and neck.

Suddenly, the hubcaps on Roger's car appeared to loosen.

The other guy was playing dirty, he pushed a button and oil spilled from his car and covered the roadway.

Roger was unable to dodge it; his car peeled through the oil and spun out of control. Roger avoided causing damage or injury to anyone.

Zack and the oil spiller were neck-and-neck until they entered the home stretch. Kelly clung on for dear life, sporting the biggest smile on her face. Zack gave her a wink and goosed it.

Zack sped across the finish line first, leaving the crowd outside roaring. They swarmed the car as Zack stepped out. Kelly ran towards them and leaped into Zack's arms, showering them with kisses. Hoots and hollers erupted from the crowd.

"That was so much fun," Kelly said, beaming with joy. "You're my lucky charm." Zack told her.

Duffus approached as Zack set Kelly down and she walked off; she didn't like Duffus.

"That was the greatest race I have ever witnessed."

"Thank you, Duffy."

"I think I might need a little more modification to qualify to race against you. You know I have to use my jets. These guys are playing dirty."

"Yeah, we don't normally play like that. I don't know what that cat was thinking."

Duffus became upset and asked, "Oh, so you don't know that cat who spilled the oil?"

"No, never seen him before," Zack replied.

"My associates and I will gladly get rid of that scum, for you, as a favor," Duffus offered.

"I have people to handle that for me."

"I know, but please allow me, it would be my honor." Zack smirked and shrugged.

Duffus cracked his neck and his knuckles. He and his crew confronted the oil spiller. Duffus swiftly seized the guy and delivered a series of punches to his face. He then struck him in the stomach, causing him to double over, and forcefully kicked him into his car. His crew pelted the car with bats, causing damage.

"Get the hell out of here and don't come back!" Duffus screamed.

The guy burned rubber as he sped away. The crowd cheered for Duffus, who was loving it with his arms raised; all psyched up.

After the races. The Lipsticks took center and performed a hip dance routine to Chuck Berry's "*Roll over Beethoven.*" The crowd circled around looking on, enjoying the dance. Black and White gangs were all together, no fighting just enjoying the Lipsticks' performance.

Freddie was dancing with some handsome fella. Val and Maria were dancing while Robin and Lisa were making out.

Everyone seemed to be having the time of their lives. Zack and Kelly were right in the center, dancing and having a great time. Kelly's face was lit up with joy and absolute love, anyone could see how much she enjoyed being with Zack.

Zack was singing along to the Chuck Berry track, Kelly admired how happy Zack seemed.

"You really like Chuck Berry huh?" Kelly teased.

"He's the greatest. It's a dream of mine to see him perform live someday," Zack admitted. Kelly smiled, noticing the excitement in Zack's eyes.

Dennis approached Zack, interrupting their moment. "Zack, we need to talk," he said solemnly.

Zack could see the urgency in Dennis's face, they knew it had to be important. Turning to Kelly, they said, "I'll be right back, okay?" After giving Kelly a kiss, Zack walked off with Dennis, leaving Kelly looking worried.

The two of them spoke privately.

"There is a guy who saw everything that happened that night with your brother. But he said he will only talk to you."

"Okay, so bring him to me."

"I'm looking for him. He travels from town to town. I'm working on locating him, but it will take some time."

"Is this for real?"

"This dude is scared shitless. Whatever he witnessed that night has him fleeing for his life."

"Find him and bring him to me. I'll pay whatever you want."

"I'm on it."

Suddenly, a Bronxville gang came speeding in, making donuts around the circle, screaming out profanities and egging the gangs to engage. The gangs reacted and chaos ensued. Freddie forcefully kicked out their window, causing them to quickly exit the car and attack him. In the meantime, Lisa broke a bottle and pressed it against some guy's neck.

"Beat it," Lisa said.

He ran off.

Val jumped on a guy's back, but he quickly knocked her off. Maria pulled out her switchblade and menacingly brandished it at him. "Is that any way to treat a lady?" she said before slashing him across his face.

Another guy cornered Lisa.

"Nowhere to go, Missy," he said, cradling a bat in his hand. Lisa took a step back. He could smell her fear.

Robin tapped the guy on his shoulder, he turned around and she knocked out his tooth with her knuckle ring. "You okay, baby?" Robin asked as Lisa jumped into her arms and kissed her.

Zack attempted to go join the fight, but Kelly grabbed their arm, stopping them. "Zack, don't!"

"Kelly, I can't let these punks run up in my turf disrespecting me," Zack scolded.

"Why, not? They're just a bunch of thugs that are trying to interrupt our night, don't let them. You don't always have to engage."

"Yes, I do. Because if I don't, there'll be another crew here tomorrow, then another. You're only as good as your reputation, out here. What do you want me to do?"

"Be better than them. You don't have to stoop to their level. You don't have anything to prove."

"That's where you're wrong, Kelly. I have everything to prove. Do you get it now? This is who I am."

Zack ran off to join the rumble. Kelly looked on and she realized there were two sides to Zack, the sweet soft side that only she got to see and the stubborn badass everyone feared. She didn't know if she liked that side.

* * *

Sandy was at work, replenishing napkins and refilling ketchup bottles. She wiped down the countertops and bar stools, while the jukebox continued playing.

A slow doo-wop song came on and Sandy decided to have one last dance for the night. She performed a sensual solo dance in front of the jukebox.

Unbeknownst to Sandy, a mysterious figure lurked outside the diner, seemingly watching her every move. Little did she know she was being stalked.

O Town, USA

Max had been severely beaten and was covered in blood. He staggered into his room and slumped onto his bed.

After hearing the commotion, Mrs. Hamilton came to check on him. She was startled to see Max slumped on the bed, hurt. "Oh my god, Max, what happened?" she dashed over to Max.

"Oh, my goodness. Max! Hank, come quick," she shouted.

CHAPTER 7

Kelly visited Max in the hospital the following day. Max had been fully bandaged up and was looking and feeling much better. Mr. and Mrs. Hamilton were in the hallway conversing with the doctors. Kelly sat by her twin's bedside watching as her parents entered, shaking their heads. "Hey, Max, how are you?"

"I feel like I got hit by a milk truck," Max groaned.

Mr. Hamilton was suspicious about what had truly happened to Max. "Well, did you son? What the hell happened?"

After a lengthy pause Max gave his family a serious look. He was ready to come clean about what he had been involved in.

"I got into some trouble with some guys."

"Did those Queerville punks do this to you?"

Mr. Hamilton asked angrily. "Dad!" Kelly interjected defensively. "Oh, those animals," Mrs. Hamilton sighed, clutching her pearls. Max shook his head, frustrated with his parents' unwarranted paranoia and blind hatred of Queerville.

"No, Dad, it wasn't anyone from Queerville. It was me, ok, I did this to myself." "Well, that's just silly," Mrs. Hamilton scowled, unable to comprehend.

"No, mom! You guys are not listening. I owe some people a lot of money and if I don't pay them back... Let's just say this won't be my first trip to the hospital."

Kelly couldn't believe her brother could get himself mixed up with loan sharks. They were rich kids; she couldn't fathom why he needed the money or why he didn't just ask their parents.

"Oh, dear Max," Mrs. Hamilton sighed in disappointment. "Well, who do you owe, son?" Mr. Hamilton asked.

"A lot of people, Dad," Max said as he lowered his head ashamed. "Well, which one did this to you?" Mr. Hamilton inquired. "His name is Machete Mike," Max snitched. Mr. Hamilton couldn't believe his ears. "Machete Mike?" he repeated in disbelief. Max nodded his head yes.

Mrs. Hamilton noticed the stunned look on Mr. Hamilton's face and asked. "Do you know who that is, dear?"

"Yes," Mr. Hamilton replied.

"Well, where is he from, who is he, Dad?" Kelly asked.

"He's from O Town and he's bad news. He's scum, a wannabe gangster, but he's dangerous," he growled.

Queerville, USA

The gangs had gathered at the club, still upset about the reception they had received in O Town. The *No Queer* signs posted were terrible enough, but the racial and homophobic insults from the people were even worse. Main Street stretched from Queerville through O Town, leaving both towns vulnerable to such attacks. Charlotte stepped forward to discuss a plan.

"We are gathered here today to discuss what we all witnessed in O Town the other day. First, congratulations to our basketball team for bringing home the victory."

The room cheered in celebration.

"Now I'm going to open the floor to all of you, so you can speak your peace," Charlotte said, and the room erupted in chatter.

"Where are all the missing kids?" someone in the crowd asked. "Yeah, and why haven't the police done anything about it?" shouted another person.

Maria jumped up and shouted, "We can't go to their town; we can't shop in their stores. I say we ban all those O Town squares from Queerville."

The crowd exploded in applause in agreement with Maria. Zack took notice of the various responses from the crowd.

"Heard, Maria. I understand your point. However, implementing that idea would only lead to further division. Too much division, and we'll be in an all-out war," Charlotte explained.

"We're already at war," Freddie responded.

"No, no, I have the mic, shush."

Freddie gestured apologetically.

Charlotte confidently walked back and forth across the stage, ensuring to establish eye contact with everyone. She spoke into the microphone with a stern tone, "Queerville has always been a safe haven for anyone to come seeking acceptance and understanding. This is where the kids find solace after being rejected by their own families. I will never close Queerville to anyone in need. Now, that is off the table."

Dee, the leader of the House of Prosperity, rose up and addressed the crowd, saying, "I propose that we arrange a meeting with their committee to find a resolution."

The room moaned and booed...

"Cut the gas," Charlotte yelled, banging her gavel.

"I say we fight fire with fire. Right Zack?" Freddie said as he turned to Zack for approval.

The room fell silent...

Zack took a long look around at their people; they were all thirsty for vengeance. Vengeance Zack themselves was in search of. *How could they deny them?*

"Let's light the match," Zack said.

The gangs roared to their feet and surged out, ready for war.

"I suppose the decision has been made. Be safe out there. Don't forget to cover your faces!" Charlotte yelled.

O Town, USA

The Baker House was cold and empty, any signs of a happy family were nonexistent, just the shadow of what once was.

Mr. Baker, isolated in his den, was the last straw for Johnnie. After following his dad to the motel where he met with a mysterious blonde woman, Johnnie had been struggling to keep this secret, and it was tearing him apart. His whole life, his dad had placed the pressure of perfection on his shoulders, only to turn around and contradict everything he stood for. The cape had finally fallen off its hero. *How could he ever respect his dad again?*

"I saw you, Dad," Johnnie said as he burst into the den. "Johnnie, get in here. I want to talk about your terrible performance against Queerville Friday night," Mr. Baker said, not hearing Johnnie's outburst. "Did you hear me, Dad?" Johnnie asked frustrated. "Hear what Johnnie?"

"I said I saw you."

Mr. Baker was clearly confused. Johnnie walked up to his dad, looking threatening.

"At the motel with that woman."

Mr. Baker stared at Johnnie as if he had just seen a ghost, his face filled with panic. He swiftly concocted an excuse.

"Son, you have no idea what you saw. I was merely assisting that woman." "Enough, Dad. Stop lying!" Johnnie shouted, raising his hands in frustration.

"Now, mind your manners, young man," Mr. Baker warned, pointing his finger at Johnnie's face. "How could you do this to Mom?" Johnnie paced back and forth, consumed by anger.

"I told you son, it's not what you think. I was helping that woman." Johnnie didn't believe his dad for a second.

"Does Mom know about this woman you've been helping?"

Mr. Baker tried to persuade him.

"Your mom doesn't have to know anything because there's nothing to know," Mr. Baker said, placing both hands on Johnnie's shoulders.

"Yeah, right Dad. I'll just keep your dirty little secret."

"Now, look son…" "Don't call me your fucking son. I don't want your fucking last name. I don't want anything from you," Johnnie shouted angrily.

Mr. Baker struck Johnnie in the face. He fell to the ground, clutching his chin and looking up at his dad. Mr. Baker stood over Johnnie, assuming a boxing stance, prepared to pound on his own son. Nursing his chin, Johnnie struggled to his feet, seized his dad's gun from the desk, and aimed it at him… he didn't want to kill his dad; he simply wanted to inflict the same pain he was causing his mom. Johnnie let out a scream and then bolted out of the house.

THE CALM & ROUTINE NORMALCY OF O TOWN WAS shattered by the influx of Queerville gangs. Pulling up in their custom jalopies, wreaking havoc on Main Street. Wielding bats and wearing masks to conceal their identities. They stormed the shops, defacing the *"No Queers"* signs with spray paint and leaving behind explicit words and imagery. They emptied the trash cans onto the streets, knocking over anything that was not tied down, causing fear among the square O Town citizens.

Queerville, USA

Back at Charlotte's, Dee stayed behind to express her displeasure with Zack and their leadership, hoping to get Charlotte's support. "This is not right," Dee growled. "What do you want me to say? The gangs all voted." "No, they all did what they were told to do."

Charlotte was always defensive about Zack, but in her role as the gang coordinator, she had to be open to listening to everyone.

"What are you saying?" Charlotte asked, her tone defensive. "We need to talk about stripping Zack of their rank." "Not this again," Charlotte said, rolling her eyes and annoyed by the request.

"Listen this is not the direction we need to be going. We should be trying to find a way to coexist with O Town, not terrorize them," Dee urged.

"Cool your jets, Dee. Those people do not want to coexist with us, they want us to not exist. Like literally."

"Charlotte, you can't say that you agree with this."

"Absolutely not."

"Then let's call a council meeting with all the heads and have a vote for a new leader." Charlotte chuckled hard and grabbed her chest. "You want to have a vote with Zack's best friend, their ex and all the people that looked up to their brother? Yeah, good luck," Charlotte jeered.

"Queerville needs a better future. The one we're headed to now is going to self-destruct."

"What do you want me to do? Even if we had a vote and made someone else leader, the people would still look to Zack. Zack is a Calhoun whose name alone has kept this town safe for almost a decade." "Zack listens to you, they respect you. Maybe you should really have a talk with them," Dee suggested.

Charlotte pondered it.

O Town, USA

Queerville gangs were still terrorizing the town. Zack shattered window displays and removed the homophobic signs.

The police sirens rang out, causing everyone to disperse and flee. Zack quickly jumped into Freddie's car, and they sped off in the opposite direction.

They were soon traveling along a country road. For two melanated people in the 1950s, the open road might be a terrifying and deadly place. Zack looked ahead at the road, apprehensive about entering uncharted waters.

"Where are we?" Zack inquired.

"I don't know, Dorothy. Looks like we're not in Kansas anymore," Freddie sneered.

"Maybe we should turn back," Zack suggested feeling a bit uncomfortable. "So, the fuzz can get us?"

They continued down the road, cautiously looking around.

"Do you really think we should ban folks from Queerville?" Zack was curious to know how Freddie felt. They were beginning to consider the idea of a ban, but they wondered what that would mean for them and Kelly. "Not all of them," Freddie said.

"Oh, look at that chariot," Zack exclaimed as they spotted a classic black Chrysler Imperial, that was parked off the road, "Wow, she's a beauty. Pull in there," Zack said, motioning to the side of the road. Freddie pulled in, and they got out and approached the black Chrysler.

An awful smell emanated from the car. Zack held their nose and grunted, "Aw, what's that smell?"

"Was that you?" Freddie asked Zack, who gave him a blank stare, and said, "It's coming from the car you goof."

As they moved closer, they spotted a dead body in the driver's seat. "Aw man, this guy reeks," Freddie said, pinching his nose. Zack looked further and examined the dead body; they came across a bullet wound in his chest. "He was shot. He must've pulled in here and bled out," Zack assumed.

"Why didn't he drive to a hospital? How did he get all the way over here?" Freddie inquired.

"I don't know, maybe he knew he was dying and wanted to get off the road."

"He was afraid someone would hit his corpse? No, this guy didn't want to be found."

"You might be right," Zack said as they opened the passenger door and climbed in.

"Ewe don't go in there," Freddie muttered.

Zack searched through the car, hoping to find anything the deceased guy may have been trying to hide. They checked his pockets and stumbled upon a note. Zack stepped out of the car to show Freddie.

"What is it?" Freddie asked.

Zack unfolded the note, revealing a map of sorts.

Freddie's eyes grew big. "It's a treasure map!"

"No, Freddie, this isn't a treasure map."

"Then what is it?" "It seems to be a map of this area," Zack replied. "Ok, maybe it's a map to the dead body," Freddie suggested. "So, then who shot him?" Zack asked. "The dead guy," Freddie replied. "So, the dead guy shot another dead guy?" Zack said confused.

"They both shot each other. Like a standoff," Freddie clarified. "Look around, we're not in the wild wild west." "Well, what do you think?" Zack suddenly had a thought and blurted out, "Bank robbers!" Freddie looked around anxiously, "What? Where?"

"No, from the news. It said the bank robbers escaped in a black 1940s Chrysler Crown Imperial. Three of them were later captured, but one managed to elude the police." "Holy shit, I never seen a bank robber before," Freddie remarked.

"Well, this will be your first dead bank robber."

"Yeah, I'll cross that off the bucket list."

"What does this mean?" Zack asked, showing Freddie the X on the map, which was located in the middle of nowhere. Freddie examined it closely.

"It's a scavenger hunt. We have to reach the first X, and then we'll find another clue that we'll need to match with the map. That should lead us to the loot," Freddie explained eagerly.

"What if this doesn't lead us to any loot? What if it's just some scribble?"

"Zack, you said this guy could be one of the bank robbers, right?"

"Yeah," Zack replied.

"A dead bank robber plus a map equals loot," Freddie murmured, placing his hands on Zack's shoulders. He continued, "Loot that no one else is searching for." Zack gave Freddie a skeptical look as he tried to convince them.

"You once told me that a man who is afraid of living, is already dead. If the loot is there, we'll split it, and then you can finally open that auto shop you've been talking about."

Zack liked the idea of finally having something of their own, and no longer seeing disappointment on their mother's face. "Okay, let's do it," Zack said, as they shook hands.

Zack took another look at the map.

"It seems like we have to continue down this road for a few miles, and we should come across something where this X is."

"We're about to become Queerville's first hardened criminals," Freddie exclaimed excitedly.

JOHNNIE DROWNED HIS SORROW AT A WATERING HOLE. It was a seedy establishment that didn't bother checking ID's. Johnnie couldn't stop replaying the fight he had with his dad. He knew that revealing this secret would devastate his mother, but he couldn't bear to see his dad continue lying to her. Perhaps he and his mom could leave and start fresh somewhere else, he pondered. After losing that crucial Queerville game in front of the college scouts, all his prospects had vanished. A new beginning, free from his father's constant pressure for perfection and academic excellence, sounded just right.

He downed his shot and forcefully placed the glass on the counter, "Another one," Johnnie grumbled.

The bartender promptly refilled his glass with another shot.

KELLY REMAINED AT THE HOSPITAL TO SPEAK WITH MAX. She needed some quality time with her twin brother. "I'm sorry I took your necklace and snitched you out to Mom and Dad," Max expressed his regret.

Kelly treasured her brother beyond any material possessions. She forgave him the moment he took it.

"I don't care about those things. I never even wore that necklace. All I want is for you to be safe."

"Awe, you do care about your younger brother," Max teased.

"You were born twenty seconds after me, not that much younger." "Either way, I'm happy to have you as my big sister." They exchanged tender smiles before Max asked, "Have you talked to Zack today?"

Kelly immediately blushed and grinned brightly.

"What do you mean?" She pretended to be clueless.

"You know what I mean and you're a terrible liar. I saw you jump on Ronnie's back after he hit Zack."

"Ronnie is a pig," Kelly blurted out, irritated.
Max noticed his sister's radiant expression.

"Are you happy?" he asked.

"Yes, I am Max," Kelly responded, grinning from ear to ear. "Zack makes me so happy. When I'm with Zack, I feel overwhelmed with joy. My heart starts pounding so fast that I think it's going to leap out of my chest. I get nervous, but it's a good kind of nervous, you know? Like I don't want to mess this up."

"I can't believe you're talking about Zack Calhoun." Max had a hard time hearing his sister swoon over the most feared person in town.

"I know you think Zack is dangerous, and maybe they are. But when I'm with Zack, I feel safe and seen.

Zack has shown me nothing but kindness and respect," Kelly confessed.

"Maybe I was wrong about Zack," Max confessed.

"Everyone has Zack wrong. There's so much more to them," Kelly added.

"Are you sure you know what you're getting yourself into?" Max asked.

"I know what the world thinks about people like Zack, and I don't care. We have something special. It's bigger than either one of us," Kelly explained.

"I just want you to know that being with Zack will not come easy. You will always be at war with the world because of who you love," Max reminded her.

"Wow," Kelly said, having an epiphany.

"What?"

"I understand what it's like to be one of them now," Kelly murmured, revealing her newfound revelation.

Max's expression became serious. "Kelly, you can't trust Mom and Dad. They can never know about you and Zack. They'll never let you be with them," Max exclaimed with a worried look came across her face.

FREDDIE AND ZACK PULLED UP TO THE SPOT ON THE MAP to find it was a watering hole—a whites-only watering hole. "You see this racist shit?" Freddie growled in frustration. "Yes, I see it," Zack sighed, feeling disheartened. "Damn, we came all this way. What are we going to do now?" Freddie asked, perplexed.

"What do you mean what are we going to do? We can't do shit but tuck our tails and head back home," Zack replied, wanting no parts of the racist establishment. "Zack, c'mon, it's right there," Freddie pleaded.

"In case you haven't noticed, we don't have a certain pigmentation," Zack jeered.

"I say we run in there, grab the map and run out."

Zack looked at Freddie as if he had lost his mind, "That map could be anywhere in there."

"No, no, look. The X is right there just a few feet from the door," Freddie showed Zack the map.

"Freddie, these white folks will kill us and hang our bodies in their yard for the dogs," Zack warned Freddie.

"Zack, we'll be in and out. You know how much loot is probably buried. We're so close, we can't turn back now," Freddie pleaded with Zack.

Zack sighed but ultimately got out of the car. They cautiously entered the watering hole. As they stepped foot through the door, a dozen white folks looked up, giving them hostile stares. The place resembled a KKK gathering, and the expressions on those white people's faces could have turned Medusa to stone. Freddie couldn't help but feel nervous.

"How's everyone doing?" he said in his best attempt at a friendly, non-threatening voice. However, all they received in response were sullen stares from all corners of the room.

"This is a bad idea," Zack whispered to Freddie.

"Just smile and don't scare these white folks," Freddie whispered back. "Our skin color is already doing that."

They scanned the room for any clues. It was difficult to see through the dim lighting and the empty dreams that filled the place.

"You niggers must be lost," the bartender shouted. Freddie motioned towards a painting on the wall with a huge X on it, and Zack looked over.

161

"Yes, actually, we are lost. Could you kind folks point us in the right direction?" Freddie and Zack took small steps toward the X.

"Boy can you read? Did you see the sign on the door?" "Actually, no, I can't read. Probably why I didn't see the sign on the door," Freddie retorted.

"Well, this here is a Whites only establishment."

"Clearly!" Freddie chuckled.

A White man cast a disparaging glance at Zack.

Zack tried to stay calm, taking bigger steps toward the X. "I suggest you and your... friend here get."

"We most certainly will. But first, do you mind if we just use your washroom?"

An awkward silence and a sense of audacity filled the air. Zack and Freddie kept walking toward the X.

A figure emerged from the bathroom, slowly approaching Zack and Freddie who had their backs turned. The bartender grabbed a shotgun from behind the counter, cocked it, and aimed it at Freddie.

"Take one more got damn step and I'll paint these walls with nigger blood."

Zack and Freddie froze in their tracks, their bodies tense. Freddie gulped.

"Maybe I should just shoot you two for bringing your stench in here," he said, his voice dripping with menace, "I could just tell the police you were trying to rob the place. They'd probably give me a damn medal."

Zack and Freddie took deep breaths, their hearts racing. The bartender's grip tightened; his gaze fixed on Freddie.

Suddenly, Johnnie appeared behind Zack and Freddie, wielding a gun of his own. "I'm sorry, I can't let you do that. Just let them leave, okay? I don't want any trouble," Johnnie said, his hand trembling. Zack and Freddie looked at each other in disbelief.

"Are you willing to die for these niggers?"

"Nobody's dying. We're just going to leave," Johnnie shouted. "Oh, it's too late for that," the bartender said, motioning to another white man, who stood up and locked the front door.

"Oh shit!" Zack mumbled as they quickly ran towards the painting with the X, while Freddie took cover. Johnnie fired shots to keep the bartender at bay.

"Go... Go... Out the back!" Johnnie screamed.

Zack removed the painting and put their fist through the wall but couldn't find the clue. They frantically searched through the wall until they finally spotted it. The bartender returned fire but missed.

Johnnie, Zack and Freddie quickly dashed out the back and jumped into Johnnie's car. The bartender followed suit and fired one more shot, hitting Zack in the shoulder. Johnnie sped off while the bartender continued to shoot, leaving bullet holes in the back of Johnnie's car.

"Shit, man what the hell was that?" Johnnie could hardly catch his breath as he asked Zack, "Do you need a hospital?" Zack and Freddie both screamed. "No!" Zack checked their shoulder. "It's just a flesh wound. I'll be fine." Freddie was relieved. "Johnnie boy! Thanks for saving our asses back there." Freddie placed the maps on top of each other and discovered the next location for the loot.

"Do you want to tell me what that was all about?" Johnnie asked insistently. "It's a scavenger hunt for school, and we have one more stop to make if you don't mind," Freddie said with a sneaky grin.

SOMEWHERE ON A FARM MILES OUTSIDE OF O TOWN, Zack and Freddie were digging in a barn when they stumbled upon the loot. Zack opened the sack and money spilled out. Zack and Freddie celebrated. "How much do you think is in there?" Freddie asked.

"More than enough for me to open my shop," Zack replied. "Should we cut Johnnie boy in?" They looked at each other and shook their heads, "Nah."

* * *

Sandy was at work listening to the radio, when she first heard about the heinous murders that were taking place.

"Another body was discovered today, marking the fifth dead body in five days. The police believe that the killer is on a mission..." the radio announcer reported.

Feeling uneasy, Sandy switched off the radio, put on some tunes, and began to dance.

Little did she know, she was still being stalked by the mysterious man lurking outside the diner.

CHAPTER 8

The sun shone brightly into the bathroom, highlighting the floral wallpaper, penny tile floors, and clawfoot tub. Zack sat still as Sandy bandaged their arm, while they grunted in pain.

"Sorry, if I'm hurting you," she said, being careful as she wrapped the bandage around Zack's arm.

"It's okay. Your hands are soft."

"Don't try to soften me up. You could've gotten yourself killed, Zack."

"I know. I don't know why I let Freddie talk me into it," Zack had to admit it was a dumb idea.

Sandy finished bandaging Zack's arm and they handed her a syringe containing testosterone.

"Can you give me my shot?" Zack asked.

"Sure." Sandy took the syringe and injected Zack in their thigh.

"Thanks."

"Here, do me, please," Sandy said, handing Zack her syringe containing her estrogen shot.

Zack palmed her thigh and injected her into her hip. Feeling a sense of nostalgia Zack raised their head and said, "I'm glad I get to share this experience with you."

Sandy's gaze drawn to Zack's green eyes as she smirked and said, "Me too." They shared warm glances before continuing to dress. Sandy slipped on her dress while Zack put on their business attire. She turned around and motioned for Zack to zip her up.

"Where are you off too?" she asked.

"To the bank to get this loan."

Sandy looked at Zack with an excited smile.

"That's good, I'm proud of you, Zack. What made you want to open a shop?" "Kelly. She convinced me to work for myself. Turn what I do into an actual business." Sandy seemed impressed. She had Kelly pegged as just some young, naïve girl. She was starting to feel like maybe she was wrong about Kelly. "I see Kelly is having a good impact on you."

"Yeah, she is. What you got buzzin today?"

"A few errands to run, then work."

Zack was surprised to hear that was all Sandy had planned for the day. Sandy usually lost herself into whatever man she was dating, but this didn't seem to be the case.

"Oh, so no Rickey today?"

"No, I think I'm going to end things with him," Sandy said sadly.

"Why? I thought you liked him."

"I do. I just... I don't know; something's missing. There's no spark; everything feels forced. It's a shame because he's really dreamy." Zack gently cupped Sandy's face and said, "Never settle for dreamy. You deserve to be with someone who makes you feel alive every second of the day." Sandy smiled in response.

"I suppose I won't have to give him my classic warning," Zack continued. "You know I gave Kelly the big sister warning. I almost scared her out of her sweater."

"You did?" Zack said, shocked.

"Yes, I don't play about you," Sandy replied, playfully winking at Zack before asking, "Has Kelly ever dated a..." she trailed off. "No, she's only ever dated squares," Zack answered.

"So, she wants to take a walk on the wild side?"

Sandy, as usual, was being the overprotective best friend. She had seen firsthand how some individuals use trans people to feed their own sick fetishes. She wanted to be certain that Kelly was not doing this with Zack.

"No, it's not like that for her. She genuinely likes me," Zack reassured Sandy.

"I'm just joshing you, Zack. Of course, she likes you. What's not to like?" Sandy said, planting a kiss on Zack's cheek. "Good luck at the bank," she added before heading out.

ZACK WAS AT THE BANK, PATIENTLY WAITING TO SPEAK with someone. They felt a little out of their element, as starting a business was a huge decision for them. However, if Kelly believed in them enough to do it, Zack knew they had to give it a try. Being a high school dropout with no business experience, the odds were stacked against them. Eventually, a banker approached Zack.

"I see your account is in good standing. However, with your mother's loan on her house, you would need another cosigner for the shop," the banker explained.

"Even with the cash deposit?" Zack inquired.

"Yes, the deposit would serve as the down payment. But the bank would still require some form of collateral for the mortgage." "Okay," Zack replied, feeling disappointed.

"Do you happen to know anyone else who owns their own business or home?" the banker asked trying to help. Zack pondered for a moment.

* * *

THE PRIDE FLAG FLUTTERED IN THE WIND AT QUEERVILLE High school. Cars, bicycles and students on foot poured down the driveway and into the parking lot. The cars were adorned with 50s emblems, while students hung out of car windows, sitting on convertible backs, roofs and running boards, exuding youthful energy.

Restlessly, Freddie observed the scene from his biology class. The students were sitting at long desks that were set up for dissecting, Freddie and Lisa sat together while Robin and Val sat across the aisle. Lisa blew kisses to Robin from across the room, and Freddie played with his partially dissected frogs. He took one out and dangled it in the air, causing several students to laugh; the teacher paid no attention.

Suddenly, Principal Shafer's voice came through the P.A system. *"Tomorrow night we'll be hosting our prep rally and bonfire, in celebration of defeating those O Town boys..."*

The students roared; their voices echoed down the halls as the teacher blew a horn to quiet the class.

"...I want to see all you students out there with lots of spirit and support for Coach Barry and the Queerville basketball team."

Freddie held the frog aloft and began to dangle it behind an unsuspecting girl. It lightly grazed her shoulder; she brushed it away at first, but her curiosity piqued, and she turned around to see what it was, letting out a bloodcurdling scream.

The teacher sprang up, but Freddie quickly tossed the frog to Lisa, who deftly caught it and hid it under the table. Both of them froze their eyes glued forward. Just then, a police officer entered the room.

Freddie appeared worried as the officer conversed with the teacher. The teacher gestured towards Freddie, prompting the officer to approach him.

"We need you to come with us," the officer said, standing over Freddie with one hand resting on his gun. "Yeah, what's this about?" Freddie asked, although he already had an inkling.

"You're under arrest for vandalism."

"Vandalism? I don't even litter," Freddie said sarcastically. The police cuffed him and took him away. Lisa and Robin exchanged a worried look.

O Town, USA

Mrs. Baker was washing dishes in the kitchen when Johnnie observed his mother. He was struggling with the urge to tell her the truth, and shatter her world, or keep his dad's secret. In that instant, he made a decision. He came barging in saying, "Mom, after graduation, I'm leaving, and I'm not coming back here."

"Oh, Johnnie, what do you mean you're not coming back? O Town is your home," Mrs. Baker responded, confused.

"This place isn't my home," Johnnie said solemnly, taking his mother's hand, which was snug in a yellow rubber glove, "It's where I'm provided for and sheltered, but it's not a real home."

Mrs. Baker removed her rubber gloves and cradled Johnnie's face softly in her palms.

"Johnnie, what is bugging you? Where is all of this coming from? O Town is where all your friends are," she asked, showing concern.

"Mom, these people are not my friends. This town just screws with people's minds and changes them," Johnnie grunted, grabbing his head as if he had a headache. "Johnnie, what is going on?"

"You should leave too Mom. There's nothing here for you anymore," Johnnie said, his eyes welling up with tears.

"Your father is here, Johnnie. I have a duty to serve my community. We still have folks in the war. I can't leave O Town." Mrs. Baker untied her apron.

"Mom, I saw Dad. I saw Dad with another woman."

Mrs. Baker stood there transfixed, feeling embarrassed. "You shut your mouth," Mrs. Baker snapped, turning her back to Johnnie.

"I'm sorry, Mom, but I saw it with my own two eyes," Johnnie replied sympathetic.

"You should stay out of grown folks' business." Johnnie noticed his mother's peculiar behavior.

"Oh my god, Mom. You knew?" Johnnie was baffled.

"Yes, I knew," Mrs. Baker said, turning around to face Johnnie with a blank expression.

"Now, I have errands to run. Don't you have studying to do?" Johnnie was taken aback by his mother's strange behavior.

KELLY, ROSE, DAWN AND MARY SUE WERE AT THE MALL shopping for a prom dress. The girls had been at the mall for hours in search of the perfect dress. Rose tried on a red dress – the girls gave it a thumbs down. Dawn tried on a pink dress, but the girls didn't like that one either. They decided to try another dress shop.

While Mary Sue was trying on her dress, Dawn, Kelly and Rose waited in the sitting area.

"Did you guys hear about the killer on the loose?" Dawn inquired enthusiastically.

"Oh my god! Yes, they said his trail is leading here to O Town," Rose added.

"What? Do they know who it is?" Kelly asked, feeling uneasy.

"No, they have no clue," Rose gave the girls a frightened look.

"How do they know it's the same person that's been killing all these women?" Kelly hadn't felt this spooked since Max placed a fake spider in her bed last Halloween.

"All the women were about the same age, and he cut them all the same way. The news says that he removes their hearts and takes them as some sort of souvenir. They're calling him the broken heart killer," Dawn explained.

"Oh my, that's just awful," Kelly said, saddened.

"Apparently, he uses some medieval knife to do it," Dawn added to her already eerie exaggeration, creeping the girls out.

"My parents want me home before dark tonight," Rose confessed. "Yeah, me too," Dawn remarked.

"We all should get home before dark," Kelly said, being cautious. Mary Sue burst from the curtains in a beautiful teal dress that complemented her tones. The girls loved it and gave it a thumbs up. "Oh, you just look so beautiful, Mary Sue," Kelly hugged Mary Sue. Rose took a closer look at the dress, "You have to get this dress, Mary Sue," she said. "You think so?"

"Yes!" They all said in unison.

"One down, three to go," Dawn sighed.

Queerville, USA

Zack and Charlotte were in the middle of a conversation in her office. "As for the bank loan, yes, I will gladly cosign for you. I'm glad Miss Kelly inspired you to open your own shop. I really like her; she has a good head on her shoulders," Charlotte said, expressing her fondness for Kelly, which made Zack realize how much they missed her. It's been days since they've seen Kelly. The last time they were together, Kelly was understandably upset with them.

"Now, back to this Dee issue," Charlotte said, trailing off. She didn't want to have this conversation, but she knew it had to be done, and she needed to be the one to have it with Zack.

"I didn't know Dee was so dissatisfied with my leadership," Zack admitted. "Zack, where do you want Queerville to go? What is the future you see for us?"

"The issues we face are bigger than Queerville," Zack replied.

"Yes, they are, but change starts at home. So, what future do you envision for your home?"

"I just want us to live without fearing for our lives every day. That's why we started the gangs - for protection and community." "You just said it yourself, protection. We formed the gangs to protect our home. Now what do you think those O Town boys will do when they find out it was us who trashed Main Street?" Charlotte questioned.

"They'll never find out," Zack murmured.

* * *

Freddie sat in a dimly lit interrogation room, taking in the sight of the dark, and chilly cement walls. He couldn't help but ponder how many hardened criminals had occupied this space before him. Freddie didn't appear to be afraid; he considered himself an outlaw, and being in that room only fueled his sense of pride. However, his irritation grew as the new Sheriff, fresh from the prejudiced states of the South, entered the room.

"Why am I here?" Freddie exclaimed.

"Main Street was vandalized by a group of thugs. Now, we know you were one of them. We just want the names of your buddies that were with you," the sheriff informed Freddie.

"I told you; it wasn't me."

"See, now, we know it was you. We have an eyewitness."

Freddie sat up in his chair and blurted out, "An eyewitness that saw me. Bullshit!" Freddie was amused.

"No, not you. Your fancy blue car. You know, the one with scorpions painted on it. I've seen that car. I must say that thing is a beauty," the sheriff teased as he watched Freddie's expression turn to worry, he added, "Still want to keep saying it wasn't you?" Freddie shrugged and said, "Yeah, my car was stolen."

"Don't give me that stolen car nonsense. Look, we know it was you. Just give us your friends and I'll let you walk."

"I'm walking anyway, because I didn't do it. Now am I free to go?" They tossed Freddie in a cell and shut the gate. Freddie quickly gripped the bars tightly, a panicked grimace on his face. His big mouth had landed him in jail.

O Town, USA

Rose and Dawn were trying on their dresses, while Kelly and Mary Sue anxiously waited for them.

"How have you been Mary Sue? I haven't seen you around school much lately. Have you been ill?" Kelly asked with genuine concern for her friend.

Mary Sue squirmed uncomfortably before saying, "Yeah, I think I might've caught a bug from one of the girls at Sunday school." "Have you picked a college yet? My parents want me to pick one soon, but I can't make up my mind." Kelly was overwhelmed with all the pressures of college. She didn't really want to attend.

"Oh, Kelly, a woman's place is at home. I just want to be a good mother and wife, with a husband who takes care of me."

Kelly's expression turned sour; she was appalled.

"I don't want any of that. I don't want a man to take care of me. I don't want children. I simply want to travel the world with someone I love, someone who

175

makes me feel safe and brings me happiness," Kelly responded firmly.

Mary Sue gasped and clutched her chest in disbelief as she blurted out, "You don't want children?!" Before Kelly could answer, Rose and Dawn popped out of the curtain with their dresses on. Rose had on a haltered, sleeveless, polka dot cocktail prom dress. Dawn had on a black and white square-cut neckline and bouffant skirt. Kelly and Mary Sue gave them a thumbs up.

"Those dresses are beautiful," Mary Sue said in awe. "I need to find my dress now, before you guys take all the pretty ones," Kelly said, anxious to find the right dress.

She grabbed her selections to try on... some were bad... some were awful... some were awfully bad. The girls gave a thumbs down to every selection. Kelly crossed her fingers and went back in to try on her final selection.

"Did you guys hear what those Queerville thugs did to Main Street?" Mary Sue scowled.

"They don't know who it was," Rose sighed and rolled her eyes. "That's just a rumor," Dawn told Mary Sue. "No, it's true, it was them," Mary Sue shouted.

Kelly poked her head out, anytime Queerville was mentioned she was all ears. "What about Queerville?" she asked.

"They trashed Main Street and wrote all kinds of ungodly things. Shame on them," Mary Sue answered.

Kelly was not pleased with what she heard, but she continued trying on her dress.

"You mean they wrote over all the No Queers signs, oh gee what a shame," Rose retorted.

"It's just not right and Johnnie told me..."

Before Mary Sue could finish her sentence. Kelly popped out in a beautiful pale pink frosted with tiers of ruffles on net, boned bodice, haltered gown that matched her perfectly.

Rose and Dawn were stunned, Kelly looked like a real-life princess. "Where was this dress at?" Rose asked, jealous.

"I want to change my dress now," Dawn commented.

"Kelly, you're going to have all the boys going crazy over you," Mary Sue teased. "In their dreams," Kelly whispered.

Rose got up and hugged Kelly, "You look so beautiful. Zack is going to be blown away when they see you," she said causing Kelly to blush and giggle. Mary Sue looked puzzled, trying to remember where she had heard that name before.

"Zack? Is that the fella that was shot?" she asked.

"What?" Kelly seemed confused.

"Johnnie was with someone named Zack and apparently this fella was shot yesterday," Mary Sue explained. Kelly suddenly got lightheaded and was struggling to catch her breath. "Who told you this?" Dawn asked.

"Johnnie," Mary Sue replied.

"What..." Kelly could barely speak, her voice barely a whisper.

"Kelly, are you okay? Take a seat dear. You probably need to eat something," Mary Sue suggested.

The room spun around Kelly as the news of Zack being shot overwhelmed her. She felt nauseous, like she was about to barf.

"I have to go... I have to go," Kelly panicked, attempting to rip off her dress. The other girls rushed to help her out of it.

AT THE POLICE STATION, OFFICER WHITEY CASUALLY strolled by the holding area where Freddie was impatiently waiting. He spotted officer Whitey and flagged him down.

"Officer Whitey, funny meeting you here," Freddie shouted from the cell. Officer Whitey looked like a deer caught in headlights, appearing uncomfortable as he nervously ran his hand through his hair and walked towards the cell.

"What are you doing in here?" he whispered to Freddie. "Some bullshit accusations," he replied.

"Oh, accusations, huh?"

"Look, you need to get me out of here," Freddie demanded. "What? I can't do that. I don't have the power to drop charges."

"Well, get me bail or a desk ticket," Freddie insisted.

"Freddie I can't..." "I could tell the sheriff about what goes on in the secret lives of his deputies," Freddie stated, his voice tinged with a hint of malice as he threatened to expose both his own secret and those of the officers'.

Officer Whitey's face turned pale, beads of sweat formed on his forehead, and his eyes darted around nervously.

"Okay fine. I'll see what I can do," Officer Whitey said before rushing off. Freddie felt relieved.

Queerville, USA

Sandy was working late, taking orders. She felt worn out and eager to get home. Rickey unexpectedly showed up, making her night even more exhausting. She motioned for him to go to the back so they could speak in private. "I haven't heard from you, so I thought I'd come and check on you," Rickey remarked shyly.

Sandy felt awkward.

"Thank you, Rickey, that's sweet. I'm sorry I haven't given you a ring. I've had a lot going on but I'm glad you're here because," Sandy paused briefly, inhaled deeply, and said, "I don't think we're right for each other."

Rickey was taken aback and giggled awkwardly. "Come on, we're perfect for each other. We have fun together. We complement each other well. I like you a lot Sandy," Rickey implored.

Sandy felt flattered, but she couldn't continue pretending that she was content. Although it pained her to say goodbye to Rickey, she knew it was the best decision for both of them.

"I don't have those feelings for you, not like that. I think you're a swell guy, Rickey," Sandy stated. But before she could finish, Rickey's eyes grew wide with hope, and he blurted out, "Then why can't we make this work?" "I don't want swell, Rickey. I don't want just like," Sandy said with soulful eyes.

"What do you want?" Sandy took a moment to collect her thoughts before answering, "To feel alive."

She gently held Rickey's face and added, "We're just two people who are not aligned."

Rickey swallowed his pride. "Okay, Miss Sandy, if you ever change your mind, you know where to find me." Rickey clasped Sandy's hand in his and kissed the back of her palm softly before walking away. Charlotte came up behind Sandy. "Girl are you in here breaking hearts again?" she chuckled.

FREDDIE WAS SITTING ANXIOUSLY IN JAIL WHEN AN officer entered with keys. He unlocked the cell and pointed at Freddie, saying, "You're free to go. You must have some good friends."

Freddie stood up, relieved to be free. Officer Whitey watched from a distance as Freddie winked at him.

"Had to be the president or vice president. I can't keep track. You know I'm going to call him and tell him what a bang-up job you're doing," Freddie sneered. The officer was not amused. "Yeah, I'm sure that'll mean a lot coming from you," he snarled.

Freddie glared at the officer, giving him a scrutinizing look. "Well, maybe I won't," Freddie shrugged. "You'll be back. Remember we have an eyewitness." "Later fuzz," Freddie shouted as he walked out the door.

As he exited the station, he spotted Lisa and Robin waiting. "My girls!" he yelled, thrilled to see them, and ran into their arms.

THERE WAS LOUD POUNDING ON SANDY'S FRONT DOOR. Zack managed to open the door partially before Kelly burst in, visibly upset, yelling, "Do you have anything you want to tell me?" Zack was bewildered, having no clue as to why Kelly was so upset. "Uh, no. What's wrong? Are you okay?" "No, I'm not okay. I have to hear from my friends that you're going around vandalizing the town with your thug friends," Kelly said, plainly agitated, causing Zack to feel attacked.

"Oh, I see. The real Kelly is coming out," Zack remarked sarcastically. "And who is the real Zack? Because it certainly isn't the person who just trashed Main Street or had a fist fight in the middle of Paradise Road," Kelly shouted.

Zack became furious, shouting, "How would you know? You don't even know me!"

Kelly flung up her hands in frustration. "I'm trying! I'm trying to get to know you! But you make it so damn hard. You keep pushing me away," she muttered.

"Maybe it's because I'm just a thug. Maybe you should go find one of those cookie cutter white boys with the sweaters," Zack said, glaring at Kelly with an expression she had never seen before. Kelly attempted to peer into those emerald eyes, searching for any trace of the Zack she knew, but they were as dark and distant as she felt. "You don't mean that," she said quietly.

"You have no concept of how it feels to be us. You sit up there on your hill, looking down on us. Do you have any idea what I go through every day? Men look at me with disgust. Women clutch their pearls and tuck their purses when they see me. They hide their kids, like I'm some kind of monster," Zack's voice was hoarse with pain.

As Zack spoke, Kelly began to tremble with anguish. It felt like a sharp blade, drenched in salt, slicing through an open wound and piercing her heart, as if someone had torn it out. She hated seeing Zack in so much pain.

"I'm sorry that you go through that. I truly am. But I am not like them. You hate them so much that you can't see it," Kelly wept, her voice breaking as she pleaded, "Please, look at me, Zack." Zack refused to make eye contact. Kelly took a deep breath and exhaled before speaking, "I heard you were shot. I came to see if you're okay." Zack grabbed their bandaged arm.

"Yeah, it was just a flesh wound. Sandy patched me up. I'm fine," Zack said nonchalantly. Hearing Sandy's name only intensified Kelly's grief. She had expected to be the one Zack turned to for help, and it broke her to see that wasn't the case.

"So, let me get this straight. You were shot, and you went to her?" Kelly asked, her voice faltering and her eyes brimmed with hurt. She took a few steps back, expecting Zack to stop her. However, Zack did not. Kelly ran outside, crying and clutching her stomach. Fighting with Zack made her physically sick. Meanwhile, Zack ran into the bathroom and puked in the toilet.

THE NIGHT SKY WAS CLOUDY, BLANKETED IN A THICK layer of fog. A calm silence filled the air as the moon partially illuminated the O Town motel off the highway. Inside, the mysterious blonde woman had just finished taking a shower. As she was prepared to lotion her body, she heard a knock at the door. She wrapped herself in a bathrobe and opened the door, only to find no one there. She poked her head out and cautiously looked left and right, but there was nothing but dark skies and fog. No one could be seen for miles. With a sense of unease, she went back inside.

A loud clunk came from the bathroom. Startled, she peered into the bathroom from a distance but didn't see anything. She took cautious steps toward the bathroom, her heart racing and hands shaking. As she walked in, a breeze blew through the wide-open window. Feeling relieved, she closed the window and turned around, only to come face-to-face with a masked figure.

A blood-curdling scream escaped her lips as the masked figure forcefully drove a silver knife into her stomach, then proceeded to slit her throat. Gasping for breath, the woman was tossed onto the bed. Without hesitation, the figure climbed on top of her, repeatedly thrusting the knife into her chest. Finally, the figure removed her heart and placed it in a glass jar.

CHAPTER 9

The doctor's office had just opened for business. It was a typical 1950s family practice, dull and pastel. On the counter, there were jars of tongue depressors with lollipops placed beside them. Mary Sue anxiously awaited the doctor's return. Her palms were sweaty, and she could hear a throbbing in her ears. She took deep breaths trying to ward off a panic attack, when finally, the doctor entered the room.

"Mary Sue are your parents here with you?" the doctor asked. "What is it, doctor?" Mary Sue already had an idea, but she wanted confirmation. The doctor sighed, "Mary Sue, I don't know how to tell you this but...you're pregnant." Mary Sue was devastated, "What? No, that can't be."

Queerville, USA

Zack and Sandy were enjoying their breakfast, which consisted of hotcakes, sausages, biscuits, eggs and a pitcher of orange juice that was only half full. Sandy was savoring the delectable breakfast that Zack had prepared. "Have you ever cooked for Kelly? Once she tries your food, she won't let you go."

"I made her some fish once. You know her taste buds are a bit different from ours," Zack replied.

Sandy chuckled before replying, "You're right. I totally forgot you got yourself a white girl. She got flavor though, I heard she stood up to Lisa."

"Yeah, she did. It completely surprised me."

"Good for her. Lisa's bark is louder than her bite anyway."

They shared a laugh, then Zack's expression turned serious. "I don't think I'm going to my mother's birthday dinner this year," Zack said dismally.

Sandy's face lit up, she became extremely joyful, ignoring Zack's change in tone. "Is it that time already? I'm coming. What time should I be there? Is she making those yams? Ugh, I love her yams!" she exclaimed with excitement.

Zack was irritated by Sandy's lack of concern for their change in mood. "Oh, gee Zack you're not going to your mother's this year. Oh, please tell me why," Zack mocked Sandy.

Sandy laughed. "I'm sorry. You mentioned food and I got distracted. Why aren't you going?" she asked, trying to be empathetic, but still seeming unconcerned.

Zack shook their head. "I didn't mention food, you did. Forget it. Right now, all you're thinking about is food. I know it."

Sandy laughed again.

"Speaking of significant others, how did Rickey take the breakup?" Zack asked, changing the topic.

"Pretty well," Sandy admitted, leaving Zack shocked to hear that Rickey handled the split well.

"He would be the first man in history to ever take losing you well," Zack acknowledged, causing Sandy to suck her teeth as if a dreadful recollection had crossed her mind. "Did you give him your flowers?" Zack inquired. "Nope. He didn't even smell them," Sandy confessed.

"Now, I know he's somewhere banging his head against the wall." Sandy laughed so hard that she spewed up her orange juice. "I'm glad you didn't waste your time," Zack remarked, becoming sentimental. "Life is too short; you shouldn't settle for someone who isn't going to make you happy," Zack added.

"I concur. Why do you think I made Maria break up with you?" Zack's face froze in shock. "Wait. You had Maria break up with me?" Zack asked, feeling baffled. Sandy was amused by Zack's ignorance.

"She was cheating on you with some greaser chick from Bronxville."

"She was?" Zack murmured, scratching their head. "Zack, you didn't know?" Sandy inquired. "No," Zack admitted. "That's funny, because everyone knew."

Zack shot Sandy an intense look. "Sandy, are you for real?" Sandy nodded her head yes and said, "Your brother wanted me to fight her." "Sounds like him. Were you really going to fight for me?"

"I'd cut a bitch for you, absolutely. Don't forget, I was the original leader of the Lipsticks," Sandy said as she stood up and placed her plate in the sink. She kissed Zack on the cheek before saying, "Thank you for breakfast."

"How about a movie night tonight?" Zack suggested, knowing it was their favorite thing to do together.

"That would be fun. I'm on the late shift tonight though." "I'll wait up for you."

"I'll bring the popcorn. See you tonight," Sandy yelled, rushing out the door. "Be careful out there, there's a killer on the loose!" Zack shouted back.

THE POLICE DELIVERED FREDDIE'S CAR TO THE CLUB ON a tow truck. When Freddie stepped outside, he was overjoyed to find his car arriving. The sheriff stepped out of the truck and approached Freddie with a smug expression. "Is this your vehicle?" the sheriff asked. Freddie answered, "Yes, it is."

"Well, that's interesting because this vehicle was found abandoned, outside a store that reported an attempted robbery," the sheriff stated. "Well, like I said, it was stolen," Freddie shrugged.

The sheriff removed his sunglasses and looked directly into Freddie's eyes, "The shop owner claimed it was two little Negro boys," he said, accusingly.

"Maybe it was the same Negro boys who stole my car and vandalized the city," Freddie stated condescendingly. The sheriff smirked and tipped his hat.

"Good day, son."

O Town, USA

Max was at home, suffering from a terrible headache. Desperately, he began searching the house for money or anything he could sell. Sneaking into his parents' room, he decided to snoop around. He entered the bathroom and opened the medicine cabinet, where he noticed his mom's amphetamine pills. Without hesitation, he started popping them.

Queerville, USA

Sandy was having a solo dance session in front of the jukebox, lost in her own little world. She swayed her hips and wrapped her arms around her curvy body, completely unaware of the effect she was having on those watching. Men gaped at her, their dates slapping them, while the single guys drooled. When she finally opened her eyes, she noticed all the men admiring her. She couldn't help but giggle before returning to work behind the counter, where Charlotte stood poised to pass judgment.

"How many times do I have to tell you? I can't put you on the menu. Stop teasing these men," Charlotte scolded. "I was just dancing. I can't help it if these married men look at me," Sandy defended herself.

"I guess. Well, as long as they're paying customers." "Well, you do know, if I were on the menu..." Sandy playfully grinded her hips against Charlotte, adding, "...these men couldn't afford me."
"How about that secret lover of yours? How much is he paying?" Sandy's mouth dropped as she rolled her eyes and sighed, "I don't know what you're talking about," pretending to be clueless. "Child, you think you're nickel slick, but I got your penny change," Charlotte retorted. "Where do you get all these old quotes from?"

"Who is this fella you've been hiding?" Sandy dramatically grasped her chest and claimed, "A lady never kisses and tells."

"Well, what does a hussy do?" Charlotte shot back.

Sandy sucked her teeth and replied, "Well, clearly, I wouldn't know." "And why are you always dancing by yourself? You don't ever dance with any of these fellas,"

Charlotte asked. Sandy swayed her hips and said confidently, "Because I don't be dancing. I be flying, and this is a first-class flight. Not everyone can come aboard."

"Okay, Pan Am, go take some orders," Charlotte snarky remarked. Sandy sucked her teeth in annoyance.

O Town, USA

Mary Sue sat in her room, tears streaming down her face, clutching her Bible tightly. Suddenly, there was a gentle knock on the door. Johnnie entered the room, concern etched on his face. "Hey Mary Sue, are you okay?" he asked, noticing her tear-stained cheeks. Trying to compose herself, Mary Sue replied, "Oh, I must have dozed off while reading my bible." She quickly adjusted her clothes, hoping to hide her slightly protruding stomach.

"I didn't see you at school today. Is everything alright?" Johnnie inquired; his voice filled with genuine worry.

"Yeah, Johnnie, I'm fine. I skipped a day, it's not the end of the world." Confused by her response, Johnnie sat down next to her.

"You skipped a day of school just to read your bible?" he asked, his eyebrows furrowing.

"No, Johnnie. What's going on? Why are you here?" Taking a deep breath, Johnnie began to open up.

"My dad is cheating on my mom with another woman," he confessed, his voice filled with pain and anger.

Shocked by this revelation, Mary Sue exclaimed, "No! Adultery is a sin." Feeling hurt by Mary Sue's quick

189

judgment, Johnnie retorted, "So is premarital sex. Can you stop being so judgmental and just listen? I have a lot on my mind right now."

"Well, so do I," Mary Sue said, leaping to her feet.

"Do you think the world just stops because Johnnie has things on his mind?" "Mary Sue, I came here to talk to you," Johnnie pleaded. "Well, I don't want to hear it." "What's wrong with you? Why are you being like this?" Mary Sue snapped, "You. You're what's wrong with me," she said, pushing Johnnie. "Mary Sue, what's gotten into you?" Johnnie was startled by Mary Sue's alarming behavior. She continued pushing him, shouting, "It's your fault." She pushed Johnny out of her room and slammed the door.

"Gee whiz, Mary Sue," Johnnie muttered.

ZACK PULLED UP TO THE BONFIRE AND THE GIRLS immediately flocked to them. Zack acknowledged them with a nod, but that was all. They walked toward their gang, who were much more excited to see Zack than they were to see them.

A few minutes later, Freddie drove up, relieved to have his car back. Zack and Freddie hugged, thrilled to see each other after the events of the other day.

"What's buzzin, cuzzin? I heard the fuzz got you," Zack inquired with an excited grin. "These pigs can't hold me. I'm slick as a dime and quick as lime. You dig," Freddie quipped. "How did you get your ride back?"

"The pigs dropped it off at the club."

"Oh, you stuck it to 'em," Zack confessed.

"Have you spoken with Johnnie boy? We need to make sure he keeps his mouth shut," Freddie remarked.

"Nah, Johnnie's solid. He's not going to squeal."

"Johnnie is a square, and we don't trust squares."

"I'll talk to him. I was going to offer to fix his ride for free." Freddie gave Zack a cold stare. "Don't do shit for free. Johnnie got it made in the shade. Why do you think his last name is Baker? All they do is bake bread. You better take that square's money," he advised Zack before getting distracted by a tall handsome boy from across the field. "I see something sweet. I'll be right back."

O Town, USA

Kelly was returning home after hanging out with her friends when she discovered Max in her room, rummaging through her drawers. "Max, what are you doing?" she asked, perplexed.

"Kelly, I need something, anything to sell. Please, I'm in trouble," Max pleaded. "I don't have anything for you to sell, Max."

"Please Kelly, please help your little brother out," Max begged.

"What's gotten into you?" Kelly inquired, worried, having noticed Max's bloodshot eyes and unpredictable behavior. Kelly hardly recognized him.

"Did you take something?" she asked, concerned.

"No, I didn't take something. I need something."

Kelly grew increasingly concerned for her brother and screamed out to her dad. "Dad, it's Max, Dad!"

"Kelly, please, I know you have something. What about that prom dress?" Max turned to go to the closet. Kelly tried to stop him, but he slammed her into the wall. She fell as Mr. Hamilton came storming in. "What is this ruckus? What is going on here? Max, did you hurt your sister?" he asked as he helped Kelly up from the floor.

"There's something wrong with him, Dad."

"I need money. Why won't you listen to me!"

"It's okay, son. We're going to get you some help."

"I don't need help. I need money," Max shouted, shoving his dad and rushing out.

Queerville, USA

The pep rally began, with Principal Shafer and the team standing before the students. Lisa and Robin exchanged flirtatious glances as Principal Shafer addressed the massive crowd.

"We kicked those square boys hard. We are the new high school champions of the Midwest! And we look forward to seeing all of you back here next year. Queerville forever!"

The school band started playing their victory song, while the cheerleaders performed their routine. Val and Zack were on the sidelines in a clumsy parody of the cheerleaders.

A blue chariot suddenly rolled down the entrance to the parking lot. Ronnie was driving with his head partially out the window. Several other guys were also in the car, each wearing O Town letterman sweaters. The blue chariot slowly and almost tauntingly circled around the bonfire area. The gangs watched them, tensing up like male animals whose territory had been invaded.

At that moment, Freddie was engaged in a passionate kiss with a tall handsome boy, he looked up to see what the commotion was about and immediately joined his friends. They all spread out, assuming aggressive stances to make it clear that they were not afraid.

* * *

Back at the diner, Sandy was being stalked by a mysterious figure watching from outside. She continued taking orders, unaware of the danger that awaited her.

O Town, USA

Mr. Hamilton and Kelly anxiously waited in the corridor for the doctor who was examining Max.

Finally, the doctor emerged with a relieved expression. "Most likely, whatever your son took will be out of his system in twenty-four hours. However, if this behavior continues, I suggest considering a long-term course of action," the doctor explained.

"What does that mean? Are you suggesting we put my brother in a facility?" Kelly inquired.

"Max is in good health. I believe he can overcome this on his own. But if he is unable to, you should consider all your options." "What about his headaches? He constantly complains about them and experiences blackouts," Kelly asked the doctor.

"We will have to conduct more tests... Mr. Hamilton, has your son ever undergone electroconvulsive therapy?"

* * *

Queerville, USA

RONNIE AND HIS FRIENDS WERE STILL CIRCLING THE bonfire. "Hey! What are the squares doing here? This isn't their territory," Freddie shouted to Zack. "They want a knuckle sandwich?" Zack replied while clenching their fist. "Well, we have enough for everyone," Val added, ready to rumble. The blue chariot turned and accelerated toward the gang.

No one budged.

Ronnie and his friends got out and rushed straight toward Zack. The Red Dragons immediately stood by Zack. "If it isn't the Queers," Ronnie snidely remarked. "Watch yourself," Zack said sharply. Ronnie shrugged it off and shouted, "We're here to collect what's ours!"

"An ass whipping?" Freddie exclaimed.

Ronnie looked at him and gave a phony laugh.

"Ha, funny guy. We want the trophy that belongs to us," he said bitterly.

"You guys lost and have the nerve to show up here frosty. Get bent!" Zack waved Ronnie off.

"You guys cheated. Everyone knows that's what you people do," Ronnie stated harshly. The gangs tried to surge forward and attack him, but Zack held them back. "You guys lost because your boy Johnnie is trash, and your point guard Max is a juicehead," Freddie stated coldly with a matching look, but it couldn't melt the heat from Ronnie's glare.

"Don't you have a penis to play with!" Ronnie sneered.

"Is that an offer?" Freddie asked, smirking.

Ronnie rolled his eyes and refocused on Zack.

"We want a fair shot and entry to the races. All I hear around town is how fast Zack is. The car that moves like lightning. I want to race you," Ronnie declared.

The gangs all burst out laughing.

"You don't just come to our turf and ask to race the champ. That's not how it works!" Val shouted.

"We have cars just like you," Ronnie said, gesturing towards his friends. Zack responded, "So, why don't y'all race each other?"

Freddie chimed in amused. "What do you think this is, Queers versus Squares?" Ronnie disregarded Freddie's remark and addressed Zack.

"And here I thought Zack was about business," Ronnie trailed off, raking Zack up and down in disgust, before asking, "What the hell are you anyway?"

Zack cold-cocked Ronnie, and Freddie instantly struck one of Ronnie's buddies. "It's Queers versus squares!" Freddie yelled as a brawl broke out between the gangs and the squares.

POLICE VEHICLE'S SURROUNDED THE MOTEL WHERE THE body of the mysterious woman had just been discovered. Her bare body laid crossed the bed, her heart removed from her chest. Detective Hobbs and Officer Whitey stood alone beside the body, completing their initial examination. Detective Hobbs sat in a chair writing his notes. "She looks like some kind of religious sacrifice," Officer Whitey suggested.

Detective Hobbs looked outside toward the shadows, the low valley between them a desolate flatness.

"We need more men for a grid search. I need you guys to set up a perimeter," he pointed back through the fields, indicating the far convergence of rural highways. "...as wide as possible on those three roads. One of you post up and take down the license plates of anything that passes."

Officer Whitey pulled out his radio. "A42. We need trooper assistance on that 419. Send as many as you can spare for a canvas." "*Roger, A42.*"

Detective Hobbs put on latex gloves and crouched down to examine the body. "There are ligature marks at the wrists and ankles, as well as Hemorrhaging around the throat. None of this makes any sense," Detective Hobbs stated, clearly perplexed.

"Why not?" Officer Whitey inquired.

"Well, there are no signs of a struggle, no defensive wounds. In fact, everything here suggests that she was killed forcefully and quickly."

"Meaning what exactly?"

"Meaning, why was she tied up after she'd already been killed?" Detective Hobbs questioned.

"This is a good Christian town. We can't have a killer on the loose who is capable of such brutality towards another human being," Officer Whitey expressed, visibly shaken.

"Where else do you expect the devil to play, if not in God's own backyard?" Detective Hobbs responded, giving Officer Whitey an eerie stare.

Queerville, USA

Darkness was falling over the diner, the eerie night sky consumed by fog. Sandy was leaving work alone, heading down the abandoned road. There was a silent calm on the road, reminiscent of every horror movie right before the killer strikes.

Sandy continued walking down the dirt road oblivious to the fact that she was being followed by the Broken Heart Killer, the mysterious figure who had been stalking her.

Her body snugged perfectly in her dress, accentuating every curve. The mysterious figure was undressing her with his eyes. Sandy heard a twig snap and swiftly turned around, only to find nothing but looming shadows, not a soul in sight. She turned back, resuming her walk.

ZACK WAS WAITING UP FOR SANDY, SITTING ON THE couch watching "*I Love Lucy*," when the phone rang.

"Hello... No, she's not here. She should be getting off now. I'll tell her you called," Zack hung up.

A weird feeling washed over them, and worry started to set in. Zack glanced at the clock. *Sandy should've been home by now.* Zack quickly put on their sneakers, grabbed their gun and rushed out.

Fog dimmed the light over the empty road as Sandy's footsteps echoed down the street. A shadowy figure lurked behind her; she could sense its presence. She turned around, but once again, there was nothing there. Turning back around, she was suddenly face-to-face with Rickey, causing her to jump in surprise.

"Oh, Rickey, you scared me," she exclaimed, sighing in relief. Sandy couldn't help but notice the vacant look on his face.

"Is something wrong? Were you on your way to the diner to see me?" Sandy inquired.

"I did everything I could to make you happy. But all you did was tease me," Rickey muttered, his words tinged with bitterness. An unsettling feeling settled in the pit of Sandy's stomach.

"Do you want to talk about it?" she asked, her voice trembling slightly.

"I wanted so much for this to work. I thought you were different from all the others. I wanted you to live. But it seems I'm not good enough for you. I suppose I'll have to steal your heart some other way now!" Rickey shouted with a sinister tone, brandishing a knife in his hand.

Reacting instinctively, Sandy kicked him in the groin and bolted, screaming for help, "Help! Somebody, please help me!" she screamed as loud as she could, terrified for her life.

Rickey pursued her, kicking her legs out from under her, forcing her to trip and fall. He quickly climbed on top of her, using his legs to pin her down. "Get off me! Help! Someone please!" Sandy cried out desperately, struggling to push him off, but he had her arms trapped with his legs. Rickey raised the knife, prepared to thrust it into Sandy's chest, before shrieking, "I'm going to cut out your fucking heart and hang it on the wall with the others."

Rickey forcefully drove the knife down, when suddenly, Zack emerged from nowhere and tackled him. Rickey dropped the knife. Zack rose up and stomped on him. Rickey grabbed Zack's leg and threw them to the ground. Determined, Rickey retrieved the knife and attempted to climb on top of Zack, but Zack swiftly shot him in the chest. Rickey collapsed onto his back and Zack hurried over to comfort Sandy who was visibly shaken up.

"It's okay. You're safe now," Zack assured her as they held a sobbing Sandy in their arms.

———

At the police station, Zack continued to console Sandy as Detective Hobbs entered the room with their statements. "Okay, your statements look good. Both your stories match, but even if they didn't, it wouldn't matter," he revealed.

"Why?"

"We believe the person you know as Rickey killed another woman at a motel yesterday. Furthermore, we believe he is the infamous broken heart killer we've been looking for."

"What?" Sandy sighed, feeling horrified, she squeezed Zack's arm. "The broken heart killer, the one responsible for the gruesome murders across the state. We have reason to believe Rickey is the culprit," Detective Hobbs confirmed.

Sandy was filled with shock and disbelief.

"How do you know that? How can you be so sure?"

"Well, the knife he had in his possession is the same model that was used in the murders. There is still some blood on the blade which I'm sure will match one of the victims. And somewhere, he has all the hearts he removed from..."

"Oh God," Sandy whispered shakily.

Zack felt concerned for her and just wanted to get her home. "Are we free to go?" Zack asked.

"Yes and thank you. You saved a lot of lives tonight. You're a real hero." Zack offered a helping hand to Sandy.

CHAPTER 10

It had been days since the attack on Sandy. The town was still in shock and on high alert. Nothing like this had ever hit so close to home. Sandy refused to leave the house, afraid of the dangers that lay in wait. Zack was in the kitchen and had just finished plating some food for the two of them. Sandy was lying on the couch, under the covers like a scared child afraid of the boogeyman. Zack handed her a plate, but she refused to eat.

"Sandy, you have to eat something. You need to keep your strength up," Zack urged.

"I'm not hungry, Zack," she mumbled, hiding her face under the cover.

Zack decided to go cruising around looking at potential shops to buy. They saw a glimpse of Kelly crossing the street. Zack couldn't believe their eyes; they hadn't seen Kelly for weeks. Zack hopped out of the car and ran over to get a better look, but it wasn't Kelly. Zack laughed at themselves, *am I losing my mind?* The separation was getting to be too much. Zack had been so worried about tending to Sandy they hadn't realized how much they missed Kelly.

At the diner, Kelly, Rose and Dawn were having burgers and fries. Rose and Dawn were engrossed in a deep conversation, while Kelly's mind was miles away. She looked up and caught a glimpse of Zack, she got excited, upon looking again, she realized it wasn't Zack. Kelly had never experienced such longing for someone before. All these emotions she was feeling were all new to her and she could barely control them. One thing was clear: she missed the hell out of Zack. She ached to see them again, but she was stuck with a dilemma, could she accept all of Zack?

It was a rainy night in Queerville, and the streets were flooded. The rain gushed into the sewers, and people hurriedly ran to seek shelter from the storm. Raindrops fell against the window as Zack looked out, wearing the loneliest expression on their face. They glanced back at Charlotte, who was caressing Sandy's head as she wept in her lap. Zack couldn't help but wonder what Kelly was doing at that very moment.

O Town, USA

Kelly was crying in her brothers' arms. She missed Zack tremendously and it was killing her. Max held his sister as she wept, he was getting a front row seat to his sister's first heartbreak. He didn't know how to help her or how to ease her pain. So, he simply held her tightly and allowed her to cry until she eventually fell asleep.

Queerville, USA

Sandy heard rattling on the front door and noticed someone attempting to enter. Frightened, she quickly retrieved a knife from the kitchen and retreated into a corner. Suddenly, the door burst open, causing Sandy to scream. Zack rushed over to her. "Sandy, it's me. It's me." Sandy's screams persisted. "You're safe, Sandy," Zack embraced her, but she continued to sob uncontrollably.

———————————————

The next morning, Kelly was still in bed, when her mother poked her head in. "Sweetheart, are you still feeling ill?" "Yes, mom," Kelly spoke softly, trying to hide the hurt in her voice. "Maybe get up and take a shower. It might make you feel better," her mother suggested.

Kelly pondered the idea and then peeled herself out of bed. She went to start the shower, stepping in and feeling the water wash over her. If only it could wash away the pain she was feeling, she thought. Deciding to make an effort to look presentable for the day, she blow-dried her hair. Afterwards, she went to the kitchen to force herself to eat. Pouring herself some tomato juice, she noticed a stack of magazines and old newspapers on the table. She briefly looked through the magazines, but it was something in the newspaper that caught her eye. She grabbed it and read the headline...

"KILLER CAUGHT"
"Zack, Queerville's hero, fought with the Broken Heart Killer and won."

Kelly's eyes grew wide; and she fainted!

Queerville, USA

Zack opened the door, and Kelly leaped into their arms, clutching firmly. Zack wrapped their arms around her. Boy, did they miss her and that sweet aroma of hers. Kelly had a lovely, delicate, powdery scent with a tinge of fresh citrus. It was the type of scent you couldn't get enough of, almost addicting. Such as some people's fascination with the smell of gasoline. Kelly was Zack's fuel. Zack took a long breath, enjoying her aroma and held her tightly.

"I'm sorry, I'm sorry. I just found out. I can't believe I almost lost you. I don't want to fight anymore," Kelly wept.

She lifted her head up, with tears in her eyes. Zack looked at her and murmured, "I don't want to fight anymore either. It's making me sick."

"So, I'm not the only one?" Kelly whispered. Zack shook their head and said, "No. I missed you so much, Kelly." "I missed you, too," Kelly replied with a smile.

They shared a gentle kiss that quickly escalated into a heated, passionate exchange. Afterwards, neither of them could open their eyes for a few moments. They snapped back to reality, and Zack took Kelly by the hand and escorted her inside. Kelly cast Zack a compassionate glance. "I gave you so much grief about being a badass, but I'm truly grateful that you are one." Tears fell from Kelly's eyes with each word, leaving her pristine sweater damp and soiled with tears. Zack offered her a tissue.

"How is Sandy holding up?"

Zack returned their gaze to Sandy's bedroom.

"She's not doing well. She's been in bed for days now. She's too scared to go out. Every time I leave, she calls me to come back. I don't blame her, that man nearly killed her... If I hadn't been there," Zack was visibly shaken up.

Kelly knew right then with certainty that she accepted all of Zack, the good, the bad, the violent. She wanted every bit of Zack. She had no more doubts.

"I said some awful things to you, Zack. I regret every single one of them. Can you forgive me?"

Zack nodded in agreement.

"We both said some awful things to each other."

"I never want us to speak to each other like that again. I feel so guilty for being mad at you, especially when you were out there fighting for your life. I swear, when I saw that article in the paper, my heart stopped," Kelly confessed.

"I thought you never wanted to see me again." Kelly moved closer and gently caressed Zack's face. "Don't ever think that again, okay? It was just a fight, that's all it was. You can't get rid of me that easily." Kelly gave Zack a loving look. Zack took her hand and said, "I have something I want to show you." Kelly's face lit up with a big smile.

* * *

Zack pulled up to their shop and assisted a blindfolded Kelly out of their car. "Are you ready?" Zack asked enthusiastically. "Yes," Kelly replied. Zack carefully removed the blindfold and Kelly's smile vanished. It was an old run-down car shop that was in desperate need of some tender loving care. Kelly felt underwhelmed. "Oh," Kelly uttered.

"Well, I'm going to fix it up," Zack sighed.

"Oh, okay," Kelly said, feeling relieved, "This is wonderful. Zack, I'm extremely proud of you," Kelly hugged Zack tightly.

"Charlotte signed for me with the bank. But it's all mine, can you believe it?" "Yes, I can," Kelly replied, as she looked proudly at Zack.

"I spend most of my time here fixing up the place." "Is that your way of telling me you won't have time to see me?" Kelly teased. "Well, if you help me fix it up, we can spend loads of time together." Kelly gazed at Zack affectionately. "After what you just went through there's no way I'm leaving your side," Kelly said softly to Zack. Zack reciprocated the tender look.

"What have you and the girls been up to?" Zack inquired, cradling Kelly in their arms. "Just the same silly stuff. Oh, I found the most beautiful prom dress. I can't wait for you to see it."

"That's right, your prom is coming up. So, who are you taking?" Zack inquired humorously. Kelly chuckled at first but then became serious. "I want to take you... but since that would start a world war. I'm just going with my girls."

Zack sensed Kelly's sorrow. "What if, after your prom, you come back here? And we'll have our own prom night," Zack suggested.

Kelly giggled, "What? Here?"

"Yeah. Kelly, you're only going to have one prom. I want to make it special for you. I'll have this place looking new by then trust me."

"In five days? My prom is in five days."

"Yes, the plumbing and electrical are all fine. It's mostly cosmetics. All I'll need to do is strip the floors, knock out some walls, paint, and get new appliances," Zack explained.

"Oh, yeah that's it? You're crazy!" Kelly was amused by Zack's determination. "It's an auto shop, it's just one open space. Most of the work will be done upstairs. I'm turning the office into a loft."

"You have flipped your lid, Zack. And I am so proud of you. How can I help?" Kelly was excited about being a part of this moment in Zack's life. She believed in them so much, and now she was witnessing what she already knew. Her only wish was for Zack to see themselves through her eyes.

Zack and Kelly began pulling up carpets, knocking down walls, removing old shelving, stripping up the floors, repairing fixtures and taking breaks to make out.

Over the next three days, Charlotte, Freddie, Lisa, Val, Robin and others came to help. Zack installed new windows, helped put up new drywall, sanded and painted the walls, waxed the floors, wallpapered the bathroom, and tiled the floors.

Zack and Kelly took a break outside the shop.

"This is the most work I have ever done in my entire life," Kelly said proudly. "How does it feel?" Zack asked her. "Satisfying, Validated," she replied.

"Welcome to working class America."

Charlotte brought some ice-cold drinks over.

"It's hotter than fish grease out here. Here you go, love birds, stay hydrated." "Thank you, Charlotte."

"Yes, thank you so much."

They both guzzled their drinks as if they had just been saved from the desert. "Miss Kelly, when am I going to see you in that prom dress? I just know you're going to look absolutely stunning."

"Aww, thank you. I'm sure I'll still be wearing it the next time you see me," Kelly replied, giving Zack a seductive glance.

"Oh, I like her," Charlotte chuckled.

Zack jumped up, ignoring Kelly's comment.

"We should get ready," Zack told Charlotte.

Kelly admired that Zack never pressured her to have sex. The mere mention of sex, they would get uncomfortable, which was a huge difference from the boys she usually dated. Zack was naturally seductive without ever trying, stimulating her mind without even touching her body. It only made Kelly want to give herself to Zack even more.

"Get ready for what?" Kelly felt lost.

"It's Mama Zack's birthday. We go to her house every year to have dinner," Charlotte explained.

Kelly's disappointment was evident, as she realized she wasn't invited. "Oh, that sounds lovely. I bet she appreciates it," Kelly replied, trying to hide her disappointment.

"Yeah, but she'll never admit it," Zack sighed.

"I hope she made those yams. I've been looking forward to those yams all damn year. Well, let me go home and change. I'll see you guys there," Charlotte said excitedly before leaving.

Zack had a strange look on their face.

"What's wrong?" Kelly asked, concerned about how quickly Zack's mood had changed. "This will be the first time I see my mother since she kicked me out," Zack admitted.

"No matter what you go through, no matter the distance, none of that changes the love she has for you, Zack. Parents are often blinded by what they believe is best for you and what actually is best for you. But that is for us to decide, not them. Just give her some time; she'll come around," Kelly reassured them.

"I just always feel like a disappointment to her. Like nothing I do is ever good enough."

"This can't be Mama Zack we're talking about," Kelly questioned. "Don't get me wrong, my mother has always supported who I am. She's always accepted me. But she still applies these hetero, conservative, white ideologies. You probably don't understand."

"No, I do. White parents, remember? They tried to raise me with those same views. But you can still love your parents without changing who you are."

"I'm working on it," Zack said looking at Kelly before asking, "What are you doing later?"

"Studying for my exams," Kelly replied.

"I want you to come with me."

Kelly's eyes widened, "You want me to meet your mom?" Kelly beamed with joy.

"Kelly, you've already met her," Zack pointed out.

"That didn't count because you weren't there. This time you'll be introducing me. I'm so excited. I need to go home and change," she said as she sprang up from her seat.

Zack couldn't help but be amused by Kelly's excitement. She began to ramble, "How are you going to introduce me? As your friend? Your steady partner?"

———————

Zack slicked their hair back and tugged on their rock-abilly bowling shirt, which was neatly tucked into their denim pants as they waited outside of Mama Zack's house. Zack swooned over Kelly, who looked stunning in her black and white plaid boatneck cocktail dress.

"You look beautiful," Zack whispered as Kelly blushed. "Aww, thank you. You look so handsome Zack," Kelly said as she kissed Zack on the lips, being careful not to ruin her lipstick.

Mama Zack opened the door.

"Zack, you made it! I'm so happy to see you."

"Hey, Mom. I wanted to officially introduce you to..." Zack placed a hand on Kelly's back, and she anxiously waited to hear what she would be referred to as.

"...Kelly. You remember her, right?" Though Kelly was disappointed that Zack didn't introduce her as their girlfriend, she still managed to crack a smile.

"Yes, I remember Kelly. She came here like a sad little puppy looking for you," Mama Zack hugged Kelly, "Nice to see you again dear. I'm glad Zack brought you along. Come in you two." Mama Zack took a step back and let them inside. They could hear Charlotte's voice echoing outside. "Who ate all the damn yams?" she exclaimed, angrily.

Dinner was ready to be served inside. Charlotte, Val, Lisa, Freddie, and Robin drooled over the spread: collard greens, potato salad, baked mac and cheese, fried chicken, ribs, stuffing, roasted garlic mashed potatoes, black eyed peas, corn bread, pitchers of Kool-Aid, all spread across Mama Zack's best China. Everyone passed bowls, made their plates, chatted, and ate, while soft tunes played in the background.

211

Kelly gazed at Zack, feeling elated to be in their space surrounded by their friends and family. She longed to share this experience with Zack and her own family. Zack kindly helped her plate her food, and they shared a giggle, lost in their own little world. Freddie cast a peek across to the two and felt compelled to ask Kelly an awkward question, "So, Kelly, have you ever had negro food before?" Freddie asked boldly, which caused everyone to gasp in shock at his audacity.

"Do you mean soul food? If so, then no," Kelly replied respectfully. Everyone was impressed with how Kelly corrected Freddie. Charlotte snapped her fingers at Freddie, delivering a classic burn from a drag queen.

"Okay, have you ever had soul food?" Freddie sneered, quoting himself with his fingers.

"Well, Zack made me some delicious fish by the pond," Kelly admitted, and everyone burst out laughing, teasing Zack.

"Oh so, you fish?"

"That's the Indian in their blood."

Mama Zack looked at Kelly. "So, dear, is this your first-time having soul food?"

"Yes ma'am," Kelly replied.

"Oh, child everyone calls me Mama Zack."

"Yes, Mama Zack," Kelly corrected herself shyly.

Lisa kept giving her side eye glances, clearly disapproving of her for Zack. "So, what do you think, Miss Kelly?" Lisa asked with a vindictive tone. She tried to put Kelly on the spot, but Kelly could hold her own.

"I haven't had a bite yet," Kelly smirked. Zack sensed the tension and took control of the situation.

"You all won't let her eat. You keep grilling her." Freddie waved his hands, silencing the room.

"Everyone be quiet. Let her have her first bite. This is Black history."

Kelly scooped some baked mac and cheese and collard greens onto her fork. She looked up to see every pair of eyes on her, feeling like a fish in a bowl. She took a bite and chewed. Everyone waited in anticipation. There was an awkward silence as Kelly finished chewing. "So, what do you think?" Zack asked.

"It's good, really good," Kelly smiled, while savoring the food in her mouth. Everyone sighed in relief.

"It has so much flavor. It's so good," Kelly whispered to Zack.

"I'm convinced she has some black in her," Freddie snickered.

"What are these again?" Kelly whispered to Zack.

"Those are yams," Zack whispered back.

Kelly was delighted. "Mama Zack, these yams are amazing."

Charlotte was so upset that she dropped her fork.

"Now, how did the white girl get some yams and I can't find any?" Everyone burst out in laughter.

After dinner, Zack sat nervously at the table, while Kelly caressed their back like a proud girlfriend. Mama Zack joined them at the table. "Thank you dear, for the gift it was thoughtful."

"You're welcome, Mom," Zack replied.

Kelly sensed the tension between Zack and their mother and tried to lighten the mood.

"Mama Zack, have you heard? Zack is opening their very own auto shop."

"Oh, is that right?"

"Yeah, I've already purchased the place and we're currently renovating. It should be open in just a few

213

days," Zack said nervously. Kelly held Zack's hand, hoping to calm them.

"The place already has a back log of orders. It seems like everyone wants their car customized by Zack," Kelly added.

Mama Zack was impressed. She looked at Zack with proud eyes. "Did it all on your own. Your own shop building it with your bare hands. That is truly something special."

Zack grew uncomfortable. "Excuse me," Zack said as they got up from the table.

"So, Kelly, how are you? How is school?" Mama Zack asked.

"School is wonderful. My GPA is up to 4.0 and I'm looking to graduate early next year."

"What colleges are you looking at?"

"I guess whichever one is the closest."

"The closest, huh? Tell me Kelly, are you smitten with my Zack?" Kelly paused for a bit, taken aback by the question. She locked her gaze on Mama Zack and replied, "Smitten? No. I am absolutely, unequivocally, in love."

Mama Zack wasn't too surprised by Kelly's response but still admired her for being honest. She gave her a warm smile as Zack returned to the table.

"Zack, this one here is a keeper," Mama Zack said.

Kelly smiled while Zack took her hand and gazed into her eyes and said, "I know, Mom." They shared a loving look.

"I'm proud of you, about everything, the shop, you stopping that killer. How is Sandy holding up?"

"Not too good, Mama."

"I'll come over and visit her tomorrow."

"She'll like that."

"Do you know Sandy as well?" Kelly asked Mama Zack. She hadn't realized how close Zack and Sandy really were. Hearing Mama Zack ask about Sandy triggered her jealousy.

"I've known Sandy for years. She was Zack's first girlfriend," Mama Zack replied.

Kelly's stomach sank, and she struggled to maintain a smile on her face. She had suspected that there was something more between Zack and Sandy. How could anyone be friends with someone as gorgeous as Sandy and not explore more? She felt crushed and furious with Zack for not being honest with her. She didn't want Mama Zack to see her upset so she forced a fake smile. "Oh, was she?" Kelly said through gritted teeth.

Kelly turned away and shot Zack an angry glare. Zack sat frozen, avoiding eye contact. Zack would rather have been anywhere else in that moment.

KELLY AND ZACK SAT IN SILENCE IN ZACK'S HUDSON Hornet. Zack was stiff behind the wheel, scared to look in Kelly's direction. The tension in the air was so thick you could cut it with a knife. Kelly had her arms folded in her lap, shaking her head in disappointment.

"Okay. What is it?" Zack finally broke the ice.

Kelly slid away and looked at Zack, her back against the passenger door. "You and Sandy were together?"

"No," Zack replied.

"I can deal with a lot of things, Zack. But I can't abide a liar." "I have never lied to you, Kelly."

Kelly sat up straight, meeting Zack's gaze.

"Your mother says otherwise."

"My mother said what she thinks she knows."

"What?" Kelly was confused.

"I can't tell you, someone else's truth."

"Even if it means losing me. I don't want to know anyone else's story. I want to know the truth, your truth Zack. You keep shutting me out. I must look like a fool to your mother."

Zack caressed Kelly's face. "My mother adores you. She kept whispering that in my ear all night. But I don't need her to tell me how amazing you are or how lucky I am to have you."

"Don't try to butter me up, Zack."

Zack pouted at Kelly. "It was only a few days ago when we promised we wouldn't fight anymore."

"Okay. This will be our last fight after you answer me." Kelly was relentless on her quest to learn the truth.

"I already did." Zack scooted closer to Kelly, lifting her chin up to meet their gaze. "Kelly, I have never lied to you."

Kelly studied Zack's eyes. The sincerity in those green eyes scorched her to the core. She knew the violence Zack was capable of, and yet she saw so much love and tenderness in their eyes. Only she knew this side of Zack and it made her treasure them even more. She could feel Zack was telling the truth, she softened up.

"Then why did your mother say that?"

"Because it's true."

"What?" Kelly was perplexed.

Zack looked away sheepishly and then began to explain, "When Sandy and I were younger. We would tell people we were together. You know, pretend we were an item. Just so people wouldn't know what we... who we really were."

Kelly took a moment to process what Zack had just shared with her. "Oh, I think I understand. This was before both of you had transitioned?"

"Yes. We never did anything sexual. We never even kissed; it was all just lies. It kept my father happy and her mother happy. Until we got tired of pretending."

Kelly gently caressed the back of Zack's neck.

"My mother paid for Sandy's surgery."

Kelly was shocked. "Really?"

"Yeah, her mother never accepted her, and her father disowned her, so she stayed with us for a while. She's like a sister to me." "Wow, I'm glad you had Sandy, and you weren't alone. I'm sorry I've been acting so jealous lately."

After hearing what Zack and Sandy had been through together, Kelly realized their bond wasn't a threat to her. Zack had never shown her anything other than kindness and loyalty. And she would no longer feed into any jealousy. She trusted Zack with her whole heart.

"No more fighting please. I can't take it when you're mad at me," Zack said, feeling emotionally exhausted.

Kelly climbed onto Zack's lap to discuss a plan.

"Let's make an agreement to always hear the other one out. No more getting mad, no more fighting."

"No more leaving," Zack added.

"I'm never leaving you again, Zack."

Kelly said as she cupped Zack's face. The joy and love she felt for Zack was unbelievable. Closing her eyes, she kissed Zack deeply. The heat burning between them fogged up the windows. They succumbed to their passion; Kelly tilted her head back as Zack softly kissed her neck. Kelly breathed heavily; her hormones were

217

racing. Zack devoured her lips, kissing her passionately, and lightly biting her lip. Kelly enjoyed it.

Zack attempted to unfasten Kelly's bra, but she stopped them. Kelly struggled to catch her breath.

"Wait. I'm not ready for that quite yet," Kelly sighed, adding, "I just don't want my first time to be like this. I want it to be special."

Zack was surprised; they had no idea that Kelly was still a virgin. "Your first time should be special, Kelly. I'm sorry, I didn't know."

"I know, it's okay. I want to save myself for you. I really want you, Zack. Like, really badly. But I'm just not ready."

Zack gently picked up a curl from Kelly's blonde hair and moved it away from her face. "There's no rush, Kelly. I'll be right here waiting for you no matter how long it takes."

Kelly smiled. For the first time, someone had made her feel special.

————————

Zack arrived home to find Sandy on the couch watching *The Little Rascals.* She was happy to see Zack. "I'm so glad your home," she said, with a faint smile. "How are you holding up?" "Better now," she murmured, feeling a sense of security now that Zack was home.
"My mother says hello." "I'm sorry I missed it," Sandy frowned. "It's okay, she understands. She sent you a plate with some yams." Sandy's eyes grew wide as she reached excitedly for the plate of food.

"I just love Mama Zack," she said smiling broadly.

Zack handed Sandy the plate, and she immediately began to devour it. Zack was happy to see Sandy in better spirits. They took a seat next to her. "You know, Sandy, it's been a few days now. You think you're ready to go outside?" "No, Zack, I'm not ready."

"What if I hold your hand and go with you?"

Zack extended their hand to Sandy; she hesitated then took Zack's hand. Zack walked Sandy outside. She seemed shaky but took small steps down the stairs. The night sky was clear, a full moon beaming down. It was a perfect warm night.

"It's okay, just keep squeezing my hand."

Sandy held on to Zack tightly as they took small steps down the street. "You're doing good, Sandy," Zack was trying to be encouraging. Sandy tried to crack a smile while a car turned the corner, flashing its headlights in Sandy's face. It triggered a flashback of her attack, causing her to panic and her body to start trembling. Zack grabbed her and held her as she wept in their arms.

THE SHERIFF AND DETECTIVE HOBBS WERE HAVING A conversation about the woman that was killed at the motel in town. "The woman from the motel has been identified as Abagail Wright. She was thirty-nine years of age, divorced, with no kids. We went through Abagail's belongings looking for anything that might explain what she was doing here in O Town. All we found were a lot of articles and documents, we have no idea what any of it means," Detective Hobbs explained. "Well, at least we got that sick bastard behind bars."

"I don't think so," Detective Hobbs sighed. The sheriff gave Detective Hobbs a stare. "Are you shitting me, son?"

"No. The victim from the motel wasn't killed with the same knife as the others and she was tied up post-mortem." "Ok, so what does that mean? He was a sick, twisted individual." "I think someone else killed Abagail and tried to make it look like the other murders." "You're saying she was killed by someone from O Town?" "Yes," Detective Hobbs replied.

"Who would want that woman dead?" the sheriff said, baffled.

CHAPTER 11

IT WAS THE GRAND OPENING OF ZACK'S AUTO SHOP. Cars were lined up for blocks, and the street was filled with Queerville citizens who came to show their support. Kelly stood front and center with Charlotte, Freddie, Lisa, Robin and Val, looking like a proud girlfriend, even though she didn't officially hold the title.

Zack stood before the crowd at the ribbon.

"I want to express my gratitude to everyone who came out today. To all those who helped in fixing up this place, and to this incredible, beautiful human being right here..." Zack pointed at Kelly, who shyly waved. Lisa couldn't stomach it. "...who believed in me and gave me the idea to do this. Thank you, baby. And now the moment you've all been waiting for; the grand opening of Zack's Custom Auto Shop." Zack cut the ribbon, eliciting cheers from the crowd.

The banner dropped...

The shop looked like a completely new place. The exterior was trendy and perfect for the neighborhood, with red brick, neon signs, and glass garage doors. Zack, holding Kelly's hand, led everyone inside. The interior was spacious, filled with new tools, appliances, and gadgets. The floors were checkered, and posters of popular cars and wheels hung on the walls. The crowd flooded in and marveled at the shop.

"I have something I want you to see," Zack said as they whisked Kelly upstairs to their live-in loft.

The loft perfectly reflected Zack's style, with a colorful, exposed brick wall behind a queen-sized bed, a large red sofa, a 40-inch floor model television set, wood floors, posters of black pioneers hanging on the walls, a dining table for two, and a nicely remodeled kitchen. Kelly was speechless at how Zack had been able to transform the shop into such a nifty pad.

"Oh, my goodness, it looks amazing. I can't believe you did all of this on your own," Kelly said, in awe.

"I had a lot of help," Zack replied, as they led her towards the bathroom. Inside, she saw vintage floral wallpaper, painted wood paneling, chrome finishes, roll-top bath, double sinks, and striped vinyl flooring.

"Wow, how did you manage to do all of this? That tub looks amazing. I love the wallpaper and tiles. Oh, you even have two sinks!" Kelly exclaimed.

"Yeah, one for me and one for you. You know, for when you come over," Zack said with a smirk.

Kelly looked at Zack and smiled back. She felt wanted.

"I have something for you." Zack reached into their pocket, pulled out a set of keys, and handed them to Kelly. "What is this?" Kelly asked confused.

"The keys to my heart," Zack joked, though Kelly would have gladly snatched them up and opened that lock.

"Keys to my loft, silly. So, you'll always have some-where to go. You can always come here."

Kelly stared at Zack, her love for them exploding through her. She moved in closer, looked deep into their eyes, held their face and softly whispered…

"I love you, Zack."

Zack was surprised and speechless. Those syllables were still ringing in their ears when Kelly kissed them. Zack was still trying to process it.

"You don't have to say anything. I just wanted you to know. I couldn't hold it in any longer," Kelly confessed.

Zack kissed Kelly passionately, this kiss was differ-ent. It was the kiss of two people trying to tell each other how much they love the other without using words. Allowing their mouths to speak for them. Their moment was interrupted by noise from downstairs, which was fortunate for Zack, as they were becoming a bit too excited.

"I think we better head back downstairs," Zack sug-gested, while adjusting their self.

"Zack, I want to come back here tonight," Kelly ex-pressed, her eyes filled with desire.

"Yeah, I know, I thought we already agreed you would." Zack clearly didn't pick up on Kelly's subtly. Kelly found it endearing.

"No, I want to come back here… and spend the night with you," Kelly nodded at Zack, subtly alluding to sex.

"Oh! Um, okay yeah. I would like that," Zack tried to keep cool. Kelly chuckled, finding Zack's bashfulness adorable.

O Town, USA

The Baker home was cold and quiet, Johnnie's parents were helping him get ready for the prom, but there was a noticeable distance between his parents, making the atmosphere awkward. Mrs. Baker was putting on a façade for the sake of her son.

"You look so handsome, Johnnie," Mrs. Baker said as she buttoned up his shirt. "Thanks, Mom," Johnnie replied.

"I took him to my barber and told him to fix him up good," Mr. Baker interjected. "That's great, dear. Can you help him with his bow tie?" Mrs. Baker asked dismissively.

Mr. Baker walked over and tied Johnnie's bow tie. Johnnie didn't want his father's hands on him, but he endured, giving his father the coldest look.

KELLY BURST INTO HER ROOM WITH THE BIGGEST SMILE. She grabbed her dress from the closet and laid out all the things she needed on her bed. She was excited for prom, but even more excited about spending the night with Zack. She thought she would feel nervous about possibly losing her virginity, but surprisingly, she wasn't. Max walked in, frowning. "Hey, Kelly, I never apologized to you for the other day."

Kelly was still beaming from seeing Zack, so she was in a very forgiving mood. "It's okay, Max, you weren't yourself. Hey, do you want to go to the prom with me?" "The prom? I'm not going to that dullsville." Kelly bear hugged her brother and pleaded with him, "Please go with me. I would like you to be my escort."

Mrs. Hamilton came in. "That's a wonderful idea. Max, you're going to the prom with your sister."

"Great." Max rolled his eyes and went to get ready.

"I think it's great that you are going to the prom with your brother. But are there no suitable single fellas at your school dear?" "No. There aren't any, Mom," Kelly replied, irritated.

"Don't worry, dear, I'm sure you'll meet a great guy soon," Mrs. Hamilton assured her.

Kelly gave a cheeky grin. "Yes, Mom, I'm sure I will," she replied as she jumped into the shower.

Queerville, USA

Zack was proudly showing Freddie and Charlotte around the shop, grinning from ear to ear. They were thrilled to finally have something of their own and not have to answer to anyone. People were flipping through the look book that Zack had, showcasing all their custom work. A bidding war had broken out over Zack's designs, which amused Zack as they watched everyone desperately vying for their work.

Sandy walked in, looking around in awe. She was still not over her trauma of being assaulted and nearly killed, but she wouldn't miss Zack's big day. Sandy tapped Zack's shoulder, and they were always happy to see her, giving her a big hug. Sandy handed Zack a gift bag. "Thank you. I'm glad you're here. I didn't think you were going to make it," Zack confessed. Sandy smirked and replied, "I couldn't miss your big day, Zack."

Zack smiled at their friend knowing the courage it had taken for her to come out. Zack appreciated Sandy coming. "How are you doing?" Zack asked. Sandy seemed uneasy, not quite feeling comfortable being outside. "Honestly, not too good since you moved out," Sandy admitted. Zack took Sandy to the corner to have a private conversation. "Look, if you need me to move back in. Just say the word." "No, no, that's not fair. You've done enough. I want you to enjoy your space."

Zack lifted Sandy's chin up, she nodded, and added, "Really, Zack I'll be okay." Sandy didn't convince Zack, but they decided to stop pressing the issue. "C'mon let me show you the loft," Zack said taking Sandy's hand.

O Town, USA

Mrs. Hamilton was doing Kelly's hair while she sat doing her make-up. "Mom, Rose is having a girl's night tonight. Is it okay if I stay the night over there?" Kelly squinted her eyes and crossed her fingers hoping her mother would say yes.

"Yes Dear, that's fine. Just get back here tomorrow at a decent hour young lady."

Kelly was pleased that her mother had said yes, but she was already working on a plan to sneak out if she had said no. Nothing was going to stop her from spending the night with Zack.

"Yes, mother, I will."

Mr. Hamilton came in, hiding something in his hand. "I have something for you baby girl," Mr. Hamilton handed Kelly a beautiful corsage.

"Oh, Dad, it's wonderful. Thank you." Kelly hugged her father, "Okay everyone out. I have to finish the final touches." "Okay, dear, we'll be downstairs," Mrs. Hamilton said.

They waited rather patiently downstairs for Kelly to come down. Max's patience had run out. His old white suit jacket, black pants and bow tie were starting to itch him. "Kelly, hurry up. I want to get this over with."

"Max don't rush your sister," Mr. Hamilton spoke sternly.

"Okay are you ready?" Kelly shouted from the top of the stairs. "Yes, dear, I have the camera ready to go," Mrs. Hamilton said, waiting with her Kodak Brownie camera. Kelly descended the stairs in her pale pink dress, adorned with tiers of ruffles on net. The dress had a crisp, filmy nylon texture, with a boned bodice; bouffant style. Her hair was elegantly styled in a braided bun, with thin bangs framing her face. She looked gorgeous.

"You look beautiful, Kelly," Max remarked.

"Thank you, Max," Kelly replied.

"Oh, my baby. You look so beautiful," Mrs. Hamilton said, her eyes welling up with tears. "Mama, don't cry," Kelly pleaded.

"You look absolutely stunning, baby girl," her father chimed in. "Thanks, Dad," Kelly said, smiling.

"Let me get a photo. Max, stand with your sister," Mrs. Hamilton said as she snapped a few pictures of them. "Mom, we have to go, now," Max said, annoyed.

"Okay, just one more," Mrs. Hamilton replied, snapping one last photo of the two.

Queerville, USA

Sandy cried in Zack's lap, and they gently caressed her head, providing her with comfort as she let her emotions out. Sandy wept, saying, "I'm sorry for ruining your big day." "Sandy don't be silly," Zack responded. "Being alone in that house, I'm terrified in my own skin. I jump at every squeak and gust of wind that hits the window," Sandy said as she sat up and wiped her tears with her hands.

"Sandy, Rickey is in jail. He can't hurt you anymore." Zack reminded her.

"I know that, but how many more Rickeys' are out there?" "I get it. He took away your power."

"What does that mean?"

"It means you need to find a way to feel safe again and I'm going to help you. You don't have to go through this alone."

Sandy cracked a smile. "You're such a great friend, Zack. I love you." "I love you too, Sandy. Come here."

Zack hugged her tightly.

O Town, USA

The Prom was a perfect representation of a classic 1950s prom: in black and white, lackluster, dull and boring. The band were all white debutantes, wearing black suits, white shirts and bow ties, with gleaming brass instruments. They were performing the blandest rendition of *Tooty Fruity*. They continued with their homogenized, slow and off-key melody of Little Richard's nasty hit, but without the nasty.

Kelly and Max entered the prom with an air of excitement. Principal Skinner grabbed a microphone, tapped it and got an ear-splitting buzz. The teens let out a collective groan.

"Welcome juniors and seniors to your nineteen fifty-five prom. We're going to have a night of good clean fun. The chaperones will be keeping an eye on things, but let's not forget that God is always watching. Therefore, let us ensure that there will be no sinful dancing or fornication tonight."

The teens collectively rolled their eyes.

Johnnie and Mary Sue entered, both looking like they would rather be anywhere else. Johnnie was dealing with family drama, while Mary Sue was keeping her pregnancy a secret from everyone. She still hadn't made a decision about whether or not to keep the baby, and she felt guilty and ashamed about having had sex.

Rose and Dawn entered sheepishly with Ronnie, who had his arms around them in a proprietary fashion. The other boys looked hostile, as if their girlfriends had deserted them. The girls noticed each other and quickly ditched their dates.

The band played a slightly hipper song and the girls hit the floor to dance with each other. Principal Skinner noticed the girls dancing together and was mortified, in a panic she rushed over to the mic and motioned toward the girls, "Remember, all couples must be boy, girl!" she blurted out.

A hand jive dance started, with Kelly, Rose, and Dawn participating. Max and Johnnie looked on. The girls seemed to be having the time of their lives.

Mary Sue and Johnnie fought all night. Max was dancing with a pretty brunette; he looked happier than he had in a long time. Kelly was dancing with a random guy, more so forced to. She couldn't tolerate having his hands on her and ended the dance abruptly. "Excuse me, I'm going to get some punch," she muttered.

Kelly rushed off, feeling creeped out. She shook off the sensation, as if something was crawling on her. The other girls decided to accompany her to get some punch.

"This prom is so lame. I want to slit my wrist just for it to be over already." Rose said, expressing her dislike for the prom.

"They could've just booked a church choir if they wanted us all to die of boredom," Dawn added sarcastically.

"Dawn don't make fun of the house of the lord." Mary Sue scolded her. Dawn rolled her eyes in response.

"I have something to tell you guys," Kelly said pausing for dramatic effect.

"You're pregnant?" Rose blurted out.

"What? No, Rose, why is that the first thing that comes to your mind?" Kelly sighed.

"I forgot we have Saint Virgin Kelly over here."

"What is it then?" Dawn asked.

"I told Zack those three magic words," Kelly revealed. "I Love You?" Rose guessed excitedly.

Kelly nodded yes and they all screamed in excitement. Mary Sue was a bit confused. "Now, I must keep asking, who is this, Zack?" No one wanted to explain who Zack was to Mary Sue due to her toxic religious beliefs, so they ignored her inquiry.

"Shush," Dawn hissed to her.

231

"Aww, I'm happy for you. Did Zack say it back?" Rose asked. "No, but it's okay. There's nothing cornier than an 'I love you too'. I want to hear it at the right time and in the right moment," Kelly explained, holding her hands to her chest, as if she were manifesting Zack saying it.

"I saw you two together at the last race, and judging by the way Zack looks at you, it's safe to say the feeling is mutual," Dawn reassured her. "I hope so Dawn," Kelly confessed, then turned to Rose, "I told my mom that I was staying the night with you."

"Wait, are you actually staying with me?" Rose asked. "No silly. I just said that so I could spend the night with Zack." Rose gasped, and Dawn's eyes widened.

"Is tonight, the night?" Dawn asked.

"Yes!" Kelly responded enthusiastically.

The girls screamed and jumped in excitement.

Mary Sue, however, didn't understand what was going on. "Kelly, are you sure? Don't let this Zack fella pressure you into having sex," Mary Sue cautioned.

"Oh, Mary Sue. Zack would never pressure me into anything. This is my choice. I always dreamed that my first time would be with someone I love, who loves me back."

"But does Zack love you? This is why you shouldn't have sex until you're married. You could get pregnant," Mary Sue said, visibly shaken up.

"Well, she doesn't have to worry about that," Dawn whispered provoking Kelly to poke her.

"Mary Sue, what's wrong?" Kelly asked, concerned about her friend. Mary Sue wiped her tears and took a moment to compose herself. She looked at Kelly and blurted out, "I'm pregnant," as she continued to weep.

They all looked flabbergasted.

Rose couldn't believe it. "How? Wait, you had sex, Mary Sue? With whom?" "Johnnie, of course. You got me so worked up listening to your escapades. I gave into my pleasures for the flesh. Now God has punished me." Kelly tried to console her.

"Did you use protection?" Rose asked.

"No," Mary Sue admitted.

Principal Skinner's voice came over the microphone, interrupting their conversation.

"Ladies and gentlemen, it's time to crown your prom King and Queen."

The teens gathered around the stage, eagerly awaiting the announcement. Principal Skinner opened the envelope.

"After counting all of your votes, your new prom Queen is... Kelly Hamilton and your new prom King is Johnnie Baker."

The crowd erupted in cheers as the girls congratulated Kelly. She and Johnnie made their way to the stage, getting congratulations along the way.

Kelly's face was radiant with joy, her pink dress gracefully glided vividly across the room, making her a true vision of beauty. Johnnie, on the other hand, forced a smile, his mind preoccupied with other thoughts. Eventually, they reached the stage where they were both crowned, and Kelly graciously accepted her bouquet of flowers. They posed for the crowd, who responded with enthusiastic cheers for their new King and Queen.

As the prom was coming to an end, Ronnie and his flunkies confronted Johnnie. "Where were you, huh?" Ronnie scolded. "What?" Johnnie replied, confused.

"When we pounced on those Queerville freaks. Where were you?" "Didn't you get your butt kicked by Zack. Twice?" Johnnie asked, snarkily.

Max rushed over and stepped between the two. "Guys, cool it." Ronnie directed his anger toward Max now. "And you, why didn't you step in?"

"I was helping my sister," Max replied.

"Your sister was in Queerville? She must like those freaks." Johnnie punched Ronnie in the mouth. His flunkies jumped on Max, and they fought.

As Kelly, Rose, and Dawn were leaving the prom, Rose spotted Zack standing in front of a white 1950 Chrysler Crown Imperial Limousine in a brand-new tux, holding a stunning bouquet of red pearl amaryllis flowers. "Oh my gosh! Kelly, is that..."

"Zack!" Kelly shouted before Rose could finish her sentence. Kelly's face lit up with glee as she tossed her prom queen flowers onto Rose and dashed over to Zack.

"Wow. Zack looks dreamy," Rose admitted.

"Okay, I'm officially jealous now," Dawn sighed.

"Goodnight, ladies!" Kelly shouted back at the girls.

"Have fun, Kelly."

Kelly approached Zack with a beaming smile, as if she were surrounded by a halo of light. Zack, on the other hand, was eerily silent, as if they were gazing at an angel. Kelly noticed Zacks' frozen and dumbfounded expression, so she decided to initiate the conversation. "You look so dreamy right now," she commented, her eyes brimming with passion. Zack was astounded by her beauty but managed to snap out of it.

"Kelly, you look..." Zack trailed off, rendered speechless. Kelly smiled at Zack's torment to find the appropriate word. "...you look breathtaking." Zack marveled at Kelly's ensemble.

"Normally, I wouldn't believe you, but after seeing your response. I suppose it's true."

Zack handed her the flowers. "These are for you, Ms. Prom Queen." Kelly touched her crown, momentarily forgetting she had it on. She took the flowers and hugged Zack. "My gosh Zack, these are beautiful. Where did you find them? Thank you."

"They're Amaryllis, native to Africa. The name comes from the Greek word *amrysso*, which means to sparkle. I wanted to find something as beautiful and rare as you."

Kelly beamed with adoration. "That is just the sweetest thing I ever heard." Kelly sniffed the flowers.

"They smell amazing, just like you."

"Forget the flowers, you look absolutely gorgeous." Zack remarked causing Kelly to blush.

"Just like you in that suit," she replied.

Zack opened the limousine door and assisted Kelly inside before climbing in and taking off. Kelly was so fascinated with the car, she felt like a movie star with her own chauffeur. Zack poured a drink for them.

"I can't believe you did all of this for me," Kelly said. "Well, your prom is supposed to be an unforgettable night. And since this will be your only prom, I wanted to make it special for you," Zack said as they handed Kelly a drink.

"It is now, thanks to you," Kelly winked at Zack.

Zack raised their glass up, and said, "Here's to a memorable night. One I hope you'll never forget."

They clicked their glasses together and flung it back. Kelly, being such a lady, coughed. Zack burst out laughing.

Zack led Kelly into the shop, which they had converted into a prom wonderland. Red balloons covered the floor, strobe lights flashed, doo wop music played from the jukebox, and a banner proudly displayed the words, *'Zack and Kelly's Prom.'* Overwhelmed with astonishment, Kelly buried her face in her hands. She couldn't believe that Zack had gone to such lengths for her. This was a stark contrast to the prom she had just left.

"You did all of this for me? This looks like a fairy tale, Zack," she murmured.

"No, this is better than a fairy tale because in this story, you saved me. You freed me from this darkness that was eating me alive. It's because of you that I believe God is real. I feel his love every time, I see you smile and every time you touch me, I can feel his mercy," Zack said softly, lost in Kelly's eyes.

She cradled Zack's face and kissed them gently as the jukebox played *"Earth Angel" by The Penguins*. Zack took Kelly's hand and led her to the dance floor. Kelly wrapped her arms around Zack, and they locked eyes, completely absorbed in each other's presence.

"So, you just had a tux hanging in your closet?" Kelly asked. "No. This is brand new," Zack replied.

"Did you buy this tux just for tonight?"

"Yes."

Kelly shook her head. She was astonished how often Zack went to great lengths to make her happy. No one had ever been more concerned about her happiness, not even her own parents.

"You are truly unpredictable," she remarked.

"I like to keep it that way."

A question that had been weighing heavily on Kelly's mind popped into her head. She was scared to ask it, scared to find out that none of it was real. She read Zack's eyes; *how could this not be real?* To the rest of the world, Zack appeared brutal, but to her, they were kind and sweet. Knowing that gave her the confidence to ask the burning question.

"Am I your girl, Zack?"

"No," Zack replied.

Kelly's heartbeat skipped a beat, and she froze for a split second. Zack drew her closer, causing her to sway once more.

"You are far more than just some girlfriend."

"Then what am I to you?" Kelly desperately wanted to know.

Zack gazed deeply into Kelly's eyes, feeling incredibly vulnerable. However, Kelly held such significance in Zack's life that they couldn't bear to keep their emotions hidden. They wanted her to understand the depth of their feelings. Swallowing their pride, Zack poured their heart out in the best way they knew how.

"Girlfriend is just a label given to someone who has your attention at the time. Kelly, there aren't enough years I could live to show you how much you mean to me; there aren't enough lifetimes or galaxies to express what I feel for you. What we have is endless. You're the perfect picture to my shattered past. You are my stars that shine brightly in my darkest times. You're my reward for all the pain. You're the happiness I was promised. You are my twin flame; you are everything," Zack quavered.

Those words ignited Kelly's soul. She was gone to Zack; there was no hope for her. There was no way in hell she would ever give Zack up. She couldn't talk as tears cascaded down her cheeks, her eyes filled with undying affection. Zack tenderly wiped her tears away with their finger and whispered, "Say something."

"When you told me what a twin flame was. I knew that you were mine. But I was too scared to say it. I thought it was too soon to feel that way about some-one. But the more time we spent together, the more I knew it was true. You are everything to me, Zack. And I want to be with you in this life and the next one and the next one," Kelly spoke softly as her hand skimmed over Zack's face. Kelly had accomplished something that no one else had; she had found her way into Zack's heart, which was no easy task, Kelly truly owned it, and Zack would willingly give it to her a thousand times.

Zack had never been in love before. They succumbed to these new emotions, gazed at Kelly with soulful eyes and murmured, "I love you... I love you, Kelly." Kelly was overcome with joy, not only were she and Zack of-ficial now, but they had just confessed their love for her. She was on cloud nine. She drew Zack in, and they shared an intense kiss. Zack cradled her face as their tongues gently danced.

Before their lips fully parted Kelly softly whispered...

"Make love to me Zack."

Zack gently ran their thumb across her full, peach lips before leaning in for a kiss. After pulling back, Zack looked down at her, tracing the line of her cheek while their gaze was locked to hers. "Are you sure?" Zack asked.

Stepping back, Kelly unzipped her dress, allowing it to gracefully fall to the floor and revealing a sexy tight silk slip. Zack took off their bow tie and jacket, while Kelly unfastened Zack's belt and tossed it aside.

Zack lifted Kelly into their arms, and they shared a passionate kiss.

The loft was decked out with flickering candles and scattered rose petals. Zack's white button-down shirt lay discarded on the floor. Zack and Kelly were making out in bed when Kelly removed her slip and clutched it against her body, feeling a slight self-consciousness.

"You've probably been with a lot of women before," Kelly uttered. "I've been with women before, but none as Zack." "So, I would be the first since..."

"Yeah. And I would be your first?"

Kelly nodded yes.

"We don't have to do this, Kelly. If you're not ready."

"No, I want to. I really want to. I'm just nervous, I've never had sex before," she admitted.

"What do you know about sex?" "All I know is that if it's good, it'll put you to sleep."

Zack chuckled. Kelly playfully hit Zack, "Don't laugh at me. I'm scared," she confessed.

"You don't have to be scared. I would never hurt you, Kelly," Zack spoke softly.

"I know Zack. You make me feel so safe."

"You are safe. If at any time you want me to stop, just say it, and I will."

Kelly nodded her head in agreement as she pulled Zack in and kissed them, but after a few moments, her eyes popped open.

"I'm scared I won't compare to those other girls you've been with," Kelly blurted out.

Zack traced Kelly's face with the back of their hand and said, "It doesn't matter how many women I've been with. All I care about is you and the way you make me feel. The way your body feels when I touch you; your peachy lips against mine when we kiss and how it would feel to be inside of you."

That comment set a fire in Kelly. She dropped her slip, forgetting her fear, and kissed Zack.

"Are you sure?" Zack asked.

Kelly removed her bra and freed her breasts, they were plump and perky, her nipples were responsive to the touch of Zack cupping her breasts in their hands. Kelly let out a breathy sigh, this was the first time anyone had ever touched her this way. Her hormones were racing.

She craved to feel Zack's lips on them…

Zack leaned in and planted soft kisses over each breast, Kelly's heart was fluttering, the touch of Zack squeezing her breast put her at their mercy. She longed for the touch of Zack's tongue on them. Kelly sucked her breath in sharply as Zack took her left breast into their mouth and suckled them, chills rushed over her, she thought she would orgasm just from that.

Her love for Zack burned intensely within her, spreading to every cell in her body. Kelly breathed heavily. Zack kissed her, then removed their T-shirt, revealing their masculine chest.

240

Kelly's gaze fell upon the scars from Zack's top surgery, and she delicately traced them with her finger. She gently pushed Zack on their back and kissed their scars. She wanted Zack to feel beautiful, regardless of their scars. She would kiss any scar Zack had, physically or emotionally. She wrapped her arms around Zack, and they melted into one another. Zack rolled on top of Kelly, moving slowly over her body, kissing and caressing every inch of her. Kelly was overwhelmed with pleasure, feeling as if she were intoxicated, and the room was spinning. Zack was like a drug to her, one she would happily indulge in. Despite imagining her first time to be vulnerable and exposed, with Zack, she felt safe and secure.

Zack's gaze focused on her lips, which were parted by her rapid breathing. They took Kelly's lip into their mouth. Kelly felt a need she had never felt before. She wanted Zack, her body was aching for them. She felt herself becoming wet between her legs, her clitoris throbbing with anticipation. She was ready, she was ready for Zack. As she locked eyes with Zack, her emotions took over. "I love you, Zack," she softly whispered.

Zack left soft kisses to the trail of her neck, and back up to her gaze. Zack waited for permission; Kelly nodded yes. This was Zack's first experience with intimacy in their new body, and they were thrilled to share it with Kelly. Zack gently slid inside; Kelly shrieked and squeezed Zack's arm, digging her nails into their flesh. She cried out. They were much bigger than what she was expecting, but she was so wet it made it easy for Zack to fully enter her. Zack began thrusting slowly and gasped as their tip penetrated her. Kelly cried out again at the sudden fullness inside her. Zack was taken aback

241

by her tightness and groaned. Zack had never felt anything better than this; it was intense, and they couldn't believe they were finally inside Kelly. Zack gently stroked; their gaze remained fixed on Kelly.

She couldn't believe how amazing it felt. Her eyes glowed with longing as she let out soft moans.

"Does it hurt?" Zack asked sincerely.

"A little."

"Do you want me to stop?"

"No, please don't," Kelly panted, then kissed Zack as she widened her legs around them, drawing them in even deeper.

Kelly groaned loudly, grabbing onto Zack's back. Zack drew energy from the pleasure evident on her face. They delved deeper inside her, and Kelly moaned Zack's name. She wrapped her legs around Zack, they rolled, with her ending up on top. Zack leaned up and sucked on her neck. Their hands gripped tightly around Kelly's hips. Kelly swayed in Zack's lap, moaning as Zack sucked on her breast. She loved being on top, being able to look down at Zack and see the pleasure she was bringing them. Zack grinded in time to her thrusts. Kelly moved her hips like she was riding a bull. Zack was surprised how quickly she caught on. Kelly was experiencing pure ecstasy. She cradled Zack's head and kissed them passionately as she rode atop. Zack wanted to come so badly but didn't want it to end. They drew back.

Zack laid Kelly on her back as she held onto them while they stroked deeper. She moaned softly; her lips bitten in pleasure. Zack loved watching Kelly's expression as they quickened their strokes. Kelly shivered with each long stroke Zack delivered, feeling her clitoris clenching tighter... Zack's rhythmic strokes intensified the heat building inside her, like a pipe about to burst... she dug her fingers into Zack's back... her body convulsing with pleasure as she reached her orgasm. She screamed out, clinging to Zack as they continued to stroke, her body still trembling. Overwhelmed with bliss, tears streamed down Kelly's face. Zack kept stroking and sucking her breast as her body remained in the throes of orgasm. Kelly screamed Zack's name as her body exploded into ecstasy, her entire being quivering wildly with pleasure.

* * *

Zack was awake, watching Kelly who was fast asleep. She looked so incredibly innocent and beautiful. Zack had just experienced something they never thought would happen. They had finally made love to someone in the way they had always desired, and it was absolutely worth it. Zack couldn't wait to do it again.

But more importantly, they had the opportunity to make love to someone they loved so deeply. It wasn't just the sex; it was being able to experience Kelly and the intimacy they shared. Their souls were now connected, something they would treasure forever. Zack was struggling with the decision of whether they should stay in town or not. The moment they laid eyes on Kelly, the choice was clear. Zack knew it, they couldn't leave now. They were trapped in the town that held the most painful memories for them.

Zack's love for Kelly was enough to replace every bad memory with a good one. On Paradise Road, when Zack was seventeen, they got into a bad crash and almost died. That memory was now replaced with the first time they saw Kelly. The diner, where their father used to humiliate and berate them in front of people, was now replaced with the first time they held Kelly and danced. The loft, where they first made love, held a new significance.

How is it possible to love someone this much? Zack wondered, gazing at Kelly as she slept. She had so much power over Zack. They didn't care. Zack would gladly do anything for her, and they were hers to own. Zack surrendered to their love for Kelly. They climbed back into bed. Kelly turned over and laid on Zack's chest, wrapping her arm around them. Zack smiled and held her tight.

* * *

The sunshine beamed on Kelly's face as she woke up. She looked around, realized where she was and smiled. Flashbacks of the previous night popped into her head, and she let out a scream into the pillow. She was no longer a virgin, but she felt happy to have given herself to her true love. Zack came over with breakfast in bed. "Good morning, beautiful. I made you some breakfast."

Kelly gazed at Zack in awe and asked, "Why are you so amazing?" "How did you sleep?" Zack asked.

"I had the best sleep of my life thanks to you," Kelly replied.

Zack leaned in for a kiss, but Kelly quickly covered her mouth with her hands. She jumped up, snatched Zack's shirt off the floor, covered herself and hurried to the bathroom.

Kelly swiftly brushed her teeth and wiped her face with a washcloth. She teased her hair, pouted her lips, and checked herself in the mirror before returning. Zack placed the food on the table and took a seat. Kelly approached and sat on Zack's lap. She gave Zack a kiss before saying, "Thank you for the food. It smells amazing." Kelly took a sip of orange juice. "Are you not eating?" Kelly asked. "I have a craving for something else," Zack said licking their lips.

"What?"

"You."

Kelly smiled and pulled Zack in for a heated kiss. Zack took Kelly into their arms, stood up and laid her onto the bed, still in a heated kiss. Zack opened the shirt and caressed her breast. Kelly breathed heavily as Zack fondled her breasts, before exploring them with their tongue. Kelly thoroughly enjoyed every minute of it. *A replay of last night, sign me up,* she thought. But Zack had other plans. Zack kissed Kelly from her breast to her stomach, licking her down to her vagina, Kelly gasped.

These were places she had never been kissed before. Zack tenderly kissed each of her lips, she was already so wet, that her juices were streaming down her thighs. Zack skillfully captured every drop with their tongue, savoring the taste in their mouth. Kelly shrieked, her heart raced, and her eyes rolled back from the intense desires she was experiencing. She had never felt such pleasurable sensations before.

No one did this... in an era where husbands and wives slept separately in twin beds. What Zack was doing to Kelly was a mere folktale. Zack craved what was between Kelly's legs. They wrapped their arms around her hips and lifted her up from the bed as their tongue delved deep inside her. Her eyes big from the intensity

245

of the warmth of Zack's tongue, and she couldn't bear it, she cried out.

Kelly gaped as she looked down at Zack, trying to comprehend how it was possible to experience such pleasure. Her mouth hung open wide, and she buried her hand in Zack's hair as they continued to taste her. The heat of Zack's mouth and the strokes of their tongue were blinding. Zack hummed, enjoying the taste of Kelly as she let out soft needy moans. The sound of her pleasure filled the loft. She looked down to meet Zack's gaze and shivered as they continued to stimulate her clitoris. She felt her body clenching tighter, and Zack's strokes quickened. Kelly gripped onto the sheets and screamed out, unable to contain herself, as Zack continued to tease her.

"What are you doing to me? Oh my... Yes!... Please don't stop," Kelly wailed.

Zack could spend the rest of the day like this, just savoring her. Zack loved the way Kelly tasted. Kelly's body trembled... her mouth wide open... but she was unable to speak... she couldn't utter a sound. Kelly couldn't stand it any longer... her body burst into Zack's mouth as she screamed out, her voice echoing outside.

CHAPTER 12

O Town, USA

Kelly had just finished recounting her sexually charged evening to the girls. Rose, Mary Sue, and Dawn's faces were frozen in complete shock, their mouths agape. Kelly's night had surpassed any of Rose's lustful nights, leaving even Rose herself mesmerized. "No one's ever done that to me before," Rose said in disbelief. How could she not have tried that before. She was going through her mental rolodex for a prospect to try it with.

"I didn't know you could do that," Dawn said, mystified. "What did it feel like?" Mary Sue asked, curious.

The girls were hung on to every word, taking mental notes. Kelly sighed as she replayed the emotions she had experienced.

"Like Nirvana. Your body experiences so many emotions. It's like a sensory overload that keeps getting better and better until you feel like you're about to explode with bliss and then, pure ecstasy," Kelly explained.

"Oh my god, yes!" Rose blurted out.

Rose quickly covered her mouth in embarrassment, and the girls looked at her and burst out laughing.

"I'm so jealous, Kelly. Your first time sounds magical. My first time was at the drive-in," Dawn sighed.

"My first time was at Lover's Lane," Mary Sue added.

"I don't even remember my first time," Rose admitted.

"I wish I had learned about this before. Maybe I wouldn't have gotten pregnant," Mary Sue stated.

"Are you keeping it?"

"Well, of course I'm keeping it, Kelly. It's the Christian thing to do." "Are you and Johnnie going to get married?"

"Does Johnnie know?"

Mary Sue's heart dropped because she hadn't told Johnnie yet. But that wasn't their business.

"Yes, he knows," Mary Sue lied.

"He was never going to make it with basketball anyway," Dawn murmured. "Dawn!"

"What? He sucks."

"Johnnie is picking me up in a few. We will discuss our future and what we plan to do," Mary Sue responded.

Mary Sue was petrified to tell Johnnie she was pregnant because she didn't want to ruin his future. She also didn't want him to feel obligated to commit to her just for the baby.

Johnnie pulled up and honked his horn.

"Well, that's Johnnie."

The girls hugged Mary Sue goodbye.

JOHNNIE & MARY SUE SAT IN AN AWKWARD SILENCE. Neither of them knew how to begin the conversation. Mary Sue glanced at Johnnie and finally spoke up.

"Johnnie, I have something important to tell you..." Before she could finish her sentence, Johnnie interrupted. "Mary Sue, I don't think we should see each other anymore."

Mary Sue was thrown for a loop, "Wait, what?"

"I just have a lot I'm dealing with right now. I don't think I can be a good boyfriend to you, that's all." "Where is this coming from? We just went to prom together." Mary Sue's head was spinning.

"I know, Mary Sue and all we did was fight. I'm tired of fighting with you, my parents, and myself. I'm just exhausted."

"What are you trying to say?"

"We should take a break. This is for the best, Mary Sue. You'll see."

Mary Sue couldn't believe she had just been dumped while carrying Johnnie's baby. She was devastated but didn't know what to do.

"Okay, Johnnie, if that's what you want." Mary Sue replied, opening the door to get out.

"Wait, Mary Sue, what did you want to tell me?"

"Nothing Johnnie, it was nothing." Mary Sue wept as she stepped out and closed the door.

JOHNNIE RUSHED HOME TO FIND HIS DAD IN THE DEN. He took a deep breath and knocked on the door. He was already expecting him. "Come in Johnnie."

"Dad, I just wanted to tell you that I'll be moving out once school is over. I'm a man now, and I need to set my own pace."

Mr. Baker looked irritated. "You went running your mouth to your mother."

"You were having an affair. So yeah, I told her, Dad. How could you, how could you do that to Mom?"

"You have no idea what you've just done!"

Mr. Baker shouted angrily. Police officers suddenly stormed the house. Officer Whitey took out his cuffs. "Mr. Baker you are under arrest for the murder of Abagail Wright. You have the right to remain silent. Anything you say can and will be used against you..."

"What? Dad, what's going on?" Johnnie asked, baffled. Mr. Baker remained silent. Officer Whitey took Mr. Baker away in cuffs as Johnnie freaked out.

* * *

Zack brought Sandy to their secluded pond hideaway, which served as their shooting range, in order to help her reclaim her power after her attack. Sandy was in good spirits, largely due to Zack. She always felt safe with Zack, she knew they would do anything to protect her, a fact they had already proven.

Zack opened their shed.

"Zack, why do you have a shed? You know you're claustrophobic," Sandy asked.

"I don't sleep in it, Sandy," Zack snided.

Sandy stepped inside and her eyes widened. Zack had an arsenal inventoried. Every gun that had been manufactured in the past ten years was stored there. Sandy had never seen so many guns in her life.

"Zack, why do you have so many guns? Are you planning an invasion?"

Zack chuckled. "They're not all mine, Sandy."

Sandy looked pensively at Zack for an answer.

"They're my dad's." She rubbed Zack's back; she knew too well the toxic relationship Zack had with their father. Zack's father was a violent man with a bad temper, and Sandy had spent many nights staying up with Zack hiding, trying to escape their father's wrath.

"You're nothing like him, Zack," she reassured Zack.

"Tell that to the rage inside me," Zack replied.

Sandy gave her best friend a caring glance and caressed Zack's face. Zack nodded, and they opened a crate. "Pick your poison," Zack said.

Sandy looked overwhelmed by the array of choices. "I don't know anything about guns."

Zack rifled through the firearms and selected a Browning model pistol. "This one is good for you. It's easy to hold and has less kick back." Sandy had a scared look on her face. "I've never held a gun before."

"C'mon." Zack urged.

Zack guided Sandy out of the shed to the back, where a makeshift shooting range had been set up. Standing behind Sandy, Zack placed the gun in her hand. Feeling the cold steel, in her hand, startled Sandy, causing her to jump.

"It's okay, don't be afraid," Zack whispered in her ear, intertwining their hands, providing warmth and comfort. Zack's hand relaxed her; Zack was her safe place. "I'm good now, Zack. Show me."

Zack positioned Sandy's fingers on the gun.

"It's already cocked. Look at the target and when you're ready, take a deep breath, and squeeze the trigger, don't pull."

Sandy nodded and Zack stepped back to allow her to line up her shot. She took a deep breath, exhaled, and fired, hitting the edge of the target.

"Wow, that was loud!" Sandy shouted.

"Yeah, that's why I shoot outside."

"I hit the target!" Sandy was excited that she hit anything. She thought she would miss and shoot a tree. "Yeah, that was a decent shot. Let's keep going and work on your aim." Sandy was eager to try again.

They spent most of the day target practicing. Sandy's accuracy improved, and she started to feel confident with the gun. They took a break from shooting.

"How do you feel?"

"About seventy five percent better."

"We're getting there. You just have to take it slowly."

"I can't believe you have me outside. Thank you, Zack. I don't know what I would do if I had to go through this alone."

"You ain't never alone, Sandy. I've known you since I was eight years old. I've lost count of how many times you've been there for me when I needed you. I would never turn my back on you. Now c'mon, a few more rounds. Then I'll drop you off at home."

MR. BAKER WAS BEING INTERROGATED BY DETECTIVE HOBBS. "How much longer are you going to keep me here?" Mr. Baker asked in a rush to get home.

"Until you stop lying. It's been hours and you still haven't told us the truth. I don't want to believe you committed murder, Jim," Detective Hobbs replied.

"I have told you the truth," Mr. Baker insisted.

"We have an eyewitness who saw you at the motel with the victim the same day she was murdered. Your name was in her appointment book." Detective Hobbs stated.

"Fine, yes. I met with Abagail once or twice at the motel. But I was not having an affair with Abagail, and I did not kill her. I'm a lot of things, but a killer is not one of them," Mr. Baker explained. "I believe you Jim. Now I need to know what you were meeting with Abagail about," Detective Hobbs inquired.

* * *

Lover's Lane was lined with rocking cars, with various limbs and articles of clothing hanging out of the open windows. Moans of pleasure drifted through the air as the pond glistened in the distance. Rose found herself in the back seat of a convertible with a guy's head between her thighs. She moaned with her eyes wide open, as she watched him eagerly satisfy her. Feeling an overwhelming sense of pleasure, she screamed out, "Oh my … Yes!" In every car, a girl was receiving oral pleasure, their cries of ecstasy echoing into the night. And it was all thanks to Kelly.

———————————————

Zack was sleeping in bed when they were awakened by the ringing phone. Still groggy, Zack got up and answered, "Hello…" "Can you come over?"

"Sandy?" Zack asked.

"Yeah," she replied.

"I'm on my way." Zack hung up and quickly got dressed. Sandy could always rely on Zack to drop everything and be there for her, and that's exactly what they did. Zack rushed over.

* * *

Detective Hobbs returned to the interrogation room to speak with an anxious Mr. Baker.

"Okay, Mr. Baker, it appears that your story checked out." "Thank you. Am I free to go?"

"Yes, you are. However, please do not leave town. We may have some additional questions." Detective Hobbs removed the cuffs, and Mr. Baker rushed out.

* * *

Zack arrived at Sandy's. She opened the door wearing her nightgown, looking like the most beautiful damsel in distress. "Thank you for coming," she muttered.

Sandy escorted them to the sofa where she rested her head on Zack's lap, while they buried their hand in her hair, caressing her until she drifted off to sleep.

O Town, USA

Kelly was at home, it was late, and she couldn't sleep. So, she went downstairs, plopped on the couch, picked up the phone and called Zack. The phone kept ringing, but there was no answer. Kelly hung up and began to worry.

Queerville, USA

The next morning, Zack was working on their first custom order, dirty and greasy underneath a car. Music played in the background. Suddenly, the sunlight streaming through the open garage doors was blocked. Zack rolled out to see what the shadow was, it was blurred at first, then their focus settled on Kelly.

"Hey, I called you last night," she said.

Zack, happy to see her, replied, "Good morning, beautiful."

Zack stood up and wiped their hands clean; telling Kelly about going to the shooting range and staying overnight at Sandy's house.

"Wow. I thought she was getting better. She was out of the house and about again," Kelly said.

"She's scared to be alone in that house," Zack responded. "Poor girl. My heart goes out to her," Kelly admitted. "I told her she could come stay with me, but she won't do it. She says she doesn't want to intrude. I even offered to move back in," Zack confessed.

Even though Kelly was over her jealousy, the thought of Zack and Sandy staying together was unsettling to her. But she knew Zack was simply trying to be there for their friend, she admired that. "You're such a great friend, Zack. One of the many reasons why I love you," Kelly said with a smile.

"I'm sorry if I scared you last night."

"It's okay, it's not like you can ring me that late. My parents would've had a heart attack. I just worry about you."

"I know you do. I need to work on making you worry less." "I'm really worried about something right now," Kelly said with a mischievous grin.

"What?" Zack asked.

"Well, I'm worried that you haven't kissed me yet," Kelly remarked.

Zack grabbed Kelly to kiss her, she pretended she didn't want it, but didn't put up much of a struggle. Zack planted one on her. Kelly wrapped her arms around Zack. "Did I tell you how amazing the other night was?" she asked. Zack shook their head no.

"It was an experience I'll never forget. You did things to my body I didn't know were possible," Kelly murmured.

Zack looked away sheepishly, but Kelly returned Zack's face back to her gaze.

"Aww, don't be coy with me. You are incredible. Thank you for making my first time so special. I'll never forget it," Kelly said before taking Zack's lips into her mouth, they shared a sensual kiss, and Kelly was instantly turned on. She drew back and asked, "Are you busy today? I want to take you somewhere," Zack was surprised that Kelly thought to do something for them. It was a first for them. "You want to take me somewhere?" Zack asked, surprised.

"Yes. I can be spontaneous too," Kelly replied.

"Do I have time to take a shower?"

"A quick one."

"Where are we going?" Zack asked.

"Why? Are you writing a book? Go, hurry, now." Kelly blurted.

Zack rushed to take a shower.

CHARLOTTE CAME TO CHECK ON SANDY, SHE USED HER spare key and let herself in, there were noises coming from the back. Charlotte searched for Sandy. As she got closer, the sounds grew louder. Charlotte made her way towards the back, where the noise was coming from. She opened the bedroom door and was surprised at what she walked in on... Sandy and Johnnie in bed having sex.... Sandy quickly covered herself.

"Oh dear, talk about a walk on the wild side." Charlotte said, gaping at the scene.

Johnnie was mortified and jumped up, hurriedly got dressed. "Charlotte!" Sandy shouted, clearly annoyed.

"Don't rush out on my account, Johnnie boy," Charlotte jeered. "I have to go," Johnnie growled as he stormed out.

"I'm sorry, Johnnie!" Sandy shouted after him. Sandy threw on her gown and turned to Charlotte.

"Charlotte, what are you doing here?"

"I came to drop off my keys to the diner before I head out on tour... I didn't know you were waiting on someone else to cum."

"Charlotte!" Sandy was appalled.

"So, is this your secret that you've been hiding?"

"It wasn't a secret; it just wasn't anybody's business."

"Well, how long has this been going on?" Charlotte continued to ask. "Not long," Sandy answered.

"I would've thought of anyone else in all the land before I thought you were sexing captain square man."

"Clearly, he's not so square."

"How did this happen? Where did you even meet? Does he know?" Charlotte rambled on.

"Charlotte, calm down," Sandy said, trying to bring some order to the conversation. They both took a seat.

"When my piece of shit car broke down on me. He pulled over to help me." Sandy explained.

"And you wanted to thank him with some..." Charlotte trailed off. Sandy gave Charlotte a blank look.

"Is it serious? Isn't he kind of young?"

"Johnnie is eighteen and no I don't know what it is, Charlotte."

"Isn't he seeing that Bible fanatic, what's her name, Betty Sue, Susie Lue...?"

"Mary Sue, and no, he ended things with her."

"To be with you?"

"God, no! That's not what I want. They were never official. Johnnie said they weren't serious."

"Does he know you're..."

"Yes, he knows I'm trans."

"Does he even know what that means?"

"Yes, Charlotte!"

"I thought Sandy didn't play second fiddle?"

"Who said I was second?" she smirked and gave Charlotte a mysterious look.

O Town, USA

Mary Sue sat in the waiting room of the abortion clinic, torn between her soul and her religion. She had been raised with strong values and had always followed the teachings of the Bible. However, she had made one mistake and given in to the desires of the flesh, and now she was paying the price. She observed the other girls entering and leaving the clinic, heartbroken. She knew deep down that she wasn't ready to become a mother.

There were so many things she wanted to accomplish before starting a family. But she didn't want to kill her baby. She didn't want God to punish her more. She didn't want to disappoint her mother. Overwhelmed with emotion, Mary Sue wept. Just as she was considering leaving, the doctor called her name.

Northside, USA

Zack pulled into a lot, packed with parked cars. There was something significant happening, but Kelly refused to reveal the secret. Smirking, Kelly enjoyed the suspense that was tormenting Zack. Eventually, they found a parking space and got out.

Hand and hand, Kelly led Zack through the entrance gate of the event. The sounds emanating from the stage were strikingly familiar to Zack. Observing Zack closely, Kelly eagerly anticipated their realization. And if that didn't give it away, the enormous poster hanging outside surely would. As Zack looked up and froze, a massive smile spread across their face. They turned to Kelly and lifted her off her feet, planting a big kiss on her. Zack was beyond excited. It was their favorite singer, Chuck Berry.

"What? No way!" Zack exclaimed.

Kelly loved seeing the joy on Zack's face. She would do anything to make Zack happy. They ran to the front of the stage, where a young Chuck Berry was on stage with his guitar performing *"Maybellene."* Zack and Kelly joined the crowd and danced. Kelly was amazed at how happy Zack was. There was no rage in Zack's eyes anymore. She wanted them to always feel this at peace.

After the concert, Zack was pumped up, they grabbed Kelly and hugged her. "That was so rad, thank you Kelly. No one's ever done anything like this for me before." "You're welcome. I've had these tickets for you for a while now," Kelly admitted.

"I had no idea," Zack replied.

"Good. I wanted to surprise you."

"You're the best girlfriend ever," Zack declared. Kelly beamed; hearing Zack call her their girlfriend for the first time. "Say that again," she requested.

Zack cupped Kelly's face and repeated, "You're the best girlfriend ever." "I like the sound of that," Kelly said, blushing. They shared a loving kiss.

After some making out, Kelly dragged Zack to the ice cream stand. They got two cones and enjoyed them standing next to a tree in the shade. As Zack was enjoying their cone, Kelly looked on finding it very enticing. She wondered if the ice cream was that good or if Zack was just skilled with their tongue. *The things that mouth can do.* She was getting turned on.

"Can I taste yours?" Kelly asked.

"No," Zack grunted as they continued to savor their cone. "You're selfish," Kelly scowled.

Kelly shoved her cone in Zack's face, getting ice cream everywhere. Zack was stunned. Kelly laughed and jumped on Zack, proceeding to lick the ice cream off their eyes, nose and lips. It turned into a heated kiss. Zack dropped their cone and held Kelly up against the tree, kissing her neck. Kelly glanced over at the children looking on. "Do you want to get out of here?" Kelly asked, giving Zack a tantalizing glance. "I know the perfect place," Zack whispered. They rushed out with both their hormones racing.

DET. HOBBS WAS VISITING RICKEY AT THE JAILHOUSE. "Rickey, how has your stay been?" Detective Hobbs inquired. "Pretty fine, officer," Rickey said dismissively. "It's Detective," Detective Hobbs said as he flashed his badge.

"Oh, detective, you fancy yourself a bunch."

Detective Hobbs brushed off Rickey's snarky remark. "The state is charging you with five cases of first-degree murder, which carry heavy penalties."

"I'd assume so," Rickey chuckled.

"I'm here to offer you a chance to escape the death penalty."

"You must be really desperate coming to a killer hoping to find mercy. I have no answers for you. I am what I am," Rickey said, depraved.

"I do not care to learn what your reasoning was; or the voices you hear; or how your mama touched you."

"Don't you dare speak on mother! She was an angel."

"You cut your mother's heart out of her chest as she slept."

"I'm getting bored, detective. It's almost lunchtime maybe we should wrap this up later."

Detective Hobbs ended the interview and ordered Rickey some lunch, in hopes he would later continue talking.

* * *

AT THE SECLUDED POND...

Zack and Kelly were kissing and stumbling over their feet, desperately trying to remove their clothes. They finally made it to the sleeping bags that Zack had set up for them on the soft grass. They clumsily fell to the ground and quickly stripped off their clothes. Zack then climbed on top of Kelly, kissing her with intense passion. As they did, Zack gently cupped both of Kelly's breasts in their hands. Kelly playfully bit Zack's lip. Zack's tongue traced a path from her breasts all the way down to her soft thighs, finally reaching between her legs.

Zack sucked her clitoris into their mouth, causing Kelly to arch her back and gently caress Zack's head between her legs. Zack moaned with pleasure as Kelly's juices flowed down their throat... teasing her clitoris with their tongue, Zack savored the taste, finding it even sweeter than the ice cream cone they just had eaten. The sound of Zack's tongue teasing and sucking her made Kelly flood like a torrent. Zack rubbed her clit with their fingers; Kelly jumped in pleasure and gasped. Zack gently sank their fingers inside of her, while moving their tongue like a water snake, causing her to scream out in pleasure, making her body tremble until she reached her climax.

Her body convulsed as Zack came up and slid inside. Kelly was captivated by the intensity in Zack's eyes. She sighed, and grabbed Zack's face, and devoured their tongue with her mouth. Zack delivered quick strokes, allowing their tip to open her up, which elicited moans of pleasure from Kelly. In that moment, she couldn't discern how she went through her entire life without ever feeling these urges and now craving them.

Looking at Zack, she felt like they were the only person she would ever give herself to in this way.

"I love you, Zack," she panted.

Zack kissed her in response, and Kelly eagerly widened her legs to allow Zack to penetrate even deeper.

Zack glanced down to where their bodies were joined and marveled at the sight of their shaft stroking Kelly. With each thrust, Zack could feel every ripple of her walls, intensifying the pleasure. The visual of them entering her only heightened the sensation. Kelly held on tightly, panting with desire.

Zack increased their pace... grinding their teeth as they fought off their impending orgasm. They didn't want this moment to end. Zack wanted to stay inside of Kelly forever. Lifting Kelly's leg up, Zack delved deeper. Kelly screamed out in ecstasy. Zack continued to stroke harder... faster... their bodies slapping together... letting her moans be their guide. Kelly wailed, breathlessly, her body on the verge of exploding... Zack moaned as they finally climaxed... the sound of Zack orgasming triggered an even louder moan from Kelly... her body quivered as she clung onto Zack, screaming as she reached her own orgasm. They exchanged a loving kiss their connection deepening.

Afterwards, Zack and Kelly lay spent on the ground, completely satisfied, with sheets wrapped around them. Kelly turned to face Zack, caressing their face with her hand.

"I didn't know I would enjoy sex this much. I never had a desire for sex until I met you. Is that crazy? Am I supposed to enjoy it this much? It's like you can never kiss me long enough or hold me tightly enough. I just can't get enough of you, Zack."

Zack cradled Kelly's face and replied, "I can't get enough of you either, Kelly."

Kelly wanted to know if Zack enjoyed making love as much as she did, so she asked, "When we make love, what does it feel like for you?"

"Heaven, it feels like heaven on earth, and I never want to leave," Zack responded.

Kelly smiled broadly, blushing red.

"I can't believe we just made love outside in public. I never imagined I'd do such a thing," she admitted.

"Say it isn't so. Why the sudden change?" Zack teased.

"What can I say? I'm head over heels in love with you, Zack," she replied, beaming at Zack.

"I've never loved anyone the way I love you, Kelly." Zack was lost in Kelly's eyes; they had never been happier. Kelly filled Zack's heart with so much love and peace. "If I asked you to marry me, what would you say?" Zack asked.

Kelly's face glowed with a huge smile. The thought of marrying Zack filled her with great joy. "I do," she whispered without blinking. Zack smiled and gave her an unforgettable kiss.

"I wish I could stay here with you forever," Kelly admitted.

"This could be our secret summer getaway if you want it to be," Zack suggested.

"Deal," Kelly agreed.

"You know we haven't discussed what you'll be doing after graduation," Zack mentioned.

Kelly sat up and put her top back on. She had been dreading this conversation, but she knew she would eventually have to talk with Zack about her future.

Could she and Zack's relationship survive long distance?

"There's plenty of time to talk about that," she said dismissively.

"Summer will be over soon. You're about to graduate in January," Zack reminded her.

"I don't want to think about it. I don't want to think about leaving you," Kelly confessed.

"You'll just be going away to college."

"And leave you to fall for some grease head in a leather jacket."

"Grease head in a leather jacket?" Zack mocked.

"Don't tease me, Zack. I'm serious."

Zack cupped Kelly's face with both hands. "Look at me, that's impossible. Because I've already fallen for you."

Kelly smiled and calmed down.

"I just have this bad feeling that I'm going to lose you. It's in the pit of my stomach and I can't shake it."

Zack lifted Kelly's chin up. "Don't think like that. What you speak into the universe comes to life." Zack rolled over and removed something from their jeans pocket, palming it in their hand. "I would rather give life to us. Now, because I know you're an old-fashion type of girl, I thought I would make us official."

Zack opened their palm, revealing their old high school pin.

Kelly's mouth dropped; she covered her face with her hands. She was so excited. Zack looked her square in the eyes and asked, "Kelly Hamilton, will you be my girl?"

Kelly grabbed Zack and kissed them screaming, "Yes!... Yes!... Yes!" Kelly took the pin and planted kisses all over Zack's face. "You have to reintroduce me to your mom now," she said.

Zack giggled, believing it was a joke, but Kelly made a stern face; she was serious. "Okay," Zack sighed.

Kelly became despondent. "I have to go," she said in a melancholy tone, "My parents want me home before they go to bed."

"I'll take you home. Later, give me a ring while they're asleep."

"I will; just make sure you pick up this time," Kelly said as she turned and kissed Zack.

* * *

A black Chrysler Imperial pulled up to Main Street. Three men dressed in black suits and fedoras stepped out. The leader, Mr. Cee was a notorious gangster, bank robber, and all-around bad guy. "Well, boys, it seems someone in this god-awful town has our money. We will burn this colorful place down and make a rainbow until someone coughs up our dough," Mr. Cee said with a grave tone. Armed with guns, the men stormed the shops, terrorizing the entire town.

RICKEY HAD JUST FINISHED HIS LUNCH AND WAS READY to talk more with Detective Hobbs. He took pleasure in annoying him. "You got a cig detective?" Rickey asked.

"I don't have time for this. I have another statement to take. Why don't you stop playing games and tell us about the woman from the motel."

"I've already told you people countless times that I didn't kill that woman. The night that woman was murdered. I was watching Miss Sandy... How is she, by the way?"

"Far better than how you left her. Get him out of here! I'm done wasting my time," Detective Hobbs said, and Rickey was escorted out as the sheriff entered the room.

"He didn't talk, did he?" the sheriff inquired.

"He still denies it. He'll be here for months awaiting trial. I'll take another crack at him then," Detective Hobbs replied.

"That poor woman deserves justice."

"I finally managed to speak with Abagail's employer, some editor from the city newspaper. He informed me that she was here covering a story," Detective Hobbs explained.

"A story? What kind of story?"

"About some missing children."

"Missing children? There are no missing children in O Town."

"Well, she certainly believed there were," Detective Hobbs said, feeling just as puzzled as the sheriff.

"What is happening in this town? Crime, murders, bank robbers and now missing children," the sheriff said, shaking his head baffled.

O Town, USA

A blue car suddenly shadowed the driveway of a beautiful, middle-class home with a white picket fence, the exact same house as in the "Leave it to Beaver" movie. A man emerged from the car and walked towards the front door... it was Freddie. He entered the home, clearly, he lived there. He hurried made his way upstairs to his bedroom and removed a brand-new O Town letterman sweater from a bag. At the same time, his mother happened to be passing by, she had her wig on backwards.

"Hey, is that a new sweater?" his mother inquired.

Freddie turned around, "Mom?" Freddie asked.

"Yes, silly," she replied.

Freddie proceeded to fix her wig.

"Yeah, my other one got blood on it."

"Blood? How did it get blood on it?"

Freddie dropped the sweater and took his mother's hand; he sat her down so they could have a heart to heart. "Mom, one of my friends was shot right in front of me."

"Oh my! Is he going to pull through?"

"No, Mom, he passed."

"What kind of trouble are you in? And who are these friends of yours that they're getting shot?"

"They're my friends, Mom. He didn't do anything wrong; it wasn't his fault." "Did you tell anyone?"

"No, Mom I can't."

"If you saw this boy, get shot, you have to tell the police." "I can't, Mom."

"Why not?"

"Because I saw who did it. And if the truth comes out, it will open a far bigger can of worms."

Freddie looked frightened so his mother embraced him.

Queerville, USA

Zack sat outside their shop, enjoying a beer and gazing up at the stars. They were eagerly anticipating a call from Kelly when Dennis pulled up with a visitor. Zack was pleased to see him.

"Dennis, I hope you have some news for me," Zack said. "I got something better," Dennis replied, glancing back at his car signaling for the person in the passenger seat to get out. A nervous looking white man exited the vehicle. Zack stood up and approached him.

"Who's this?" Zack asked.

"This is the guy I was telling you about. I personally found him and assured him that he would be safe with you," Dennis said.

Zack moved closer and stared intently at the man.

"So, you saw my brother on the night he was killed?"

"Yeah, I saw him, and I also saw who killed him," the man replied, his voice trembling.

Zack maintained a stern expression. "I'm listening."

O Town, USA

Kelly was cozy on the couch at home, wearing Zack's pin on her pajamas. Glancing down at it, she smiled. Just looking at the pin gave her goosebumps. She couldn't wait for her folks to go to bed so she could call Zack. She was watching her favorite show when her brother, Max, stormed in.

"I need to talk to you," he said, sounding panicky.

"Can it wait? I'm watching I love Lucy," Kelly replied.

"No, it's important." Max grabbed the remote and turned off the television. Kelly became upset, as she didn't like missing her show.

"Max! This better be important," she warned him. Max took Kelly's hand in his and made her listen to him. "I was going through a lot, and I didn't know how to deal with it. I feel like my brain has been played with and my wires are all crossed. So, I turned to alcohol and pills to deal with it all, but it got out of control. I started gambling, making bets I couldn't cover, then bets to cover other bets. I had to pay some bad people back, or they would have hurt mom and dad or even you."

"What's wrong? What are you trying to say, Max?" Kelly was confused, her brother was acting erratic.

Queerville, USA

Zack was still in the middle of their conversation with the white man who had witnessed Anthony's murder...

"...he was wearing that O Town sweater," the man said.

"Did you see his face? Who was it?" Zack was anxious to know. They could already feel the cold steel in their hands. As soon as a name left his lips, Zack was killing whoever was responsible. No talking, no apologies. Zack wanted them dead, and they wanted to do it themself.

"Yeah, I saw his face... It was that Hamilton kid." Zack froze, the blood left their face, they were in shock.

"What?" Zack was flabbergasted.

"I think his name is Max. Yeah, Max."

Zack became enraged. The fire returned to their eyes; the blood returned to their face. Zack was red with revenge. They were breathing like a raging bull. Zack stormed out, leaving Dennis and the White man in the dust.

O Town, USA

Max was pouring his heart out to Kelly. "I did it, Kelly."

"Did what Max?" Kelly asked, confused.

Max looked at his sister with sorrow. "I saw Zack's brother..." Kelly jumped up, not wanting to hear the rest. She covered her ears. "No... No... No..." Kelly stuttered.

"...he had a shit load of money, and I needed it. But he wouldn't hand it over. I must've blacked out or something. I just shot him; I shot him and took the money," Max wept.

"No... please don't say it. Max, no," Kelly's heart shattered. She was distraught.

"I killed him, Kelly," Max sobbed.

Kelly SCREAMED as she fell to the floor. Max tried to comfort her. "Get off of me! Why, Max? Why? What did you do? What did you do?" Kelly shouted as she wept.

"I'm sorry, Kelly. I didn't mean to. You have to believe me. I need your help, Kelly," Max cradled Kelly's face as she wept. "Please... Zack is going to kill me," Max seemed frightened...

Kelly's face was swollen with tears, her angelic blue eyes glistened with the ones that had yet to fall...

She cried hysterically—not for her brother, but for what this signified—the end of her and Zack.

Though she was madly in love with Zack, she would never turn her brother in... her heart shattered into a million pieces as she realized she could never see Zack again.

Suddenly, there was a knock on the door...

PRAY GAY AWAY
FALL 1956

KELLY HAMILTON

Kelly swayed into the party in her pink cocktail dress. The boys came to a halt as they turned to gaze at her. She spotted Dawn and Rose on the dance floor and joined them; the girls were overjoyed to see her. They shared a hug and danced together. Kelly was enjoying herself immensely.

She was at ease, as if her brother Max had never confessed to murdering the love of her life's brother.

She went to get a drink from the bar, turned the corner, and came face to face with Zack.

Her eyes widened, and her heart skipped a beat. Fear had rendered her immobile. Zack had a strange expression on their face. "Do you have anything you need to tell me?" Zack asked gravely. Kelly was frightened. She took a step back, her eyes filled with sadness. Max dashed in front of his sister, shielding her from Zack. "Zack don't do this," Max pleaded. Zack glared viciously at Max and murmured, "Did you really think I wouldn't find out?" Zack sighed cruelly.

"Zack, please," Kelly begged from behind Max. Zack ignored Kelly's pleas and brandished a gun, shooting Max in the head. Kelly wailed in pain as Max's body fell into her arms.

Kelly sprang up, still screaming and startled from her nightmare. Max barged in, asking, "Are you okay?" Kelly appeared to be spooked by her nightmare. "I'm just fine, Max."

"Are you planning on going to school today?" Kelly cast a scathing glance at her brother.

"It's the first day of our senior year. You can't stay in here and avoid Zack forever."

Kelly was extremely weary after learning that Max had murdered Zack's brother. "What does it matter? It's already over." Max knelt in front of his sister, imploring, "Kelly, you don't have to tell Zack. You can just act as though everything is normal." Kelly was in tears, and her brother could tell she was distressed.

"Zack is not naive, Max. I've been avoiding them all summer. Zack will discover the truth, and when they do, they'll realize I knew all along." Max was determined to help his sister. He was already struggling with the guilt of killing someone. He couldn't bear the notion of being the cause of his sister's anguish.

"You don't have to tell Zack the truth. You could simply tell a fib." Max's suggestion infuriated Kelly.

"Tell a fib? Max, you murdered someone. Someone who was very dear to someone I love. You're my brother, and I adore you. That is why I haven't told anyone. But I will not lie to Zack. I simply cannot do it." "Kelly, you can't stay in bed forever. Mom and Dad will soon realize something is wrong. What about school and all your friends?" Max stared at Kelly as she wept and wiped her eyes.

CHAPTER 13

As the sun shone brightly over O Town High School, youngsters sauntered and skipped through the doors, dressed in cult-like poodle skirts, sweaters, and short-sleeve button-downs. Principal Skinner's voice rang out across the PA system. *"Good morning, O Town finest and brightest. This year, we will be implementing a dress code. Ladies will continue with their poodle skirts and sweaters. And fellas in their button-up shirts and slacks. Anyone not in accordance with the dress code regulations will be penalized. Remember, you can't get into Heaven wearing devil colors and grease in your hair."*

Dawn was disgusted and baffled by Principal Skinner's announcement. "Did Principal Skinner just say that we're not getting into heaven because we wear colors and put grease in our hair?" Rose sighed and shook her head.

"As I've stated before, this town grows weirder by the day. Rosemary baby all over again."

"It's our senior year why enforce a dress code now?" Dawn's words were falling on deaf ears. Rose was speechless, gaping at the strapping blonde hottie with Jack Armstrong features wearing an O Town Letterman's sweater.

"Don't pinch me. I think I'm dreaming." Rose gaped at the hottie.

Dawn turned just as the hottie passed by, and their gazes locked. Dawn and Rose were both smitten by him.

"Who is that?" Dawn murmured.

Ronnie and his flunkies walked the corridor like the chosen ones. They were all dressed in their O Town varsity jackets. It appeared to be the douchebag uniform this year. They believe they're tougher than they really are.

Dawn and Rose squabble over the hottie. "Dawn, you know that I saw him first."

"Yeah, but he looked at me." "He only looked at you because you were blocking his view of me."

Rose and Dawn were engaged in a passionate yet friendly debate when something caught Rose's attention. "Oh, sweet, baby Jesus."

"What?" Dawn was perplexed, turning around to see what had captured Rose's undivided attention.

Walking down the corridor in pink slippers that pan up to pajama trousers and a white T-shirt was Kelly. She appeared to have just gotten out of bed. Rose and Dawn were stunned because neither they nor anybody else had ever seen Kelly in such a state.

Kelly approached them, a false grin on her face.

"Hey, Dawn, Rose." Dawn and Rose exchanged silenced looks. "Hey, Kelly, how are you feeling?" Rose inquired awkwardly,

"Did you and Zack break up?" Dawn asked.

"If we did, no one told me," Kelly chuckled, appearing to be on the verge of a nervous breakdown.

"I'm not sure if you noticed, but you're at school in your pajamas," Rose said softly.

"I couldn't find my goddamn poodle skirts," Kelly burst out laughing, causing Dawn and Rose to erupt in laughter as well.

Principal Skinner entered the corridor and observed the girls; she was horrified by Kelly's wardrobe choice.

"Oh, my dear Lord!" Principal Skinner clutched her chest as if she were having a heart attack.

"Kelly Hamilton, my office right now!" Principal Skinner was furious. Kelly cast a peek towards Principal Skinner before returning her attention to Dawn and Rose. "Well, I guess I'll see you at summer school, girls." Kelly bowed her head and made her way to Principal Skinner's office.

Dawn and Rose simply stared at one other in bewilderment. Principal Skinner rushed into her office with vengeance. "We have an emergency!"

TEN BLACK CLASSIC CHRYSLER VEHICLES WERE PARKED outside an abandoned warehouse. Men in black suits, surrounded by armed escorts, sat stoically at a large round table. These were clearly made men, and what appeared to be a mob meeting.

Tommy Russo, the Russo family's patriarch, spoke sternly. "There is no money to be made in Queerville. I propose you shift your focus to Chicago, New York and Florida. The Russo's control the west. Everywhere else is available for expansion. Let me state unequivocally that Queerville is protected. Anthony Calhoun gave his life to demonstrate this."

Tommy turned the floor over to Mr. Cee, who stood tall and imposing. The other men's gaze was fixed on him. Even in the presence of merciless killers, Mr. Cee was feared.

"Upon recovering my money my men and I will be headed south. There's a huge opportunity there and we want to lay our claims to the south now. Before any hoodlums catch on."

"What opportunity is that?" Tommy asked.

"Well narcotics of course. They bring in more profit than booze or gambling could ever do. You have to go out to drink booze and gambling doesn't give you a high. It just leaves you feeling like a loser."

Allen Lewis, a thirty-something weasel, sat in the back, intently listening.

"I promise you, flood a town with narcotics and watch the money pile in. That's when you step in and assume control. When a town is at its most vulnerable. Once you've established a precedent, the locals will follow suit."

Tommy didn't seem to agree with Mr. Cee sentiments. "Let's hear what the rest of the families have to say?" Tommy sighed.

After the meeting, Allen approached Mr. Cee to display his admiration. "I have to say your plan is a genius one."

"I know it is. I've done it before, and my men and I will find pleasure in doing it again."

"I want a seat at the table," Allen said anxiously, causing Mr. Cee to chuckle.

"A seat at the table of the Italian mob? Due, to my fifty percent Scottish ancestry, I barely have a seat at the table. Allen, you have a long way to go before becoming a Made man."

"What if I can do it?"

"Do what?"

"Flood a town with opioids and bring in a shit load of cash."

"The families already control every major city on the map," Mr. Cee stated.

"Yes, but not here."

"Did you not hear that Queerville is protected?"
"But not O Town and as you just stated I am not a Made man, yet."

Mr. Cee stepped back and looked Allen up and down. He was astounded by his commitment and eager to see what he might accomplish.

"I like you. If you can accomplish that without getting yourself killed. I'm certain the families will give you a seat at the table," Mr. Cee admitted, adding, "Now excuse me, I have to see a man about my money," Mr. Cee donned his hat and strutted out with his men.

Allen went to see Mayor Booker and inquired about possibly settling in O Town. Mayor Booker was eager to welcome another White Christian man to the beautiful, ideal community of O Town. "What do the people of O Town do for fun?" Allen asked.

"The fine people of O Town are into good Christian fun. We go to church every Sunday. We host bowling nights, and the kids attend the hop, under close supervision of course."

"And what do the men and women of O Town do for work?"

"Women? Well, the men work sixteen hour shifts to provide for their families. The majority of men work in the city while others own businesses here and work in O Town."

"So, their wives are just left home, lonely and bored?"

"Well, I suppose. But the women do keep busy with housework and chores, and they tend to the children."

"Is there any crime here? I want to live in a safe place, free from any criminal activities."

"No, there isn't any crime in O Town. Just typical adolescent misbehavior, nothing too severe," Mayor Booker assured Allen.

That's precisely what Allen was hoping to hear. No criminal activity meant O Town was up for grabs, and he intended on taking a chunk.

"Well, Mayor Booker, I appreciate you taking the time to chat with me. I'm going to stick around and get a sense of things to see whether O Town is a good fit for me."

Mayor Booker stood up and shook Allen's hand. Allen began to walk away but turned around with a burning question.

"What can you tell me about the folks in Queerville?" he asked with a mischievous smirk on his face.

MR. CEE AND HIS HENCHMEN BARGED INTO MACHETE Mike's illegal sports bar as if they owned it. "Who runs this joint now?" Mr. Cee inquired. The bartender indicated Machete Mike in the back. The men followed suit.

"Why do you want to know? You want to make a wager or something?" Machete Mike asked.

"Do I appear to be a man who asks for money?"

"What do you want?"

"Well, you see, a few months back; my associates and I robbed a bank for a large sum of money. When we got pinched my man that did manage to get away with the money. Well, you see he died, and someone took our money that we managed to stash."

"I'm sorry to hear that but what's it got to do with me?" "Well, supposedly, the people who are responsible live here in this town, and I'm running out of time. I can't keep going around chasing folks. No, I'd rather let them come to me."

"How are you going to do that?"

Mr. Cee gave Machete Mike an evil grin...

"By taking down the biggest scum in town."

Mr. Cee henchmen were already drawing their firearms when Machete Mike's goons attempted to make a move. They fired rounds, and shell casings fell to the ground. The place exploded with gunfire. Machete Mike stood there, terrified, as he witnessed his men get massacred.

"Do inform everyone that Mr. Calhoun is in town and until I get my money returned to me, I'm going to go to every establishment like this one and burn it to the ground."

Machete Mike looked terrified and nodded his head okay. Mr. Calhoun's henchmen poured gasoline throughout the bar and set it ablaze.

SANDY LAID IN JOHNNIE'S ARMS AFTER JUST MAKING LOVE. Now that Johnnie was attending community college, he had more time to spend with her, which he had been doing all summer long. However, their activities were limited to staying in and having sex. Sandy was growing bored. She was not used to a man keeping her cooped up in the house. Typically, men couldn't wait to take her out and show her off. She had never encountered a man who didn't want to be seen with her.

"Zack said you can drop your car off at the shop anytime. They'll fix it free of charge of course."

"Well, that's the least they can do. It's already been three months," Johnnie mumbled.

"Is something bothering you Johnnie?" Sandy asked concerned. She could tell something was weighing on Johnnie.

"Your friend nearly got me killed."

"I thought you two had worked this out already. What more would you like Zack to do?" Sandy was constantly on the defensive when it came to Zack.

"Nothing. I'll go drop my car off then head home. I have studying to do anyway."

"We've been stuck in the house all summer. I thought maybe we could go see a flick or go out somewhere," Sandy suggested excitedly.

Johnnie glared at Sandy as if she were insane.

"I can't go out with you," Johnnie said repulsed.

"Why not? You're single, I'm single," Sandy said perplexed. "Because I can't," Johnnie blurted out.

Sandy took a long look at Johnnie, "Oh, I get it. You're ashamed of me," she murmured.

"If people saw me with you, they'll..."

"They'll what Johnnie?" Sandy waited for an answer. Johnny grasped his head as though he had a horrible headache, and shouted, "I'm not Gay! Okay! Stop trying to make me like you!" Sandy leaped in Johnnie's face. "News flash, Johnnie I am a woman!"
Johnnie grabbed Sandy by her wrist and squeezed hard. "Ouch, Johnnie, you're hurting me," she groaned. Johnnie tightened his grip, "I'm not like you, you're a freak." Johnnie's eyes were completely black. "Let me go and get the hell out, Johnnie!"

Johnnie released his grasp on Sandy's wrist. She examined the damage to it as Johnnie stormed out. Her wrist was sore and swollen so she iced it before heading out for her shift at the diner.

O Town, USA

KELLY RETURNED HOME FROM SCHOOL AFTER BEING suspended. She undressed, climbed back into bed, and wept. Max poked his head in, he could see how difficult this had been for his sister. He shattered his sister's relationship with the love of her life. He would go to any length to set things right.

* * *

Zack walked into Charlotte's diner. There were a couple of teens eating and playing music, but the place wasn't packed. Sandy was trying to hold a plate with her injured wrist when it slipped and fell, breaking into pieces. Zack hurried over to help her.

"Are you, okay?"

"Yeah, just having a clumsy day today." Sandy was nervous, she didn't want Zack to notice her bruised wrist. She knew what Zack would do to Johnnie.

"Do you need help? Where's Patty?" Zack asked. They brought the broken glass over to the trash.

"No, that's okay; the place isn't busy. Don't you have a ride to repair and a bash to get ready for?"

"I'll fix Johnnie boy's car; don't worry. I just finished the Lipsticks ride today. I'm glad you're back to work, Sandy. This place is not the same without you."

"You're only saying that because I give you extra fries," Sandy cynically pointed out to Zack.

Zack spotted the bruise on Sandy's wrist.

"Ugh, that looks nasty. You need to ice that thing."

Sandy was mortified that Zack had seen her bruise. She attempted to conceal it. "Yeah, I will."

Zack took a closer look at her wrist. Sandy was frantically attempting to free her wrist from Zack's clutches.

"How did it happen?" Zack asked concerned.

"Must've happened just now. You really should go meet Johnnie at the shop," Sandy insisted, managing to free her wrist from Zack's grasp.

"Are you going to keep bothering me about this? Okay, I'll go repair your boyfriend's ride. Freddie is at the shop, waiting for me anyway," Zack surrendered by throwing their hands in the air and backing away.

"Thank you, Z." Sandy exhaled a sigh of relief.

O Town, USA

Dawn and Rose were sitting in class when Principal Skinner's voice screeched over the PA.

"Just a friendly reminder that the O Town Costume Bash is tonight. We want to see everyone dressed up in their best costumes. Remember that dressing up as the devil is not a respectable costume. Anyone seen in explicit, unchristian-like costumes will be reprimanded."

"What exactly is going on with Kelly?" Rose was concerned for her dearest friend.

"I honestly don't know," Dawn shook her head baffled. "Did she and Zack break up?"

"How would I know? I think she'd be more heartbroken." "Dawn, she came to school in her pajamas. It doesn't get any more heart broken than that," Rose lost her train of thought when the hottie from earlier entered the classroom.

He took a seat and opened his Bible. "Ugh, such a square. Well, you're shit out of luck. Squares only date Squares," Dawn teased Rose. She was disappointed to see that the hottie was a religious square.

"I can be square... enough," Rose said as she buttoned her shirt all the way up and placed her sweater on, "I wonder if he drives a convertible," Rose added with eyes full of lust.

A student passed around brochures seeking a reporter for the school newspaper. Dawn took one. "Oh, a school paper?" Dawn appeared interested. She took a long look at the brochure pondering.

"What are you wearing to the costume bash tonight?" "Oh, I'm not sure. I wasn't planning on going." "We need some excitement in our lives. This is our senior year. We should be making bad decisions and having regrettable sex with hot guys," Rose sneered.

Queerville, USA

When Zack arrived at their auto shop, Johnnie's car was already docked, and Freddie was inspecting it.

"How did you like running the shop?" Zack inquired of a frantic and agitated Freddie.

"Thank God you're back. The shop is fine. It's the people who are rude. All anyone cares about is you. *Where's Zack? When is Zack coming back?* They pull up and if you're not here they leave," Freddie quickly said. While they surveyed the damage to Johnnie's car, Zack grinned at Freddie's whimpering.

"I can fix this," Zack was eager to take on the challenge. "Gasoline and a match can fix it too."

"Johnnie saved our asses, and he never said a word. We didn't even offer him half of the money we found. So, unless you want to cough up your half, help me with this."

Freddie grudgingly got up to assist, but not before making a snide remark, "Hey, let's put a rainbow flag across the door."
Zack laughed at the thought, but they would never out someone. "You have to come with us tonight, Zack.

We're going to make those O Town squares shit their pants."

"It's a costume bash, right?"

"Yes, you can come dressed as your favorite musician, movie star, or O Town square."

"Yeah, costumes and squares aren't my thing."

"But it's a square that possesses your heart," Freddie said as he laughed. Zack turned to face him; their face solemn. "Sorry Zack," Freddie murmured.

MR. CALHOUN ARRIVED AT MAMA ZACK'S HOUSE AND knocked on the door. When Mama Zack opened the door, she felt as though she had seen a ghost. She became silent and paralyzed by panic as her face turned white. Mr. Calhoun simply stepped in, forcing Mama Zack back since she was overcome with dread.

"I do love what you've done with the place," he said in a sarcastic tone. "What are you doing here? You should be in jail," Mama Zack said shaken up.

"Oh, darling, there is no jail that can hold a Calhoun." "What do you want?" she asked.

"I came to see some old friends and to check on you, my dear. After all, we did share some amazing memories, wouldn't you say?" Mama Zack appeared to be scared. She assumed a defensive posture, encircling herself with her arms. He had clearly hurt her in the past. Mr. Calhoun enjoyed seeing the terror in her eyes. He moved closer to her, tormenting her even more.

"Last time I saw you, I was lying on the floor covered in blood. While you were taken away in handcuffs," she reminded him.

"Handcuffs, courtesy of you. I had a big score that day that I missed out on because of your... overreacting."

"What does that have to do with me?"

"Well, I'm here to collect. You've lived a very wealthy lifestyle due to my criminal activities."

"I didn't know you were a criminal. You lied to me, you lied about everything." Mama Zack backstepped into the wall as Mr. Calhoun approached her. She avoided his gaze by turning her head. He played with her hair while inhaling the fear she exuded. He enjoyed toying with her.

"And you chose to believe what you wanted to believe. Now I must run, my dear. But I'll be back tomorrow, and this time," he leaned in closer to her, instilling fear, "There aren't enough policemen in this town to put cuffs on me," he whispered into her ear, tipping his hat to Mama Zack as he left, leaving her visibly terrified.

VAL, LISA AND MARIA WERE CRUISING, IN LISA'S RIDE ON their way to crash the O Town costume party. Val was yelling at Lisa from the back seat while Maria sat on the passenger side. They were dressed accordingly for the costume bash. Val was a greaser; she wore a leather jacket, denim jeans, and lots of hair grease; Maria was Marilyn Monroe in The Seven Year Itch; and Lisa was a retro sailor.

"It's been so long since I've been laid. I need to get some soon," Maria sighed.

"I can assist you with that," Val responded.
Maria chuckled completely ignoring Val's comment.

"Yeah, well I don't have that problem," Lisa said with a cheeky look.

"Yes, we know you and Robin have been going at it like rabbits all summer long."

"Why don't you go see Zack? We all know that's who you really want anyway," Lisa asked.

"What can I say? Zack has the tongue of a water snake and the fingers of a pianist," Maria groaned as she shifted in her seat, crossing her legs at the mere thought of having sex with Zack again. She fanned herself as Lisa laughed at her antics.

"So, just have sex with Zack."

Maria sucked her teeth.

"Zack is smitten with their trophy white girl. Ugh, what do they see in her anyway?"

Lisa rolled her eyes in agreement.

"Yeah, I don't know either. She's just some rich white girl from O Town."

"Well, if you were with me. We'd be someplace swapping spit right now," Val confessed to Maria.

"Gross. Val, have you ever been with a girl?" Maria asked.

"Why don't you move your bod into my chamber, where we can discuss this in private."

Maria stared back at her in the rearview mirror. Lisa noticed that Maria was considering it.

"C'mon Maria," Val begged.

Maria didn't say anything. They pulled up to a light. Maria looked at the red light and then abruptly got out of the car and jumped into the back seat with Val. "Well, slide over, I'm not sitting on your lap."

Val and Maria were talking softly. Val put her arm around Maria, and she made a face, but didn't remove it. Lisa watched from the rear-view mirror; Val saw her. "To the costume bash!" Val shouted.

"Drop dead." Lisa was annoyed.

"Unless, of course, you want to go to lover's lane and have an orgy," Val suggested, causing Lisa to roll her eyes. "You wish you were Zack."

Val's jaw was hanging open in shock.

"You guys had a threesome with Zack?"

Maria and Lisa exchanged a sly smirk.

"Aww, what's the matter? Are you jealous?" Maria teased.

Val averted her gaze; Maria returned her head back to her. Val impulsively kissed her and threw her arm around Maria.

"We're here!" Lisa shouted.

Maria and Val broke their lip lock and hopped out of the car. They adjusted their costumes and watched as the O Town teens arrived for the bash in their plain, basic costumes. A lot of cowboys, Indians, Davy Crockett, John Wayne and Buddy Holly.

"Even in disguise, these O Town squares are too obvious." Lisa grunted.

"They could've just come as themselves; it would've been much scarier."

Suddenly, a White boy appeared unexpectedly, surprising them. "Are you ready to do this?" He asked. They were puzzled by the white boy. They took a closer look. "Freddie?" Lisa inquired.

"Yeah, it's me." Freddie responded.

They all burst out with laughter. Freddie was dressed as a square, in a Caucasian mask with blonde hair, a letterman sweater, and a button-up shirt.

"Freaky, Freddie," Val chuckled.

"I didn't get pulled over once in this mask."

Robin approached the group.

She ditched her gang jacket and denim in favor of a pin-up girl outfit. "Hey, gang," Robin spoke softly. Lisa was awestruck over her girlfriend. "Wow, babe you look smoking." They shared a kiss. "Thank you. Everyone looks so amazing. Lisa and Maria, you betties."

"Thank you, doll. But I want to borrow your entire outfit,"

Maria admired Robin's look.

Freddie handed everyone brown bottles containing some type of laxative. "Just pour a little of this into any beverages at the bash." "What's going to happen?" Lisa asked. "You'll see in sixteen hours."

Freddie had a mischievous look on his face. They made their way across the street and into the party.

Teens from O Town poured into the themed celebration. Queerville gangs in costumes arrived and blended in with the crowd, with some even wearing O Town Letterman sweaters.

ZACK CAME STORMING INTO MAMA ZACK'S HOME frantically shouting, "Mom!" as they hurriedly searched the home for their mother. Zack discovered her in her bed, balled up, with a knife near her.

"Are you okay?"

"He was here. He said he'll be back tomorrow."
Zack cradled their mother as she wept.

THE QUEERVILLE GANGS WERE CAUSING MISCHIEF, spiking the punch and putting bugs in the food. Rose, dressed as Lucille Ball, arrived in search of the hottie.

O Town teens were eating and drinking all the poisoned food and drinks, oblivious to the hijinks of the Queerville gangs.

Freddie drugged the punch in the main room; Rose did a double take as Freddie passed by her. She poured herself a glass of the drugged punch and sipped it.

Principal Skinner ran after a teen wearing a devil costume, grabbing him by his horns.

"Child, you dare laugh in the face of Jesus with this monstrosity. You want to see what true hell looks like?" Principal Skinner dragged the teen away.

The Queerville gangs were heading out when they saw a group of teens dressed in KKK garb, with white sheets and pillowcases drawn over their heads. They exchanged stunned expressions before pouncing on the teens, yanking their hoods off. One of the teens was Ronnie, who was dazed from being pummeled.

* * *

Zack sat alone in the dark at their mother's house, their gaze fixed on the front door. They sipped a beer while clutching a rifle. Their thoughts suddenly reverted to a memory of their mother screaming and an old Nat King Cole song booming from the speakers. It was unquestionably a painful memory for them. Zack teared up and drifted off to sleep.

MR. CALHOUN

Chicago, Illinois
1946

Mama Zack served supper to an anxiously waiting ten-year-old Zack and twelve-year-old Anthony. They shared loving glances as they sat and ate together like one happy family. Zack dumped their broccoli onto their brother's plate while their mother's back was turned. He didn't mind it; he loved broccoli and was always willing to do anything for his little sister. Which is why he allowed Zack to wear his clothes.

Zack never liked wearing girly clothes. They made them itch and were uncomfortable. They felt most like themselves in their brothers' baggy slacks and t-shirts. Mama Zack allowed Zack to dress however they felt comfortable, but not everyone in their household was as supportive.

The sound of someone entering the home brought fright to Zack and Anthony's faces. Loud, thumping footsteps reverberate. Zack began to tremble. Anthony grasped their hand, squeezed it, and imitated breathing. Zack peered up at the door, dreading who was about to step in. Mr. Calhoun emerged from the shadows and entered the kitchen. Mama Zack sat his meal down on the table. He cast a peek toward Anthony and Zack. He observed what Zack was wearing and shook his head in practice disapproval. "What are you wearing child?" he grumbled.

Mama Zack interjected, "Oh, let her be. There just clothes." Mr. Calhoun sat down and touched his food. He was furious. "This food is cold," he scowled.

"I just took it right out the pot."
Mr. Calhoun snatched up the plate and hurled it against the wall, shattering it.

"Are you calling me a liar? I said the food is cold."
Zack and Anthony dashed into the hall closet, terrified of what was about to happen. Mr. Calhoun got up and faced Mama Zack who was terrified. He grabbed her and shook her.

"How many times are we going to go through this? I told you have my food extra hot and ready for me when I get home," he slapped Mama Zack across the face. She ran into the living room and quickly switched on the record player to drown out the noise. She didn't want Zack and Anthony to hear her being beaten. A Billie Holiday track came on…

Mr. Calhoun snuck up behind her and struck her in the face repeatedly. "Stop putting that child in those damn boy's clothes," he hollered and struck her again.

Zack and Anthony clutched one another, horrified, as they listened to their mother being beaten. The sounds of her wailing in pain over the music were too much for Zack, who couldn't bear it any longer.

They surged out of the closet and attacked him. Zack's small fist pounded on his belly, he chuckled and backhanded Zack across the room. Anthony also tried to defend his mother, but Mr. Calhoun took off his belt and beat him with it. Mama Zack screamed, pleading for him to stop. Zack got up and bolted out of the house.

Zack sprinted all the way to Sandy's house. Their footsteps between Sandy's home and theirs may have worn a path in the pavement where they had trod so often. They climbed the tree outside her window and crept inside.

Twelve-year-old Sandy was in front of their mirror practicing their dance moves when they noticed Zack crawling through the window.

"Zack, what's wrong?"

Zack was hyperventilating. "Breathe, Zack." Sandy mimic Zack to breathe. "He's beating her again," Zack panted. Sandy hugged Zack as they curled up on the floor. Sandy's home was typically a place of solitude for Zack, but today Sandy's drunk mother happened to be home.

Mrs. Myers used to be a beauty queen before she picked up the bottle. She had the kind of beauty that women would kill for. Any room she walked into left men dumbfounded and women envious of her. Her sole vice was being an alcoholic. You could smell the booze before she even approached the bedroom door; she came barging into the room.

"What's going on in here?" she slurred. Sandy leapt up, surprised since she was not expecting her. They were in girl clothes, which Mrs. Myers despised. "Look at this sissy! What did I tell you about wearing those girl clothes?"

She took one step toward Sandy, and Zack sprang up and stepped between them.

"And look at you. You've got the devil in you, child; you can't go against nature. This is not how God intended you to be. What, ya'll want to swap bodies or something?" She chuckled as she tried to maintain her balance. "Now come get this spanking." She removed her belt and glared at Sandy who didn't budge.

"I said get over here and get this spanking. No son of mine is going to be some sissy faggot." Sandy's defiance infuriated her even more. She lunged after them, but Zack shoved her into the dresser. Zack and Sandy took off out the window, and down the tree.

Zack and Sandy found themselves at the Carnival that was in town. Eyes big from all the rides and wonder. A welcome diversion from the turmoil they both left behind at home. Sandy was beaming as they explored the festivities. But their smiles would quickly change to frowns when they realized they didn't have a single penny.

"Zack, what are we going to do? We don't have any money." Sandy murmured, disappointed.

"We have something that's more valuable than money," Zack replied. "What?"

"Our youth," Zack smiled.

Sandy fixed her clothes, pouted her lips, and wet her eyes with saliva as they pretended to cry.

The big-hearted people stopped and offered help and money. On the other side of the park, Zack would do the same. One by one, the people would drop money into their laps. They quickly had enough money to buy anything they wanted.

"What do you want to do first Sandy?" Zack asked with excitement. Sandy looked up and saw the Ferris wheel and dragged Zack to get on. They rode every ride at the park and even won some prizes. Sandy was having the time of her life. She felt so free and joyful there with Zack. Zack was waiting in line to play a shooting game as Sandy wandered off.

Sandy stumbled across a palm reading tent. They were always anxious about their future—whether they would ever find love or be imprisoned within this body they loathed. They entered the tent, unsure of what to expect.

She stepped in, and a small gypsy woman sat waiting. "Welcome child, don't be afraid." The woman said. Sandy was definitely afraid, but she wanted to know her future. So, she took a seat across from the woman.

"How does this work?" Sandy asked, curious.

"Hold out your hand child."

Sandy's hand was trembling as the gypsy woman took her hand in hers. She could tell that Sandy was a boy, but she didn't pass judgment. "What should I call you?" The gypsy woman asked.

"Sandy. You can call me Sandy."

"Such a beautiful name. What is it you would like to know, Sandy?" "My future. Will I be... who I want to be?" Sandy was desperate for answers.

The woman looked deep into Sandy's eyes and then caressed her hand. She closed her eyes and traced Sandy's hand with her finger. "You are already Sandy." "Huh?" Sandy was perplexed.

"You are already who you want to be."

"I don't understand any of that. How about love? Will I ever find love?" Sandy asked smiling.

The woman looked at Sandy's hand again and took a moment. "Do you know a place called Queerville?"

"Queerville? What's that?" Sandy replied.

"Queerville will be your home. There you will fall in love with a man; he will have hell in his eyes, but you will find heaven in his arms. That's the man you will marry," the gypsy woman said as Sandy chuckled. "Marry? Yeah, okay, lady, thanks for nothing. I can't marry a man." Sandy was annoyed and thought the woman was a fraud. She tossed a dollar on the table and walked out of the tent.

Zack was outside looking for her. "Hey, there you are. What were you doing in there?"

"Getting scammed. She told me I'm going to marry a man." "A man? Ewe," Zack scoffed.

"It's not even possible for people like us to get married." "Let's get some food. I'm starving."

* * *

Zack crept back into their bedroom and changed into their pajamas. As Zack crawled into bed, they could hear footsteps outside their door. They hurried and shut their eyes, pretending to be sleeping. Mr. Calhoun entered and closed the door behind him.

"No sense in pretending to be sleeping. We both know you're not." Zack held their eyes shut tightly.

Mr. Calhoun flipped on the radio; Frank Sinatra was playing as he began unbuttoning his shirt.

"You understand that the bond between a man and a woman is sacred and natural. However, the bond between father and daughter is substantially purer. How many times must I demonstrate that men are to lay with women? And that's how it shall be." Mr. Calhoun turned around and peered at Zack in bed.

* * *

Present Day,
Queerville, USA

Zack woke up in a sweat exasperating.

301

CHAPTER 14

The following day at O Town High was unusual. All the students had fallen ill at the same time. Students ran out of each classroom one by one. Teens in Biology 101 were clutching their stomachs and fleeing the classroom, as were those in economics class. Rose sat in her homeroom, distracted by all the excitement in the hallway... her tummy started bubbling... she passed gas accidentally.

Embarrassed... her eyes widened, and she covered her mouth. The hottie made an interesting expression as if he had sensed a foul stench. He took a glance around to see where the odor was coming from. Rose broke wind again. She bolted from the classroom, clutching her stomach, humiliated.

Principal Skinner hurried over the PA, "*Any teen who attended last night's Costume party. Please consult the school nurse immediately. You have been excused for the day.*"

Rose dashed down the hall to the lady's room. Teens raced into bathrooms clutching their stomachs. The toilets were all full. Due to the crowding, several students were relieving themselves in sinks and shower stalls. Everyone was in excruciating pain from stomach cramps and diarrhea. The sound of bow movements echoed through the air.

Dawn was now officially an O Town High journalist. She was nearing the end of her interview with Betty, the school editor, who had just given out the first assignments for the academic year. "Ms. Parker I'm delighted to welcome you to the O Town Voice. Since you are the last to be onboarded, the only assignment left is an article on the history of O Town."

Dawn was disappointed. She thought being a journalist would be thrilling and satisfying. Not a travel guide for Americas' most uninteresting city.

"The history of O Town? You guys don't have anything more exciting to investigate? I'm sure there's a teacher somewhere right now, screwing a freshman," Dawn sneered.

"Language, Ms. Parker. A story is only as exciting as the person writing it. So, make it sound exciting. You can use the library for research. Don't forget that these assignments go toward your college credits." Dawn reluctantly accepted the assignment. "Okay, fine. But I'm not a happy camper." She took the assignment and slowly paced into the school hallway, where she was approached by Johnnie.

"Hey, Dawn, have you seen Mary Sue?"

"Hey Johnnie, no, I haven't seen Mary Sue since you two graduated. I thought you two were off planning the wedding."

"Wedding? Who's wedding?" Johnnie was confused and still had no clue that Mary Sue was carrying his baby. "You guys' wedding, with Mary Sue being pregnant in all. I assumed you'd be getting married." Johnnie was at a loss for words. "Mary Sue is what!?" Johnnie exclaimed, puzzled. "Well yeah.... You didn't know?" Johnnie rushed out.

JOHNNIE ARRIVED AT MARY SUE'S HOUSE. HE POUNDED frantically on the door. His mind was racing with thoughts. *Mary Sue couldn't possibly have kept a baby a secret from me.* He was incensed. Mary Sue opened the door. "What are you doing here, Johnnie?" She was shocked to see him. Johnnie noticed Mary Sue's tummy. He took a step back, astonished. Mary Sue was six months pregnant. Johnnie couldn't believe his eyes. "It's true. You're pregnant," Johnnie said, flabbergasted. "We should talk Johnnie," Mary Sue said as she stepped back and welcomed Johnnie inside.

MAX EAVESDROPPED TO HIS SISTER WEEPING IN BED. Kelly was heartbroken over her and Zack. Her hand clutched Zack's high school pin. She wished she could see Zack, but she understood why she couldn't. She was desperate for their touch. She would give anything to look into those gorgeous green eyes again. She missed Zack terribly. Kelly sobbed, her tears soaking her pillow.

Max's heart sank, hearing his sister in such misery through the door. He despised himself, knowing he was the source of her anguish. He knew he needed to set things right.

* * *

Maria and her Lipsticks gang were at the club, marveling at their custom-made ride, which Zack had built for them. The ride was pink, with plush seats and a lipstick painted on the passenger side, as well as the name *Lipsticks* engraved in lipstick on the driver's side. Halle came over with her eyes green with envy. "Zack really did a good job on your ride. This thing is going to turn heads." "Oh, baby, I already turn heads," Maria said confidently. "Yes, you do," Halle took a seductive look at Maria, who seemed to welcome the flirtations.

"Where is your dame at?"

"She's old news. I dropped that betty." Maria smiled at the news. "So, Halle is back on the market? I'm sure the girls will be excited to hear that."

"Yeah, well, I'm really picking with my women. I don't just sleep with anyone."

"Well, if you don't try the goods, how are you supposed to know if you want to purchase the package?" Maria sneered. Halle chuckled. They exchanged lusty glances. "Well, if the package is all it describes itself to be, then that should be enough," Halle explained.

"Well, you know looks can be deceiving." Maria added as she licked her lips.

"How about Zack? Are they all they pretend to be?"

"Oh, Zack is the whole package and then some," Maria beamed as she spoke about Zack.

"So, what happened?"

"We expired. Simple as that."

"And what now? Are you over them?"

Maria toyed with Halle's hair and said, "The best way to get over someone is to get under someone new." "What are you doing today?" Halle asked, her lust-filled eyes gleaming.

"Today is not good. We have to plan the holiday festivities but I'm free tomorrow."

"Okay, so your place tomorrow?"

"Yes, bring some toys."

They exchanged seductive looks as Halle walked away, eager for their romantic rendezvous.

Sandy just arrived home after her shift. She was about to hop in the shower when she heard a loud knock at her door. Sandy opened the door to an angry Johnnie. "Johnnie, what are you doing here?" she asked annoyed. Johnnie barged in, shouting, "Did you know!?"

"Know what?" Sandy asked.

"That Mary Sue is pregnant," Johnnie blurted out.

"Well, Johnnie, how or why would I know that?" Sandy responded with a snarky tone. "Because you want me all to yourself," Johnnie replied.

"I have never told you that. You just assumed that," Sandy told him. Johnnie gripped his head, as if he had a migraine. "I'm sick of you screwing with my head!" Johnnie hollered.

Out of nowhere, Johnnie punched Sandy in the ribs; she hunched over and gasped.

"Johnnie, get the hell out and don't you ever come back here again!" Sandy groaned.

"I'm sorry," he apologized as he raced out.

FREDDIE AND OFFICER WHITEY WERE AT THE MOTEL for their daily rendezvous. Officer Whitey arrived late. Freddie was already in his bathrobe, waiting. "Sorry, I'm late. There's been a lot of crime happening around the city." "What kind of crimes?"

"Arson. Several unlawful establishments have been burned to the ground."

"Well good. We don't need criminals in our town; we already have enough problems."

Officer Whitey attempted to take his uniform off.

"Don't! Leave it on." Freddie said as he stood up and approached him. He circled around him, lustfully gazing at him up and down.

"I hate cops. You know what we do to police officers?" Freddie caressed Whitey's crotch: he dropped his head back as Freddie kissed his neck. They exchanged passionate kisses.

"Get down on your hands and knees," Freddie demanded as he shoved Officer Whitey to the ground. Freddie took Officer Whitey's handcuffs and placed them on him, cuffing his hands behind his back. He stepped in front of the kneeling Officer Whitey and unzipped his pants, freeing himself. Officer Whitey's eyes got wide as he gasped while watching Freddie stroke his own cock in front of him. He licked his lips, and his accelerated breathing became louder and louder in anticipation of Freddie entering his mouth. Freddie stroked himself until he was completely erected. Officer Whitey gaped at Freddie's hard on. "Open your mouth."

Officer Whitey opened his mouth wide. Freddie took a step closer, wet his lips, yanked Officer Whitey's head back, and spat into his mouth, sliding his erection into the depths of his mouth. Officer Whitey sighed as he sucked on Freddie, his eyes overflowing with ecstasy. Freddie groaned loudly. With his hands cuffed behind his back, Officer Whitey thrust his mouth back and forth on Freddie's cock. Freddie's eyes rolled to the back of his head. He was about to burst. Officer Whitey gagged as Freddie shoved his cock further into the back of his throat.

Freddie removed himself, laid Officer Whitey across the bed, and pulled his pants down. Officer Whitey arched his back as Freddie's palm pressed into the back of his neck, forcing his face into the bed. Officer Whitey felt his thick warm flesh break through his barrier. He wailed Freddie's name as Freddie stroked him hard from the back. His other hand gripped onto the cuffs, keeping Officer Whitey restrained as Freddie stroked deeper. "You've been a bad officer," Freddie panted.

"I'm going to punish you."

"Yes, please punish me. Punish me with your big black cock," Officer Whitey groaned. The force of Freddie's thrusts rocked his body back and forth.

Freddie grabbed Officer Whitey's hair, drew him back, and kissed him as he took Officer Whitey's cock into his hand and stroked him from behind, mirroring the strokes he was giving him. Officer Whitey moaned loudly. Freddie covered his mouth with his hand and stroked faster. Their bodies trembled, Officer Whitey could feel Freddie's muscles contract inside of him and then his warm juices bursting. Freddie moaned with his orgasm, and Officer Whitey matched his cries. They were both panting and utterly satisfied. Freddie removed the cuffs from Officer Whitey's wrist. He grabbed Freddie and kissed him. "That was amazing, but I have to go," Officer Whitey sighed as he leapt up and got dressed.

"You really do, dick and dip."

"Huh?"

"Nothing," Freddie shrugged.

"I have to get home before my wife does. You can stay and get washed up. Look, I'm sorry, okay."
He kissed Freddie goodbye and dashed out the door.

ALLEN WENT TO PAY THE BRONXVILLE DEVILS A VISIT. They obviously weren't expecting him. He was hailed by a highly armed welcome. Allen, no stranger to danger, came to a halt and waited for whoever was in command to approach him with the typical intimidating greeting that all bad guys offer unwelcome guests. Right on cue, Bobby, the baby-faced Puerto Rican

Greaser and second in command, walked up to Allen with a deathly stare.

"What do you want, Daddy O?" Bobby scoffed.

"Ouch! I'm probably younger than your father."

"Shit, I wouldn't know; I never met him," Bobby shrugged.

Allen looked around and noted how many men had guns aimed at him. "Nice little organization, you have yourself here."

"You have ten seconds to tell me what you want."

"Well, I want to make you rich."

Boddy seemed interested. He waved his men down. They sat on an old, worn-out sofa surrounded by bikes and auto parts.

"There's no money here to be made."

"Surely, you don't believe that. You had to pay for all those firearms somehow."

"Who said we paid for them?"

Allen chuckled. He appreciated a youthful enthusiastic soul whose mentality was easily molded.

"You ever heard of the Chicago pones?" Allen asked.

Bobby chuckled and asked, "Yeah, who hasn't."

"Well, I organized their business model that brought in five figures a week."

"I'm supposed to take your word for that?"

"No, not at all."

"Our business is just fine. As you can see, we're not starving."

"That's where you're wrong. You should always be hungry for more. What do you have going on here? Some stolen cars, bootlegging?" Allen scoffed and shrugged. Bobby's look indicated that he was correct.

"Oh, no, that's work. With my plan, you won't have to lift a finger; the money will flow to you." Bobby was intrigued but doubtful. "If your plan is so foolproof, why do you need us?" Bobby inquired, his face suspicious.

"That's a simple answer. You have the resources, and the manpower. It's going to require a large number of soldiers and a significant number of firearms to pull this off."

Bobby pondered for a moment, but he couldn't pass up any opportunity to make money and take care of his people.

"I need to clear this with my brother Antonio first. We need to meet everyone who will be involved," Bobby spoke with conviction. "Let me introduce you to my lady. I call her Mary Jane." Allen pulled out a joint and handed it to Bobby.

Allen smirked, knowing he had just enlisted the Bronxville Devil's in his takeover plot.

* * *

Sandy was in her washroom nursing her bruised rib. She was in slight pain while trying to bandage her stomach. She couldn't believe how quickly she bruised.

Suddenly, she could feel someone's presence behind her. She turned around to see a mortified Zack. Zack became outraged and looked to Sandy for confirmation. Zack just had to glance at Sandy's terrified expression to know that Johnnie was to blame. Zack was fuming and breathing heavily before charging out.

"Zack, NO!" Sandy yelled.

* * *

Just before Freddie was about to leave the motel, he heard a knock on the door. A Caucasian woman who appeared to have been up all-night sobbing seemed to be distressed. She was clearly expecting someone else to open the door, which made her even more surprised to see Freddie do so. Her expression was somber, and Freddie was bewildered. "Can I help you?"

"Jesus, how old are you?" the woman asked him. Freddie gazed at her as if to say, *who are you, lady?* She stepped in since she didn't want strangers to overhear their conversation. Freddie began to piece together who the woman was.

"I'm Mrs. Whitey." She stated in a mournful tone. Freddie sighed, dreading the conversation. She gazed around the room, appalled by her husband's scantily clad retreat, where he held his affair.

"I assume you know my husband." She waited patiently for a response. Freddie was wreaking havoc in his mind to concoct a lie. The woman could see Freddie was struggling to come up with a response. "Please, I already know the answer. I sat outside and watched him rush out of this room, adjusting his clothes." She quavered as her eyes welled up with tears. Freddie was beginning to sympathize with the woman. He never thought about the home he was wrecking. He was so engrossed in his hormones that he didn't realize the devastation he was inflicting on people's lives.

"How long has this been going on?"

"About a year," Freddie whispered, ashamed. The woman grasped her chest in shock that her husband could cheat on her once, let alone for a year. Furthermore, with a man—or, in Freddie's case, a young boy—she was dumbfounded and at a loss for words. In a fit of mania, she broke out laughing.

"Here I was expecting some young, dumb blonde." The woman scoffed. Freddie felt foolish and didn't know what to do, so he let out an awkward laugh.

The woman composed herself, wiped her tears, and calmed down. She took a deep breath and turned to face Freddie. "I'm going to ask you to stop seeing my husband. Please, if you have any humanity, put an end to it. I will not raise a child with a homosexual."

"You're pregnant?" Freddie was shocked.

"Yes, six months."

Freddie took a moment to contemplate everything, and he knew in his heart he needed to end his affair with Officer Whitey. He nodded, assuring the woman that he would end things. She turned to walk out.

"Just so you know. That won't change him; he's still what he is." The woman paused for a second, then continued out the door.

JOHNNIE OPENED HIS FRONT DOOR TO A FLYING FIST. Wham!—an instant blackeye. Johnnie collapsed to the floor. Zack repeatedly struck Johnnie in the face until they grew tiresome. "Stay away from her. If I ever see, you anywhere near her again. I'll fucking kill you, Johnnie!" Zack said gravely then stormed out. Leaving Johnnie bruised and bleeding on the floor.

———————————

The next day, dark clouds gathered, casting long shadows over O Town. Principle Skinner entered her office to find Kelly's parents waiting.

"Mr. and Mrs. Hamilton thank you for coming today. We need to have a serious discussion about Kelly." Principal Skinner closed the door slowly and with an uncanny grimace on her face.

* * *

Zack and Freddie were disassembling Johnnie's car. Freddie was animatedly telling Zack about the mischief at the costume party. "Principal Skinner was frosted," Freddie chuckled.

"I can't believe you guys did that." "Principal Skinner grabbed some kid up in a devil costume and she almost had a heart attack. I thought the grim reaper was coming for her."

"Who would do that? Principal Skinner is a Bible groupie. That kid is definitely, not graduating this year."

Freddie eyes focused on the black Chrysler that had just pulled up out front. Mr. Calhoun stepped out, as intimidating as the car.

Zack stopped what they were doing and took notice. Freddie looked scared shitless. Zack was traumatized, trying to snap out of it. Mr. Calhoun entered the shop through the open garage doors.

"I came to town looking for the punks who stole my money, and what do you know? It led me here."

"You got it wrong. We ain't steal no money," Freddie replied. "Well, your friend Johnnie says otherwise." Mr. Calhoun looked at Freddie.

"I knew he was a rat," Freddie whispered. Mr. Calhoun chuckled. "I like this kid he has some balls." Freddie grinned hard like a fan meeting his idol. Mr. Calhoun turned to Zack, "What about you? I bet you have yourself the biggest set of balls now," he sneered. "Stop! You don't get to speak to me that way," Zack informed him while casting a harsh glare.

A highly intense and awkward silence left Freddie feeling confused. "Um, Zack, do you know this cat?" Freddie asked, seeking clarification.

"No, not really. I just share his DNA," Zack replied nonchalantly. Initially puzzled, Freddie eventually pieced it together. His mouth fell open in disbelief.

"This is your father?" Freddie exclaimed, stunned by the revelation.

"How about you let me and my... offspring speak in private," Mr. Calhoun suggested, urging Freddie to leave.

Freddie glanced at Zack, who nodded reassuringly, signaling that it was alright. Warily, Freddie stepped away, peering up and down at Mr. Calhoun.

Mr. Calhoun paced around the shop.

"Zack's Auto Shop huh? I see you have your mother's DNA. She liked to work for her money too. I prefer to take mine. You know, how you took my money."

"What do you want?" Zack's patience was running thin. "I'm just trying to catch up on lost time. I heard you've got yourself one fine-ass white girl. What's her name? Kelly. And how is Sandy? I heard she turned into one hell of a knockout. I must say you do have my taste in women," Mr. Calhoun said with a sly smirk that aggravated Zack.

Zack slammed the hood of the car shut and stepped closer to their father with a threatening demeanor, locking eyes with him. "If you so much as look at Sandy, I will gouge out your eyes. Utter Kelly's name again in my presence, and I'll cut out your tongue and feed it to you," Zack declared gravely.

The intensity in Zack's gaze was piercing.

"Now that's my DNA in you talking. So, I know you mean it," Mr. Calhoun said, finding amusement in the situation. However, Zack did not. "Relax," he sighed.

"How do you want to handle this?" Zack asked.

Mr. Calhoun chuckled and said, "You are your fathers' child. Meet me in an hour, you know where."

* * *

Queerville skies gave way to gray clouds. The wind was a tyrant, bending tree trunks and splintering branches. A tremendous roar rang out as Freddie's car was parked alone outside the diner. Freddie walked into the deserted diner, finding Sandy wiping down the countertop, so he went to chat with her.

"Where is everyone at?" he asked. "Bad weather keeps people inside," Sandy replied. "Yeah, looks like a storm is coming." "I might just close up early."

"Is Charlotte still on tour?"

"Yeah, she should be back next week."

"I wanted to go with her but with my mother in all. I can't leave the state."

"You know Freddie, I have never met your mother."

"Because she ain't nothing to meet."

Sandy chuckled, prompting Freddie to ask, "Have you ever met Zack's father? Now, he's intimidating." Confusion filled Sandy's face. "What do you mean? You've never met Zack's father, Freddie." Sandy was perplexed as to why Freddie was referring to Zack's father. As far as she knew he was in prison, where he belonged.

"I have today," Freddie said. Sandy's fear grew.

"What? Zack's father is in town?" Sandy was scared and rightfully so. Mr. Calhoun was a violent and dangerous man, who had tormented and tortured Zack throughout their entire childhood. "Yeah, he came into the shop, and it got very uncomfortable. He's kind of a wet rag."

Sandy hurried and untied her apron, "Freddie, we need to get to Zack, now." Freddie jumped up and they rushed out and went straight to Zack's shop; it was closed. Sandy banged on the door; Zack was not home. "Where too now?" Freddie inquired.

"I think I know," Sandy insisted.

315

MR. CALHOUN ARRIVED AT THE HILLTOP, COCKY. Zack was waiting pensively. He crept up behind Zack whose back was turned. "Are you alone?" Zack asked.

"I sent my crew ahead and told them I had the money." Zack turned to face their father. A long awkward silence in the middle of a stare down.

"You couldn't come to your own son's funeral?" Zack asked disappointed. "I'll be sure to go to yours."

* * *

Freddie and Sandy were in the car racing to Zack. Sandy's leg was trembling; she was anxious to get to them. She was all too aware of the anguish Mr. Calhoun had inflicted on Zack as a kid. What scared her the most was knowing what he was capable of. "If I know Zack's dad, there's only one place he would go to torment them," Sandy suggested. "To think I was starting to like this guy," Freddie mumbled.

THE THUNDER ROARED THE SKY AS IT DOWN POURED on them. Zack and their dad were discussing old memories. Mr. Calhoun seemed to have a different recollection of events; Zack, on the other hand, remembered everything precisely. They were both drenched by the rain that had fallen on them.

"Do you remember when I used to bring you up here and push you on the swing? Then I'd take you to go get ice cream. You were such a beautiful little girl," Mr. Calhoun mockingly smirked.

There was a surge of rage flowing through Zack. They smirked and looked straight into Mr. Calhoun's eyes.

"Let me tell you what I remember. I remember the Billie Holiday track mom used to play to muffle the sounds of you beating her, and that Louis Jordan song would blast through the speakers. So, we wouldn't hear her screaming from her bruises as she took a bath," Zack voice broke.

Ashamed to hear of his own transgressions. Mr. Calhoun turned around and put his back to Zack.

"But you know what I will never forget, DAD? Is that Frank Sinatra song that would play when you would come into my room at night," Zack shivered as tears raced down their cheeks, their body attempting to release the trauma they had been carrying for so long.

Mr. Calhoun spun around defensively.

"Now, child, you matured too quickly..."

Suddenly, Bang! - a bullet went clean through Mr. Calhoun's head. His body dropped to the ground. Zack was left shaking, holding tightly onto the gun, and hyperventilating.

Freddie's car pulled up, and Sandy rushed over. She cradled Zack's face, "Breathe, just breathe... Breathe Zack. It's okay. Give me the gun." Sandy removed the gun from Zack's shaking grasp. Freddie glanced at Mr. Calhoun lying on the ground.

"What should we do with him?"

Zack was in a state of shock. Sandy put them in the car, and then she and Freddie stood over Mr. Calhoun's body. "We have to get rid of the body," Sandy replied.

"Okay. Let's ask Zack..."

"Zack is in no shape to help us." "Well, what do you suggest?" Sandy turned around and spotted the swing with the murky water below it. The downpour was intense. "I have an idea," Sandy said. She understood they had to hide the body. You don't just kill a Made man; you need permission for that. If word spread that Mr. Calhoun was killed, it would be hell for Queerville, not to mention that the other Mob families would place a hit on Zack. Sandy couldn't let that happen.

THE NEXT MORNING WAS A BRIGHT AND SUNNY DAY. The storm that had gone the night before had left no trace. Max paced back and forth outside the police station. Despite his reservations, he decided to turn himself in. He could no longer continue to be the source of his sister's pain.

He stepped inside and approached the front desk. "Excuse me, Officer," he mumbled, nervously. "What is it son?" the officer responded irritated. "I want to report a crime." The officer appeared irritated, he sighed, and grabbed a notebook. He just knew it was a hoax. "What's the crime you want to report?" "Murder," Max whispered.
"You saw someone get murdered, son?" the officer was shocked. "No... I murdered someone," Max confessed.

ZACK WAS ASLEEP ON SANDY'S COUCH WHEN THEY WERE awakened by the noise coming from the kitchen. Zack sat up and took a moment to take in their surroundings. Feeling a bit groggy, Zack slapped their drowsy face to wake up. Sandy walked in with a tray of food. "I'm sorry, Zack. I didn't mean to wake you," Sandy said apologetically, still concerned for Zack's mental state. "What time is it?" Zack grumbled. "It's a little after nine," Sandy replied.

"I don't even remember coming back here."

"That's because I brought you here. Zack, you were traumatized. I didn't want you to be alone," Sandy kissed Zack on the forehead and placed the food down on the table in front of them. "I made you some breakfast," she said proudly.

"Sandy Myers, cooked for me?" Zack said in astonishment. "Hey, I cook," Sandy responded defensively. Zack took a seat at the table with Sandy.

"In all the years I've known you, Sandy. You have never cooked for anyone else. Hell, you don't even dance with anyone else," Zack remarked.

"Dancing is very intimate to me. I don't do it with just anyone. You know this already Zack." "Okay, Sandy the dance virgin. When will she ever give her feet to another," Zack sneered, making Sandy laugh. Zack chuckled and ate a few bites of food before mentally repeating the events with their dad. "You know he had the nerve to go see my mother," Zack spoke solemnly.

"Oh, is that what drove you over the edge?"

"She was in shambles. After everything he had put her through. After all he put me and Anthony through. He shows up here and terrorizes us."

"When Freddie told me your dad was in town. I just knew I had to get to you. I'm just sorry I couldn't get there sooner."

"I'm glad you got there when you did. You got there right when I needed you."

"Do you remember when you were nine and he locked you in the closet, threatening not to let you out until you were normal?"

"Yeah, you came and broke me out." Zack's face lit up with a warm smile at the memory of their best friend rescuing them from their father's torture.

"Anthony was too petrified to defy him. But I knew I had to get you out of there."

"You've always been there for me Sandy," Zack acknowledged gratefully.

"I've known you since I was ten years old. You were the first person I ever cared for outside of my family. You're my best friend; I'll always be here for you, Zack." They exchanged warm smiles. "Now, eat!" Sandy blurted out.

ROBIN WAS IN THE KITCHEN MAKING BREAKFAST. She was creating more of a mess than she was cooking. She was burning the eggs while Lisa looked on, amused. "Cooking isn't your strongest suit I see," Lisa teased.

"Hey, I'm making these eggs with love," Robin confessed proudly. "Well, if those eggs are a symbol of our love we're doomed," Lisa joked. Robin couldn't help but feel a bit serious. She was falling hard for Lisa and wanted to see if they were on the same page. "You know we still haven't said those three words," Robin said sheepishly. "Let's move in?" Lisa was puzzled. "No, silly. Those three magic words."
Lisa continued to be clueless, "Huh?"

"I love you," Robin remarked.

"Aww, you just said it," Lisa smiled. Robin gave her a blank stare realizing Lisa had just duped her. Lisa stood up and came over to her, wrapping her arms around her.

"If you have something to say, just say it," Lisa smiled enticingly at Robin.

"You first."

"I can show you better than I can tell you," Lisa whispered.

Lisa leaned in and kissed Robin passionately. Robin hoisted her up and sat her on top of the table, knocking the plates to the floor. Still in a heated kiss. Her hands ran down the curve of Lisa's spine which broke her out in goosebumps. Her panties filled with wetness. Robin sank her fingers into Lisa, she moaned into her mouth in pure surrender. Robin drew back and ran her tongue across Lisa's firm breast. Still stroking her, Lisa dropped her head back and moaned as Robin's mouth encircled her nipples and she tugged at them.

Robin kneeled and spread Lisa's legs wider. She extended her tongue and slid inside of Lisa; she let out a small shriek. Her tongue stroked Lisa's clit: the sensation was unbearable.

Lisa swung her legs around Robin's shoulders. Robin held her by the hips and hoisted her into the air. She arched her hips reflexively as Robin's tongue probed her pussy; frantically trying to match her rhythm. Her wetness trickled down Robin's chin and onto her neck. Lisa's fingers dug into her scalp, clutching her hair, as she cried out in ecstasy. Robin laid her down on the bed.

Lisa snatched Robin's gown and ripped it off, yanking her onto the bed. She tugged Robin's leg, urging her to wrap it around her. "You know my favorite number is 69." Lisa smirked. Robin sat backwards on Lisa's face before plunging down and devouring her. Robin stroked Lisa's warm pussy with her tongue while Lisa buried her head deeper, smearing Robin's juices across her face. The intensity of wanting desperately to satisfy the other stimulated their hormones even more.

Robin's heart was thumping as she moaned and breathed loudly. She had always lusted after Lisa and now it seemed it was mutual. She was intent on discovering just how wet she could make her. Robin's tongue rasped over her pussy circling with pinpoint accuracy on her clit. Lisa closed her eyes and let the sensation build. Robin licked and sucked on her clit; the tension exploded in one long spasm. Lisa came hard; her juices trickled down into Robin's mouth. She sucked her dry.

Lisa, determined to make Robin orgasm, climbed on top of Robin and spread her legs wide. Thrusting her tongue deep inside her, Robin groaned loudly, like a wolf at night howling at the moon. Lisa sucked up her juices like soup...she slid her fingers inside of her...she waited for her to react; no response, she slid another finger inside of her. Robin let out a gasp. Lisa filled her with three fingers. It was a tight fit but Robin's juices sooth the pain her fingers left behind. Robin arched her back and clutched on to Lisa. She groaned right on the edge of climaxing.

"Tell me," Lisa whispered.

She sucked on Robin's nipple; her teeth teased them. It was both pleasurable and painful.

"Say it," Lisa demanded, trying vigorously to get Robin to say those three words. Robin was stubborn in her ways; she refused to say it. She clenched her teeth and fought the urge to say it and the urge to come; she didn't want to give in to Lisa. Even coming would establish its veracity. She resisted it.

Lisa's fingers hadn't stopped - they were still fucking her insanely hard. She was so near that her orgasm was intensifying. Lisa kissed her, fucking her pussy relentlessly as her pelvis erupted and she released heat like a volcano exploding through her core.

"I LOVE YOU!" Robin screamed, and moaned as her body was convulsing uncontrollably. Lisa grinned knowing she had won. "I love you, too, baby." she kissed Robin deeply before whispering, "But I'm not done with you," into Robin's ear.

ZACK AND SANDY WERE IN A DEEP DISCUSSION ABOUT Sandy's continued poor choices in men. "Okay, what about Jimmy?" Sandy laughed hard and covered her face in embarrassment. "Jimmy was cool," Sandy said with denial. Zack's eyes grew big; they were flabbergasted. "What? He had a unibrow."

"I thought he was adorable," Sandy said defensively. Zack laughed and gave Sandy a cheeky look.

"And Daron?" Zack added. Sandy immediately sucked her teeth and rolled her eyes. "Okay, I had no business dating that man, but in my defense, his girlfriend was cheating too."

"And you slept with him too."

"No, I did not," Sandy said shockingly.

"Sandy, don't lie."

"I did not sleep with that man," Sandy assured Zack. Zack gave Sandy a blank stare.

"Okay, he might've given me fellatio, but that's it." Zack busted out laughing. "Why did you despise that woman so much, Sandy?"

"Who Cheryl? I didn't despise Cheryl; I just wished her eternal damnation," Sandy admitted.

"Are you ever going to forgive that girl for stealing your first love?"

"Oh, we're even now," Sandy shrugged.

They both laughed.

"Is that why you developed the motto; Sandy, don't play second fiddle?"

"Actually, that was based on all the men that cheated on me."

"What do you mean?" Zack asked curiously. Sandy inhaled deeply and exhaled.

"Men see me as a sexual toy that they can play with until they grow bored, then they go find a shiny new toy. Every man I ever dated cheated on me, and each time I got cheated on, I changed something about myself. My look, my body, the way I talk, dress, and walk—I thought it was me. Why can't a man stay faithful to me?" Sandy teared up as her voice became brittle. Zack held her hand to comfort her as they wiped away her tears.

"You are beautiful Sandy. The word beautiful exists solely because of you. Those dudes were fools, they didn't know how to love you. They've never had anything as precious as you."

"Yeah, well, that just goes to show you. No matter how beautiful or sexy a woman is, a man will still cheat on her."

"Those aren't men; those are boys. A real man would worship the ground you walk on and never let you go a day without feeling his love and loyalty. Don't you ever settle for anything less." Sandy smiled at Zack's kind words.

"Even after they cheated, I wanted them to choose me, but they didn't. No man has ever chosen me. They just sleep with me; discard me, then it's back to their ex."

"The right one will and you're right—you should never play second fiddle to anyone. You should always feel like the most important person in your partner's life."

"Like you do for Kelly?" Sandy's words irritated Zack: she could see they were being evasive. She was perplexed as to what had triggered the sudden change.

"Yeah, something like that," Zack jumped up, "I got to go and see my mom," Zack insisted.

"Okay, tell her I said hi. I'm headed into the diner now, but if you want to talk later, I'll be home around ten." "Alright. I'll see you later," Zack hugged Sandy goodbye.

O Town, USA

Johnnie walked outside to find his car disassembled and vandalized. The doors and wheels were missing; seats scorched. He looked across the street to see Freddie and his gang. They laughed and mocked Johnnie's bruised face.

"Snitches get stitches," Freddie shouted.

324

Johnnie ducked back inside, cowering behind the curtains. Freddie hopped in his ride. "Scorpions, roll out!"

HALLE ARRIVED AT MARIA'S PAD WITH A BOUQUET OF roses. Maria opened the door in a silk robe with a big smile that quickly vanished the moment she noticed the roses. Not one for romance, she was instantly irritated. "Here I got these for you," Halle exclaimed excitedly.

Maria put on a phony grin and murmured a thank you as she accepted the roses and tossed them into the cupboard. She brought Halle to the living room, where she had a fruit tray waiting, but they weren't for merely indulging but rather as an aphrodisiac: strawberries, chocolate, figs, and watermelons.

"I'm loving the spread."

"I haven't even opened my legs yet," Maria replied humorously, leading Halle to laugh.

"What's so funny?" Maria grabbed Halle and pushed her onto the couch, where she climbed on top of her. She took Halle's hands and placed them around her hips while she kissed her. She then reached up and took a chocolate-covered strawberry and fed it to Halle. "You like getting right into it, huh?" Halle asked. "You know what you came for. Why play games?" Maria said seductively.

Halle rolled over on top of Maria and kissed her fiercely. Her tongue traced her neck, her collarbone, to her shoulder, and then down the center of her chest. She tugged her robe apart and kissed her hips and her pelvis. She lingered near her groin and flipped her over. Nipping and biting the small of her back, then down to her ass. Her entire body was scorching, as if it were on fire from within. Her pussy was swollen, heated, and gushing. She licked every drop before burying her face deep inside Maria. Maria's phone rang, she moaned and reached over to answer it while Halle continued to taste her. "Hello," she panted, "What!?" Maria shouted, angrily, pushing Halle off.

* * *

Lisa had Robin tied up and blindfolded in bed. When they were interrupted by a phone call. Lisa picked up the phone. "Hello," she breathed. Lisa's excited look faded into pure rage. "What!?" Lisa shouted.

* * *

A swarm of teenagers burst into the diner. Sandy was about to come over and take their order when she overheard the news.

"Max Hamilton has been arrested for the murder of Anthony Calhoun," a teen blurted out.

The diner went silent; you could hear a pin drop, along with Sandy's heart that was in her stomach.

"What?" she said flabbergasted.

The teen looked up at her.

"Yeah, he turned himself in this morning. He's at the jailhouse being processed."

The other teens gasped in disbelief.

"Let's go!" Teens shouted out.

They dashed out of the diner and took to the streets. Sandy hurried to the phone and dialed Zack's number. She wanted them to hear the news from her firsthand. There was no answer. She became concerned, she knew this news would devastate them. This was the last thing Zack needed to deal with after last night. She hung up and called Mama Zack's home.

* * *

Freddie was waiting for Officer Whitey in his usual room at the motel. He was determined to finally put an end to their affair. Freddie didn't want to be responsible for ruining someone's marriage, and he longed for a genuine connection instead of being treated as a mere sex object. Officer Whitey barged in, appearing flustered.

"Boy am I happy to see you," he sighed. Freddie stood up, facing him. He was eager to get this conversation over with and leave expeditiously.

"Listen, I'm done with this whole dick and dip thing we got going on." Freddie stated firmly. "What? What are you talking about?" Officer Whitey asked, confused. "Us, this motel. I can't continue like this anymore." "Freddie, you know this is how it has to be." "No, it doesn't have to be this way. If I knew my worth, I would realize that I deserve more than a cheap motel twice a week. And I definitely deserve more than being your BBC fetish."

"BBC? Freddie, you lost me. Come on, you know that I'm married." "You white men see us as fetishes. It's not about your marriage. You wouldn't be caught in public with me," Freddie argued. "That's not true. I'm just not out to my family or anyone."
"You're not out to your damn self," Freddie retorted.
"We have sex. We never said it was serious."
"Yeah, that's exactly what it was—nothing serious."
"I don't want to lose what we have," Officer Whitey pleaded. "No, you don't want to lose your BBC," Freddie shot back. "Can you please stop making everything about race?"

"News flash, Officer Whitey, it's nineteen fifty-six; everything is about race," Freddie snapped.

"What do you want from me? Tell me and I'll do it,"

Officer Whitey said, taking Freddie's hand. However, Freddie pulled away. "Nothing. I don't even know your first name," Freddie confessed, shaking his head and headed towards the door.

"Well, I thought you should know that Max Hamilton was arrested this morning for the murder of Anthony Calhoun," Officer Whitey revealed.

Freddie was dumbfounded, stunned by the news. He cast Officer Whitey a worried look before stating hastily, "You need to get back to the station."

"Why? What for?" Officer Whitey asked puzzled.

"This town is about to go up in flames," Freddie murmured.

* * *

As the sun began to set over Queerville and O Town. The word that Max had been detained in connection with Anthony's murder spread swiftly. People were whispering in each other's ears, spreading the story all the way from Queerville to O Town to Bronxville.

Angry Queerville residents began marching through the streets toward the jailhouse. Torches in hand, they were enraged and thirsty for blood at the same moment as O Town residents, creating a scene straight out of West Side Story. Both sides were angry and desperate for answers.

Freddie, Val, Maria, Lisa, Robin, and other Queerville gangs led their side.

Ronnie and his goons led O Town residents to the jail. They came head-to-head, more like mob to mob, in front of the jailhouse.

"Folks, there's no need for protest. Max has turned himself in willingly and has confessed to the murder of Anthony Calhoun," the sheriff hollered over his megaphone.

"We're here to make sure justice is served. And his parents don't buy their way out of this one!" Freddie shouted. The Queerville people cheered.

"I assure you, there's nothing to buy here. We will review Max's confession, and he will wait to be transported to a state facility along with the other prisoners," the sheriff explained.

"What happened to innocent until proven guilty?" Ronnie shouted. The O Town people cheered.

"Well, he confessed son. He's guilty," the sheriff responded sarcastically.

Kelly and her parents emerged from the jailhouse into the unruly crowd. The Queerville folks booed them as they stood on the O Town frontline.

"Everyone, please return to your homes. There's nothing you can do here," the sheriff pleaded.

Zack made their way through the Queerville mob to the frontline, where they locked eyes with Kelly. The instant she saw Zack, her eyes brightened and the melancholy on her face vanished. She almost ran to Zack, but she stopped herself. She was well aware that she couldn't. She didn't blink once at Zack.

Bottles were being THROWN, TORCHES were lighting FIRES, and chariots were BURSTING into FLAMES as the crowd became violent. Gang fights and brawls were happening all around them. Despite the chaos, Zack and Kelly couldn't take their eyes off each other; as the world crumbled around them.

Zack took a step back towards the jailhouse, still maintaining eye contact with Kelly. She followed, mirroring every stride. They continued until they reached the back of the jailhouse.

Zack and Kelly emerged from the back of the jailhouse simultaneously. They stopped and gazed at each other before Kelly sprang into Zack's arms.

She wrapped her arms tightly around Zack's neck, and they shared a passionate kiss, as if their lives depended on it.

Her attraction to Zack had ignited her fire, but it was Zack's kiss that made her burn. Zack drew back and lowered Kelly to her feet. "I'm sorry. I'm sorry about my brother." Kelly apologized profusely. "Thank you for coming to me that night and telling me the truth. I know how difficult that must have been for you. But I gave you all the time I could, Kelly. I told you this would happen." "Well, it's over now. We can be to-gether again." Kelly wrapped her arms around Zack, but they yanked her arms from around their neck.

"Kelly, it's not over. As long as your brother is still breathing it's not over," Zack said sternly.

"He's in jail, Zack. What more do you want?"

"Yeah, jail! My brother is in the dirt; he ain't coming back. I can't go visit him and bring him pies whenever I want!" Zack shouted angrily.

Being torn between her brother and the love of her life had taken a toll on Kelly. She broke down sobbing. "You promised that you wouldn't hurt him."

"I said I would give you time. You asked me, you begged me, to give you time."

"He's my brother, Zack!" Kelly shouted.

INSIDE THE JAILHOUSE WHERE RICKEY WAS WAITING, officers were being called to the front to disperse the mob outside. Rickey remained in jail, awaiting trial. An officer attempted to escort Rickey from his cell to an in-terview room. However, Rickey stumbled over a desk and lifted a paper clip. The officer proceeded to escort Rickey. Once inside the interview room, the officer sat Rickey down and locked the door behind him.

Rickey seized the opportunity to escape; he utilized the paper clip to jimmy the door lock and cautiously poked his head out to check if it was safe. With the coast clear, he slipped out of the room and quietly made his way into an adjacent restroom. There, he skillfully jimmied the window latch and leapt out to his freedom.

* * *

Kelly was furious with Zack; she felt betrayed.
"I came to you and told you the truth. I betrayed my own brother," Kelly shouted, shoving Zack and pounding on their chest, like a child throwing a temper tantrum.

"I didn't lie. I came to you because I hoped that you loved me enough to trust me," Kelly said hysterically while giving Zack a firm shove. "You don't love me! You don't know what love is!" Kelly shouted and shoved Zack again, but this time Zack grabbed her arms.

"He's still alive, isn't he? He walked himself into that jail. That should tell you how much I love you. Don't you ever question my love for you. Ever!" Zack shouted.

In the heat of the moment, Kelly became engrossed and kissed Zack. They were madly in love, fighting with their emotions and hormones.

They kissed aggressively but passionately, their hands all over each other; tongues, struggling to absorb each other as if starved for the other. Panting and grinding, Zack pressed Kelly up against the wall and left hickeys on her neck. Kelly breathed heavily and drew Zack in closer, her hands tenaciously grasping onto them.

Zack pulled Kelly's panties to the side and gently caressed her warm and wet tightness. Kelly latched onto Zack and moaned as their fingers stroked her pulsating pussy. She breathed Zack's name in their ear as she left soft kisses on their neck. Zack removed their fingers and licked them one by one; it's been so long since they've tasted Kelly's sweet juices. Kelly was so enthralled that she took her panties off. She wanted more of Zack; she pulled them into a deep, devouring kiss. Zack unbuckled their pants and hoisted her up against the wall as they entered deep inside her. Kelly gasped as Zack's erection filled her…she rotated her hips, riding atop Zack.

Zack's hip pounded against her body, fucking her hard against the wall. Kelly screamed Zack's name. The more breathless pleas she uttered; the deeper Zack drove inside of her. She ran her hand through Zack's hair, her gaze riveted on theirs. Those enticing emerald eyes pierced her core. The world around them was crumbling, but they had no other desire but to please each other. She groaned with ecstasy as Zack stroked her harder; they were almost there, and so was she.

All she felt was Zack inside of her, nothing else existed; she screamed with a wanting, a want for it to never end. There was nothing left of her body for anyone but Zack. Her eyes lusted for them, her ears adored them, her mouth yearn for them, but her pussy craved them. Kelly whimpered in a voice Zack had never heard before…she cradled Zack's face and plunged her tongue into their warm, sweet mouth.

Zack pressed Kelly against the wall, using it as support as they stroked her faster. Their body collided with her pelvis, creating a rhythmic pounding sensation. Zack growled as they tried to suppress their moans. Every lick, every kiss, and every stroke caused an electric surge—a tiny, sharp, painful, but pleasing flash through their bodies. Zack peered into Kelly's blue eyes, such purity, the innocents in her moans. It was as if she craved the intensity that Zack's inner rage provided, a dangerous element that seemed to fuel their connection. Both of them were on the verge of climax. They locked eyes, panting heavily, and then reached their peak together. Even after the climax, they stayed engrossed in one other, sharing a passionate kiss.

Zack let Kelly down, and they adjusted their clothing. They allowed their emotions to settle down.

"You asked me to give you time. What for Kelly?" Zack asked breathless.

"My brother, something isn't right. I don't think he did it." "Kelly, he just confessed and there's an eyewitness who saw your brother do it."

"Please, just trust me, Zack. I'm asking you to trust me. Do you trust me?" Kelly asked desperately.

Zack studied Kelly's eyes; they were begging them to trust her. They knew Kelly wouldn't ask if there wasn't a good reason. "Yes," Zack answered. Kelly smiled, happy to have Zack's trust.

"Kelly!" Mrs. Hamilton yelled as she and Mr. Hamilton rounded the corner.

"Get away from my daughter," Mr. Hamilton yelled.

"Daddy, don't you speak to Zack that way."

"Kelly, I will drag you out of here kicking and screaming."

"No one is going to lay a hand on her," Zack interjected. "This doesn't concern you," Mr. Hamilton said.

"Yes, it does," Kelly screamed, standing in front of Zack, shielding them from her parents.

"I love Zack. Do you hear me? We are in love and there's nothing you can do about it."

"You've corrupted my daughter. This isn't her talking," Mr. Hamilton told Zack.

"Yes, it is daddy, for the first time. This is the person who's been screaming to come out. The girl you tried to keep hidden is tired of being locked up. I finally let her out, and it feels amazing. I owe that to Zack. So, don't you dare speak to them that way." Kelly felt empowered and ready to take on her parents for Zack. She would defend their love till the death.

"Enough of this. Kelly let's go."

"No, Mom."

Mr. Hamilton looked at Zack and pleaded, "If you truly love my daughter. You would tell her to get in the car and come home. We can discuss this matter tomorrow." Zack took a moment to reflect before turning to Kelly and grasping her hands in theirs.

"Kelly, he's right..."

"No, don't listen to them, Zack. You can't trust them," she warned Zack.

"Kelly, go with your folks tonight, and tomorrow we'll go to the hop or go watch a flick. How does that sound?"

"Zack, you can't trust them, please," Kelly begged.

"It's going to be okay. I'll see you tomorrow."

"You promise, Zack? I need to see you," Kelly sobbed as she stared desperately into Zack's consoling eyes. Zack cupped her face with both hands.

"Yes, baby, I promise. Nothing in this world and everything in it could ever keep me from you. Remember that," Zack stated lovingly. Kelly beamed with adoration after hearing Zack declare those words.

"I love you, Zack."

"I love you, Kelly."

They hugged tightly; Kelly stared into Zack's eyes, as she slowly let go of their hand. Zack watched as she walked to her parents.

"Kelly!" Zack yelled.

Kelly spun around...

"If I asked you to marry me. What would you say?" Kelly's cheeks dimpled into a wide smile, and she hid her face in her hands as she gushed, then placed her palms over her heart.

"I do," she said enthusiastically, kissing her hand and blowing it to Zack. Zack was beaming with affection. They felt relieved watching Kelly walk away with a smile.

* * *

SANDY WAS JUST WALKING IN THE DOOR WHEN HER phone began to ring. She rushed to answer the call hoping it was Zack. "Zack?" she said gleefully but her countenance quickly turned to terror once she heard Rickey's ominous southern voice. "Hello, miss Sandy, I sure do miss you. Your heart still belongs to me. I'll see you real soon," Rickey said eerily.

Sandy slammed the phone down, terrified. Her body trembled with fear as she backed up into the corner and sank down the wall, knees to her chest, encircling herself in her arms.

CHAPTER 15

A sea of gang jackets and teen smoking; greasy hair and colorful Cadillacs; lesbians and gay boys displaying affection just another day at Queerville High School.

A substitute teacher was lecturing the class and writing on the board, but no one was paying much attention. Val was seeking to get Maria's attention.

"Maria. Hey, Maria."

Maria turned and looked at Val who was sitting right across from her. "What, Val?" Maria sighed annoyed.

"When are you going to let me take you out?"

"Never. I don't date the help."

Val was perplexed, having just finished playing backseat bingo with Maria, who was now suffering from selective memory.

"I'm second in line to the Red Dragons."

"And I run my own gang."

"But when you got with Zack, they didn't have a gang," Val reminded Maria.

"Yeah, but it's, Zack. They don't need a gang."

Val sucked her teeth.

Freddie and Lisa leaned in to join the banter.

"We got those O Town squares really good," Freddie snickered. "I heard they had to repaint the walls," Lisa said. "Principal Skinner had to call in a plumber," Val added. "They're still cleaning up poop."

They all shared a good laugh.

Suddenly, there was an explosion outside. They scrambled to their feet and peered out the window to see Freddie's ride in flames.

"My RIDE!!" Freddie shouted, mortified.
Freddie, Val, Maria and Lisa raced outside.

Freddie ran as fast as he could to his flaming ride. He wailed and put his hands on his head, puzzled. When he turned around, he noticed Ronnie and his goons giggling.

"Hey, it was those O Town punks," Val blurted. They sprinted in their direction, but they cowardly hopped into their ride, flipping birds while laughing and speeding off.

"This isn't over SQUARES!" Freddie shouted angrily.

O Town, USA

As the day continued, Dawn began to regret signing up for the school paper. She sat exhausted in the school library at a round table covered in books, researching the town's history for her first article. She was intensely taking notes when she came across something alarming in one of the books. "What?" In shock, she muttered to herself. Dawn gathered all her books and hurried out.

* * *

337

Rose sat in her biology class, intensely gawking at the new guy. She ditched her usual colorful attire for something a little more conservative today. The teacher was placing the students in pairs to complete today's assignment. "Rose, you can partner with James." The teacher pointed to the new guy. Rose's face brightened up as she discovered James was the new guy she'd been smitten with. Rose wasted no time and hurried to sit with James. "Hello, Rose, I'm sure glad I got partnered with you."

"Oh, geez James, I didn't think you noticed me," Rose said, turning cherry red. "Yeah, kind of hard not to with you staring in all." "Oh, James, did I make you feel uncomfortable?"

"No, I just figured you were shy overall, being such a keen conservative girl like yourself." Rose chuckled at first but then replied sarcastically, "Yes, that's exactly it. I'm such a devout Christian conservative whose nuts for Jesus." Rose fought to keep a straight face.

"I knew it," James exclaimed excitedly.

ZACK ARRIVED AT THE HAMILTON'S TO SEE KELLY. They rang the doorbell, ecstatic to soon see her. Mr. Hamilton answered the door, unprepared to see Zack standing there. "Zack, you're here," Mr. Hamilton muttered. "I'm here to check on Kelly and make sure she's alright."

"That's not possible at the moment."

"Why not? Just go get her."

"I can't just go get her..."

Zack grew angry at Mr. Hamilton's attempt to keep them from Kelly. Zack shouted into the house, pushing Mr. Hamilton out of the way and calling Kelly's name throughout the house.

"Excuse me," Mr. Hamilton was taken aback by Zack's intrusion. Zack ran upstairs searching every room.

"Kelly, baby, where are you?... Where's her room?"

Zack entered Kelly's room, and to their amazement, everything was gone. The drawers were empty, in the closets were empty hangers, and the sheets were removed from the bed.

Zack was stumped.

"I was trying to tell you it's not possible because she's gone." "Where is she?" Zack asked.

"She left town with her mother."

"Kelly would never leave town without telling me," Zack reassured Mr. Hamilton.

"You don't know my daughter as well as you think you do."

"I know Kelly better than you could possibly imagine. This isn't our first lifetime together."

"She was forbidden to do so. Her mother took her to her aunts. Where she will remain until she graduates. She will thereafter attend college."

"Tell me where she is!" Zack shouted angrily.

"Your love affair with my daughter is over," Mr. Hamilton drew closer to peer into Zack's eyes and murmured, "You will never see her again. She'll be better off without you."

Zack felt hurt; their blood was boiling, and they wanted to strike Mr. Hamilton. But Zack respected the fact that he was Kelly's father. Zack stormed out, refusing to believe anything Mr. Hamilton had just said.

They set out to find Kelly on their own.

* * *

Freddie, Lisa, Val, Robin, and Maria were having a heated discussion over burgers and fries at the diner. "We got to hit those O Town Squares back and hard," Freddie scoffed. "Forget Ronnie. What are we going to do about this Max thing?" Maria asked.

"Yeah, I can't believe it was Max. Why would he kill Anthony?" Robin added. "I knew Kelly was trouble. I tried to warn Zack," Lisa sighed. "You weren't the only one. So did I," Maria added.

"Zack isn't going to listen to anything concerning Kelly," Freddie stated. "I say we ban those squares from coming here."

"Zack is never going to let that happen."

"Who says Zack needs to know," Val blurted out.

"Look, Zack chose Kelly over us. It's time we started protecting Queerville. That's what Anthony would have wanted." Lisa felt portrayed. "I know just how to stick it to those squares." Val grinned.

Zack charged into O Town High where Dawn spotted them in the corridor. Dawn was surprised to see Zack at her school since Kelly had been suspended. "Hey, Zack!" Dawn shouted. Zack turned and looked at Dawn, she could tell Zack didn't recognize her. "I'm Kelly's best friend, Dawn." "Have you seen her? Is she here?" Zack inquired frantically. "No, Kelly hasn't been to school," Dawn replied. Zack grew frustrated.

"Is everything alright?" Dawn asked.

"Her father sent her away," Zack stated.

Dawn was shocked to learn that Kelly's father had sent her away so abruptly.

"What? He did? What a turd. She didn't say goodbye to you?" Zack shook their head; no. Dawn could see the hurt in Zack's face.

"Well, that's not right. I know Kelly, and she's just keen on you. There's no way she'd ever leave without saying goodbye to you." Dawn was concerned, and she was correct, leaving Zack to contemplate.

* * *

Johnnie had just finished telling Mary Sue about his affair with Sandy. They both sat in silence, dazed. Mary Sue turned to look at Johnnie, whose face was still bruised from his altercation with Zack.

"Look at what they did to you Johnnie. Those people prey on those weak in faith. We just need to get you to church and wash your sin away."

"Mary Sue, I still have those desires."

"You can't give in to the flesh. You must strengthen the spirit." Mary Sue took her Bible, and they got down on their knees, bowed their heads, and clasped hands.

"Heavenly Father. We ask that you remove this sin from Johnnie's mind. Make him pure again. Cleanse his body of this disgusting disease. We come to you now to pray away Johnnie's twisted attraction and return him as you meant for him, Amen." Mary Sue turned and faced Johnnie. "Now, you must tell your mother. She will help you reset." Johnnie nodded in agreement.

ROSE AND JAMES WERE CHATTING AT HER LOCKER. In an attempt to swoon James, Rose flicked her hair and toyed with her lips. But James appeared oblivious to all of Rose's desperate advances. "Class was really great. I love biology. What did you think of it?" James asked.

"Well, I've had quite a few lessons in, biology lately. I'm feeling more like a chemistry girl," Rose retorted.

"This school is really rad. What about that principal Skinner she's awesome."

"Yeah, she would make a wonderful warden," Rose sneered, causing James to chuckle and say, "You're such a funny girl, Rose." "I'm glad you think so, James," Rose replied.

"Well, Rose, I'm off to pray." James walked off with a smile. Leaving Rose standing alone, annoyed. She was losing tolerance with James' nonchalant demeanor.

———————————

 Johnnie had just confided to his mother his desire for same-sex attraction. Mrs. Baker sat in an uneasy silence, clutching her pearls. She appeared very frigid and distant. "Much like you, I was seduced into sin... by all sorts of Godless people. I knew in my heart I had forsaken Jesus for Satan. I won't let him have you. We must fight for your soul," Mrs. Baker said as she cast an unsettling glance at Johnnie.

* * *

Dawn arrived at Town Hall to investigate further into a bizarre story she believed she'd just uncovered. She cheerfully approached the main desk. "Hello, I'm a student at O Town High, and I'm doing an article about the history of our town. I would like to see the city archives."

Dawn received all the necessary documentation from the clerk. She was meticulously checking over school registrations and deed ownerships. She seemed perplexed. She returned to the front desk for more assistance. "Is it possible for me to see Queerville's archives as well?" She began comparing O Town archives with Queerville archives and discovered something; her eyes grew big. It was a photo of Freddie in an old O Town yearbook. "Freddie?" she said baffled. Dawn glanced up at the clock – she gathered her belongings and hurried out.

THE BAKERS WERE HAVING AN INTENSE ARGUMENT. Mrs. Baker was at war with Mr. Baker. "How long have you been preaching this garbage to our son!?" Mr. Baker shouted. "Garbage? His soul is in damnation we must save him. I did it once we can do it again." "How? You tell me how and I will do it. But there must be a better way," Mr. Baker pleaded. "This is the only way."

Johnnie peeked through the crack in the kitchen door. He observed his father seated in the kitchen, embraced by his mother. She lifted his head up to meet her gaze. "I promise you; you don't want to get in my way." Johnnie heard a vehicle approaching and walked to the window. He was taken aback when he saw Mr. Booker and Pastor Peter enter the house. Mrs. Baker welcomed them. It was unequivocally conspiratorial, and it had everything to do with Johnnie. He crept to the landing to watch them, careful not to be spotted.

O Town, USA

The prep valley had all the girls in their pastel colors, poodle skirts, and sweaters, and the guys in their white, short-sleeve button-up shirts and letterman sweaters. Rose and Dawn performed their cheer routine. As usual, Ronnie and his goons harassed the nerds. Principal Skinner delivered warnings and enforced her rigorous dress code. A watered down 50's track played out the speaker. It seemed more like a baptism than a prep rally. Principal Skinner took the stage.

"Thank you all for coming out to support our football team and their upcoming game against those Bronxville greasers…" the teens booed.

"…We're going to kick those filthy grease heads butt. Slap them with the hand of the lord and rip those leather jackets clean off," the crowd roared.

Suddenly, Val sped through the gates with Freddie, Lisa and Maria in her red convertible. Ronnie took notice. "Look, it's those Queerville freaks. What are they doing here?"

Val raced towards Ronnie before slamming on the brakes. They climbed out the ride. "You must've made a wrong turn. The end of the rainbow is that way," Ronnie scoffed, pointing east. "You're always on repeat, never saying anything original," Freddie sneered.

"Look, you said you want to race, so I'm here to see what you've got?" Val interjected.

Ronnie laughed. "You? You're not the one to beat. I want to race the champ. Where is Zack?"

They all laughed.

"You don't get to Zack without racing me first."

"I call bullshit," Ronnie responded.

"Aye, you want a knuckle sandwich?" Lisa asked.

"Listen, broad…" Ronnie moved forward to get in Lisa's face, but Robin stepped in front of him.

"If I was you, I wouldn't finish that sentence," Robin growled. Ronnie looked Robin in the eyes; he could feel the violence in her gaze. He took a step backward.

"It's true. So, in order to race Zack, you must first defeat Val." Maria chimed in. Ronnie stared lasciviously at Maria and smirked. "Ok, on one condition." Ronnie winked at Maria.

Paradise Road River Basin

Val's '53 red Ford convertible and Ronnie's '55 sea mist green Chevy were waiting side by side, their front wheels resting on a weather-beaten starting line. The sky was getting lighter as the radio played, *Green Onions.* There were about six to eight other cars parked off the road to watch the race.

Everything was quiet now, only the crickets ignoring the solemnity of the scene, and still singing. Freddie jumped out of Val's car. Val handed him a flashlight, and he took a position in front of the two cars. Val looked over and spotted Maria on the passenger side of Ronnie's car.

"Hey Maria, what in the hell are you doing in there? Is she gonna ride with you?" Val was concerned for Maria's safety.

"Mind your own business, Val. How many times do I have to tell you? I'm not your girl." Maria was aiming to make Val envious.

"Yeah, she's with me. She's done playing with pancakes, she wants the sausage now," Ronnie sneered.

"Is everybody ready?" Freddie shouted.

Val settled back in the driver's seat and positioned her hand on the gearshift. Both drivers started revving their engines, and tension was building. Freddie looked nervous; the engines began to roar, and his hands on the flashlights shook, but he managed to switch them on. Freddie waved both flashlights in the air. "Get ready," he held the flashlights up…"Get set," he dropped his arms as he screamed… "GO!"

Both cars sped off the line, their tires burning and screeching. As they passed, Freddie had his hands over his head and coughed in a cloud of smoke. Out on the strip, as they hit third gear, the cars were practically neck and neck. Maria looked scared to death.

"Let me out!" Maria shouted. Ronnie refused to stop and let her out.

Ronnie looked insane as he tromped it. Val hit fourth at about eighty-five. Ronnie did likewise but started to fishtail. Maria closed her eyes, almost crying. Ronnie regained control nervously. Ronnie engine was winding out incredibly and he began to get the edge on Val. The cars rocket through the dawn light along the flashing white line until suddenly Ronnie's car blew a tire, his front wheel slipped off and the car hit an irrigation ditch and began flipping over wildly in a horrifying cloud of dust and smoke.

Val saw the Chevy leaving the road and screamed to a halt, swimming through an unbelievable U-turn and high tailing it back to the crash site. She was out of the car like a bullet, running across the dirty cloddy field.

Ronnie's car was beginning to burn in the engine compartment and Val panicked. Meanwhile, the spectators arrived, including Freddie, who jumped from Lisa's ride and ran across the field. Freddie and Val arrived at the fire at approximately the same time. They came to a standstill as the flames were getting higher and burning up into the trees. Val looked around furiously—she spotted Ronnie and went after him.

"You stupid son of a bitch, she was in that car! Why did you have to drive like that?"

Val took a couple of swings at Ronnie, and finally managed to take him down. They both got up and looked at the flaming wreckage. Freddie moved around the side, crouching, trying to see past the flames.

Suddenly, he stood up and motioned for Val to come over. They both circled the wreck. Around behind the flaming car, Maria stood in a state of shock, watching the car go up in smoke. She saw Ronnie and went for him, screaming and beating him with her fist.

"I said, Let me out—you lousy, square jerk! You could have killed me—what's wrong with you? You clubfoot."

She beat at his chest, crying hysterically. Val ran over and grabbed her, pulling her away. She fought with Val, too, not knowing what was going on.

"No, no, no. Please, don't come near me. No, please. I think I'm going to be sick," Maria said.

Standing in the early light, Val held her. Maria threw her arms around Val as the crowd developed along the irrigation ditch to watch the flaming car.

Freddie, Val, Lisa, Maria, and Robin sat at a booth in the diner after a long and challenging night; they appeared a little worn out and aloof. Zack walked in and approached the table.

"Hey, have you guys seen Kelly today?" Zack asked with a worried look.

"Nope," said Freddie.

"Nope," Maria replied.

"No, Zack she hasn't come in," Val added.

There was an awkward silence.

"I don't think it would be a good idea for her to show her face around here again," Lisa muttered.

"What?" Zack asked, agitated.

Lisa refused to repeat herself. Zack noticed their demeanor.

"Anyone else have something they want to say? Anthony was my brother. I'm the only one who gets to decide who pays for his death."

The gang hung their heads like an embarrassed disobedient kid. "Go burn rubber, all of you!" Zack shouted. They got up and hit the streets; Maria stayed behind, with Zack.

"You do understand why they're mad, right?" Maria asked but Zack didn't respond.

"You knew. There's no way; you didn't know. You chose her over us. Over your own brother."

"You have no idea what you're talking about. Yes, I knew; Kelly came to me and told me her brother confessed. Knowing what I would do to him, she still told me. She betrayed her own brother for me. All she asked was that I give her time. She thought something was off and that maybe there was more to his story, so I did," Zack explained and took a seat.

"So, Kelly told you?" Maria said baffled.

"And she's paying the price right now. Her parents sent her away." Maria could hear the hurt in Zack's voice. Even though they were no longer together, she still cared deeply for Zack and never wanted to see them in pain. "Are you okay?"

"No, I feel like I'm losing it. None of this makes any sense. Max, Kelly, her parents. She told me not to trust them. I just let her go with them." Zack was crushed.

Maria took Zack's hand in hers.

Val stood outside the diner, taking in the scene. They were growing deeply attached to Maria. But Maria's

heart was with Zack, and Val was well aware of that.
"Do you know where they sent her?"
"No, they won't tell me."
"You could go to the jail and ask her brother."
"If I see Max, I might kill him."
"The town would throw you a parade," Maria sighed.

"Nothing happens to Max until I say so. Make sure
everyone else knows that too," Zack said sternly.

Patty came to take their order. "Hey, guys, sorry for
the wait. We're a little short on staff. What can I get for
you?" "Patty, where is Sandy?" Zack asked.

"I don't know. She didn't come in today. No one has
heard from her," Patty replied, leading Zack to feel concerned.

ZACK USED THEIR KEY TO ENTER SANDY'S HOUSE.
The place was pitch black; Zack walked softly through
the apartment. You could hear their footsteps squeak-
ing. Suddenly, there was a bang! A muzzle flashed, and
Zack collapsed on the ground. "Oh my god, Zack. Are
you okay?" "Yeah, lucky for me you're a lousy shot."

"Well, it's dark in here." Sandy helped Zack up off the
floor. "Why are all the lights off?" "Zack, I'm so sorry. I
could've killed you." Sandy hugged Zack tightly.

"I'm okay. Why are you walking around your pad
with a gun?" "I thought you were Rickey," Sandy
sobbed. "Rickey? Sandy, Rickey is in jail." Zack assured
her. "Then how did he call me?" Zack looked baffled.

"What? Rickey called you?" "Yes, late last night."

Sandy was visibly shaken up; the man of her night-
mares had escaped from prison and was out to get her.
She resembled the frightened little girl from six
months ago. She didn't want to face Rickey ever again.

CHAPTER 16

Johnnie was staring at himself in the mirror with his shirt off; he didn't recognize the person looking back. He washed his face, patted it dry, and looked intently at his reflection in the mirror. His bruises from Zack's brutal attack were hardly visible. He felt stinging aches in his head, similar to a nasty headache; violent visions flashed across his mind without warning. He clenched his teeth and held his head till they subsided before washing his face once again.

Mrs. Baker knocked on the door. "Johnnie, we need to head out now." Johnnie patted his face dry. "Ok, Mom, I'll be right out." He hung up the washcloth and put on his shirt, covering up the mysterious lashes on his back.

ZACK AND SANDY SPENT THE WHOLE NIGHT UP TALKING about Kelly's parents sending her way. "Oh, Zack, I know this must be tearing you up inside right now." Sandy was empathetic. "It is, but they underestimate Kelly. She's resilient, and she's smart. She'll find a way to get back to me; I know it." Zack was optimistic.

"I certainly hope so, Zack, for your sake." Sandy appeared worried for Zack.

O Town, USA

Rose was putting her books in her locker when her crush, James, approached her. "Hello, Rose," he said while flashing his huge Pepsodent smile. *This guy is a dreamboat.* She thought to herself.

"Well, hello, James. Are you off to pray right now?" Rose said with a fake huge smile.

"No, Rose, don't be silly. What are your plans for after school?"

"I'm pretty much free." "I heard of a place where we might find some fun," James said with a huge smile on his face.

"Really, you found fun?" Rose was being sarcastically witty.

"Yeah, a place called Lover's Lane. Have you ever been?" Rose's eyes grew big, and she slammed her locker shut.

"No, I can't say that I have. But if fun is there, I want to go get some."

"Oh, Rose, I'm glad you said yes. I just have to get my Bible from my locker. Then we can take off."

Rose rolled her eyes.

Queerville, USA

Freddie was at the diner, enjoying himself a big breakfast when Dawn came barging over. "Hello, Freddie, nice yearbook photo," Dawn said as she tossed the O Town yearbook on the table with Freddie's photo circled. Freddie looked mortified. He snatched her arm and forced her into the booth. "Would you keep your mouth closed. How did you find out?" Freddie whispered.

"I'm the new reporter for the school paper."

"You guys have your own paper? Gee Whiz you guys are squares. Well, what's it to you?"

"My first piece is on the history of O Town. And I was rather shocked to learn how many students had previously attended Queerville before abruptly becoming O Town's smartest and brightest. But this one specific boy, who was a freshman at O Town one year, and was leading the Scorpions by his senior year." Dawn grinned; with her arms crossed, she gave Freddie the *I got you* expression.

"You didn't get left behind twice Freddie. You missed a whole year of school. Why?" Dawn was inquisitive.

Freddie rolled his eyes irritated.

"How much do you want to keep your mouth closed?" Freddie asked with clenched teeth.

"Oh, I don't want your money. I need your help."

THE SHERIFF WAS LEADING THE MAN HUNT FOR RICKEY. The officers had never experienced anything like this before. They were completely overwhelmed and unprepared for the situation.

"Rickey Doe was awaiting trial for a slew of heinous killings he committed across the Midwest. He was scheduled to be transferred to a state facility for his trial date. Somehow, he managed to escape during the protest last night."

The sheriff held up a photo of Rickey.

"We have an escaped prisoner on the loose. Don't let this pretty boy face fool you. This man is pure evil he will not hesitate to kill you."

"We'll be assigning units to the Queerville diner; that's where we suspect he's headed," Detective Hobbs added.

The officers mumbled their disgust. They had an issue with safeguarding the very people they loathed.

The sheriff took note of the frowns, rolled eyes, and harsh stares.

"I see that some of you find that objectionable. How you feel about the residents of Queerville is irrelevant. They still need our protection. And we have a duty to protect and serve ALL people. Now, if you still have an issue, you can hand in your badges and go work as a milkman," the sheriff spoke sternly. The room stood silent.

MAX WAS SLEEPING IN HIS CELL, HAVING A NIGHTMARE about Anthony's murder, which felt more like a flashback. Everything was a bit hazy. He could see himself conversing with someone, but it wasn't Anthony. He could hear voices but couldn't understand them. Then there was a skirmish with two men fighting, but it wasn't him. He was watching, staring up at the commotion, when three gunshots rang, and Anthony's body plummeted to Max's feet. Max awakened in a cold sweat, his breathing erratic.

ZACK AND SANDY FINISHED UP WITH THEIR BREAKFAST. Zack cast Sandy a long, concerned look. "Sandy, why didn't you tell me Johnnie was hurting you?"

"It wasn't like that, Zack. It only happened once, and I ended it immediately," Sandy said defensively.

"And your wrist? You still want to tell me you fell on it." "Okay, the wrist thing was in the middle of a heated argument," Sandy said, completely in denial.

"Just stop it, Sandy. You're in denial," Zack shouted, getting up to kneel in front of Sandy.

"I'm not in denial," Sandy insisted. Zack refused to back down and looked deeper into Sandy's eyes searching for a trace of truth before asking her again, "Has he been putting his hands on you this entire time?"

"No, Zack. You know I wouldn't stay with a man who puts his hands on me," Sandy's eyes welled up with tears, and her voice cracked. She grew emotional. Sandy had endured domestic abuse for most of her adult life. She vowed never to let a man put his hands on her ever again. She broke down.

"I don't know why I keep attracting these abusive men," she sobbed as Zack hugged her.

"It's not your fault. You have a beautiful soul and sometimes that can attract the ugliest of people. Certain people live in a world of darkness, and any indications of light can be blinding. It's not you they're fighting, but their own demons. None of this is your fault," Zack reassured her.

———————————

A wide swath of blue sky over the open road. The only sound was the distant American flag being blown by the wind. A car pulled up on the graveled asphalt that led up to a large facility, with a cross on a spire atop a steeple. The initials P.G.A. were inscribed above the door.

Gray-blue carpet covered a huge section of the floor. Walls that were white and unadorned. A few empty, simple chairs flanked one side of the wall. Secured doors that led to unknown rooms. It had the impression of a juvenile detention center of some kind.

Through the glass of the aluminum-framed doors, Johnnie and Mrs. Baker approached uncertainly, then entered. Johnnie's white shirt was tucked into a pair of brand-new khakis with no belt. On his feet were rubber-soled black shoes. "Are you checking in today?" Aaron asked without looking up. His eyes were glued to his Seventeen magazine.

Aaron was a young man with an unusual haircut. He placed a clipboard on the reception ledge for them to sign in, his eyes still glued to his magazine. Mrs. Baker removed her sunglasses and cleared her throat in an attempt to catch Aaron's attention. Aaron looked up and immediately recognized Mrs. Baker; he hurriedly tossed the magazine.

"Mrs. Baker, sorry, I didn't realize it was you. Are you here for worship or..."

"Worship. My Johnnie boy here needs to hear some testimony."

"Okay, well, right this way, Mrs. Baker, Johnnie." Aaron escorted them through the secure doors.

ZACK WAS COMPLAINING TO SANDY ABOUT NOT BEING able to find Kelly. Zack was desperate to find her but had no idea where to start their search. "Have you checked with her friends?" Sandy asked Zack.

"Yeah, they haven't seen her either."

"What are you going to do?"

"Check every motel from here to the border. If they're driving, they're going to need to stop and rest."

"Are you sure you want to do that? It's a scary place outside of Queerville."

"I know. That's why I need to get to her, and I want you to come with me."

"What? Zack, I..." Sandy was hesitant.

"Sandy, I'm not leaving you here alone while Rickey is on the loose. I won't be able to look for Kelly if I'm worried about you. Please come with me and help me find her," Zack pleaded. Sandy gave Zack a sympathetic look and asked, "When do you want to leave?"

Lover's Lane

Rose sat like a church girl, her shirt button to the top, sweater button tight, stiff in the passenger side of James car.

"You know, Rose, this place is not what I thought it was. I guess kids love coming up here for the view."

Rose looked at James and gave him some dopey countenance. "Oh, gee, James I wouldn't know. I've never been here before. I'm usually home reading my Bible and holding my crucifix," Rose sneered, she was keeping up this facade effortlessly.

"You're a good girl Rose. I was so shocked to hear you weren't going steady with anyone."

"We'll James I just don't want to rush it. You don't want to make a mistake with something that important." James agreed before admiring the view.

"It sure is pretty."

"Oh yeah... gorgeous." Rose said as she made goggle eyes at James.

"To be honest Rose. I didn't think you'd want to come here until we'd been going steady for a little while."

"Well, James, we can just pretend to have been going steady for a while and get to the more serious part of our relationship."

"Rose, how would we do that?"

"I can show you how." Rose was more than eager. She leaned back a little more, draping her arm across the top of the seat. Her tits pointed toward the sky. Rose took his hand.

"See, we're already holding hands."

"You're a funny girl, Rose."

James took out his pin.

"Rose, would you like to wear my pin?"

"Oh, gee, James so soon? Yes, sure," Rose pretended to be surprised as James pinned her.

"Well, James, now that I'm wearing your pin. I have to thank you," Rose said seductively.

He looked over at her a little confused, then burst into his goony laughter.

"That's too kind Rose. You don't have to thank me." He was still guffawing when he looked over at Rose, who was licking her lips, and suddenly froze. His eyes widen.

ZACK & SANDY WERE CRUISING DOWN THE OPEN ROAD... Zack was dead set on tracking down Mrs. Hamilton and finding Kelly. Zack and Sandy scoured every motel within twenty miles, showing Kelly's photo around. A lot of '*Whites only*' motels; restricted Zack's search for Kelly. They checked gas stations and diners along the highways; no one had seen them. It was getting late; they hadn't eaten since brunch, and they were getting fatigued.

"Zack it's getting late. Let's find some food and call it a night." Sandy suggested.

"Just one more place."

"Zack, we did all we could for today. We need to eat and refuel." Sandy's earnest look persuaded them to agree. "Okay, you're right. Let's find some food." Zack sighed.

* * *

A Letterman's sweater hung over the door. The windshield was completely fogged. Rose's sweater was draped over the backseat. The car was rocking as Rose moans rang out across Lovers Lane.

They were clasped in a tense embrace, all arms and hair entwined. James pulled back for a moment, gasping for air. His face was covered with lipstick and there was a crazy look in his eye. He was stuck somewhere between passion and fear as he clung desperately to the steering wheel.

"Rose, what about saving ourselves until we get married?" James panted.

"Oh, James, we're not getting married. So, it's okay." "I don't think it works like that."

"It seems to be working just fine."

She glanced down at his crotch. He was stunned at the sight of his erection. She grabbed a handful of his hair. "Do you want to stop?" Rose asked breathily. James shook his head, no. She drew him down again and kissed him fiercely.

* * *

Zack and Sandy stepped inside a black-owned speakeasy lounge. Comfortable chairs angled side by side with petite tables between them. The place was swarming with gorgeous, melanated women dressed to the nines, but Sandy's beauty stood out among a crowd. Every fella's head swiveled to catch a glimpse of her as she walked in with Zack.

They took a table, and the hostess immediately greeted them and handed them menus. Zack was in no mood to eat and was still worried sick about Kelly. Sandy, on the other hand, was prepared to consume the entire menu.

"What are you getting?" Sandy asked with her eyes wide as she perused the menu.

"I'm not hungry."

"Zack, you need to eat something. You can't keep this search for Kelly up on an empty stomach. You'll be no use to her."

Zack grew frustrated.

"Fine, just order me something. I'm going to the restroom." Zack got up and took notice of all the men gawking at Sandy as the hostess came over and took Sandy's food and drink orders. The place was very intimate, with dim lighting, antique furniture, and there was a live band on stage performing a slow doo-wop tune.

A bold soul with a pop belly and crooked teeth felt compelled to approach Sandy. She spotted him coming from a mile away and was already annoyed.

"If I had a nickel for every time, I saw a woman as beautiful as you, I'd still only have five cents. What does it feel like to be the most gorgeous girl in the room?" He used his finest pick-up lines on her. Sandy flashed a phony grin and rolled her eyes, hoping the man would go away.

"What are you doing here with that wimp?" he scoffed, referring to Zack; a tactic that would never win Sandy over. She sat up straight and gave him a menacing stare.

"I can assure you, there isn't a drop of wimp in their entire bloodline. If you care to find out, keep talking."

Sandy stated firmly.

Her warning stunned the man. He huffed and walked away. She grinned as the waitress delivered their drinks, just as Zack returned to the table.

"I got you a gin so you could relax."

"Thanks." Zack picked up the glass and downed the gin in one long gulp. "Zack, they have a live band," Sandy exclaimed with a wide grin.

"No, Sandy," Zack said firmly.

"C'mon, Zack. I haven't heard you sing in ages," Sandy pleaded with Zack. Sandy was Zack's biggest fan; she loved dancing to Zack's electrifying voice. She was proud of them and encouraged them often to pursue a singing career. But Zack was in no mood to sing. Sandy pouted her lips and batted her eyes, which was usually enough to convince guys to do what she wanted, but Zack wasn't having it.

"Ugh, fine then," Sandy gave up, sank back into her chair, and scanned the room. She felt like a fish in a bowl, with all the men staring at her. She groaned and sipped her martini. Zack was amused by Sandy's ire.

"I hate it here," Sandy murmured.

"Oh, come on, you should be used to it by now."

"I assumed because we aren't in Queerville. I would-n't draw as much attention."

"There isn't a man within a hundred miles who wouldn't give his right arm to be with you, Sandy."

"Please, these men don't want to be with me. They all just want to fuck me."

The waitress eventually brought their food over. Sandy was about to dive in when a shadow cast over their table. "Sandy Myers, as I live and breathe, is that you?" Sandy couldn't believe her ears when she realized it was Cheryl, her archenemy. Zack instantly dropped their fork, knowing that things were about to get nasty. Cheryl was a very attractive woman; on the slimmer side, but she couldn't hold a candle to Sandy.

Sandy rolled her eyes and refused to acknowledge her presence. Cheryl greeted Zack with a warm smile.

"Hello, Zack, well aren't you just a dream boat. You should come and sit at my table. That's where all the good-looking, nice folks are," she snidely remarked.

Zack spat out their food at Cheryl's attempt to antagonize Sandy; that was just her first jab at Sandy.

"Thank you for the invite, Cheryl, but I have the best view in the house," Zack said winking at Sandy.

Sandy smiled at the compliment.

"Awe, you two are still besties, I see. You could never go without each other," Cheryl glanced at Sandy.

"I see you've gained a few pounds, Sandy. You won't find a man with all that weight."

"That's ironic considering I had two of your boyfriends at this same weight."

"Oh dear, those men would fuck anything. Besides, none of them were my first love."

Sandy was struggling desperately to keep her composure, but she didn't want Cheryl to see her sweat.

"I, on the other hand, prefer a strong, handsome man with alluring eyes." Cheryl sighed as she massaged Zack's arm and stared into their eyes.

That was the final straw. Sandy had reached her breaking point; she sprang up to confront her, but Zack stepped between the two.

"Cheryl, maybe you should go join your friends. I'm sure they miss you," Zack suggested.

"You are most likely correct. I do leave an impression. I'm sure my presence at the table is valued once more. Have a pleasant time, you two," Cheryl winked at Sandy and sashayed away.

Sandy sat back down in her seat, exasperated. Her leg twitched, her arms crossed, and she rocked in her chair. She was furious. Zack wanted to cheer her up, so they decided to hit the stage with the band.

"Okay, I'll do one song." Zack gave Sandy a sneaky grin, and her face brightened with a smile. She began clapping before Zack even took the stage.

Zack spoke with the band before picking up the guitar. They fiddled with the strings and adjusted the microphone. The spotlight shone on Zack as they played the initial key strings to *Mannish Boy by Muddy Waters*, and the band followed on drums and harmonica. The patrons immediately recognized the tune and flocked to the dance floor.

Sandy moved in front of the stage, swaying her hips to the beat of the drum, showing her support for Zack. The men were mesmerized watching her hands encircle her body, caressing her curvaceous figure. Cheryl envied Sandy as the men at her table gawked at her.

Zack and Sandy eventually enjoyed their meal following Zack's impromptu performance. Cheryl approached them to say her farewell, just as they were about to leave.

"Zack, are you two leaving so soon?"

"Yeah, we had a long day." Zack took a step forward, but Cheryl stood in Zack's path, blocking them from leaving. She licked her lips and stared at Zack seductively in a desperate attempt to flirt with them. She traced Zack's shoulder and arms with her finger. Sandy was growing increasingly irritated with each touch.

"Well, I must say that was one hell of a performance, Zack. You are so good with your hands. I'm curious to know how you handle other parts of the body."

"Bitch!"

Sandy yelled as she grabbed Cheryl by her hair and struck her in the face. Zack yanked Sandy away and they fled the scene.

Zack accelerated down the road while Sandy adjusted her clothing following her altercation with

Cheryl. The car ride was silent but not awkward. Sandy soon gathered herself and regained her composure. Zack chuckled as they glanced at her. Sandy looked at them, and they both burst out laughing.

"Now, that's the Sandy I remember. If you keep this up, I might have to re-appoint you as leader of the Lipsticks." Sandy grinned, amused by her own behavior.

* * *

James had a frozen smile on his face as he drove up to Rose's house. "Gee, Rose, tonight sure was fun."

"I bet it was for you," Rose said with a smirk.

"You're so different than the other girls."

"That's because God only created one Rose; the others are from my seeds."

"See, another joke. You're so funny. Can I see you tomorrow?"

"I have best friend duties tomorrow. Dawn has uncovered the aliens in area 51 or something of the sort. But I'll ring you when I'm free."

"Ok, Rose," James smiled excitedly.

Rose leaned over and gave James a kiss to remember, leaving him stunned. Rose winked at him as she exited the car. "Goodnight."

* * *

Zack and Sandy arrived back at her place. Sandy kicked off her shoes and dropped onto the couch.

"I'm exhausted," she sighed.

"Yeah, we covered a lot of ground today."

"Zack, I don't think you're going to find Kelly this way. Half the places we go to are for whites only, and the other half won't speak to us because we're queer. We're not getting anywhere. I think you need to go see Max." "I can't look at Max. I don't want to see him."

363

"I know Max confessed to killing Anthony, but I also know there's a reason why he's still alive."

Zack gave Sandy a questioning glance.

"Yeah, I catch on quick. Whatever the reason, you've allowed him to keep breathing and to voluntarily turn himself in. Remember that and go see him." Zack wasn't surprised that Sandy had figured it out; there was no one in Queerville who knew them better than she did.

The police lights blared in from outside, catching Sandy's attention. "I see my police protection is here. Zack, go home, get some rest, and go see Max in the morning, please." Sandy pleaded, giving Zack a concerned look.

"Alright fine. Are you sure you'll be, okay?" Zack asked. "Yes, Zack, I'll be fine. Ring me tomorrow." Zack kissed Sandy on the forehead. "Goodnight."

"Drive safe," Sandy responded.

* * *

The phone rang as Zack walked into their loft. They rushed to pick up the call. "Hello," Zack answered.

"Zack! Zack, you have to get me out of here!" Kelly shouted frantically.

"Kelly? What's happening?" Zack asked anxiously.

"Zack, please help me, Zack. ZACK!" Kelly sobbed.

"Kelly, where are you?" Zack felt helpless as they listened to Kelly's terrified cries, not knowing where she was. Zack overheard a scuffle.

"Zackkk!!!" Kelly screamed and the phone went dead. Zack immediately hung up and called the operator.

"Operator."

"Yeah, I was just disconnected from my last call. Could you please reconnect me?" Zack eagerly asked the operator.

After a brief moment the operator said, "I'm sorry it looks like that number was private." Zack hung up the phone and paced back and forth.

Zack's heart was racing; they were worried for Kelly. Kelly pleads reverberates in their mind.

Zack, help. Help me, Zack.

For the first time in Zack's life, they felt powerless. All their training and abilities were futile. The idea of Kelly somewhere cold and frightened; infuriated Zack; they would burn down the town just so Kelly might feel its warmth. Their love for her was endless. They would do anything to find Kelly and Zack knew exactly what they had to do.

CHAPTER 17

Zack sat uneasy in the visiting booth the next morning as an officer escorted Max in. Max seemed pleasantly surprised to see them waiting. He took a seat across from Zack.

"Zack, look I just want to say thank you…"

"Max, you turned yourself in because you saw how much your sister was suffering. For that, you have my respect. That's the one thing we have in common: we both love her. But make no mistake; that's as far as it goes. There is no world in which I will let you live," Zack promised Max.

"Why are you here then?"

"Kelly, called me last night. I don't know where your parents sent her. But she was scared, Max. I need to know where she is."

"My parents did what?" Max was perplexed; he was unaware that his parents had sent Kelly away, but he knew why, and that meant there could only be one place she could be.

"Wherever they've sent her, she's alone and terrified. Help me find her and bring her back, Max."

Max grew enraged and grasped his head as he experienced sudden, violent flashbacks out of nowhere. He became irate as his consciousness was invaded with horrific memories that he had attempted to forget; they all came pouring in, making him fearful and afraid. He began to act erratically.

"Max, where is she? Where's Kelly?" Zack inquired.

"They sent her to the camp. You have to get her out of there. You don't know what they do to you in that place!" Max said, clearly spooked. He began acting hostile, banging on the glass.

"Save her Zack!" Max shouted desperately.

"What camp? What camp, Max? Where is she?" Zack inquired frantically.

The guards came and dragged Max out of the room, with him screaming, "Please Zack! Save my sister. Get her out of there. ZACK, SAVE MY SISTER, PLEASSEEE!!!"

His voice echoed. Zack stood there, baffled. Their hands trembled, and their fear for Kelly intensified. They could only imagine the misery Kelly was going through if Max was so worried about her. Zack's heart ached; they had no way of finding Kelly.

* * *

KELLY WAS LOCKED IN A TINY DARK ROOM WITH Biblical artifacts adorning the walls. She was clad in a hospital gown. Her eyes were dark circles, as if she'd been awake all night and hadn't gotten much sleep. She was barefoot and furious, pounding on the door, insisting on being let out.

An older, frail, White woman opened the door; it was obvious she was the one in charge. Two male staff members dressed as orderlies joined her side.

"There is only one way out of here, Ms. Hamilton. We've already explained this to you," the woman said.

"Let me out of this place now," Kelly demanded.

"Ms. Hamilton, we are trying to save your soul."

367

"I demand to speak with my parents!" Kelly shouted.

"And your parents would love to speak with Kelly. Not this corrupted, sinful version of their daughter. Now you know what you must do. Resisting only makes it harder."

"Zack will find me," Kelly muttered with a smug grin.

The woman motioned for the male staffers to restrain her. Kelly resisted and fought back. "Zack will find me. Do you hear me? Zack will find me, and they're going to make you pay!" Kelly screamed as the staffers strapped her down. The woman gave Kelly a sedative, and she drifted to sleep. The woman turned to one of the staffers. "We need to find out who this Zack person is; they could be trouble," the woman murmured menacingly in the midst of an ominous silence.

DAWN WAS BACK AT TOWN HALL CONTINUING HER research into the history of O Town. She was going through the records, comparing the dates of families who had relocated to O Town. Strangely there were no dates going back further than 1945. Dawn compared the dates to the public facilities, which stretched back 100 years. She found it suspicious, and she started to get an eerie feeling...

THUMP! Rose crept up behind her startling her.

"Rose, jeez..."

"Why are you in this creepy place?" Rose asked.

"It's the town hall, Rose." Dawn replied.

"Why does the town need a hall?"

"Rose, look at this." Dawn showed Rose what she had discovered. "What is this?" Rose had no clue what any of it meant.

"No one in O Town has been here longer than ten years. In fact, I can't find any articles or documents about O Town dated before nineteen forty-five," Dawn said, puzzling Rose.

"What are you saying Dawn?" Rose gave Dawn a blank stare, "We don't exist?" in her best spooky voice as she pinched Dawn. "Ouch! Rose. Yes, we do exist," Dawn hissed. Rose gasped and murmured, "Invasion of the body snatchers." "Would you be serious for one second, Rose." "Well, Dawn, clearly, we are in O Town. We've lived here our entire lives. What are you trying to say?" Dawn gave Rose a cryptic glare.

"Ten years ago, Rose, O Town, and its residents did not exist." They looked at each other bewildered.

POLICE CARS PATROLLED OUTSIDE THE DINER ON HIGH alert and vigilant for Rickey. Inside the diner a police officer was present to keep a close eye on Sandy. His presence had Val and Lisa nervous. "Why is the fuzz in here cruising? I thought the diner was off-limits to pigs," Val said annoyed. "You didn't hear? Rickey escaped," Lisa informed Val.

"What? When did that psycho get away?" Val was stunned.

"During the protest. He jimmied a lock and jumped out of a window in the restroom."

"We should be out there looking for him."

"Zack wants us here to keep an eye on Sandy."

"The heat is here; she'll be fine. I say we go find this cat and give him a bruising."

"Oh, are you calling the shots now? Ice it!" Lisa was getting peeved by Val's rebellious behavior.

Sandy and Patty were at the counter looking on. "This whole thing must make you a nervous wreck." Patty empathized with Sandy. "I'm trying not to think about," Sandy said.

"Not to think about it? You have a killer out to get you. That should be all you're thinking about."

"I gave Rickey too much power over me the last time. I'm not doing that again," Sandy spoke boldly.

"Sandy don't be a fool. We're not talking about some psychotic ex here. This is the same man who tried to slaughter you in the middle of the street," Patty reminded Sandy.

"And I haven't forgotten that. But I will not allow him to make me live in fear." Sandy spoke confidently.

"I just don't want anything to happen to you, Sandy. I love you, girl." "I know Patty, thank you," Sandy gave Patty a hug.

DAWN AND ROSE PAID FREDDIE A SURPRISED VISIT AT his O Town home. Freddie opened the door and was stunned to see the girls. He rolled his eyes and sighed, "What are you two doing here?"

"Does your gang know that you live in O Town?" Rose sneered. Freddie narrowed his eyes at her before Dawn interjected, "Freddie, I have some more questions for you."

"Listen, Nancy Drew, I told you everything I'm going to tell you," Freddie said, attempting to close the door, but Dawn stopped him. "It's not about your double life in Queerville. Please, I think there's something bigger going on."

Freddie sighed then let them in and offered the girls a seat on the couch.

"What is this about?" he asked hurriedly.
Freddie's mother walked in, she had very distinctive features, no eyebrows, and fierce projecting eyes.

"I didn't know you had friends over," she remarked, pleased to see new faces.

"Mom, please go lay down," Freddie appeared embarrassed. Freddie's mom ignored him and welcomed the girls with a big hug. "It's always nice meeting some of Freddie's friends. He never has guests over."

"Nice to meet you," Rose replied.

"His grandmother will be out with some tea and cookies."

"Great, sounds yummy," Dawn responded.

"No, mom, please," Freddie pleaded with his mother. The teapot began to whistle from the kitchen.

"The tea is ready. Excuse me dears." Freddie's mom went into the kitchen.

"Girls, this is really not a good time."

"Freddie, I have to show you something."

"It will just take a second," Rose added. Freddie sighed then took a seat between Dawn and Rose. Dawn took out her research. Before she could show Freddie, her notes his 'grandmother' came out with tea and cookies.

"Oh, hey girls, would you like some tea and cookies?" The girls glanced up, puzzled yet amused.

The 'grandmother' was just Freddie's Mom in a different wig with glasses.

The girls looked at each other then back at Freddie's grandmother.

"Am I hallucinating or is that..." Rose whispered to Freddie. "It's the same person. My mother has DID, it's a dissociative identity disorder," Freddie sighed.

The girls didn't know what to do.

"Should we..." Dawn whispered to Freddie.

"Yes, just go along with it." Freddie suggested. Dawn smiled and took a cookie.

"Thank you." Dawn smirked.

"Yes, we would love some," Rose followed Dawn's lead, trying hard not to laugh. Freddie got up and helped his mother back to bed.

"Come on, grandma, let me put you back to bed." Dawn showed Freddie all her notes once he returned. "Why are you digging this up?" Freddie asked. "Because people need to know if something weird is happening in this town."

"Freddie, does any of this mean anything to you? What is going on? I have lived in O Town my whole life. I can't make sense of any of this." Rose asked.

"Are you certain you've lived in O Town your whole life? Do you have any proof? Have your parents ever shown you, your birth certificate?" Freddie was being cryptic.

"No. I'm afraid I can't say they have." Rose responded.

"Neither have mine."

They were dumbfounded; an eerie, mysterious feeling pervaded the room.

Freddie's mom, disguised as a man, burst in, speaking in a strong, masculine voice, startling them.

"Which one of these girls is yours, son? I bet it's that little red head," she grunted.

The girls erupted in laughter after being startled. Freddie leapt to his feet, humiliated, and walked his mom back to her bedroom. "It's time to go to bed."

ZACK TOLD SANDY ABOUT THEIR STRANGE VISIT WITH Max. "What? Where?" Sandy asked. "I don't know." Zack answered. Patty overheard the conversation and decided to chime in. "You have to go speak with him again and make him tell you where it is," Patty suggested. "Max was placed on suicide watch after his break- down. They're not letting anyone in to see him."

"What kind of camp is it? Is it for juveniles? Some kind of behavior facility?" Patty asked.

"I just know it's bad. She sounded so scared, begging me to help her. I let her go with her parents. She warned me not to trust them... she told me, and I just let her go with them," Zack was devastated. Sandy caressed their hand. "What are you going to do?" Sandy asked. "I don't know what to do. I don't even know where to look," Zack said, feeling helpless.

"I do," Freddie exclaimed loudly.

Zack spun around to see Freddie, Dawn and Rose. In some cheesy Charlie's Angels pose here to save the day. "I know where they sent Kelly. We're going to need the rest of the gangs. Sandy, can you grab us some milkshakes? We're going to need a pick-me-up."

Freddie captured everyone's attention while narrating his story as he stood in the middle of the diner. Zack, Sandy, Patty, Lisa, Val, Maria, and Robin were all attentively listening, as were Dawn and Rose.

"If I'm correct, Kelly was taken to the P.G.A. facility... It's a conversion camp," Freddie confessed.
Patty gasped. "Oh, dear god. That poor girl," Patty clutched her chest. "What's P.G.A.?" Sandy asked.

"It's an acronym for Pray Gay Away," Freddie revealed. "Oh God, no," Zack quavered.

"What are they doing to her in there?" Dawn asked but was afraid to know. "Those people will do anything and everything to break you and brainwash you. I witnessed people being tortured, beaten, and starved. The weak ones take their own lives to escape the torment," Freddie grew emotional.

"Why are they doing this? For what reason?" Rose asked, afraid for her friend. "To teach you that being Queer is a sin. A sin you must renounce and ask to be forgiven."

"And if you don't?" Zack asked.

"There's no if, Zack."

Zack became agitated as they imagined what Kelly was going through. Sandy caressed Zack back, calming them.

"Freddie, how do you know all of this?" Lisa asked.

"Because I was one of them. They beat me, tormented me, and tried to brainwash me. I saw teens come in looking just like us. But when they left, they looked like the poster child for O Town."

"So, you're saying these sick fucks are snatching teenagers and turning them into some kind of brainwashed squares?" Zack asked. "Wow, it's like invasion of the body snatchers," Val sighed, prompting Rose to point at them in agreement.

"That's my best friend in that place. We have to do something," Dawn said concerned.

"We are. We're going to break her out of there." Zack said as they leapt up and poured a drink from Charlotte's secret stash behind the counter. Sandy followed behind. "If we hit the road now, we should get there before night fall." Zack told Sandy.

"Zack, I'm not going with you."

"What? Sandy, I need you close…."

"Zack, no, I'll be a distraction. You need to be focused on Kelly, not worrying about me. I can't keep following you around everywhere, afraid of the big bad wolf."

"Sandy, I can't leave you here."

"I'll be fine. I need to do this on my own. I have enough police cars following my every move."

"No, Sandy, I don't trust…"

"Then trust me. I'm not living in fear any longer, and I'm not some damsel in distress."

Zack cast Sandy a worried look. Sandy cupped Zack's face with both hands before saying, "It's ok, Zack; you can't save everyone. Go get your girl."

Val observed the innocent embrace from afar.

Zack came over to regroup with the gang.

"Let's head out now before it gets too late." Rose and Dawn jumped up, but Freddie, Val, Lisa, Maria and Robin didn't budge.

"What's going on?" Zack inquired.

"Zack, there's no getting Kelly out of that place. The doors are locked, and the hallways are heavily guarded. There's nothing you can do. I'm sorry, I can't go back to that place. I can't." Freddie wept as he rushed out.

"Freddie!" Zack yelled after him.

Zack looked back at Val and Lisa. "And you two?"

"Zack, listen, I know that's your girl in all, but her brother killed Anthony. What happens to her has nothing to do with us," Lisa said bluntly.

"Nothing to do with us? Did you not just hear Freddie? They're only doing this to people like us. It was you and Val that first told me about the missing kids, remember?" Zack reminded Lisa who refused to make eye contact and didn't respond back.

"Are you speaking for all the gangs?" Zack asked.

"Yeah, they feel the same way," Maria interjected.

Val stood up and faced Zack. "We're not about to risk our lives for some square," Val stated harshly, prompting Zack to punch her in the mouth.

"We'll finish that when I get back," Zack muttered. Val held her bleeding lip.

Zack turned to face the room. "I want people at the school, the square, and the club. We made these gangs to protect the town, so how about you do just that," Zack demanded, then raced out with Dawn and Rose.

Sandy shook her head disappointed at the others. "You should all be ashamed of yourselves. Get out, all of you," Sandy said furious. "Sandy, we're here to protect you," Val remarked.

"I don't want or need disloyal flunkies protecting me. Now get out!" Sandy jeered. They walked out of the diner with their heads lowered.

MR. BAKER CAME TO SEE THE SHERIFF WITH SOME NEWS. "Mr. Baker, what can I do for you?" Mr. Baker placed a paper on the sheriff's desk. The sheriff picked it up and gave it a glance.

"Well, what do we have here?"

"That's all you need to… arrest my wife for the murder of Abigail Wright."

The sheriff was dumbfounded. They were still investigating Abigail's murder and Mrs. Baker wasn't even on their list of potential suspects. The sheriff skimmed over the small piece of paper; it was a receipt. He looked back up to Mr. Baker. "Well, have a seat," he said.

* * *

Rose was driving fast down a dusty road. Zack sat on the passenger side with Dawn in the rear, studying the map. "Ok, so what's the plan?" Rose asked.

"Yeah, I don't have one. I'm sorry I might've jumped the gun. I just want to get to her," Zack replied. Rose gave Zack a heartfelt glance. "No, I understand," Rose said sincerely. Dawn looked over the map.

"Okay, Freddie said it would be about twenty miles out through a forest sitting on top of a hill."

"That means they'll see us coming. We have to park away from the facility," Zack added.

"The only thing I see twenty miles out is a mountain range. However, there is no facility on the map," Dawn was puzzled.

"There wouldn't be. For this facility to exist, it must be privately owned," Zack stated.

"Which means?" Rose inquired.

"They're some powerful people involved. We really could've used some back up," Zack sighed.

THEY ARRIVED FROM A DISTANCE TO THE FACILITY. A massive white building with a church steeple ascended from the structure, soaring like a clock tower with a cone-like spire topped with a lone cross scraping the sky. "There it is."

"Creepy!" Rose got chills.

"Zack, what are you going to do?" Dawn asked.

"I have no clue. I'll figure something out," Zack replied. "Should we come to?" Rose was eager to help. She couldn't stomach knowing Kelly was in that horrible place. "No, I need to make sure she's in there first. You two find somewhere to hide the car, and I'll find you." "Ok, Zack, be careful," Rose pulled over and let Zack out.

Zack climbed up the mountain toward the facility. Through the glass of the aluminum-framed doors, Aaron spotted Zack approaching. Zack took a deep breath then entered.

"Hello, how can I help you?" Aaron asked.

"I'm here to check myself in," Zack stated.

"Are you experiencing same sex attraction and want to be cured?"

Zack appeared hesitant before mumbling, "Yes."

"You've come to the right place," Aaron said with a cryptic smile.

CHAPTER 18

Aaron led Zack on a tour of the facilities. As they turned
a corner Zack looked back and noticed another young
adult being led to the check-in area. They moved
through a door and under an awning toward a larger
room that seemed to be some sort of main auditorium.

Zack, wearing a name tag, found a seat and settled
into a semi-circle of chairs with ten other young adults
and a half dozen teens—a few from the costume bash,
three girls, the rest mostly boys. They all took out their
handbooks and recited the rules out loud, starting
with Thomas, an older, super conservative White male.

"Sobriety. No smoking. No alcohol, or drugs."
Zack looked around the room at all the historical religious paintings and other images. The Last Supper by
Dagnan-Bouveret, Jesus holding up a wine glass stood
out amongst the others.

Zack spotted Carmen, who was all of sixteen, yet she
appeared to be almost twenty something. Zack would-
n't have recognized her without the scar on her chin.
She got that from climbing a tree with Zack. Andrew,
17, was fidgety and freckled; read his section of the regulations, "Restrooms. Members must be supervised by
staff during restroom visits."

Larry, 20s, even under the crisp khaki and white uniform Zack could still tell he was a greaser: slick black

hair; pale complexion, and black boots. He was slight of frame, handsome and super smart.

"Sexual misconduct. No viewing of pornographic material..." Larry recited. His reading carried a thinly veiled cynicism that told Zack he did not believe in P.G.A. and did not want to be here.

"No masturbation. No physical contact with any members or non-members at any time," Larry continued.

Zack looked tight at the various faces as they listened to Sarah; the older, frail, white woman who was the coordinator and ruled P.G.A. with an iron fist. "I am using sexual sin and homosexuality to fill a God shaped void in my life..." Sarah sermonized.

"I am using sexual sin and homosexuality to fill a God shaped void in my life," the group repeated.

Zack looked around to see a dozen or more people that had entered and lined the back walls. Various men and women of all ages, some as young as twelve. A similar cross section to the seated group.

"But... I am not broken, and God loves me..." Sarah continued. They repeated.

"God does not love, lesbians, gays, bi people, transgender, queers and the retarded."

On the board was a circle with several words inside of it: Marriage, Children, family, support, caring. In an opposing circle is another list: Rape, child molestation, promiscuity, AIDS, loneliness, zero children. Sarah wrote heterosexual over the *Good/Life* circle, and *Homosexual* over the other.

It was time for the next exercise. Sarah set up the *Truth Chair*: a role-playing exercise. Two empty chairs faced each other. Carmon took one of the seats and waited with dread.

"Go Carmen. There he is in that chair..."

Zack watched Carmen be berated by Sarah to engage with her invisible father. Carmen gripped the side of her chair. Her wrists were scarred from previous suicide attempts.

"...staring right back at you," Sarah continued. Opposite her was literally an empty chair. Zack turned and noticed Mark, 18, Black, a hulking young man, a linebacker in the making with a baby face. He didn't want to be there either. He looked just as mortified as Zack did. Larry beside him, leaned back biting his nails.

"He's right there. Make use of your words. Spit them out with intent. Tell him how he led you to sin." Sarah continued to antagonize Carmen, who appeared to be emotionally depleted.

"I don't want to do this!" Carmen shouted.

"Okay, let's take a tea break," Sarah suggested.

During the tea break, Zack walked over to a shaken Carmen. She was so excited to see Zack that she almost jumped into their arms. But she didn't want to break the rules, so she stopped herself. "Oh my god, Zack. What are you doing here? Did your dad send you here?"

"No, I came in voluntary."

"Why on earth would you do that? This place is hell," Carmen was bemused.

"Is this everyone? Are there more teens somewhere?" Zack was anxious to find Kelly.

"Well, yeah, this place is a castle. There are about twenty kids on each floor."

"How do you find someone in this place?"

"They don't let newbies just roam around. You have to be a staffer to walk freely. They escort you everywhere even to the restrooms."

"I see," Zack's gaze flew around the room, searching for any entrance that might bring them to Kelly.

"You're looking for someone, aren't you? Here to break someone out? It's not going to happen. This place is locked up like Fort Knox. There's only one exit, and that's through the front door," Carmen elaborated. Zack was disappointed.

"Anything else I can help you with?"

Zack gave Carmen a sneaky grin.

"Yeah, there is."

Zack slipped out into the corridor and cautiously crept about, evading the staff. They made their way to the records room and used a tool to Jimmie the lock and gain access. They looked around frantically, searching the desk and file cabinets before discovering admission records, birth and death certificates, and other vital documentation. Zack seized the documents and stuffed them into their jeans.

Carmen approached the front entrance to flirt with Aaron, diverting his attention away from Zack, who was preparing to sneak by him and depart from the facility.

"Hey, Aaron, I bought you some tea and cookies," Carmen grinned. "Oh, that's so kind of you, Carmen. Thank you. But you know, you should not be strolling about by yourself. What happened to your escort?"

Carmen walked behind Aaron, forcing him to turn his back on the door. Allowing Zack to make a hasty escape.

* * *

In the car, Rose and Dawn were making every effort to remain warm. It was dark; there was not a star in the gloomy sky. They heard howling. Fearful, they stared out into the night, trying to pierce through the darkness to whatever was creating the sounds.

"Oh my, what is that?" Rose asked, spooked.

"I think it was a cat or some sort."

"That was no cat. It sounded more like a tiger."

"Nevertheless, it's a feline but tigers don't howl."

"Yeah, they moan while they chew on your bones."

Dawn glared at Rose. "Rose, stop trying to scare me."

"We're sitting in a car in the middle of nowhere in the dark, surrounded by some beast, waiting for one of us to die so that it may consume our dead carcasses. Why aren't you scared?"

"Rose! Just stop it. There's nothing to be afraid of, okay?" Dawn felt valiant.

Rose peered out the window, looking for any activity. Her eyes fought to see through the dim darkness. There was a moment of complete silence and calm. She could hear herself breathing.

Suddenly, BANG! The girls leaped and scrambled to the opposite side of the car, screaming.

"It's, Zack!" Rose hollered.

Rose hurried and opened the door. "Zack, are you okay?" Rose asked concerned.

"Yes. I stole some records. Maybe this can help you guys uncover what's going on in town and make a connection."

Zack handed Dawn all the records they confiscated.

"Good thinking, Zack. I'm sure there's something in these documents that will shed light on what's going on in town."

"How is it in there?" Rose was curious.

"It's not good. There is a lot of psychological and emotional abuse." "Did you see Kelly?"

"No, that place is huge. I need more time."

"What are you going to do?"

"I checked myself in. I'm going to play along until I find her."

"Zack, that could be dangerous. These people are brainwashing teens. God only knows what else," Dawn was worrisome.

"That's why I'm staying. I got to find Kelly. She doesn't deserve to be in that place."

"Oh, Zack," Rose admired Zack's fortitude.

"Be careful," Dawn sighed.

"You guys hit the road and get back into town. Be careful; we don't know who is involved or who we can trust. Go see Sandy; she will help you."

"Find our girl and bring her home," Rose urged.

"I will, or I'll die trying... If I don't make it out of there..." the uncertainty caused Zack to halt, "...tell Kelly I will always love her, and I'll see her in our next life."

Dawn gave a heartfelt nod as she watched Zack take off.

"That was so sweet," Rose was tearful after witnessing Zack make the ultimate sacrifice to save Kelly. She wished she had someone who genuinely cared for her in the same manner.

Thomas came in and started counting the teens; he noticed one was missing. He looked puzzled as he searched around for Zack. He spotted Carmen.

"Carmen, have you seen the newbie?"

"Yeah, the tea must've gone right through. You know..." Carmen grabbed her stomach, mimicking bowel movements.

"Still, no one is allowed to move without an escort." Carmen signaled for Thomas to turn around as Zack came strolling in.

"Because it is your first day, I will not penalize you for your disobedience. However, you are not permitted to leave without an escort," Thomas scowled.

"Um, sorry, I didn't know," Zack grinned slyly.

"Supper is in thirty minutes. Then I will show you to your room," Thomas informed Zack.

* * *

Zack had no appetite to eat; they were worried sick about Kelly. She wasn't at supper, which meant they had her somewhere starving. That infuriated Zack even more, but they knew they couldn't revolt if they were to save Kelly. Zack had to contain all their resentment and rage and assimilate.

Thomas escorted Zack through the secure doors and up the stairs to the patient quarters. A lengthy corridor with locked doors on both sides. Zack trailed from behind, gazing into every room through the tiny window, in search of Kelly. Thomas recited more rules and regulations, but Zack was preoccupied with finding Kelly.

"Hygiene. Men must shave their facial hair every day, while women must shave their underarms and leg hair regularly. Attire. Only short sleeves and pants are permitted for men. Poodle skirts and bras must be worn at all times for the ladies."

Thomas stopped at a room and opened the door. The room was tiny, a few feet short of a jail cell. The twin bed took up the majority of the space in the room.

"This is your room," Thomas informed Zack.

Zack's claustrophobia intensified as they peeked inside. Zack had a tremendous dread of being in tight spaces as a result of their father. Zack was hyperventilating and sweating profusely; their head was spinning. Zack felt like they were about to pass out.

"Are you feeling alright?" Thomas inquired, although he wasn't particularly concerned.

"I just don't like small spaces," Zack breathed.

"Awe, that's the devil talking. God is with you in all spaces, big and small."

Zack glanced down the hall, realizing Kelly could be in any of the rooms. Zack mustered up some courage; they had no other choice if they were to find Kelly. Zack took a deep breath and entered the room. Thomas quickly shut and locked the door behind them.

Zack sat on the bed, staring at the door, attempting to keep their breathing calm. Gazing at the walls, they appeared to be closing in. Zack took a long breath and exhaled, but the walls looked to be closing in still. Zack was sweating and breathing erratically, reflecting their mental instability. They closed their eyes and visualized Kelly. Zack could almost smell her sweet perfume and feel her soft lips on theirs. They found some solace in imagining Kelly's smile. Just as they were ready to drift off to sleep, a horrifying scream echoed across the halls, startling Zack.

THE NEXT MORNING DAWN AND ROSE RUSHED INTO the diner and dumped all their books and documents onto the counter. Sandy turned around and gave the girls a bewildered stare. "Zack, sent us," Dawn blurted out. "Yeah, Zack said you would help us," Rose elaborated. "Just tell me what you need, ladies," Sandy replied.

The three of them sat in a booth, skimming over all the documents from the facility, hoping to find a link to O Town, when Sandy came across a large, suspicious file. The title on the file stood out to her. "Look at this, opposition town."

"What does that mean?" Dawn was puzzled.

"O Town?" Sandy suggested.

"Is that what the O stands for?"

Sandy opened the file. *The folder contained OPPOSITION TOWN NOTES, BLUEPRINTS, and DATES.*

"Opposition Town, which dates back ten years. There are blueprints for houses and a high school. This is it; this is proof that O Town didn't exist until ten years ago."

"Oh, my..." Dawn couldn't believe they actually uncovered something, she was starting to feel like a real investigator reporter.

"Sandy, can I speak with you?" Val asked, interrupting their triumphal moment. Sandy turned around and glanced at Val, standing there.

"Yeah, sure. Excuse me ladies." Sandy was hesitant to speak with Val. They moved over to the jukebox to chat privately.

"I wanted to apologize for yesterday. We should've had Zack's back." "Val, tell this to Zack, not me."

"When Zack returns here with Kelly, they will have no intention of seeing anybody. Those two will be confined to Zack's bed for the next week," Val assumed.

"If I know Zack, you're probably right. There's no way they're letting Kelly out of their sight ever again."

"So, are we cool again, Sandy?"

"Yes, Val, we're cool," Sandy said with a smile.

"Man, that smile." Like every other man and woman in town. Val was enchanted by Sandy's gorgeous smile. Val couldn't stop herself; she leaned in and attempted to kiss Sandy.

Sandy leaned back, rejecting Val's advances.

"What are you doing?" Sandy was both shocked and irritated. "C'mon, Sandy. You can't possibly still be holding out for Zack." Val gibed. "Zack?" Sandy was dumbfounded. She laughed as if that were the most absurd thing she had ever heard.

"I've noticed how you always have your hands all over them."

"I've known Zack for more than half my life, longer than anyone else in this town. Don't you dare pretend to know me or what's in my heart."

"You're right, Sandy; as we all know, you don't play second fiddle to anyone," Val smirked.

"You're obviously going through something or on something. So, I'm going to pretend this never happened. Because you and I both know, Zack would not be too pleased with your comments." Sandy's tone was stern. Val felt Sandy's ire rise with each syllable. She cut her eyes at Val and strutted off.

* * *

Zack was sitting at breakfast. The words *God is watching* were written on the board. Sarah stepped into the room. The bewildered faces of the group staring back. It was time for another group activity.

"Who's ready to do the real work? Catalogue your sins and ask God's forgiveness for your wrongs. Carmen?" Sarah inquired, her voice commanding. Carmen hesitated to get out of her chair; she stood up and faced the group, reading from a crumpled-up piece of handwritten paper. She was mid-flow. It was painfully awkward hearing her read. She was trying to motor through it as fast as humanly possible.

"And it was then where my sinful thoughts of other girls started happening. I renounce these sinful thoughts and actions and I ask God to forgive me all these things," Carmen spoke impassively. Zack watched. Knowing that they would be up there soon cataloging their own sins.

"Carmen, don't you know it's a sin to lie?" Sarah questioned Carmen's honestly.

"I'm not lying," Carmen assured Sarah.

"That's not what your parents tell us. But we don't need them to tell us how sinful you are, Carmen. You and that other girl, in the room last night. You thought no one was watching..."

Male staffers stormed in and grabbed Carmen, held her down, and ripped her shirt open. Sarah pulled out a whip and began to whip Carmen. Zack leapt up to stop her, but Mark grabbed them and pulled them down.

"That will only make it worse. Trust me," Mark warned Zack.

Sarah continued for punishment, "...but God sees all. God is always watching. We must rid the body of sin. Rid the flesh of sin. Only then can God come in..."

Carmen screamed in excruciating anguish. Zack looked on, horrified. What kind of person would do this to another human being? Zack looked away.

* * *

Rose and Dawn were still deep in the investigation. Sandy supplied them with complimentary food and drinks. "Look, these kids all lived in Queerville, originally. But after they attended P.G.A. they came back and moved to O Town," Dawn told Rose.

"Okay, so they moved?"

"Rose, think about it? Who are the people that live in Queerville?"

"Queer," Sandy interjected.

"Right, so the parents sent their kids to that conversion camp to be tortured and brainwashed. To conform to their beliefs and thereby 'cure' them of their homosexuality," Dawn was appalled. "Is it the whole town?"

"No, not everyone. But others had to know what was going on, or else why would our parents lie to us?" Dawn looked at Sandy. "Sandy, what if you're right and they just created O Town to house all their square conversion graduates."

"How can they just build an entire town in the middle of nowhere and no one notices?" Rose had a hard time believing the secrets that they were uncovering.

"They didn't. They built it in Queerville. When I moved here with Zack and their family, O Town was already established, but Queerville had a lot more land than it does now. We were young and didn't think much of it," Sandy explained.

"Yes! That's the only thing that makes sense. Queerville dates back fifty years, and the land expands through O Town. They must've taken over half the land in Queerville and established their own community with like-minded people," Dawn was excited she had just cracked her first huge case. "That would explain why we share the same police department, hospital, and postal service. Oh, and Main Street; they're all connected. How have we never seen this before?" Rose was starting to come around.

"And in order to accomplish such a thing, you would have to have top-level approval. Zack was right. We don't know who could be involved," the girls exchanged troubled looks.

"Ok, now, I'm getting worried. Zack hasn't come back yet or called," Sandy was anxious. She looked up at the clock. "I need to make a phone call; excuse me, ladies," Sandy stood up and walked to the front of the diner. She reached behind the counter for the phone and dialed a number.

"Hey, I'm sorry to bother you, but I think Zack could use your help."

* * *

Zack was in the midst of a group session where everyone sat in a circle. Sarah took the reins. "We have a newbie with us tonight. Please introduce yourself to the group," Sarah motioned for Zack to take the floor. Zack nervously cleared their throat. "Hello, I'm Zack." Zack felt tense. "Remember to tell the truth always," Sarah reminded Zack. "I am telling the truth."

"Your parents did not name you Zack."

"My name is Zack!" Zack replied agitated.
Sarah wrote notes in her notepad.

"Please tell us why you are here."

"Um, I wanted... I want to be saved and welcomed into Gods kingdom," Zack was sick to their stomach for having to say such a thing. "And how are you going to do that?"

"Um, by asking for forgiveness."
Zack was not one to pretend, which is why they were struggling so badly with this revelation. Sarah gave Zack a long judging glance. "Tell us your name," Sarah insisted once more.

"My name is Zack!" Zack shouted defensively.
Sarah threw down her notepad and stormed out. She let out a shout into the adjacent office.

Mark leaned over to Zack. "You seem smart. You want my advice? Play the part; tell them everything they want to hear. Fake it till you make it. Resisting only makes it worse."

Zack appreciated the advice and nodded their head for confirmation.

Sarah, Thomas, and two hulking male staffers charged in and grabbed Zack, dragging them out.

"Where are you taking me? Let me go! Get off! Let me go!"

"You do not want to face your sin. So, you will face your fears. Until you realize they are one in the same," Sarah muttered.

They dragged Zack into some sort of chapel. The room was cast in darkness; the windows blacked out. Candles flickered, and dim lamps illuminated the room. The centerpiece was a casket that they dragged Zack toward; they freaked out.

"No, don't put me in there. Please, no. Don't put me in there! Pleaseeee!" Zack begged as they tossed them into the casket. Zack resisted, but the staffers struck them repeatedly, and slammed the casket shut. Zack yelled and pounded on the casket, begging to be let out.

"God is with you, child. Always," Sarah whispered. Zack screamed at the top of their lungs. Pleading to get out.

———————

Later that night, the staff returned to remove Zack from the casket and transport them to therapy. Sarah was waiting for Zack with a sadistic smirk on her face. They seated Zack on a chair, looking like a shell of themselves with vacant eyes and a lifeless face. Zack was withdrawn as they stared down at the floor.

"Well, you made it through your first cleansing. Now, we can start the work. But first, we need to be truthful. What happens to you on the outside can affect who you are on the inside. We know who you are… Zackia Calhoun…"

Zack was unresponsive and emotionless as Sarah continued to reveal her revelations about Zack.

"…Your daddy molested you for years…"

Zack raised an eyebrow at Sarah, puzzled as to how she'd uncovered their deepest, darkest secret. They felt dizzy and were seeing two of her.

"…he violated your body over and over again…"

Flashbacks of Zack's physical abuse replayed in their head—their father sexually assaulting them and beating them night after night. Zack was taking their moral inventory as tears flooded down their cheeks. Their hands were clammy, and their chest was constricted, making it difficult to breathe. Zack was on the brink of breaking.

"…he programmed you to reject men. You don't dislike men; you dislike what he did to you. But you associate that with all men…"

Zack was mentally fading, and breathing was hard. Heavy on their chest. Their heart pounded in their ears. Their hands trembled, and their eyes welled up with tears, which distorted their vision as if they were looking through a fish-eye lens.

"…You were using sexual sin and homosexuality to fill a void in your life that only God can fill…"

Zack was in utter anguish. Their rage was building, like a teapot brewing.

"You want to release it. I can see it. Let it out."

ZACK SCREAMED!!

"Heavenly Father. Look down on us now with your wisdom and unleash your power for one of your flock. Zackia, has lost her way. We pray, Lord, that you make her pure again."

Zack continued to scream...

"Repeat after me...I renounce these sinful thoughts and actions and I ask God to forgive me of all these things... say it. Let the sin out," Sarah encouraged Zack to recite the mantra.

Zack stopped screaming and gained their composure, their breathing steadied. They made direct eye contact with Sarah, and their vision cleared.

"I renounce these sinful thoughts and actions and I ask God to forgive me all these things," Zack repeated as they rocked back and forth in their chair.

"Now, let the healing begin," Sarah grinned, elated that she had finally broken Zack.

ZACK CALHOUN

Chicago, Illinois
1947

Zackia, also known as, Zack was climbing a tree, clothed in the boyish attire that their father detested. Zack spent most of their adolescence climbing, running, building, and engaging in other masculine activities. They didn't have a feminine bone in their body, regardless of how much their father wished otherwise.

On this particular day, Mr. Calhoun decided to finally treat Zack like the boy they wish to be.

Mr. Calhoun pulled up to the park where Zack was playing. He was accompanied by four gruff and rugged teenage boys. Zack took notice; they smirked, wondering whether their father had brought the boys to play with them. Judging by the wicked expression on his face, Zack knew otherwise. The boys surrounded Zack in a menacing manner.

"This is my child, and though you can't tell by looking at her, she is in fact a girl. You see, boys, my daughter is a bit confused. She appears to believe she's a boy, and since none of my efforts to convince her differently have been effective, I reasoned that it was past time to treat her as one. So, boys, let's welcome the new boy to town. Show him how Chicago treats degenerates," Mr. Calhoun said vindictively.

The first boy hit Zack, and they refused to exhibit any emotion. Zack took the blow without flinching. The other boys were offended, so they all jumped in and hit Zack and kicked them. They kept kicking Zack as they were on the ground. Zack curled up, grunting in agony, but didn't say a word, nor did they cry. They didn't want their father to get the pleasure of seeing them weep.

The boys grew tired and winded; they came to a halt. Zack stood up despite their pain and bruises; they refused to show weakness; instead, they stared their father in the eyes and spat forth the blood from their swollen lips and muttered, "One of these days, I'm going to put a bullet in your head."

"You don't have the balls..." he chuckled, "But witnessing you take that beating; I will say you certainly have my heart."

"I HATE YOU!" Zack screamed.

"Good. Use it," Mr. Calhoun grabbed Zack up.

* * *

Mr. Calhoun took Zack into a dilapidated gym. Nothing except sweaty older men hitting punching bags. An older Italian man approached them. "Who exactly do we have here, Giovanni?" the Italian man asked. "This here is my daughter. Who would have predicted that my son would inherit his mother's heart while my daughter would inherit mine? She has my spirit in her, and I want you to teach her how to use it." "Well, this has to be a first. A girl fighter?" the Italian man was perplexed. "Not just a girl. A Calhoun. I want you to train her. Teach her how to fight back and defend herself."

"Mama, said fighting is bad," Zack murmured.

Mr. Calhoun crouched in front of Zack. "You should never start a fight, child, but you for damn sure better be prepared to finish it," Mr. Calhoun informed Zack. Those statements stayed with Zack and subsequently led to Mr. Calhoun's fate.

Zack trained relentlessly for months, day and night. They had no intention of defending themselves but rather of striking first at anyone that caused them grief or made them fear for their life. They would never allow another person to beat them or anyone they loved ever again.

Each week, Mr. Calhoun would put them to the test. He would send boys to fight Zack, and if they lost, he'd beat them again, but much worse. He thought if Zack found it hard to be a boy, they would start acting more ladylike. Zack, on the other hand, was eager to prove him wrong. They used every black eye and bruised rib as fuel. But the catalyst for unleashing Zack's inner beast had been there in front of their eyes the whole time.

In his last attempt to break Zack. Mr. Calhoun felt it would be funny to invite Zack's best friend to see what the cost of living a homosexual lifestyle was.

Just like the first time the biggest boy struck first, Zack went down. But they were not beaten; instead, they were waiting for the right moment to strike back more effectively. They pummeled Zack; they were merciless. The only thing Zack saw was a swarm of feet stomping on them. Zack was startled to hear someone yell, "Come on, Zack! Fight back; you can do it!" It was Sandy. Mr. Calhoun clutched her tight as she struggled with him to get to Zack.

"Hey boys, this one here wants to join in the fun. Show this sissy how to be a man." He let go of Sandy, who instantly assumed a defensive stance despite being clothed in feminine attire. Sandy was prepared to fight. She knew she couldn't take them all, but she was determined to make at least one of them hobble away.

Suddenly, this fire came over Zack, and they saw black. Zack sprang up with the ferocity of Superman and grabbed one boy by his shirt. He swung, but Zack dodged it, and in one swing, Zack knocked the boy unconscious. Another boy whirled around to kick Zack, but Zack caught his foot and twisted it, breaking the boy's ankle and causing him to scream in pain. A third boy attempted to go blow for blow with Zack; he threw a couple jabs and missed each one. Zack repositioned their feet and landed a lean hook and an uppercut, knocking the boy down, disoriented.

Zack looked at the fourth boy, who gasped and fled in terror. Zack raced up to their father and drew Sandy behind them to protect her. Mr. Calhoun was taken aback by Zack's violent side.

"Dear child, I'm going to make a killer out of you yet."

"I'll never be anything like you," Zack growled.

"Whether you like it or not, that killer instinct runs through your bloodline. I'm a mobster, but your granddaddy was a gangster, and so was his daddy. But you, child, you just might be the deadliest one," Mr. Calhoun snickered. Zack stepped back, shaking their head, unable to believe it. They raced off with Sandy.

When Zack and Sandy arrived at her house, an ambulance was parked outside, and her mother was being carried out on a stretcher. Sandy ran to her.

"Mommy?" Sandy wailed as she clutched her mother's lifeless body. She was gone. Her mother died of alcohol poisoning; she had drunk herself to death. Sandy's father came home and found her unresponsive in a puddle of booze. After all of her mother's psychological and emotional abuse. Sandy was still heartbroken over her death. Sandy adored her mother no matter how badly she made her feel about herself. And she'd never get the chance to tell her. More significantly, she will never replace the gap left by her desire for her mother's approval.

Her parents had long separated. Her mother abandoned them a year ago because she couldn't bear the thought of raising a devil child, as she called it. As a result, it was just her and her father. He grappled with Sandy's identity as well, but he never said anything harsh to her. Sandy's mother would parade men in and out of her home in front of Sandy. Not one of them ever treated her right, which is how Sandy developed such poor taste in men.

Her mother was only there to see her on the weekends. Sandy wanted so much to look like her mother. She would peek through her door and watch her apply make-up and sculpt her body with corsets. Sandy spent hours in front of the mirror, mimicking her mother's gestures and how she walked. She would later inherit her mother's sense of style. If her mother was a bombshell, then Sandy was the explosion. She succeeded her mother in beauty, an honor she cherished.

That night Zack stayed with her. Sandy wept all night in Zack's lap. Though Zack was always willing to comfort Sandy, they welcomed the escape from their own household. Mama Zack had discovered that Mr. Calhoun had been sending Zack to fight at the gym, and she was not pleased. They argued about it for days. She did not want Zack to fight. Mama Zack wished desperately for her children to be nothing like their father. But it was out of her control. Anthony was to be the successor to the Calhoun throne, but he didn't have the guts. Zack, on the other hand, was forged into it.

Mama Zack had their things packed and in the car by the next morning. She told Zack and Anthony to get in the back. Zack looked sadly out the window at Sandy; they didn't want to leave her. Zack and Sandy both sobbed for each other while Mama Zack continued to load up the car with the rest of their belongings.

Mr. Myers came over and chatted with Mama Zack. He asked her to take Sandy; with her mother gone, he didn't know the first thing about raising a child. But it was mainly because he had no idea how to accept his queer child. He loved Sandy, but his religious views and ignorance prevented him from understanding, let alone accepting, her. Sandy, like any other little girl, needed her father's love; the little boy within her had already lost their mother's love.

Sandy would grow up believing that no one wanted her and that she was never enough. She clung to her father, pleading with him not to leave her. He was the last blood relative she had. He placed Sandy in the back of the car and promised he would come visit; he never did. He hugged her, wiped her tears away, and kissed her on the cheek. Sandy waved at her father as the car pulled off and he faded into the distance. Zack wrapped their arm around Sandy.

"Don't worry, Sandy. I'll never leave you," Zack whispered as Sandy rested her head on their shoulder; and for the first time in her life, she felt loved.

They drove for hours down rural roads to a solitary road, passing a sign that read... *Welcome to Queerville.*

Queerville was a strange utopia as you may already know. A place Zack and Sandy could finally be themselves. It was shocking to see so many individuals who looked like them live so openly. Gays, lesbians, transgenders, drag queens, and allies all living together. There was no shaming, hostility, or name-calling. Queerville was a vibrant community full of freedom, peace, and happiness. It was like living in a rainbow.

One day after school, Anthony, Zack, and Sandy came across Charlotte's diner, where they all encountered the formidable Charlotte herself. She instantly fell in love with the three, and so did they. Charlotte's diner became the official hangout for all the teens. Like Zack, Mama Zack and Anthony adored Sandy as if she were family, and she loved having two siblings now.

They did everything together, including going to the beach, watching flicks, and when the carnival was in town, they all attended as a family. Sandy grew to appreciate carnivals as her happy place; it was the only place that held nothing but good memories. It was a magical wonderland that made her feel like anything was possible. They had talent shows in the living room; Anthony would do magic tricks, Sandy would showcase her dancing, and Zack would serenade them with their soulful voice.

As the years passed, Zack and Sandy delved deeper into their transition with the support of Mama Zack and Anthony. Mama Zack taught Sandy how to apply her make-up and how to style her hair. Sandy cherished having a mother figure once more, and Mama Zack relished having a daughter again. Zack and Sandy would stay up all night discussing their potential future as the opposite sexes. Listening to Sandy gush over her expectations of becoming a woman left Zack unsure about their own identity. Sandy could sense Zack's mood.

"What's wrong Zack?"

"I don't know. I just don't feel like a woman. I feel caged in this body."

"Yes, I know that's what we're talking about. Me becoming a woman and you becoming a man."

"That's it though. I don't want to be... a man."

"Huh? So, you want to stay a girl?"

"No. I just... I don't want to stay in this body, but I also don't want to be called a man."

"Well, what do you want to be called?"

"Just Zack. All I want to be is Zack. I don't want to identify to any gender."

"I don't get it. So, you don't want to be a girl and you don't want to be a boy?"

"Yeah, exactly."

"Zack, you have to be one or the other. You have to choose a gender." "Who says? You know how we talk about someone in the third person and say things like, *they went to the hop, they didn't ring me, or they went home*. It's a gender-neutral word; it doesn't mean either a boy or a girl."

"So, you want us to call you a they?"

"I just know that gender does not always have to be mentioned. I'm not sure why I feel this way. I just do," Zack was struggling with their identity.

Mama Zack who was eavesdropping at the door stepped in to give her opinion. "Because you're an angel, baby. When God created angels, they didn't create male or female angels. They just created a spirit. A genderless spirit. They can present themselves as masculine or feminine, but they are neither, and neither is God," Mama Zack explained.

"Mom, I'm no angel. If I were an angel, why would God put me through so much pain?"

"To test you. Remember, God gives the most difficult battles to the most powerful soldiers. The pain that you're experiencing is to prepare you for the reward that God will bestow upon you."

Zack rolled their eyes.

Despite Mama Zack's greatest efforts to make Zack feel loved, all they had ever felt was misery. Zack began to suspect that love was, in fact, suffering.

After their enlightened conversation, they all agreed to refer to Zack as they. Sandy struggled at first but eventually got the hang of it. They were finally happy and living in their truth. Till one day they got an unexpected visitor.

Mr. Calhoun had tracked them down and they were back to being one miserable family. He was not a fan of Queerville's homosexuality on display, but he admired the town's uniqueness and resources. Queerville had the potential to become a major city, but it lacked security.

Anthony wanted to impress his father, so he started a gang, the Red Dragons. After speaking with Charlotte, she also agreed that the town needed protection from those who might want to disturb its tranquility. However, the gangs would have to be tailored to the resident's social identity.

As a result, Anthony devised a system and tailored the gangs to each group's identity. Anthony chose Charlotte as the town's coordinator, and Sandy as the leader of the Lipsticks. And with Mr. Calhoun's agreement, Queerville was officially under the protection of the Calhoun Mob Family. No one quite understood why Mr. Calhoun would agree to such a thing, given his homophobia, but the town was grateful to be under his protection.

Zack, on the other hand, did not trust him, and for good reason. After Mr. Calhoun put his name on the line to safeguard the town. He wanted to be certain that it was secured in the hands of his children. He wasn't too concerned about Anthony since he knew Anthony was a man and would be just fine. But Zack would have to toughen up. The torture he had previously inflicted on them was insufficient. He persisted in physically abusing Zack, or as he described it, "fixing them."

Each time he caught Zack in boys' clothing, he would beat them. He dragged Zack out of the diner by their hair and whipped them in front of the entire town with his belt. When Zack got home, he would strip them naked and dunk their head in the bathtub.

Zack ran away from home one night and stumbled upon a secluded pond area hidden from everything. It was serene and had the most spectacular view of the city. This would be Zack's secret hideaway, where they would go to escape from their father. Zack would spend endless nights there, sleeping and eating fish from the pond, leaving Sandy and their mom worried sick. When Zack eventually returned home, he locked them in the closet for hours to keep them from leaving.

Zack would scream and pound on the door to get out, he would just sit and laugh. Sandy came home and heard Zack weeping; she didn't fear Mr. Calhoun, and she wasn't about to sit and listen to her best friend cry. So, she flung open the door and let Zack out. Zack leapt into her arms; Sandy was bigger than Zack at the time, so she felt she had to protect them. Mr. Calhoun got enraged when he discovered Sandy let Zack out, but before he could unleash his punishment, Mama Zack arrived home in the middle of the chaos, and she took a frying pan to his head.

Zack went to their room and attempted to recover from the horrible ordeal they had just gone through. Sandy was right beside them.

"I'm so weak... I can't beat him... I can't take this anymore," Zack sobbed.

"You're not weak, Zack. You're stronger than you know, that's why he keeps trying to break you. Because he knows he can't," Sandy assured Zack of their resilience.

"Look at me, Sandy!" Zack was feeling defeated. Sandy cupped Zack's face. She could see the fire burning inside of them as she gazed into Zack's eyes.

"Never let them win. Feed that rage burning inside of you. Use that fuel, put it in a bottle, light a match, and throw it back at them. But never let them break you," Sandy spoke with deep sincerity.

That was the last time Mr. Calhoun ever put his hands on Zack. Mama Zack, on the other hand, would not be so fortunate.

CHAPTER 19

P.G.A.
Present Day.

Zack sat at the table with the other teens, who were rushing through their breakfast. Zack didn't seem like themselves; they were withdrawn. Carmen came and sat next to them she was not her normal chatty self; she had no fight left in her. She seemed distant and frigid. Zack's attention was drawn to a *bing* sound as the elevator doors opened on their floor. Zack turned their head to see a male staffer pushing a young girl in a wheelchair. Zack couldn't get a good look at who it was.

The staffer swung the wheelchair around and rolled it through the double doors backwards. The young girl's head drew back, and her hair slipped off her face revealing that it was Kelly. She appeared unconscious, possibly drugged or having received some kind of treatment.

Zack became indignant, and life returned to their face as they remembered why they were there. Zack sprang up and dashed over, but the doors shut on them. Zack looked through the glass on the double doors and noticed the room the staffer took Kelly to. Mark approached Zack. "I know that look. Whatever you got planned I want in," Mark said.

"I don't know what you're talking about," Zack was skeptical that Mark could be trusted, and they had no intention of allowing anyone to interfere with their efforts to save Kelly.

"Yes, you do. You've been on a mission since you came here."

"What happened to 'fake it till you make it'?" Zack sneered.

"I was wrong. I figured it out; they don't want you to renounce your sin. They want you to completely forget."

"Forget what?"

"Everything that made you sin. You don't leave this place if you remember," Mark said frightened.

They heard shouting coming from the kitchen, Zack and Mark ran back to see what was causing the uproar. It was Carmen, she was holding a shard of glass to her neck. Zack rushed to her.

"Carmen don't do this. I can save you. Okay, I can get you out of here," Zack pleaded.

"No, you can't. There's no getting out of here." Carmen was inconsolable, her eyes devoid of all hope. She would rather die than be indoctrinated to adopt their beliefs. The staffers stormed in and attempted to plead with her. "Carmen, put the glass down," Thomas begged her. Zack and Mark watched in terror as Carmen wept, her hands bloodied and trembling from clutching the glass.

"I won't live the way you want me to. I won't conform. I won't spend my life trying to please everyone else while I hate myself. I don't want to forget. I'm going to die, being me," Carmen wailed, then plunged the glass into her neck; blood squirted out. The staffers rushed to her and administered first aid.

Zack lifted one of the staffers keys as he sprinted past them. They backstepped out through all the chaos and rushed to the corridor, frantically trying to find the appropriate key before anybody spotted them. They tried several keys until one of them eventually worked.

Zack dashed to the room with Kelly and glanced inside; she was out cold. Zack used the key to enter and ran to Kelly. Zack gently raised her head.

"Kelly, wake up. Come on baby. Wake up, Kelly."

Kelly's eyelids were twitching; she was a little groggy. The brightness blinded her as she attempted to open her eyes. Her vision was blurry, but she managed to focus on Zack. She'd spot those emerald eyes from a mile away. She cracked a grin.

"Zack, you came for me," she mumbled.

"Of course, I did. Come on, let's go."

Zack wrapped Kelly's arm over their neck and hauled her up; she was in and out of consciousness. Zack carried her through the double doors and down the long corridor. The front door was a few steps away. Zack dashed for it and was met with force. The staffers grabbed them; Zack's keys flew across the floor and landed at Mark's feet; he scooped them up discreetly.

The staffers snatched Kelly from Zack's arms.

"Get off, let her go. Let us out this fucking place!" Zack shouted. "Oh, Zack, I thought we had a breakthrough," Sarah shook her head disappointed.

"My father touched me, so now I'm gay. Yeah, I heard that shit before, and you have it backwards; my father did what he did to try and fix me. You all are just as sick as he was," Zack sneered. "Oh, I see you enjoy lying. Well, here at P.G.A., liars get preferential attention," Sarah stated gravely.

JOHNNIE AND MRS. BAKER WERE AT CHURCH TO CLEANSE him of his same sex attraction. Pastor Peter and a few other town members were present to witness the cleanse. "We are gathered here today to cleanse brother Johnnie of his sin. The heavenly father in the wisdom of his mercy hasn't had his last word on this boy's soul." Pastor Peter preached his sermon.

They circled around Johnnie, issuing an ultimatum. He nodded his head, completely surrendering. Pastor Peter rested his hand on Johnnie's shoulder. In a frantic, jolting motion, he shoved Johnnie, attempting to cast the devil out. Others followed his lead.

Mrs. Baker shoved Johnnie's head aggressively. Johnnie fell backwards to the floor. Mrs. Baker struck Johnnie with her Bible. Johnnie's anguished face as he rolled over was flushed and wet with tears.

Other parishioners were encouraged to strike Johnnie with Bibles and other books. Harder and harder, they struck him.

Pastor Peter signaled to the baptistery. Johnnie stood at his feet with the help of those around him. Mary Sue was by his side.

Johnnie stepped into the baptismal pool. Where he was baptized by Pastor Peter, who plunged him into the pool while encouraging others to place their hands on Johnnie, holding him beneath the water. His big body shuddered, and his strong arms reached out from the water. Like a massive baby. Fully surrendered. The only thing that made this even remotely bearable was that Johnnie seemed ecstatic and accepting of his rebirth. His arms clawing for God, reaching for a loving embrace.

* * *

Zack was hauled into a disciplinary room, where their
arms were outstretched, and they were shackled up by
their hands. The staffers ripped off their shirt, exposing
their masculine chest. Sarah was taken back by Zack's
scars from their top surgery. "Dear God, you are an
abomination. This is just unholy," Sarah was appalled.
A staffer came in with a whip.

"Why would you do this to yourself? God made you
perfectly fine in his image, child," Sarah implored.

"I want to be made in my own image," Zack grunted.

"And you shall be," Sarah replied, with a devilish
grin.

* * *

Johnnie in his white robe stood center as everyone
kneeled around him, their hands reaching toward him,
praising him. Pastor Peter delivered his sermon.

"Look at this living testament. Give praise to Johnnie
for fighting his demons and let him be the proof…"
While Pastor Peter was delivering his sermon, Zack was
being lashed in the back, screaming in agony. Their
back was smeared with blood and bruises as Sarah continued to whip them repeatedly. "…that you can, pray
gay away. You can renounce your homosexuality. If
you just ask God to remove your sin. God will heal you
of your same sex attraction, but you must ask him. Repeat after me…"

Pastor Peter, Mrs. Baker, Johnnie, Mary Sue, and the
other parishioners marched down Main Street into
Queerville holding signs with religious scriptures and
the quote… *"YOU CAN PRAY GAY AWAY."*

Queerville folks were not pleased; they threw rocks
at the religious zealots. Such a demonstration of hatred
in their own community clearly affected some people.

How could this be occurring in a place that had been a safe haven for decades?

They passed by Charlotte's, and people emerged from the diner in astonishment. As Freddie stood there watching, he instantly became furious. *They have no right to tell us who to love or how to look.* He'd had enough of hiding and remaining silent. His blood was boiling, and he was ready to go to war.

"...I renounce these sinful thoughts and actions and I ask God to forgive me of all these things," Pastor Peter continued. The sheriff approached the mob and arrested Mrs. Baker.

* * *

The staffers were finally done torturing Zack. They left them shackled up, by the arms.

"Now, what image does this remind you of?"
Sarah chuckled as Zack blacked out from the pain.

* * *

Kelly was strapped into a stretcher. Principal Skinner sat on a stool next to her. "Miss Kelly, now what am I going to do with you?" Principal Skinner sighed. Kelly looked at Principal Skinner shocked, she couldn't believe she was the one behind this. "This is what happens when you don't wear your poodle skirts. There is a purpose for all of this. We are God's chosen and he wants a pure breed to bring in the second coming."

"What...Where is Zack?" Kelly murmured.

"Zack, Zack, Zack. You are a beautiful, White, Christian woman; you have no business frolicking around with that... that freak," Principal Skinner expressed her disgust which infuriated Kelly.

"Don't you call Zack a freak!" Kelly shouted.
She was angry, fighting to get out of her restraints.

"If you won't rid yourself of the sin, we will have to rid it for you," Principal Skinner said eerie.

"Stop! Please, not again... Not again," Kelly begged. Sarah attached the ECT to Kelly's head and shocked her as she pleaded for them to stop.

––––––––––––––––

Mark showed up late at night to check on Zack and discovered them still shackled up. He entered using the keys he had confiscated. He freed Zack's arms and assisted them to the floor. Zack groaned in agony; their arms ached, and their back throbbed. Mark scrambled to get some medical gowns and applied pressure to Zack's back to stop the bleeding.

"Are you okay?" Mark asked, but based on Zack's condition, he knew the answer. Zack was partially conscious; Mark tapped their face to rouse them up and squirted water into their mouth.

"Look, I don't know who that girl is to you. But right now, she's downstairs, getting her brain fried. I'm not sure how much more she can take. So, if she means anything to you, she could really use your help right now, and so could I," Mark pleaded.

Zack breathed heavily; Mark gave them more water.

"Where is she?" Zack exhaled heavily.

Zack and Mark crept outside the therapy room, waiting for the staffers to clear out. Zack spotted Principal Skinner and Mr. Booker talking. *Of course, these two were in cahoots*, they thought. Zack glanced around and noticed a supply closet. They signaled Mark to follow them inside. Zack started wildly rummaging through all the goods.

"What are you looking for? Why are we in here?"

"They're not going to just let us stroll out the front door."

"Okay, so what do you suggest?" Mark was curious. Zack came across lighters and some flammable liquids. They turned and gave Mark a wicked grin.

"We burn it down," Zack stated.

Zack and Mark gathered all the flammable liquids and lighters from the supply room. They doused the drapes and other furnishings with accelerants and set them ablaze. The room quickly became engulfed in red-hot flames.

A male staffer emerged and tried to apprehend Zack, but they punched him in the face. Thomas intervened and grabbed Mark, but Mark broke free. Zack and Mark found themselves pitted against Thomas and the staffer. They briefly scuffled before Zack knocked Thomas unconscious. "Zack, go! I got this one!" Mark yelled as he wrestled with the male staffer.

Zack hurriedly returned to the therapy room, only to be confronted by another staffer. They traded blows, leaving Zack weary and in excruciating pain. They were nearly depleted of strength. Desperate, Zack picked up a lamp and smashed it over the staffer's head, rendering them unconscious.

Zack entered the room and barely recognized Kelly. Their heart broke at the sight of her in such a state. Outraged, Zack noticed that Kelly didn't appear to be breathing. Panicking, they checked her pulse and found that she was still alive. Zack let out a relieved exhale. Kelly looked pale and sluggish, with parched lips and dark bags under her eyes. Zack removed the ETC wires and gently scooped Kelly into their arms. They carefully carried her up the stairs to the main hall, intending to make their way towards the front door.

As Zack approached the front door, they were suddenly blocked by Sarah and four other staffers. Holding Kelly tightly, Zack swiftly scanned the room, desperately searching for another escape route. However, the windows were nailed shut, and the doors were chained, leaving them with no way out. Exhausted and disheartened, Zack felt defeated. "You are truly the work of the devil. You just won't quit! I think it's time we put you down for good," Sarah said maliciously as she signaled the staffers to go after Zack.

Suddenly, there was a deafening BANG! A shotgun shell blasted through the door, splitting it apart. Sarah spun around, stunned, and took a slow pan of Charlotte stepping in, wielding a shotgun in her hands.

"Give me back my babies or I'll burn this mother fucker to the ground!" Charlotte yelled angrily.

Zack was overjoyed and relieved to see Charlotte. Molotov Cocktails smashed through the windows, setting fire to everything. The staffers looked terrified.

Outside, all the Queerville gangs were storming the facility, while Val, Robin, Lisa and Halle threw Molotov cocktails through the windows.

Back inside, Charlotte spotted Sarah. "What have you been doing to these babies?" "You all will burn in hell," Sarah grumbled as she swung at Charlotte and missed. Charlotte landed a right hook that left her dazed and had her scrambling to keep on her feet. Maria pounced on her and finished the beatdown with a one-two combo that left her sprawled across the floor.

"I guess we'll see you there," Maria chuckled.

Freddie caught one of the staffers trying to flee. He pulled him back and gave him a lean hook, hurling him outside into the clutches of the angry mob. The other staffer tried to sneak up behind Freddie, but he spotted him approaching. Freddie turned around; his eyes wide; he recognized the guy.

"I remember you. You're the one who forced me to eat my supper off the floor after you pissed on it. Oh, I'm going to enjoy this," Freddie took off his jacket and went toe-to-toe with the staffer. He dodged all his blows and waited for an opening. Freddie broke his nose with a jab before striking him in the gut and landing an uppercut that sent him flying up in the air and to the ground. Freddie spat on the staffer before relieving himself on him and rushing over to Zack.

"I'm sorry it took me so long. I had a few fears to face," Freddie said apologetic. "I'm just damn glad to see you, Freddie," Zack smirked.

Zack walked outside still carrying Kelly in their arms. Rose and Dawn rushed to them.

"Oh my, is she alive?" Rose asked.

"Is she okay?" Dawn was concerned.

"We need to get her to the hospital," Zack said, breathless. They managed to hand Kelly over to Freddie before passing out. "Zack!" They all shouted.

Rose sped down the road with Zack and Kelly barely hanging on in the back seat. Freddie desperately tried to keep them conscious while Dawn held Kelly's hand from the passenger side. Zack's eyes were barely open, but they could still see Kelly struggling to speak. In a tender moment, Zack reached out and gently stroked her cheek.

"Nothing in this world could ever keep me from you," Zack mumbled. A faint smile crossed Kelly's face, but then her eyes rolled back, and she lost consciousness. "Oh my God, Kelly!" Dawn shouted in panic. Suddenly, Zack also slipped unconsciousness.

"Rose, hit the gas. We're losing them!" Freddie yelled urgently. "I'm going as fast as I can," Rose assured Freddie, her foot pressing harder on the gas pedal.

The gangs trailed behind Zack and Kelly as they were rushed into the hospital on stretchers. Doctors immediately began treating them. Zack regained consciousness and reached for Kelly, who doctors were desperately working to save. The nurses rolled Zack over and examined their back, which was badly bruised and bloodied.

Sandy rushed in; she was devastated to see the severity of Zack's injuries. She wept in Charlotte's arms, her heart breaking for Zack.

* * *

 Zack was treated and sent to a private room. Sandy was right by Zack's side, resting her head on their chest. Mama Zack sat at the foot of the bed.

After a few hours, Zack opened their eyes. "Sandy," Zack whispered. Sandy lifted her head up. "Hey Zack, you're awake? You scared me half to death," Sandy sighed.

"Hi, baby. Thank God, you're okay," Mama Zack said taking Zack's hand. "Where's Kelly?" Zack asked.

"She's okay Zack. She made it through surgery. She's going to be fine," Sandy assured Zack. Zack was relieved. They attempted to get up. "No, Zack, you shouldn't be up."

"I need to see her, mom. I have to see her, please," Zack groaned as Sandy pushed them back down.

"Lay down I will check on her. If she's awake, I will come back and get you." Sandy stepped into the hall where she ran into Charlotte. "How is our superhero doing?" Charlotte asked.

"Zack may not fully be aware of the extent of their injuries. All they want is to see Kelly," Sandy replied.

"Zack loves that girl. C'mon, her room is over here."

Charlotte showed Sandy to Kelly's room. Kelly was asleep in bed. They stood in the hall, staring at her. "Has anyone called her parents?" Charlotte inquired. "Should we? They're the ones that put her in that place."

The doctor approached the room.

"Hello, are you two family?" The doctor asked.

"I guess you can say that. How is she?"

"Well, Kelly went under massive brain surgery. There was a lot of damage done from the electroconvulsive therapy she endured." "Oh, dear God, is she going to be, okay?" Charlotte was saddened to hear the doctor's news. She truly adored Kelly.

"We won't know till she wakes up."

"And when will that be?"

"With brain surgery. It could take days, weeks, or even months. It depends on the patient and how quickly their body can recover." Sandy and Charlotte stared at Kelly, still reeling from the night's events. They stood silently.

Zack was seldom far from Kelly's side throughout the following few days. Zack held her hand for hours. Rose and Dawn kept her hydrated while also providing food for Zack. The only thing that could entice Zack away was their back treatment, which caused them to scream in agony. Sandy stood there, horrified. Zack's whole life had been nothing but pain and misery; she couldn't bear to look. She hated watching her best friend endure such torment. When will it end? When will they be free of this alleged test God keeps putting them through? Listening to Zack scream obliterated the little faith she still had in God.

* * *

Kelly's eyelids twitched while her lips parted slightly. She strained to open her eyes. Rose and Dawn leapt up. "Oh my God, Kelly!" Rose shouted.

"You're awake." Dawn was thrilled.

Kelly attempted to focus on the faces in the room, but everything was a blur, she ultimately settled on Rose and Dawn's smiling faces. She touched her lips, she was parched.

"You want water?" Rose retrieved a cup of water from the table and offered it to Kelly. She gulped the water quickly through the straw, relieving her thirst.

"Hey girls," Kelly mumbled.

"Oh, thank God," Rose said, relieved.

Rose and Dawn were happy to see Kelly finally woke and talking. "Where am I?" Kelly felt a bit fuzzy. "You're in the hospital," Dawn answered. "Why? What happened? My head hurts so bad," Kelly grunted. Dawn was alarmed that Kelly didn't seem to remember why she was there. "Rose, go get the doctor," she shouted. Rose rushed off to find the doctor.

"Do you don't remember anything?"

"Um..." Kelly attempted to recall the last thing she remembered, but her mind went blank.

"Do you remember the camp?"

"What camp?" Kelly asked. Dawn was baffled.

"Kelly, do you remember Zack saving you?"

"Um, no. Zack...? No, who's Zack?"

"Dear, God!" Dawn sighed.

The doctor came to exam Kelly.

"We're glad to see you awake, Kelly. How are you feeling?" "My head is a little foggy and I have this pounding," Kelly confessed. "That's to be expected. I can prescribe something for the pain."

"What about her memories doctor. She doesn't seem to remember anything," Dawn informed the doctor.

"Nothing is guaranteed. Only time will tell. Kelly's short-term memory was seriously compromised. I doubt she'll remember anything or anyone she's en-countered recently."

"No, she has to remember," Rose urged.

"Sorry ladies. I'll be back with some meds."
Dawn and Rose exchanged glances before focusing their attention on Kelly. She looked so innocent and clueless. She was completely oblivious that she had no memory of the love of her life.

"Do you girls want to tell me who this Zack is? And where are my mom and dad? Where is Max?"

Dawn and Rose shook their heads.
Zack, Sandy, Charlotte, Freddie, and Mama Zack were having a laugh as Charlotte animatedly recounted sto-ries about her wild nights on tour when Dawn and Rose walked in looking troubled. "Is Kelly awake?" Zack asked as they sat up.

"Um, yeah, she is Zack," Rose said sincerely.
Zack attempted to climb out of bed, but Sandy pushed them back down. They groaned in pain. "Actually, Zack, can we speak with Sandy and Charlotte for a sec-ond?" Dawn asked.

Everyone looked perplexed. Sandy and Charlotte fol-lowed the girls into the corridor. They had no idea what was going on but thought it had to be serious. "What's going on ladies?" Charlotte inquired quickly. "Kelly is awake right?" Sandy questioned.

"Yes," Dawn sighed. "That's good," Sandy said relieved. "Not necessarily," Rose whispered. "What do you mean? Spit it out ladies," Charlotte was losing patience.

"Kelly doesn't remember Zack," Dawn blurted out.

"What?" Sandy was in disbelief.

"The doctor said she lost all her short-term memories. She doesn't remember Zack, her brother being in jail, or even her parents sending her to that God awful place," Rose elaborated. "Oh, dear God, this is going to break Zack's heart," Charlotte revealed. "Maybe if she just sees Zack, she will remember everything," Sandy proposed.

"She doesn't want to," Dawn shook her head.

"She doesn't want to what?" Sandy was flabbergasted, she couldn't believe her ears.

"We told her who Zack is to her. She freaked out, she doesn't want to see them."

"We'll see about that," Sandy spoke firmly and strutted off to see Kelly.

Kelly was sitting up in her bed trying to wrap her head around everything Rose and Dawn had just told her when Sandy entered. "Hey, Kelly," she said softly. Kelly locked her gaze on Sandy; she squinted her eyes. Sandy seemed faintly familiar, but she wasn't completely sure. "Hello," she responded back.

"How are you feeling?"

"Do I know you?" Kelly asked faintly.

Sandy could see Kelly was struggling to remember.

"Yes, you do. Do you remember?"

"Um, no, I'm sorry," Kelly was still feeling foggy.

"I'm Sandy, Zack's friend. They really would like to see you," Sandy stated desperately.

Kelly's body language changed as she became uneasy discussing Zack. She was unsettled.

"Oh, no, I don't want to see that... Zack person," Kelly said repulsed. Sandy grew irritated; she leaned closer to give Kelly a grave look. "Let me tell you something... that Zack person walked into hell to find you and carried you out. You will speak with them," Sandy glared angrily at Kelly.

―――――――――――

Sandy returned to deliver the devastating news to Zack. She knew this news would break them. She struggled with finding the right words that would make sense to them.

"Sandy, did you see her? How is she?" Zack was ecstatic. Sandy sighed and took a seat next to Zack to deliver the news.

"Zack... Kelly doesn't remember you," she said with a heavy heart. "What?" Zack was baffled.

"She doesn't remember anything from the past year."

"No, I don't believe it," Zack leapt up out of bed and dashed to Kelly's room.

Zack stood at the doorway, gazing at Kelly. Zack grinned, happy to see her finally well. She looked up startled to see Zack.

"Zack?" Kelly asked.

"You do remember," Zack exclaimed excitedly.

"No, you just look exactly how Rose described you," Kelly replied. "You really don't remember me?" Zack inquired with a sorrowful heart. Zack sat on Kelly's bed; she shifted noticeably uncomfortable. Zack reached to take her hand, and she flinched. That hurt Zack to the core. "Kelly... Kelly, it's me," Zack quavered.

"I'm sorry... I don't know you."

"You just need time to remember."

Zack pleaded with Kelly. They were convinced their love was too strong for her to forget. Kelly only needed a reminder of this.

"No, I don't want to. I don't want to remember. Dawn and Rose told me everything and those things are sinful... I renounce these sinful thoughts and actions and I ask God to forgive me of all these things..." Kelly's indoctrination was taking effect.

"This isn't you talking, Kelly. This is them and their hatred." Zack continued to plead with Kelly.

Kelly ignored Zack's pleas and continued to chant the P.G.A. mantra while covering her ears.

"...I renounce these sinful thoughts and actions and I ask God to forgive me all these things," she rocked her body back and forth. "Kelly, it's me, baby," Zack quavered, and their eyes welled up with tears.

Suddenly, Mr. and Mrs. Hamilton came storming in. "Get away from my daughter!" Mr. Hamilton shouted. Zack spun around to face him while yelling, "You did this to her!" Zack struck Mr. Hamilton in the mouth. The nurses pulled Zack off Mr. Hamilton and hauled Zack out of the room. Kelly was curled up, still murmuring the P.G.A. mantra.

* * *

Dawn stormed into the sheriff's office and tossed a file containing all the incriminating evidence against those responsible for the conversion camp.

"Excuse me? What is it with everyone marching in here like it's their own personal office."

"These are the people responsible for the P.G.A. facility. You might want to bring in some reinforcements." Dawn spoke solemnly.

"What in the hell is P.G.A.?"

The sheriff opened the file and skimmed through it. He gaped in disbelief.

"What in God's green earth…"

He was confounded.

CHAPTER 20

The P.G.A. facility was utterly destroyed, with windows blasted out, furniture strewn throughout the yard, severe fire damage, and a crisply burnt P.G.A. sign. A rainbow was spray painted across the pavement. The sheriff looked on in complete dismay. Officer Whitey approached him shaking his head. "The fire department said that there were zero casualties in the blaze." Officer Whitey informed the sheriff.

"Well, thank God for that," the sheriff replied. Officer Whitey stepped back and assessed the aftermath. "Jesus, I can't believe this was happening right next door," Officer Whitey said in disbelief.

"How did I not see this? I saw so many of these kids just completely change over summer. I just thought it was hormones," the sheriff blamed himself.

"Sheriff, no one could've known they were brainwashing children like some sick cult."

"And all in the name of the church."

The sheriff sneered and pointed to the aftermath.

"This! This is why the youth have strayed away from God. Can you blame them?" he scoffed and shook his head, "We tell them that they're evil and that they're not welcome in God's house. Of course, they burned it to the ground."

The sheriff for that county approached the O Town sheriff and officer Whitey.

"Good day, gentlemen. The name is Douglas. I'm the sheriff around these parts. Look, what occurred here is simply a darn disgrace. I don't care about jurisdiction; we're here to help you in whatever manner we can," The two sheriffs shook hands.

"Thank you, Sheriff Douglas; that's good to hear because we're going to need it."

"Yeah, should we go and arrest Zack and the other Queerville gangs for arson?" Officer Whitey asked.

"Arrest them? We should give them a got damn metal," the sheriff was appalled by Officer Whitey's suggestion.

"Okay, so what now?" Officer Whitey asked.

"Now, the real battle begins. We go and arrest those responsible," the sheriff grinned.

An enraged mob had besieged the police station as the sheriff and Officer Whitey apprehended the perpetrators of the conversion camp. One by one, the officers brought in Principal Skinner, Mr. Booker, Sarah, Pastor Peter, and Thomas.

As the mob grew, they yelled obscenities, yearning for blood and attempting to grasp them. Some were parents whose children had been kidnapped and taken to the camp, while others were survivors and the last of the allies who stood with them. They all wished to inflict harm on each and every one of them.

Due to the overwhelming amount of evidence and witness statements that identified Sarah and Thomas as the perpetrators of these heinous acts, they were booked and charged right away. Their culprits were placed in dim interrogation rooms to be interrogated by officials.

Principal Skinner was in interrogation room one. She wasn't used to being on the opposite side of power. She refused to recognize the harm in what she had done. "These children were doomed. We saved them from eternal damnation and delivered them to Jesus." Principal Skinner was delusional.

"You tortured them until they broke and when that didn't work. You fried their brains," the sheriff scoffed.

"We cast the devil out," she replied.
Frustrated, the sheriff buried his head in his hand.

Mr. Booker was over in interrogation room two. He saw himself as a patriot, willing to do everything for the sake of this great America. He, like so many other imprisoned patriots, believed he was helping by murdering individuals born on the land he professed to love.

"This town has been overrun by those freaks. We did what we had to do to reclaim our town," Mr. Booker grumbled. Detective Hobbs sighed loudly in disbelief at Mr. Booker's blunder.

"Queerville, was established in 1910. They built this entire town from the ground up. This is their land," Detective Hobbs replied, with a smirk. Mr. Booker looked bewildered. "That can't be right," Mr. Booker replied.

"Sure, it is. I have the proof right here."
Detective Hobbs showed Mr. Book the blueprints to *Operation Town*. "Ten years ago, your predecessors and accomplices illegally occupied hundreds of acres in Queerville and established what you now call O Town. All to create your own all-American conservative Christian society and those who did not conform to your way of life or opposed your ideas. You sent them to that hell up in the mountains. Shame on you, shame on you

all. O Town, the place that you love so much... was built on stolen land," Detective Hobbs explained leaving Mr. Booker flabbergasted.

Pastor Peter was in interrogation room three being interrogated by the sheriff. Pastor Peter is why people say, there's no hate like Christian love. Like many other religious zealots who were so deluded by religion, he took his religious beliefs to the extreme by committing horrible acts on children to push his views onto others. So blinded by religion and driven by hatred, they inflicted violence against others in an effort to prove God's love. These zealots may know religion, but they certainly do not know God. "I do not answer to, you. I answer to God. Only he can judge me," Pastor Peter sneered with his nose in the air.

"You are responsible for twenty suicides and over fifty homicides at your conversion camp. I'm sure God will judge you accordingly."

"Well, that's what forgiveness is for," he grinned.

"Yeah, but you must first repent," he reminded Pastor Peter, who appeared to have just had a revelation. The sheriff gave him a cup of ice water. "Here you go, you're going to need this where you're going," he winked at Pastor Peter.

* * *

Zack came to see Kelly but found an empty bed. A nurse came in to change the sheets. "Excuse me, what happened to the girl that was in here?" Zack asked.

"She was discharged, so her parents took her home." Zack stormed out.

429

KELLY WAS CATCHING UP WITH DAWN AND ROSE IN HER bedroom with her dad downstairs. Dawn informed Kelly about the conversion camp and the people who ran it. "Wow, so Principal Skinner?" Kelly was shocked. "Yeah," Dawn sighed, just as surprised.

"It makes so much sense now," Rose chuckled.

"Half of the town had sent their children to that place to 'fix' them," Dawn was irritated.

"What about you guys? Were you there too?" Kelly asked. "No. Not that we would remember."

"We asked our parents and they said, no."

"Do you believe them?" Kelly asked.

"I don't know. I would like to believe they had no idea what was going on in there," Dawn replied. "Yeah, me too. I don't want to even think about it. I don't want to know."

"We checked all the records and files. There were hundreds of children that were treated there. I didn't see Rose nor my name, but I did see, Max."

"Max?"

"Yeah, your brother was treated there, Kelly. He just didn't remember," Rose added. "Is that why he's in jail? What exactly did he do?" Kelly was looking for answers. She felt as if she had awoken in an episode of Alfred Hitchcock Presents, with no memory of the previous twelve months.

Zack came speeding up on their motorcycle outside the Hamilton estate. They dashed to the door and pounded on it, shouting, "Kelly... Kelly!"

Mr. Hamilton opened the door and came storming out, charging at Zack. "Get off of my property before I call the police."

"You should be in jail right next to your son."

Mr. Hamilton struck Zack in the face, "Now, get out of here!" Zack struck him back, "I'm not leaving without Kelly."

The girls could hear the commotion all the way upstairs. "Is that Zack?" Rose asked.

Dawn and Rose sprinted downstairs and out the front door. Kelly stood at the top of the stairs; she wasn't ready to see Zack again. Dawn and Rose intervened and separated them. Rose restrained Zack.

"He did this to her. He should be behind bars not walking around free!"

"You will never see my daughter again."

"That will never happen. You can't keep us apart. No one can; we're destined to be together."

Mr. Hamilton stormed back inside.

"Zack, calm down," Rose pleaded with Zack. "I need to see her, Rose, please." "Zack, you can't see Kelly like this. You'll scare her." Dawn said. "We'll be here for Kelly. We'll make sure she's not alone, and when she's ready, we'll call you. But you have to give her time," Rose said sincerely. Zack took a moment, then nodded in agreement. Rose gave them a sympathetic embrace. "It's going to be okay."

"Just tell her I love her, please, Rose," Zack pleaded.

"I will Zack," Rose replied sincerely.

FREDDIE CAME TO VISIT MAX AT THE JAILHOUSE. Freddie wasn't exactly happy to be there. Max was already waiting in the visitor booth when Freddie took a seat. "Thanks for coming to see me." "Max, what do you want?" Max looked at Freddie with a suspicious grin. "Do you know how it feels to have your brain scrambled and not be able to remember things? The night with Anthony was so traumatizing for me that I blocked it out. But slowly, bits and pieces started to

431

flood in. I only remember half of what happened that night—just me and Anthony's dead body. I remember hearing a gunshot. So, I thought I did it. But you knew—you knew I didn't do it and you let me turn myself in."

"So what? It's not like you remember what really happened," Freddie shrugged.

"I remember, Freddie... I remember you were there... I remember everything," Max grinned. Freddie appeared to be worried. "It's time you tell the truth," Max urged.

Sandy cleaned and bandaged Zack's back. Their wounds were still raw and bleeding. She was furious that Zack had gotten into a fight with Mr. Hamilton. "I can't believe you went over there," Sandy scolded. "I had to see her Sandy," Zack confessed.

"Your back needs to heal, Zack. You cannot keep ripping your wounds open. They're never going to heal like that," Sandy advised. "More scars? Great. I must look like Frankenstein, a fucking monster." Sandy stopped and glared at Zack. "Hey, never, ever speak about yourself like that again. You are not a monster. Do you hear me?" Zack agreed with a nod then changed the subject. "How are you doing? Any Rickey sightings?" Zack asked.

"No, the police think maybe he skipped town."

"Good. Maybe now you can get a good night's sleep," Zack expressed their relief for Sandy. "Zack, I haven't been able to get a good night's sleep since you left. You had me worried sick," Sandy confessed.

"Well, you don't have to worry anymore," Zack assured her.

"Actually, I still do. Because you can't sit still. You're running on empty, Zack. You need to slow down and process everything that just happened," Sandy advised. "Process what?" Zack evaded the implications. Sandy sat down and looked at Zack sympathetically before asking, "What else happened in there, Zack? What did they do to you?"

Sandy's concern for Zack's mental well-being was genuine. She had a feeling that there was more to the story than what had been revealed. After enduring years of abuse from their father, Zack had always kept their emotions bottled up. Sandy was usually able to persuade them to confide in her, but this time felt different. She knew Zack better than anyone and could sense when they were hiding something.

Zack could see the worry in Sandy's eyes; they felt vulnerable and wanted to open up to her when suddenly, Zack became uncomfortable as a glimpse of all the brutality they had undergone at P.G.A. raced through their mind.

"There's nothing to talk about," Zack said as they sprang up to put on their shirt. Sandy exhaled in frustration at Zack's denial.

DETECTIVE HOBBS WAS INTERROGATING MRS. BAKER. Mrs. Baker was in her orange jail uniform and had been in her cell for days since the protest in Queerville.

"Mrs. Baker, are you still denying that you know Ms. Abagail Wright?"

"I do not know this woman. Now, it's been days, why am I still in here?"

"Ms. Abagail was working on a story about missing children in O Town only they weren't missing..."

Mrs. Baker became fidgety.

"...the children were at your facility. Mr. Baker gave Ms. Abagail proof of that, and that is why you are here. You killed her so she wouldn't expose the truth. The truth about how you and your powerful friends were tormenting and brainwashing the children in this town."

"I've never met this woman, nor did I kill her. Surely, you must be mistaken."

"Mr. Baker didn't want his son in that facility. But you went on and admitted him anyway. So, you know what Mr. Baker did? He came and brought us this re-ceipt," Detective Hobbs held up the receipt for Mrs. Baker to see, "...for the knife that you purchased. The same branded knife that killed Ms. Wright."

Mrs. Baker became uncomfortable.

"You didn't have to kill that woman, and you cer-tainly did not have to harm those children. You people want to preach the gospel but then go against what the Bible stands for. You forget the sixth commandment, thy shall not kill," Detective Hobbs murmured.

"You know nothing of the Bible. Those people are liv-ing in sin. They are an abomination to God," Mrs. Baker snide.

"Doesn't the Bible say that every man was created in God's image? So, what does that tell you?" Mrs. Baker looked dumbfounded. "The women in prison are going to love you. They just love meeting women who harm children," he grinned.

KELLY WAS RUMMAGING THROUGH HER SCRAPBOOK, looking at photos of her and her friends. But what re-ally shocked her were the photos of her and Zack. She noticed how happy she looked, and it was like staring at a stranger. She ripped the photos out and tore them up.

The bell rang downstairs. Mr. Hamilton opened the door, surprised to see the sheriff on the other side. "Good evening, Mr. Hamilton. I think you know why we are here." Mr. Hamilton stepped back welcoming the sheriff in. They took a seat in the living room where they were joined by Mrs. Hamilton.

"We had no idea what they were doing at that facility."

"We would've never sent our Kelly to that place if we knew that they were mistreating children," Mrs. Hamilton assured the sheriff.

"To say that they were mistreating children is an understatement. So, why did you send your daughter to that facility?" the sheriff asked.

"It was supposed to be a youth reform facility for juveniles," Mrs. Hamilton replied.

"But your daughter is not a juvenile. She is of age to consent, and from what we're told, she was placed there against her will."

"Sheriff, you must understand. Kelly was out of control. Becoming a danger to herself and others. We did what we thought was best for our daughter."

"Mr. Hamilton, I have over a hundred angry citizens down at the station. About a half dozen of this town's most influential people look to be a part of this. And you want me to believe that you had no clue what that facility really was or what they were doing to your daughter?" the sheriff scoffed. Mr. Hamilton didn't appreciate the sheriff's tone. "I think it's about time we ask for a lawyer," he insisted. "Yeah, you're going to need a good one," the sheriff replied.

Zack was at their shop working on Freddie's car when Mark walked up. "Zack's Auto Shop, see, I knew there was more to you." They stopped and greeted him with a hug. "Mark, I'm glad you made it," Zack said happily upon seeing Mark. Zack grabbed some beers and pulled up a seat for Mark. "This is a nice place you got yourself here Zack." "Thank you. How are you? Where have you been staying?" Zack inquired.

"I'm still trying to wrap my head around all of it. You know, I can't believe my own parents put me in that place. I don't want to go back home. I can't stay with those people," Mark replied, expressing his frustration.

"You know if you hadn't come and got me. I wouldn't have made it out of there, and I would've never saved my girl. I owe you, man; you can stay here. I've got a room in the back; it isn't much. It's got a window, a bed, and your own bathroom," Zack offered.

"Thank you, Zack," Mark said grateful.

"As far as cash goes, you can help me around the shop, and I could pay you a decent wage," Zack suggested.

"You are a god send Zack," Mark said gratefully. They clinked beers as a yellow taxi pulled up; Freddie got out.

"I never imagined I'd see the day when Freddie Scorpion jumped out of a yellow car," Zack remarked.

"Well, if you had worked quicker on my ride, it would have been fixed by now," Freddie scoffed.

"I got out of the hospital, yesterday," Zack said defensively, Freddie's bravado offended them. "Excuses," Freddie murmured.

Mark found himself attracted to Freddie's smooth chocolate skin and beatnik appeal. Mark was a tall drink of water himself; standing at 6'1, he towered over Freddie, but he was willing to submit. He rose to greet him. "Hello," Mark said using his sexiest bedroom voice. "Oh, hello," Freddie barely looked at Mark.

"Freddie, Mark. Mark, Freddie." Zack formally introduced the two. "Nice to meet you," Mark said to Freddie.

"It is nice to meet me," Freddie replied. Zack was amused by Freddie's humorous yet insulting behavior.

"Freddie, Mark is the one who saved me, so you may want to be a little nicer to him," Zack confessed.

Freddie gasped and turned to face Mark, "Wait. That was you?" Freddie asked excitedly. Mark nodded yes. Freddie hugged him tightly, expressing his gratitude. "Thank you. Thank you for saving my best friend."

He squeezed Mark tighter.

"Freddie don't squeeze the life out of the man, geez," Zack chuckled. Freddie released his grasp on Mark, embarrassed.

"Oh, sorry," he chuckled.

"It's okay. I can take it," Mark grinned as he gazed into Freddie's eyes causing him to blush.

MAX AND THE SHERIFF WERE REVIEWING THE NEW facts from his revised statement. "Are you sure about this?" the sheriff asked. "Yes, sheriff, I would like to recant my statement. I did not kill Anthony Calhoun," Max admitted. "Well son, I read your new statement. What those people did to you in that place sickens me to my stomach."

"It was pretty awful," he sighed.

"Regarding the murder of Anthony Calhoun, there was never any evidence to back up your confession. In fact, your confession was pretty much all we had."

"Yeah, sorry about that."

"Are you sure you don't remember who that other fella was?"

Max paused momentarily before saying, "No, sheriff, sorry."

"I have to ask, son. Do you feel safe returning home with your parents?" "I have to sheriff; my sister is there. I need to protect her," Max expressed his concern.

"Okay, son, we'll get you processed out."
Max smiled broadly.

SANDY WAS HOME WATCHING TELEVISION IN FRONT OF her open window. Unbeknownst to her, Rickey sat outside, watching her with a wicked sneer.

"Oh, miss Sandy. What do I have to do to get to your heart," he whispered eerily to himself.

CHAPTER 21

Dawn eventually published her first article, and it quickly became the buzz of the school. Open newspapers and terrified looks filled the school corridors. Dawn was greeted with a lot of pointing and staring as she moved through the halls. Everyone was reading it…

"*Dear students of O Town High: I'm sure by now you've all heard about the recent tragedies that took place a few towns over. What you don't realize is that those who were held accountable are the same people who vowed to protect you. Your mother's, your father's, Principal Skinner, Pastor Peter, and Mayor Booker. You might've been a victim and don't know it yet. Your own parents may have sent you to this hell in the hopes that you would behave and conform. Conform to the life they say is best for you. But who are we to judge what is best for someone? To pass judgment on people based on who they love, how they look, or the color of their skin…*"

Dawn marveled at their shocked faces as she made her way to class.

"*…Principal Skinner's actions will leave a mark on this town, but none greater than the one she left on her daughter, Mary Sue. Who tries so desperately to be perfect, to be this image she could never live up to. She will spend the rest of her life never feeling good enough. I want you all to break the chains, break free, and enjoy life to the*

fullest; it is the only one that has been promised to you. So, live it… on your terms."
After learning that Principal Skinner was Mary Sue's mother, students sighed in surprise. Dawn smirked then continued to her locker.

A TAXI PULLED UP TO ZACK'S AUTO SHOP AND MAX GOT out. Zack was buffering Freddie's car, when they looked up and spotted him. Zack was furious seeing Max free. "Your family really have some deep pockets. I don't need you in jail. I'll kill you with my bear hands."

Zack snarled as they charged towards Max.

Zack forced him against the wall and began to choke him. Max gasped for air while attempting to speak. Mark stood there speechless, unsure what to do. Max was turning blue as Zack squeezed his neck.

In the midst of Zack's wrath, Kelly's face popped into their head. They heard her voice; asking them to trust her. Zack released their grip on Max.

Max coughed trying to catch his breath, "Zack, I know you don't want to see me. But I have to tell you what really happened to your brother," Max panted.

* * *

Kelly returned to school, wearing her traditional poodle skirt and button-up sweater. She walked down the corridor, feeling like a new version of herself: bland, conservative, and uninteresting – like Mary Sue 2.0. As she passed by, students stared and whispered, completely oblivious to the chatter. Kelly noticed Dawn and Rose at their lockers.

"Hello Dawn, hello Rose," Kelly greeted them.

Dawn and Rose were shocked to see their friend back in school so soon. "Kelly?" Rose exclaimed.

"Yes," Kelly replied to Rose shock upon seeing her.

"We're just surprised to see you here at school," Dawn stated. "Well, I am graduating in two weeks. My folks wanted to wait till I receive my diploma before we move." "Move?" Rose said perplexed.

"Yeah, my parents thought I could use a new start. Leave all of this behind me. Maybe enroll in college early," Kelly explained.

"College?" Dawn was shocked to hear Kelly talk about college.

"So, you are going to college?" Rose inquired just as confused.

"Well, yeah, what else am I going to do?" Kelly responded.

"Oh, I don't know. Maybe go see the world with someone you love who loves you," Rose replied sarcastically.

Rose knew that had always been Kelly's dream; she never wanted to go to college. Kelly was adventurous; she believed that life lessons could not be learned in the classroom but outside, in the real world. Her best friends were having difficulty grasping this new version of her.

"Rose, that's preposterous. My parents want me to attend college and get a good education," Kelly responded.

"Kelly, your parents are the ones who put you in that place."

"Oh, they didn't know what was going on in there. I must forgive them if I want God to forgive me of my sins. Besides, they said I was completely out of control," Kelly said in complete denial. "No, you were not. You were very much in control of every aspect of your life," Rose insisted.

"What are you saying Rose?" Kelly asked, annoyed.

"I'm saying that your parents are lying to you!" Rose shouted, irritated. "Okay, let's cool it. Kelly, have you told Zack that you're leaving town?" Dawn asked. "No, why would I?" Kelly remarked.

"Perhaps because the real Kelly would," Rose sneered.

"The real Kelly?" Kelly repeated, irritated.

Dawn saw that things were escalating quickly, so she stepped between Rose and Kelly.

"Kelly, you might not remember. But Zack is very important to you. You guys are basically soulmates. Kelly would never leave without saying goodbye to Zack." Dawn attempted to persuade Kelly, but she was fed up.

"I'm so tired of people telling me what I would or would not do. I can't wait to leave this town behind me," Kelly snarled and stormed away.

JOHNNIE AND MARY SUE WERE STUCK IN THE HOUSE. Both were reluctant to show their faces around town. "I was already afraid to go out and expose my pregnancy, but now... that's the least of my concerns. My mother said that place was a youth center to help kids find their way," Mary Sue wept.

"My mother killed a woman so no one would find out what happened to me. Our parents went to great lengths to protect us. We can't turn on them now," Johnnie confessed.

"What about those kids whose souls are lost forever?"

"Mary Sue, I was one of those kids. That placed saved me, it saved me from a life of sin."

443

"This town won't see it that way. They'll paint my mother as some evil scientist. She was just trying to help," she lamented.

Confused, Johnnie asked, "What are you saying, Mary Sue?"

"I don't want to raise my child in a town full of sinners," Mary Sue scowled.

"Mary Sue, O Town is the only place I've ever known. We can't leave here," Johnnie pleaded.

"Do you see what's happening outside? Those Queerville freaks frolicking around with their homosexuality. Those are Godless people."

Johnnie remained optimistic. "They can be saved, just like I was. We should stay and help them."

"You can stay but I'm taking my baby out of this God forsaken town," Mary Sue stormed out.

* * *

ROSE WAS ON HER WAY TO SURPRISE JAMES AT THE GYM when she overheard him talking about her with Ronnie and the rest of the team. "So, then she said *No, I've never been to Lover's Lane*." James mimicked her voice. The team laughed.

Rose was devastated listening to James ridicule her and decided to continue to eavesdrop.

"Rose has visited Lovers' Lane more times than a warm breeze," Ronnie chuckled.

"So, we get there right and I'm like gee what happens here. She was like I can show you and then she plants one on me."

"Next time, tell her you don't know how to use it and see if she gives you a hand," Ronnie suggested. The team burst out laughing, slapping high fives to Ronnie.

Rose stormed in, feeling humiliated, "Well, that wouldn't be a lie." "Oh, shit!" Ronnie turned white like a ghost. The other team members ran off scared of Rose's wrath. "You're an asshole, Ronnie," Rose cut her eye at Ronnie. "Come on now, Rose. Everyone's had a 'petal' of you," Ronnie jeered. "Everyone except you, now run along, loser," Rose scolded. Ronnie sucked his teeth and took off.

"Hey, Rose," James attempted to smooth talk her.

"Don't hey me, mister. You think I'm some kind of toy for you to play with?" Rose was furious.

"What about you, Rose? You lied to me too. Who was that girl?" James replied.

"I was just trying to be someone you would like. But you didn't want to get to know me. You were only looking to get laid. Are you happy now?" Rose was crushed.

"You pretended to be someone you weren't. So, did I. I guess we're even," James admitted.

"Ugh, I can't believe I got played by a square in a lettermen sweater," Rose whispered as she walked away, rolling her eyes.

Rose had exploited sex to get boys to like her since she had never seen an example of healthy love. The only love she had ever admired was the love between Zack and Kelly, which was now in shambles. She began to believe that she would never find someone to love her.

* * *

FREDDIE ARRIVED AT ZACK'S SHOP AND COULD TELL BY the look on Zack's face, Max had told them his side of the truth. He could see the rage in Zack's eyes. Zack was sitting with a pistol on their lap, sipping a beer. Freddie immediately started talking.

445

"Look, Zack, let me explain," Freddie pleaded while Zack glared at him.

"You got until I finish this beer," Zack said, gripping the pistol in their other hand.

Freddie finally told Zack the truth about who actually killed their brother. At their feet were several empty beer bottles. Freddie was still pouring his heart out.

"Max had blacked out by that time. I couldn't react, Zack. I froze and stayed hidden. Once I realized Max didn't remember anything, I couldn't tell anyone. So, I kept my mouth shut."

"So, he left Max there to take the fall, but Max woke up and ran, and that's what the eyewitness saw, Max running?" Zack elaborated.

"Yeah, that's pretty much it," Freddie confirmed.

Zack turned and looked Freddie in the eyes.

"Do you know what would've happened if I had killed Max? Kelly would have never forgiven me. I would've lost the love of my life because of you," Zack growled.

"I wouldn't have let you kill Max," Freddie remarked.

"What makes you think I need your fucking permission?" Zack shouted; their rage was palpable on Freddie's skin. He didn't want to lose their friendship. He knew what he did was wrong. He was ready to take full responsibility for trying to hide the truth. "I'm sorry, Zack. I'm sorry I didn't tell you. I knew if I said anything, people would have wondered why Max didn't remember. Then everyone would find out about that place, that I was there, and what they did to me. And I was hiding the fact that I'm really from O Town," Freddie was pleading for his life.

"I wouldn't have cared Freddie. You should've told me... You should've told me who killed my brother," Zack grunted.

KELLY ARRIVED HOME TO FIND MAX IN THE LIVINGROOM She was thrilled to see her brother and jumped into his arms. "Max!" Kelly smiled broadly. "Kelly, I'm so happy to see you," Max exclaimed. Max studied his sister's eyes, trying to decipher this altered version of her. Something was different.

"Kelly, I'm glad you're alright. I was really worried about you," Max confessed sincerely. "You and everybody else," Kelly replied, taking a seat on the couch.

"Do you remember anything from that place?"

"I don't even remember being there," Kelly admitted.

"What's the last thing you remember?" Max inquired anxiously, hoping to aid his sister's memory. Kelly groaned as she reflected, "Last summer when we left for Virginia."

"Wow, that was two years ago, Kelly. You don't remember anything from this summer?"

"I remember being in church."

Max laughed, prompting Kelly to ask, "What? What's so funny?" "Kelly, you hate church," Max reminded her.

"No, I don't," Kelly said defensively.

"Yes, you do. You hate organized religion. You don't remember when mom and pop took your supper away because you wouldn't attend church?" Kelly attempted to recollect. "This person everyone keeps describing isn't me at all."

"No, it's you. I've known you my whole life; we're twins, remember? You've always been your own person, Kelly."

"I have to say, the more I hear about this Kelly person, the less I like her." Kelly was struggling to be both the girl everyone remembered and the person she was now. Max gazed at Kelly as though he didn't recognize her before saying, "That's too bad because she was really rad. I hope I get to tell her that one day."

447

Max walked away and stood behind the wall, grieving for his sister. He had no notion who the girl on the couch was anymore.

SANDY CLOSED UP THE DINER AND WAS HEADED HOME. Rickey stood in the darkness, far away, observing her. He trailed after her along the gravel road. Using the night sky to hide in the shadows. He enjoyed watching his prey before slaughtering them. Sandy proceeded along the dark path. He grinned, waiting for the right moment to show himself. He waited for her to move further away from the diner before creeping behind her and revealing himself.

"Hello Miss Sandy," Rickey smiled sinisterly.

Sandy froze, her skin crawling. She turned around to face him. Rickey had a malevolent look on his face, that frightened her. She backed up a few paces and Rickey matched her stride. She attempted to run, but he grabbed her and sniffed her neck. He liked the smell of fear. Rickey enjoyed toying with her.

"Now, why would you be walking home alone with a killer on the loose? Don't you know it's not safe for a pretty girl like you? I must say, Sandy, I am very disappointed that you would be so foolish to be out here all alone."

Sandy's terrified expression faded, and she began to chuckle, puzzling Rickey.

"But I'm not alone," Sandy grinned.

Rickey seemed perplexed by Sandy's sudden change.

Suddenly, whistling rang out into the air. Rickey was bewildered. He looked around to find the Queerville gangs pulling up and circling him. Some were hanging out the windows, swinging bats. "Oh, I see, your friends are here to protect you."

"No, they're not here to protect me," Sandy admitted.

"I see. They're here to watch me cut out your heart."

"Sorry, my heart belongs to another," Sandy smirked, then suddenly, Bang! Rickey's body trembled; he staggered back and tumbled to the ground. He glanced down and saw a bullet hole in his chest; he couldn't believe it. Sandy pulled out the revolver from her purse and stood over him.

"Oh, and my friends are here to get rid of your body. I hope you rot in hell," Sandy said as she stepped back and let the gangs swarm and pummeled Rickey with their bats. Beating him unconscious.

CHAPTER 22

Zack and Mark were just finishing up the last few touches to Freddie's ride when he arrived excitedly. "What'z buzzin, Zack?" Freddie greeted Zack but they were in no mood for Freddie's banter. "Your car is done. I reupholstered the inside. Replaced your parts and slapped some new paint on it," Zack said short and eva- sively, tossing Freddie the keys.

"Thank you, Zack. It looks like new," Freddie mar- veled at his ride. "And I did the wheels. Zack told me you guys are racers. So, I made sure you had the best tires to burn rubber with," Mark added. "Well, thank you Mark," Freddie smiled.

"If anyone comes looking for me. I'll be at my mother's," Zack said before hopping on their motorcy- cle and speeding off.

Freddie was disappointed that Zack was avoiding them.

"Give it time, Freddie. Zack will forgive you," Mark said. He could see Freddie's desire to make things right with Zack weighed heavily on him.

"That's my best friend they have no choice. What do you have planned on this beautiful day?"

"I can't recall what I would ordinarily do on a lovely day like this," Mark said still apprehensive about being free.

"How have you been adjusting?" Freddie asked.

"Well, thanks to Zack, it's been a lot easier."

"Have you spoken to your parents yet?"

"No, I don't have anything to say to them. They didn't love me the way I was. They're not going to love me now."

Freddie could relate far too well. Listening to Mark talk about his parents triggered Freddie's animosity towards his own mother.

"My mother admitted me to P.G.A., and shortly after, she was diagnosed with an illness. She needs around-the-clock care. I was so mad at her for leaving me in that place, but I couldn't bring myself to hate her for it. I never got the chance to tell her what happened to me after I got out. Now, I have to make sure she is safe. I have to make sure the woman who abandoned me in hell is safe," Freddie muttered, his voice laced with pain. He had never confided in anyone about this before. Mark was moved that Freddie had revealed such a personal secret with him. He felt honored as he looked into Freddie's eyes, gently cupped his face, and kissed him.

MAMA ZACK WAS IN THE KITCHEN PREPARING LUNCH when Zack entered. "Hey mama, how are you?"

"Hey baby, what a nice surprise. I'm just wonderful but I'm still worried about you dear?" Mama Zack replied with a loving smile.

"Mom, I told you I'm fine," Zack hissed.

Mama Zack hugged Zack and gently held their face in her hands. "When I think about what those people did to you. It makes my blood boil. I'm so sorry baby. I'm sorry that happened to you," she said, squeezing Zack tightly.

"There is nothing wrong with you. God loves you. They will never turn you away," she said releasing Zack.

"I know Mom. When I was younger, you used to tell me that all the time."

Mama Zack took the meatloaf out of the oven. "Are you hungry?" "Sure, Mom, I'll have something to eat."

"Oh, good I'll fix you a plate."

During lunch, Zack told their mother about Kelly. Hearing what happened to Kelly broke Mama Zack's heart. She had grown fond of her. Kelly was so young and innocent, and she truly adored Zack. Mama Zack hated that she had experienced such depravity.

"Awe, poor Kelly. I really love that girl. She's such a sweetheart, and she loves you so much," she wept as she continued, "I'm so sorry, baby. I know this must be killing you. Just stay hopeful. She may one day regain her memories." Mama Zack wiped her tears.

"No, Mom, it's not possible; that portion of her brain was completely fried."

"Fried? What do you mean?"

"Her memories of her and me. This last year of her life. It's like it's been deleted forever."

"Awe, baby. Love doesn't get deleted. Those folks may have indoctrinated her into their conservative way of life, but her love for you remains. It's hidden deep within her," Mama Zack explained. "I planned to make her fall in love with me again. But she won't even see me. Their brainwashing made her bury that part of her-self. She locked that Kelly away for good; she despises that part of herself. She doesn't want to be anything like Kelly before, and she doesn't want anything to do with me," Zack said, their voice broken.

"Do you remember when you were younger, and I told you what a twin flame is?" Zack nodded yes.

452

"Twin flames, like you and Kelly. It doesn't need memory or force; it is simply magnetic. When you and Kelly first met, you both fell in love the instant you laid eyes on each other. There is nothing in this world that can stop it from happening. I know you're hurting; focus on healing. But you and Kelly are not over. Twin Flames never are," Mama Zack said with sincerity, offering Zack hope. "I have to go, mom. There's a meeting at the club." "Okay, baby, be safe out there." Zack kissed their mother on the cheek. "Thank you, Mom."

THE GANGS GATHERED AT THE CLUB TO DISCUSS THE atrocious events that took place at the P.G.A. facility. Charlotte, at the center, led the meeting. "I want to take this time to thank you all for showing up for each other. Because no matter what we're going through with one another, we don't let anyone else come in our home and hurt our babies." The gangs clapped and cheered. Charlotte looked at Zack with her heart full. "Zack, my sweet baby, you have endured so much pain your entire life, but this past year nearly broke you. It's a miracle you're still standing. I thank God for your strength, and I pray he takes his foot off your neck."

The gangs nodded in agreement at Zack.

"When we established these gangs, it was for more than just battling each other in categories. It was to keep our town safe. But I guess we lost our way somehow. These very actions from these damn Bible freaks are why, I never closed my doors to any child..."

All the gangs listened pensively.

"Mama is back and I'm not going anywhere.

We need to protect this town and guard it with our lives because what happened up on that hill cannot happen ever again."

The room roared.

"I will be opening the club to any queer children with nowhere to go. If you find a child in need, you send them here. Now, I'll be opening the floor up to anyone who wants to be heard."

Val raised her hand. Charlotte motioned for them to take the floor. Val stood up and cleared her throat. After a long pause she said, "I challenge Zack to a race for leadership of the Red Dragons."

Charlotte sucked her teeth and rolled her eyes.

The room erupted, the gangs went berserk, and everyone was in shock, gasping. Everyone looked at Zack, who never turned around to acknowledge Val. Charlotte banged her gavel to quiet the room. "Zack." Charlotte turned the floor over to Zack for a response. Zack exhaled deeply, stood up, and turned to face Val.

The room went completely silent.

"I accept," Zack sighed.

* * *

After the meeting, Zack went to see Sandy at the diner. They settled in at the counter. Sandy was delighted to see them. "How are you?" Sandy asked. "I'm better now that I know Rickey won't be bothering you anymore," Zack replied. "Yeah, it feels good to feel safe again," Sandy admitted. "I'm glad you took your power back. How did it feel?" "Scary and exciting at the same time." "First time always is." "Have you spoken to Kelly?" Sandy inquired. Zack exhaled and hissed, "No, she still refuses to see me." Sandy could see the heart

454

break in Zack's eyes. "Just give her time Zack."

"Yeah. That's what everyone keeps telling me."

"You know what you could do in the meantime?"

"What?"

"Forgive, Freddie. He was carrying a lot."

"I'm just letting Freddie soak."

"Good, you need your best friend."

"I thought you were my best friend."

"Well, now, you have two."

Sandy smiled and then looked concerned at her friend, who appeared mentally exhausted. Before she could say anything, Zack spoke up, "I'm tired Sandy." Zack seemed frazzled. "Zack?" Sandy whispered. "I'm tired of everything... the racing, the fighting, the chasing... I'm just tired," Zack's eyes welled up with tears. "I'm worried about you Zack. You keep so much inside. You won't let anyone share the burden with you."

"I don't like being a burden on people. I never know how to verbally express my feelings, that's why I write it all down."

"Come here," Sandy said as she took Zack's hand and led them back into the supply closet. They took a squat on the floor. Sandy held Zack's hand.

"It's not always about finding the right words to say, Zack. Sometimes, the world can be so loud that we can't hear each other's cries for help. Even in solitude, the world can be deafeningly loud. But I hear you; even when you're not saying anything, I hear you. You don't have to keep everything inside; it's okay to let it out, Zack. It's the only way to heal. I just want to remind you that you're never alone."

As soon as Sandy said those words, Zack broke down. They wept, releasing their emotions. Sandy wrapped her arms around Zack, and they wailed in each other's embrace. Zack let out all the anguish and hurt from their father's murder, Kelly, and everything that had happened at the camp. Zack let it all out. Sandy held them tightly and cried alongside them. She had witnessed so much of Zack's agony, and in some ways, she was releasing it as well.

Afterwards Zack took a deep breath and felt a thousand times better. "I'm proud of you. Thank you for being vulnerable," Sandy said. "You're the only person I've ever been vulnerable with," Zack admitted. "Well, that's what sisters are for," Sandy said winking at Zack.

"Do you want to come and watch me race tonight? It might be the last time you get to see me race," Zack confessed. "Yes, I'll come to support you."

Paradise Road River Basin

Val pulled up to the starting line with more enthusiasm than anybody else, like a child on Christmas morning. Zack, on the other hand, seemed to have already made up their minds and just wanted it to be over.

The gangs lined the streets to show their support for Zack. Charlotte was in the heart of the strip, directly in front of the rides. A challenge of this magnitude required her to officiate it. She waved her white flag. "What we have here is a race challenge for leadership. This has never been attempted before. Win or lose, Zack will remain in command of Queerville and all that operates in it. Whoever wins this race will be the new leader or continuing leader of the Red Dragons.

"Are you ready?" Charlotte shouted.

The crowd erupted.

Zack and Val rev their engines. The gangs screamed as Charlotte raised her arms, and their engines roared.

Charlotte dropped her arms, Val sped off on burning tires, rushing into a cloud of smoke, and Zack rolled out after. Sandy and Freddie looked on cheering for Zack.

Zack was barely putting in any effort into winning. Just cruising for it to be over.

Val was handling her car like a pro nascar driver determined to win. She kept looking at Zack for some type of validation. Zack had a sneaky grin on their face.

The cars were neck-and-neck nearly to the finish. Zack downshifted and hit their brake to slow down their ride. Freddie and Sandy noticed their brake light was on. They looked at each other with bewildered expressions.

"Why is Zack braking?" Freddie asked. Sandy smiled she knew exactly what Zack was doing. "Zack is letting Val win," Freddie sighed and shook his head.

Val shifted gears and hit the petal speeding through the finish line. "Yeah, baby! Yes!" Val hollered. Val was overjoyed. They couldn't believe they had just defeated Zack, a feat that had never been done before. Little did she realize; it still hadn't been done. Zack rode in seconds after Val, who was celebrating oblivious to the fact that Zack let her win, but others noticed and were laughing at her. Zack came over to congratulate her, "Nice driving, Val." Val had a look of gloat on her face.

"Thank you, Zack," she replied, shaking hands then turning around to face the crowd. "Red Dragons, come and meet your new leader," Val blurted out to the crowd.

There were a few chuckles from the crowd. Some hackles of *"I'm staying with Zack."* Most of the Red Dragons stood with Zack while a handful stood behind Val.

Val looked disappointed; she thought the gang would be happy with her as the new leader.

"Not what you expected, huh?" Zack gloated and gestured to Lisa, Robin, and the few individuals who stood with Val.

"Good luck. I wish you the best," Zack murmured and walked away with Freddie and Sandy by their side.

"So, I come to see you race for the first time, and you blow off," Sandy sneered.

"We saw what you did," Freddie remarked.

"What?" Zack replied, playing clueless.

"Zack, you let her take off first and you had your foot on the brake petal," Freddie added.

Zack simply smirked, causing Freddie and Sandy to exchange a knowing glance, indicating their intention to keep this secret and support their friend.

"Let's get out of here," Zack proposed, removing their Red Dragons' jacket and casually throwing it onto Val's car.

Observing Zack's departure with Freddie, Sandy, and the rest of the gang, Val felt a wave of unexpected emotions. As she scanned her surroundings, she noticed people pointing and laughing at her. She realized that she didn't command the same level of respect as Zack did. Determined to change that, she made a silent vow that if they didn't respect her, they would sure fear her.

* * *

Dawn had a late-night visitor at her home. She was overjoyed to see Max when she opened the door.

"Max, hey, what are you doing here?"
Dawn smiled. "I read your article it was really good."

"Thank you, Max. How are you?"

"Well, I almost went to prison and came home to find out my sister is a complete stranger." Max sneered. "Yeah, all of this must be hard on you."

"I don't know if she told you or not but we're leaving town." "Yeah, she mentioned it."

"I just wanted to tell you. I was always pretty keen on you," Max murmured causing Dawn to turn cheery red.

"Well, don't you have the perfect timing."
"Yeah, I know, better late than never," Max chuckled.

"I have always been keen on you too, Max."
Max grinned. "Well, that's just swell then, Dawn. Do you think I could ring you some time?"

"Yeah, sure, Max, I would love that," Dawn said smilingly. "Well, okay then. I guess I'll go," Max said sheepishly. Dawn found his timidity endearing. "Max, come here," Max leaned in closer to Dawn and she grabbed him and kissed him.

Dawn had butterflies kissing Max for the first time. Max was a nervous wreck after their kiss. "Goodnight, Dawn," he said as he stumbled down the stairs and chuckled at himself. "Goodnight, Max." Dawn replied with a wide smile.

* * *

Zack pulled up to find a taxi parked out front of their shop. Their heart stopped when Kelly got out. "Kelly, are you okay? Is something wrong?" "No, everything's fine. I just came to tell you myself that I'm leaving town." "What?" Zack was in shock they couldn't believe their ears.

"My folks and I think it'd be better for me to start fresh some place away from all of this."

"All of this? Kelly, this is your home."

"This is not my home. I can't stay here living in someone else's shadow. I'm not that girl. I'm not the Kelly you love. She's gone."

"Kelly, just wait..."

Zack took a step closer toward Kelly, and she got startled, backstepped, and clutched her purse tighter, like some scared, privileged White woman afraid of the black guy crossing the street. It shattered Zack's heart into a million pieces.

"I gave it all the time I could. I've seen too many doctors who all say the same thing; I'll never regain those memories. So, there's no sense in sticking around here," Kelly said sternly.

"Kelly... please don't leave," Zack pleaded.

"I merely came to inform you because it was the right thing to do. Everyone keeps telling me that you're the reason I'm still alive," Kelly's tone was sarcastic.

"Don't do this. The Kelly I know wouldn't want this," Zack continued to plead.

"I hope this can give you some closure and allow you to move on now. Whatever you had with... me is over now. Goodbye, Zack," Kelly was callous. She turned and headed back to her taxi.

"Kelly!" Zack shouted.

She turned back around and faced Zack.

"You and I will never be over," Zack quavered.

Kelly shook her head and rode off in the taxi.

———————————

Max pulled up to the cemetery with Ronnie. They got out of the car. Light fog moved over the tombstones. "Are you sure this is the place?" "Yeah, this is where the team is meeting," Max assured him. They walked through the gloomy cemetery and over grave sites.

"I think it's about time we give those Queerville freaks a good thrashing. They got the whole town fooled. I don't believe any of that news."

"You do realize my sister and I were both tortured in that place," Max was disgusted with Ronnie assumptions.

"Your sister is one of them, and Max, I don't believe you were ever in that place," Ronnie scoffed.

Max struggled with wanting to knock Ronnie out. They saw headlights ahead; and continued walking toward them.

"By the way, thanks for letting me rot in jail for something you did," Max remarked.

"Noone told you to black out. You should be glad I did it. The town has one less queer freak. Besides, you needed the money."

"I didn't need the money. My family is rich. I was just some spoiled kid that got himself in too deep with some bad people. But Anthony... he was innocent."

Anthony's murder was weighing heavy on Max.

He played it back in his head...

Anthony stood at his ride, counting the money he had just confiscated from the twerp. Max and Ronnie came out of the sports bar after losing big. The flames from the fire grabbed their attention, and that's when Ronnie spotted Anthony, and his eyes went wide.

"Look at this Queerville freak."

"Ronnie, what are you doing? That's Anthony Calhoun," Max reminded him. "I know who he is, and he's still a Queerville freak. Look at how much money he has. And how much did we lose tonight? How are we going to repay it?"

"No, Ronnie. We can find another way to repay it."

Max tried to stop Ronnie. Ronnie pushed him off and approached Anthony.

"Now, what are you two doing over on this side?" Anthony inquired. "That's a lot of money you got there," Ronnie said brusquely. "So? What is O Town's finest squares doing on this side of town?" Anthony asked again.

"Looking to start trouble," Ronnie scoffed with a menacing look on his face.

Ronnie reached for the money, but Anthony grabbed him. Ronnie saw the revolver in Anthony's waistband and snatched it. Anthony sprang back, his hands in the air, as Ronnie waved the pistol. Ronnie pistol-whipped Max in the head as he tried to stop him.

Max dropped to the ground, holding his head, watching Ronnie and Anthony like shadows, tussling for the gun. Then all Max heard was BANG! BANG! BANG! —three gun shots. Anthony's body dropped; his blood splattered onto Max's sweater. After the hit to the head, he was barely conscious. His vision was hazy. He looked around; all he saw was Anthony's body and Freddie lurking in the trenches before blacking out.

Freddie looked over and saw Anthony dead on the ground. Max passed out, and Ronnie stood over him, prepared to shoot him. Ronnie looked up, noticed Freddie, and put his finger to his lips, warning him to be quiet. Ronnie decided to leave Max to take the fall.

Max finally came to, holding his head, confused. He looked around at Anthony's dead body, saw the blood on his sweater, and frantically took the sweater off and hauled ass out of there, bumping into the white man,

462

leaving behind his bloody sweater. The white man saw Anthony's dead body and took off. Freddie came over and grabbed Max's bloody sweater from the ground. He was trying to protect Max.

BACK TO THE CEMETERY...

"All I could remember was that I needed money, Anthony had it, and a gun. You left me to take the wrap."

"Well, what do you want to do about it now, Max? You want to fight me? You're not going to tell the truth. Zack would kill you too," Ronnie admitted.

"You'd be surprised what telling the truth could do... There they go, up ahead."

The headlights were blaring in their faces; they couldn't see who was standing by the car. Ronnie was shielding his eyes, trying to see through the glare. "Who is that?" Ronnie squinted his eyes.

Ronnie crept closer through the headlights... He could see someone with their back turned, he stepped closer, the figure turned around...it was Zack. Ronnie froze in place and nearly shat on himself.

"Max, what is this?" He looked at Max.

"What do you think it is? Anthony didn't deserve to die. He was good people something you know nothing about."

Ronnie pushed Max and attempted to plead his case to Zack.

"Zack, I don't know what..." **BANG!** - A bullet pierced straight through Ronnie's head, and his body collapsed on the ground. Zack moved closer and stood over his body, shooting his corpse and emptying their clip into Ronnie.

Zack looked down at Ronnie's bullet-riddled body, finally letting go of this chapter of their life, *it's finally over.* Anthony's death has been avenged.

Max walked up to Zack. "Thank you for trusting me?"

"Trust me... that was the last thing your sister asked me to do before your parents sent her to that place. She begged me to trust her; she said you needed time. I didn't trust you, Max; I trusted her," Zack explained.

"For what it's worth. I really am sorry about you and my sister. She truly loved you, Zack. She was filled with so much joy and happiness. I never seen her so happy until she met you. The girl she is now is just a shell of who my sister was. She might look like her but it's not Kelly. It's like she lost herself, her identity."

Zack and Max shared a moment both mourning their love for Kelly. "Take care of her. Tell her I just want her to be happy," Zack said tearfully. "I will, but I don't think she'll ever be that happy again," Max confessed.

Those words cut Zack like a dagger. They brushed away their tears as Max patted them on the back and took off. Zack regained their composure and grabbed a shovel and started digging...

Zack buried Ronnie's body right next to Anthony. Just like they promised.

* * *

Allen strolled into the police station and demanded to speak with the sheriff. The startled officer escorted him down the hall to the sheriff's office. The sheriff glanced up and looked right through Allen to his snakeskin. Allen was not a trustworthy man which made him the perfect candidate. "What can I do for you Mr..?"

"Allen. Allen Lewis and I hear this town is need of a new mayor." Allen had a sly grin on his face.

———————————————

Zack rushed to Kelly's home, but they were already gone, the house was locked up. Zack looked through the window and all the furniture was covered with tarps. Kelly was gone. Zack broke down in tears.

Back home, Zack sobbed looking at photos of them and Kelly…*"I remember when she walked into the diner. She brought me a milkshake—a damn milkshake. And from that moment on, she had me hooked. She never looked at me like those people do. She always saw the good in me. I never had someone love me that deeply or that unconditionally. For a long time, I carried this emptiness within my soul, but when I met Kelly, I felt whole for the first time. I don't know how to live without her, and I don't want to."*

Zack was distraught, wrecking their loft, smashing glasses, tossing dishes, kicking over furniture, and knocking over tables, staggering to the floor…

Sandy rushed in and caught Zack before they could hit the floor. She cradled Zack in her arms as they wept for Kelly in utter anguish…

All their memories of Kelly rushed through their mind. Playing over and over in a continuous loop. With every smile that popped into their head their heart would break even more…

Sandy rocked Zack in her arms as they wailed in agony at the notion that they would never see Kelly again.

RISE
OF THE
RED
DRAGONS

SUMMER 2024

Made in the USA
Las Vegas, NV
14 March 2024

87208044R00277